A SINNER WITHOUT A SAINT

THE PENNINGTONS, BOOK 4

An honorable artist

Benedict Pennington's greatest ambition is not to paint a masterpiece, but to make the country's most important artworks accessible to all. His success in persuading a noted philanthropist to donate his collection of Old Master paintings to England's first national art museum brings his dream tantalizingly close to reality —until Viscount Dulcie, once the object of Benedict's illicit adolescent desire, begins to court the donor's granddaughter, set on winning the painting for himself.

A hedonistic viscount

Sinclair Milne, Viscount Dulcie, prefers collecting innovative art and dallying with handsome men to burdening himself with anything as dull as a wife. But when rivals hint that Dulcie's refusal to pursue wealthy Miss Adler and her paintings is due to lingering tender feelings for Benedict Pennington, Dulcie vows to prove them wrong. And if wooing Miss Adler from the holier-than-thou painter also gets his matchmaking father off his back? Even better . . .

Can a sinner and a saint both win at love?

But when Benedict is dragooned into painting his portrait, Dulcie finds himself once again inexplicably drawn to the intense artist. Can the sinful viscount entice a wary Benedict into a casual liaison, one that will put neither their reputations, nor their feelings, at risk? Or will the not-so-saintly painter demand something far more vulnerable—his heart?

PRAISE FOR BLISS BENNET

"The best historical romance I've read all year. Literate, grown-up, filled with yearning and lust and beauty." —*All About Romance*

"...intelligent and inventive, poignant and gratifying, and a radiant addition to a much-lauded series."—*USA Today Happy Ever After*

"Bennet may be a fledgling author but her book stands stalwart with... *Devil in Spring* by Lisa Kleypas, *My American Duchess* by Eloisa James, and *A Lady's Code of Misconduct* by Meredith Duran.... I was very much taken with her assured writing, complex and unusual characterization, and verve for storytelling."—*Cogitations and Meditations*

"A refreshing change of pace from other historical romances." —*Romantically Inclined Reviews*

"This pleasing romance... round[s] out its story with precise historical flair and genuine feelings."—*Publishers Weekly*

"This has been the year of finding incredible new voices in Historical Romance for me and I can now add Bliss Bennet to the list!"—*Passages to the Past*

"effervescent. . . . a series well worth following."—*Historical Novel Society Indie Reviews*

"[Bennet has] the rare, and becoming rarer, ability to create main characters who reflect their times and are in turn uniquely, likably themselves."—*Miss Bates Reads Romance*

"A beautifully written love story that has everything you want in a great historical romance: heart-wrenching emotion, heartbreak and a great HEA."—*The Reading Wench*

"Catnip for the historical romance reader."—*Bookworlder*

"A cut above many wallpaper historical romances being published today, Bennet writes with flair, confidence, and style and makes the era she is writing about come to vivid life. Her characters leap off the page, the writing is crisp, and the pathos, emotion, and romance is sure to keep readers turning the pages late into the night." —*Bookish Jottings*

"Bennet creates the most enticing, delightfully imperfect characters. Watching them finally achieve their happy ever after is bittersweet—you're happy they're happy, but... you weren't done with them yet..."—*USA Today Happy Ever After*

A SINNER WITHOUT A SAINT

The Penningtons
Book 2

BLISS BENNET

Cover design by Historical Editorial
Model cover photograph © 2018 by Jessica Boyatt

This is a work of fiction. Names, characters, and incidents are the product of the author's imagination, or are used fictitiously. Any resemblance to actual events, locales, or persons, living or dead, is purely coincidental.

ISBN ebook: 978-0-9961937-6-4
ISBN paperback: 978-0-9961937-7-1
Paperback edition

For permissions requests, please contact the author: bliss@blissbenet.com

FOR MY FATHER

PROLOGUE

APRIL 1807

THE EARL MILNE, sophisticated man of the world that he was, never permitted himself to be swayed by anything as base as superstition. Turning his chair three times round had never brought him any luck at cards, nor finding a broken horse shoe unhoped-for riches. The burning of three candles in a room, or gazing at a new moon through glass, had never been followed by unexpected death. And as for spitting to avoid bad luck—well, no proper gentleman would *ever* engage in such uncouth, vulgar behavior. As a peer of George III's realm, Milne must set the example to his family and his dependents, shunning anything that hinted of the irrational, the unfounded, or the excessively credulous.

Yet each day that his only son and heir walked God's green earth, it grew increasingly difficult for him to believe it no coincidence that young Sinclair Milne, courtesy-titled Viscount Dulcie, had been born on July 14, 1789, the very same day the French rabble had stormed the Bastille. Just like those ungodly unwashed peasants, Dulcie had a penchant for questioning the natural social order, one that would not stand him in good stead when his father shuffled off this mortal coil and the responsibilities of the earldom fell to him.

Best, then, to nip this latest little rebellion in the bud, before things got dangerously out of hand.

"John, inform Lord Dulcie I wish to speak with him," the earl instructed the footman who came at his call. "Immediately."

"Very good, my lord."

Milne tapped the evidence of his son's latest peccadillo—a letter written in a looping, boyish hand—against the blotter. Only a scapegrace such as Dulcie would force his father to bring up such unsavory matters in polite conversation.

"Father! Have you changed your mind about the billiards table?" Seventeen-year-old Viscount Dulcie, all smiles and charm, strolled into the library and threw himself into its most comfortable armchair. "Surely you don't wish me to be fleeced by every boy at school just because I've not been able to practice between terms."

Dulcie's guinea-gold curls and guileless expression might lead the unsuspecting to mistake him for an angel, lit by accident upon this too mundane earth. But the earl had long ago learned to disregard his heir's beguiling mien.

"I've not summoned you to discuss billiards, Dulcie. I've already told you how much it pains me that you waste your time playing at games instead of reading or studying." The earl rose from his own seat and held out the distasteful letter between two fingers. "I wish to speak to you about this note. Do you recognize the hand?"

Dulcie's blue eyes, fringed by over-long lashes, narrowed. "Father, that letter is addressed to me. What right had you to open it, or to read it without my consent?"

"It was franked by Lord Saybrook," Milne answered, drawing the pages back before his son had a chance to jerk them from his grasp. Dulcie had the right of it, of course, but he'd never get to his point if he allowed his son to drag him down that blind alley. "Of course I assumed it was for me."

"But it wasn't. And yet you kept reading, even after you realized your mistake." Dulcie folded his arms across his chest and shook his head. "Really, father, are those the actions of a gentleman?"

"The actions of a gentleman? Who are you to preach to me of gentlemanlike behavior, sir, when you act so shamefully towards

2

poor Saybrook's son?"

Dulcie crossed a booted ankle over his knee. "Benedict Pennington, Lord Saybrook's second son and the author of that letter, is one of my fags, and is under my protection. And if I ask him to translate a passage of Greek between terms, rather than to black my boots or fetch me my breakfast while we are at school, is not that a sign of my respect for the boy?"

"Respect? When you ask him to translate such, such—Why, I hardly know what to call this!" The earl struck a hand over the letter, sending its pages aflutter.

"Philosophy, perhaps?" Dulcie said, sitting back in his chair with irritating composure. "Xenophon is, after all, standard fare amongst schoolboys at Harrow. Even in your own day, I would wager."

"Yes, the history parts, and the fighting parts. But not this immoral filth." Milne opened the letter, searching for the abhorrent passage. "*But the sweetest of all charms are the charms of a boy who yields to you willingly. The sweetest of all and the most erotic is when he fights with you and argues. To enjoy the charms of an unwilling boy seems to me to be more like robbery than lovemaking,*" he read, his voice rising with each appalling line.

"Ah, he found that passage, did he? I was hoping he would. It is the height of hypocrisy how everyone praises the ancient Greeks while suppressing the fact that their culture accepted, even celebrated, love between men."

"Dulcie, this is no harmless intellectual exercise!" Milne paced the room. "Such vile affections may have been tolerated in past times, in other places, but we live in England, a civilized, Christian country. Do you not realize, if the wrong person got hold of this boy's letter he could be set in the stocks, or even hanged?"

"For a mere translation?" His son's tone remained nonchalant, but his fingers tapped the arm of his chair. "Surely not."

"Surely so, when accompanied by such protestations of devotion to his "dearest Clair" as young Pennington has written here. Not to mention the caresses and kisses he professes to dream of sharing with you. Foolish boy, to commit such words to paper."

"Dearest Clair?" Dulcie said, a hint of color rising in his cheeks. "What else did he write?"

"That is completely beside the point!" Milne snapped, then took a deep, steadying breath. Raising his voice with Dulcie only ever led the boy to resist his elder's dictates with increasingly mulish determination.

The earl lowered himself to kneel by his son's chair. "Surely, Dulcie, you have no desire to kiss a boy, or to have one kiss you?"

His son's blue eyes met his own. "Of course not, sir."

With another man, such an unflinching response would convince one of the truth of the speaker's words. But with Dulcie, one could never be quite certain.

"And Saybrook's son," the earl persisted. "He means nothing to you, I am sure."

This time, Milne waited an uncomfortably long moment before his son deigned to respond. But at last, Dulcie gave him the words he needed to hear.

"Yes. Nothing at all."

With a sigh, Milne rose and tossed the offensive letter onto the small fire that burnt in the grate. He did not want the pain of Dulcie putting the lie to the admission he'd just wrangled from him by trying to charm the foolscap from his very fingers.

"Well, then. Sentimental romances will arise when boys are crowded all together at school. I remember my own infatuation with a young chorister during my time at Harrow. The most lovely smile, and the voice of an angel, he had. But when that boy began to take on the aspects of an adult man, and stopped resembling a beautiful girl, my infatuation naturally faded."

"Naturally, sir."

Did Dulcie's faint smile mock his father's nostalgic memory? Or was it a sign that the sentiments expressed in young Pennington's letter, the one he stared at as it curled and burned in the grate, were welcome?

Milne cleared his throat. "You are nearly eighteen, Dulcie. And as my eldest son, you have a duty to marry, and to sire an heir to carry on the Milne line. So it is time for you to put away such childish notions, before you cause real harm to Lord Saybrook's son, or to some other unsuspecting boy."

Dulcie's eyes turned from the fire to his father. "It was only an academic exercise, Father. I never intended to harm—"

"No, you never do intend, do you? Impetuous, headstrong boy. You must learn once and for all that your actions have consequences."

The earl sat behind his desk, then folded his hands on the blotter in front of him. "If you are well-versed enough in Greek to teach a twelve-year-old to translate Xenophon, Dulcie, you are surely skilled enough to sit for the entrance examinations for Oxford. And if you are not, you will study for them here until you are."

Dulcie's spine straightened. "Here? What, am I not to return to Harrow after Easter?"

"Should I allow you to go back and perhaps have this boy tempt you further astray? Even you must realize that such a course would be unwise."

"But Father, if I promised—"

"No. You will remain here, and allow poor Pennington's unfortunate infatuation to die a decent death. And we will not speak of such things ever again. Do you understand?"

"As you wish, sir." Dulcie rose from his chair, his eyes flicking for the merest instant towards the grate before returning to rest on his father. "Am I to be allowed to write to my friend Leverett, to tell him I won't be returning?"

"Yes, if your letter contains no messages for young Pennington. I will, of course, need to read it before franking it." A disgraceful demand, but one he felt he must insist upon. How else to impress the weight of his disapproval on his careless son?

But Dulcie stood straight and tall, no hint of shame marring either his features or his figure. "Of course, sir. Will that be all?"

Milne nodded.

His son, ever polite, offered him a bow, then strode from the room.

Once he was certain Dulcie was gone, the earl moved to the hearth and took up the poker. With a muttered oath, he prodded at the fire until he was certain not a scrap of that shameful letter remained for a servant—or Dulcie—to find.

CHAPTER 1

GHOSTS, IF ONE was of a turn of mind to believe in such things, appeared to best advantage in the countryside, haunting lonely lanes, picturesque tumbledown castles, or sublimely abandoned ruins. They most assuredly did not frequent the bustling ballrooms, private clubs, or public shops of the world's largest metropolis. Yet for the last two months, an apparition from his past had frequently and habitually manifested itself at the edges of Viscount Dulcie's London life, an apparition not of wisps or shadow, but of all-too-solid flesh.

Not that Dulcie would allow a mere ghost, even in the striking form of a grown-to-delicious-manhood Benedict Pennington, to distract him today. Not when he was on the verge of proving once and for all that he, not his rival Lattimer Leverett, deserved a position on the governing board of the British Institution for Promoting the Fine Arts in the United Kingdom.

"You're staring again, Dulcie."

Lattimer Leverett nodded towards the center of the Cockspur Street print shop where Benedict Pennington stood, hands tucked into the hollow of his spine. Everyone else in the room had gathered around the draped easel at the center of the shop, but Pennington's eyes were fixed on an engraving displayed in one of the several mahogany racks scattered throughout the room. His attention had always been caught by things no one else noticed.

Suddenly, a scowl roiled his handsome features, almost as if somehow that inanimate engraving, rather than a far younger Lord Dulcie, had done him some personal injury, and he was devising how best to extract his revenge.

Only a fool would find such an expression the least bit compelling.

Leverett elbowed Dulcie and sniggered.

Yes, he was gawking, and certainly not at the artwork. But instead of upbraiding his companion for so rudely calling attention to the fact, Dulcie raised his lips in a practiced smile. Containing his emotions behind a mask of dandified indifference had long become second nature, even with a companion as provoking as Leverett.

But Pennington, damn him, seemed to have the power to make that mask slip without even trying. Why had he not remembered that the gentleman had some pretensions to the paintbrush himself, and would likely be among the crowd at Colnaghi's monthly levee?

"Can't keep your eyes off him, can you? How amusing, when it was he who could not stop staring at you when we were all at school."

Dulcie quelled the urge to jerk his eyes away in embarrassment. Leverett's annoying taunt deserved no such response. Instead, he allowed his gaze to linger for just the barest moment before moving it slowly, carelessly about the room. Leverett, privileged grandson of a duke, would not appreciate being made to wait.

But the fellow would keep trying to challenge his position as leader of the connoisseur set, despite Dulcie's obviously superior knowledge and taste. Hadn't he dragged Dulcie to the print shop today in an attempt to embarrass him in front of the most influential members of the British Institution, and prove his aesthetic judgment the more acute? But if Leverett thought an indiscreetly whispered innuendo about a childhood calf-love would put him off his game, he only demonstrated that he was as bad at evaluating people as he was at judging fine art.

No, Leverett would have to try a little harder before he could discompose Sinclair Milne.

Dulcie gestured with his quizzing glass towards the easel upon which a proof, covered by a drape, rested. "An engraving commissioned more than a decade ago finally makes its appearance—is it any wonder that I stare, Leverett? In truth, I'm almost afraid to blink for fear the thing will prove the most ephemeral of mirages. Will it actually be revealed after this cover is removed?"

Chuckles, and a few outright laughs, burst from the men around them, bringing a frown to Leverett's face. Yes, that would confuse him, Dulcie making fun of the work by the very man he'd been championing all these years.

For they had come to the print shop today to pronounce judgment upon the long-awaited proof of the engraving of *Christ Healing the Sick*. To entice gentlemen to join the British Institution, each new subscriber to the fledgling organization had been promised a print of Benjamin West's renowned painting. But what engraver could be entrusted to transform the masterpiece to print?

Dulcie had supported West's controversial choice of a young, relatively unknown engraver. Leverett had disagreed, loudly and often. And he'd teased Dulcie unmercifully in the ensuing eleven years, as the engraver offered one excuse after another for his failure to complete the task.

But in spite of all Leverett's taunts and gibes, Dulcie had never wavered, as certain then as he was today that the man would soon be regarded as one of the finest engravers of their age. Now, his faith in the artist, as well as his own status as the better aesthetic judge, would be confirmed beyond doubt. He, not Leverett, deserved to be appointed to the Institution's board.

If he could just push Benedict Pennington from his mind long enough to concentrate on the task at hand.

Signore Colnaghi, the shop's proprietor, bustled out from behind the counter. "Such a one for the jokes you are, my lord. But I tell you, I have seen this engraving with my own eyes, both the plate and the proof. It is no fleeting cloud, to pass away at the merest gust of wind."

"But what of the quality?" interrupted George Norton, a recent, and eager, subscriber to the British Institution. "Is the result worth the wait?"

Other members of the Institution echoed Norton's query, buzzing about Dulcie and Leverett like drones around two queens poised to fight for control of the hive.

Dulcie crossed his arms and smiled. "Yes, Leverett, what of the quality? We await with bated breath the judgment of a true connoisseur."

Leverett's lips thinned. "Uncover the proof, *Signore*."

Colnaghi pulled the drape with a dramatic flourish. The crowd pushed forward, each struggling to catch a glimpse over Leverett and Dulcie's shoulders.

Raising his quizzing glass, Dulcie examined the engraving with minute attention. Yes, the engraver demonstrated a decided superiority in drawing the human figure. He'd cut the copper plate with firmness and precision, using fine lines to convey details that in the original had been portrayed with color. Religious subjects were not Leverett's specialty, but even he must concede that the engraver had captured both the substance and the feeling of West's painting with remarkable skill.

And that intense, well-muscled Roman warrior in the corner —did he not have something of the air of the adult Benedict Pennington?

"So, what say you, Leverett?" he asked, raising his eyes to his companion rather than allowing them to drift over the crowd in search of a far more interesting face. "A miserable failure, as you have long predicted? Or a work worthy of being hung in your own ancestral halls?"

Leverett scowled, clearly aware he'd been bested yet again. "It is tolerable," he finally acknowledged.

"Tolerable? If I am not mistaken, and these good gentlemen about us know how rarely I am, Mr. Heath has given the world a print of unrivaled excellence." Dulcie threw his arm wide. "A triumph, a clear triumph. Do you not agree, gentlemen?"

"Oh, yes, my lord. A triumph indeed!" Mr. Norton exclaimed.

To Dulcie's satisfaction, the coterie around them, which included several current members of the British Institution's governing board, hummed in agreement. Even the stately Marquess of Stafford, the group's current president, gave him an agreeable nod.

If he met with Stafford's approval, an invitation to sit on the Board would be nearly assured.

Dulcie permitted himself one last glance at the engraving, then stepped aside to allow the Marquess to take a closer look.

George Norton followed Dulcie.

It gave him no little satisfaction to see the young man's eyes shining up at him, rather than at Leverett. Earlier in the season, Dulcie had noticed his rival's interest in the boy, and had thought to pluck him out from under Leverett's wing, cultivating his taste in art, and, perhaps, if he were correct about Norton's predilections, in other, less intellectual pleasures. Lord knows he'd learn far more from Dulcie than he'd ever gain from a fellow as self-serving as Leverett. Yet something about the pup's overeager manner, or perhaps his too-artfully styled hair—did he set it in papers each night, to make it curl just so?—had given Dulcie pause.

Still, using the boy to tease Leverett offered its own rewards.

"Do you have a framer you frequent, Norton?" he asked, placing a companionable arm about the young man's shoulders. "If not, I would be happy to recommend one. A print of such excellence deserves a frame of equal quality."

"I say, Pennington, what is your opinion of the print?" Leverett interrupted, inviting the man Dulcie least wished to acknowledge into their conversation. "Although if memory serves, you were wont to agree with Dulcie's every opinion with slavish devotion when we were boys together at school."

Benedict Pennington glanced up from the rack of prints he had been examining. All dark eyes, tousled hair, and stern, unsmiling mouth, he gave the engraving a cursory glance. "When one has not had the opportunity to view the original, it is impossible to form an opinion," he offered.

"Have you not visited the British Institution, Mr. Pennington, where the original painting hangs?" Norton exclaimed. "For a nominal fee, any gentleman interested in the arts may become a subscriber."

"And join a group of collectors who come together primarily to keep the prices of Old Master paintings high? Thank you, but I'd rather not."

Dulcie suppressed a bark of laughter. Such a frank assessment of the motives of many of his fellow British Institution members had often crossed his own mind, although he'd never be so impolitic as to say so in public. But Pennington, it would seem, had no such scruples. When had the shy boy he remembered learned to give voice to his passionately held principles?

"Mr. Pennington?" A tall young woman with a surprisingly deep voice laid a hand on Pennington's arm. "Come, there is something I wish to show you."

"If you will excuse me, gentleman?" Pennington bowed, then walked off towards the back of the shop with his companion.

"Well, Dulcie, Pennington certainly shows you little regard.

How fleeting are the *tendres* of our youth. He and Dulcie were as thick as thieves when we were all at Harrow, you know, Norton."

Dulcie narrowed his eyes, but Leverett did not heed the warning. "I could understand it then, for young Pennington was quite pretty as a child. But why you continue to hold him in fascination, Dulcie, I cannot begin to fathom. Plagued by sentiment, are you?"

"You mistake the matter, Leverett," he said, his arm falling from Norton's shoulders. "Caution, not sentimentality, leads me to keep an eye on Pennington. He is, after all, brother of the lady I'm courting."

Married himself, Leverett thought nothing of a man taking on a wife while satisfying his carnal urges with younger members of his own sex. But Dulcie's courtship of Sibilla Pennington had been nothing but a ruse, designed not only to distract his father from his infernal matchmaking, but also to drive his friend Peregrine Sayre wild with jealousy. It would all come to an end before long, as soon as Sayre could be pushed into declaring his true feelings for the chit.

But if Dulcie's courtship of Sibilla Pennington had the additional benefit of making another Pennington jealous before it ended, why then, Dulcie would be the last to call attention to the fact.

Out of the corner of his eye, Dulcie spied Benedict Pennington, his careful attention fixed on the lady by his side. Merely the son and brother of a viscount, not a viscount with an earldom in the wings, as was Dulcie, yet he held his tall, classically-proportioned frame with all the confidence of an ancient Spartan warrior. Where was the diffident boy who had so quietly but fervently admired him at Harrow? Dulcie could find little sign of him in the hard, unyielding man across the room. And yet he still found himself drawn to the sight, even in the face of Leverett's petty provocations.

George Norton, wisely refusing to entangle himself in the

arguments of his elders, cut his eyes towards the couple. "Do you know the lady, my lord? I've not seen her before."

Dulcie did not recognize her, either. And he decidedly did not care for the proprietary air with which she grasped Mr. Pennington's arm, pulling him to a rack of prints at the opposite end of the shop.

Leverett laughed. "Better to ask who her grandfather is. And what glorious paintings she will inherit from him, and Pennington from her, when the old fellow goes the way of all flesh."

"A relation of Pennington's?" Dulcie asked, his brow furrowing. He could not recall Benedict ever mentioning a relative who collected art.

"Not yet. But rumor suggests he may soon be, if Adler has anything to say about it."

Dulcie's posture stiffened. Benedict Pennington intended to marry?

"Adler? Do you mean Julius Adler?" Norton exclaimed. "Why, it's said he owns the largest collection of Old Masters in all England. How could I not know he has an unmarried granddaughter? Especially a granddaughter who is one of his heirs?"

"His *only* heir. And you know nothing of her because she's been secreted away on the Continent for years. But now that she's of marriageable age, he's brought her to London, dangling the prospect of his paintings as dowry. Tempting, wouldn't you say, Dulcie?"

Norton frowned, squinting at the lady in question. "She's not so very ill-favored, though she is rather tall for a female. And if one were to get a Rubens and a Raphael along with her—"

"Indeed. But alas, I believe Adler is on the lookout for an earl at the very least. If I were you, Dulcie, I'd give over Pennington's sister and attach yourself to this one."

"But did you not just say that Benedict Pennington is

courting her?" Dulcie brushed at an imaginary piece of lint on his sleeve.

"Would you allow a little thing like that to stop you? What, do you fear to hurt poor Pennington's feelings?"

Leverett's waspish tone had begun to draw the attention of their fellow British Institution members. Sensing a fight, or at least fodder for some gossip, they drifted, singly and in pairs, away from the engraving and towards their trio.

"When has hurting anyone's feelings ever prevented me from pursuing what I wish?" Dulcie struggled to keep the annoyance from his voice.

"Then why do you hesitate? Surely a man who aspires to be the finest art connoisseur of his age would not scruple to pursue such an opportunity," Leverett goaded. "Davenport, would you marry Julius Adler's granddaughter, if her dowry included a Titian and a Correggio?"

"In a trice," answered Davenport.

"And you, Meheux?" Leverett asked, turning to another man in the crowd. "A leg-shackle in exchange for a Michelangelo and a Poussin? Even if you had to steal the lady from under the nose of another suitor?"

"Do I get the Titian and Correggio, too?" Meheux waggled an eyebrow.

"Greedy bastard," Leverett said. "Yes, yes, all of them, and more."

"*Bien entendu*," Meheux answered with a shrug. "Only an *imbécile* would allow such an opportunity to slip through his fingers."

"And yet our Lord Dulcie here hesitates."

Davenport, Meheux, and the other British Institution members looked at him askance. How far would Leverett take this?

"I am courting Miss Pennington," Dulcie said in as even a tone as he could muster.

"But I've heard no banns read, no engagement formally announced," Leverett answered. "Surely a man with as glib a tongue as yours could extricate himself from an unofficial courtship if he truly wished it. So I am left to wonder—why should Dulcie pass up such an opportunity? The only answer that makes any sense at all is that he has a— well, a womanish *care* for the man courting Miss Adler before him. Benedict Pennington."

The crowd about them stirred with unease. More than a few among them shared Leverett and Dulcie's predilection for male bed partners, but none were fool enough to wish such preferences bandied about in the street. Or in the midst of Colnaghi's print shop.

Dulcie took out a handkerchief and rubbed it over his quizzing glass. "Why, Leverett, you've always accused me of having a care for no one but myself."

"Indeed. But perhaps you've only been pining away for a long-lost boyhood . . . friend? One whose place young Norton here hopes to fill for you?"

The crowd about them buzzed just a little louder after each of Leverett's increasingly pointed hints. Even Norton took a careful step away from the pair, his eyes flickering with alarm. Damnation, they'd turn on Dulcie in a trice, no matter what they got up to in the privacy of their homes or the back rooms of public houses. On Norton, too, if Lattimer publicly tarred them with the brush of sexual impropriety.

The ghost of another young boy flickered in the back of his mind, a boy whom his impetuosity had also once put into danger. One to whom he'd never been able to make proper amends.

"Come, Leverett, you know how little I hold all humankind in regard," Dulcie drawled. "I'd pine away over a Rembrandt or Rubens, perhaps, but never over a mere human."

"Then prove it," Leverett pressed, obviously unwilling to give up this unexpectedly fruitful line of attack. "I'll wager five hundred guineas that sentiment will keep you from courting and stealing Miss Adler, and her considerable dowry of Old Masters paintings, away from poor Benedict Pennington."

A gasp rose from the knot of men crowding about them, then a torrent of whispers. Each knew Dulcie's reputation for embracing almost any wager, no matter how outrageous. If he refused this one, he'd not only be the laughingstock of the season, he'd confirm each and every man's belief in Leverett's ridiculous claims.

Dulcie's eyes flicked to George Norton. The poor boy stood resolute, but his face had paled to an alarming degree. Just up from university, he was, and far more interested in art than in the political career his father wished him to pursue. But if the miasma of salacious rumor polluted his reputation during his first weeks in town, neither the political nor artistic set would welcome him. And Norton senior would send the boy scurrying back home in disgrace.

He clenched his hands. Damn him for a coward if he allowed it to happen again. Norton did not deserve to become entangled in Leverett's net, any more than young Benedict Pennington had.

No, he had to put an end to this idle chatter before more than his own reputation was impugned.

Dulcie stepped forward and held out his hand. "Sir, I accept your wager."

As the men about them cheered and teased, Dulcie kept a smile pasted on his face, his back resolutely turned away from Benedict Pennington. No need to inform Leverett that merely accepting a wager did not mean one was intent on winning it. Perhaps, as he had done with his friend Peregrine Sayre, he might decide to help advance Pennington's courtship by feigning an interest in the object of the fellow's admiration. That is, if Adler's collection did not pose too much of a temptation.

Perhaps, if his better angels won this round in the constant battle for his tattered soul, he might even lay the ghost of that long-betrayed boy to rest.

"No, not there. A little to the left. No, no, not so far! Bring it back to the right a bit more. Now, just a touch higher . . ."

Benedict Pennington suppressed a grunt of frustration. He'd come here today to talk to Julius Adler about donating his paintings for the good of the nation, not to fuss about where to hang them in the merchant's London house. Besides, the frame Adler had chosen for this latest addition to his collection dug heavily into his hip, and his fingers were growing numb as he struggled to support its weight while keeping his grip against the prickly intricacies of its carving. This job really required more than two men, but Adler would not suffer anyone but himself and Benedict to touch his newly acquired Carracci.

But it wasn't Adler who was the current cause of his troubles. No, it was his granddaughter, Polly, who darted about the picture gallery, her face tight with concentration, examining the position of the painting from as many different angles as possible. Silly to be jealous of the girl just for having the chance to gaze so intently at the draped figure of Saint John in the wilderness. Especially as her stare was motivated by pure aesthetic appreciation, not tinged with lust, as his would be.

It was only that the saint's reclining posture and guinea-gold curls put him so much in mind of Clair as a schoolboy—Viscount Dulcie, as he kept forgetting to think of him. The similarity made the prideful part of him cringe, remembering how the older boy had befriended him, then abandoned him without a thought all those years ago. But another, more persistent part kept pulling him back, eager for the rush of feeling the painting evoked, the memories of the shock at his first sight of the stunningly handsome adolescent Sinclair Milne, the revelatory pleasures of their early days together. Memories he'd thought he'd put aside long ago, until he'd returned from the Continent earlier this spring, and caught sight of the grown-to-adulthood Lord Dulcie in all his arrogant glory.

Memories that continued to plague him now that their once separate social circles had begun to overlap as Dulcie paid court to Benedict's sister.

"Here, child?" Adler's impatient question pulled Benedict out of his fruitless reverie. Dulcie seemed on the verge of making an offer for Sibilla, and it would not do for Benedict to keep mooning over a future brother-in-law.

"A bit higher, Grandfather," Polly said, lifting her own hands and rising on her toes.

Benedict hoisted the painting a hands-width higher. "Here?"

"Yes, but now a touch to the right . . ."Adler's foot tapped with impatience. Of a less artistic, and more decisive, temperament than his granddaughter, the merchant clearly did not share Polly's interest in the finer points of aesthetic display.

Benedict's fingers tingled, longing for a piece of charcoal with which to limn the intent expression on Polly's face. Sketching could always distract him from his often turbulent feelings. And Polly's passion for this task put him in mind of his mother, a far more comforting memory than that of Viscount Dulcie. A talented artist herself, Lady Saybrook had been the first to offer Benedict a paintbrush, and to encourage his own clumsy early aesthetic efforts. During the painting lessons Benedict had given Polly since their first meeting in Italy last June, he'd taught her many of the artistic precepts his mother had imparted to him, including those about how the placement of a picture could influence the effect it would have on its viewers.

"Here?" he asked as he suppressed a grunt.

"Almost! Just a bit to the left," she answered, leaning her entire body in the direction she wished the painting to move.

"Come now, Polyhymnia," Adler interrupted. "Mr. Pennington may have once dreamed of being close enough to touch a Carracci, but I hardly think said dream included toting one about for days on end."

Polly's brow wrinkled. "I know, Grandfather, but I just cannot decide. After seeing Sir John Leicester's collection, the way he displayed his paintings so symmetrically, I cannot get it out of my head. Might we install a brass picture rail here, and hang the paintings on chains the way he has, rather than from hooks in the wall?"

Benedict had admired Leicester's new system, too. It would be perfect for the new national art museum, allowing the displays to be changed at will.

If he could but convince Adler to finally commit to serving as the museum's first, and leading, patron.

"And how much do you think such a contrivance costs?" Adler asked, gazing fondly at his granddaughter even while shaking his head at what he obviously regarded as her latest flight of artistic fancy. "Do you think I put together one of the finest art collections in the country by frittering away my money on every newfangled notion that catches the eye?"

"I would never ask you to buy anything just because it is fashionable," Polly said, her voice ripe with disdain. "But with such a system in place, you could rearrange your pictures whenever you liked. Just think of the possibilities!"

"Rearrange the pictures? Why ever would I wish to do that?"

Polly caught Benedict's eye, and the two of them grinned. Adler might enjoy collecting paintings, but he had little of the aesthetic sensibility that ran so strongly in his granddaughter, something she and Benedict, artists both, had shared many a smile over during the months since they had first met.

"Ah, yes, laugh all you will. But someone around here must

pay the bills." After a nod to Benedict, Adler caught hold of one end of the painting, then hefted it to his shoulder. "Now, Polly, pick a spot and be done with it. I've more important matters to see to before we dine tonight."

"And if you choose the spot now, we'll have time for a lesson before you must ready yourself for the evening," Benedict tempted as he raised his end of the painting once again. Parallel to its neighbor, but with a bit more space between the two than he'd given it before.

"No, not today, we've a ball to attend," Adler said. "Polyhymnia does enough already to frighten away potential suitors without staining her fingers and gown with watercolors. I shudder to think what she'd look—or smell—like if I gave in and allowed her to dabble in oils."

Happily for Benedict, Adler's eye was fixed on his granddaughter, not him. Polly had no difficulty maintaining an air of innocence, unlike Benedict, whose face tended to reveal far more than he wished. He'd long urged Polly to confess to her grandfather that under his tutelage, she'd done far more than dabble with oils. At least she took decent care not to reek of turpentine whenever she was in her grandfather's presence.

"Mr. Pennington says my work shows great improvement," Polly interrupted, clearly attempting to distract him from any further discussion of suitors. Polly had as little wish to marry as Benedict did, even if her reluctance stemmed from a far different cause.

With her most winning smile, she laid a hand on her grandfather's arm. "And you know that Mr. Pennington is the best of teachers."

Adler grunted. "The best of dockworkers is what you need here, Polly, not the best of teachers. Now choose, or I'll choose for you."

"But Grandfather—"

"No! I will brook no further dithering, nor more argument.

Footman, mark this spot, then install the proper hangers. And you, Polly, go and ready yourself for this evening's entertainment. Or I'll forbid you to pick up another paintbrush!"

"Yes, Grandfather." Polly ducked her head and turned away, but not before Benedict caught a glimpse of a familiar, stubborn set to her lips.

Benedict shook his head. He had nothing but gratitude towards Julius Adler for the way the art collector had supported him and his work since they'd met abroad nearly a year ago. But he knew how unhappy Polly became when her strict grandfather grew impatient with her disorderly ways, and how frustrated by his oft-repeated threat to keep her from painting. And how often she would agree with the older man, just to keep the peace, only to go off and do what she wanted once they were apart. Only too likely she'd rush straight back to her canvas after this latest brusque attempt to control her free spirit. Perhaps after he'd discussed this business of the museum with Adler, he'd try once again to hint to the man the value of patience when dealing with his sensitive, talented granddaughter.

"No, no, do not touch it!" Adler chided the footman, who had come too close to the painting as he reached up to mark the spot for the hangers.

Benedict and Adler lowered the frame once again to the floor, placing the Carracci out of the footman's reach. Before the older man lowered a protective cloth over the painting, Benedict caught a last glimpse of the reclining saint. Yes, St. John did look far too much like Clair—Lord Dulcie, damn it. But Dulcie shared little of the saint's charitable nature, at least as far as Benedict could see. Most men matured from their careless adolescent selves, but the only change Benedict had noticed over the past two months of circling the viscount was in Dulcie's person, somehow not just more elegant, but also more virile, than it had been even at sixteen.

"Yes, a true masterpiece. No wonder you stare," Adler said

before turning back to the footman. "Inform me when you've finished, and Mr. Pennington and I will see to the hanging."

Benedict shook his head at Adler's misinterpretation. Would he have to avoid the gallery altogether once the blasted painting had finally been hung?

"Now, Pennington, you have news about our little scheme?"

At last. "I do indeed, sir."

"Then come with me, and we'll discuss it like civilized men, over a drink."

Benedict followed Adler into a neat, if rather stark, library.

"So, you managed to meet with the king's art advisor, and sound him out about our ideas?" Adler asked as he gestured Benedict towards a chair by the hearth.

"Yes, I ran down Sir Charles Long in his club yesterday. He agrees that the time is ripe to approach the king about supporting the establishment of an art gallery for the nation."

"And well he should. How could he allow the British Empire to be outdone by the French? And by the Italians, and the Germans? Why, even the Imperial collections in Vienna are open to anyone with clean shoes! It's a national disgrace that we have no public gallery of equal stature." Adler handed Benedict a glass, then took a seat behind a desk.

"Indeed, sir. If England's support of the arts was at all suitable to her rank amongst the nations of Europe, our national establishments for the cultivation of the arts would surely surpass those of any other age or country," Benedict agreed.

Despite—or perhaps because of—being born in Russia, Adler had a strong streak of patriotism for his adopted country. Benedict's own motivations for championing a national art gallery in London were far different. Important works of art should not be hidden away in private collections—such as those owned by Lord Dulcie and his fellow British Institution connoisseurs—with only friends and family allowed to view them. How were the next generation of British artists to be nurtured and encouraged if they had no access to the finished works of the greatest painters of the past? How much more would his own mother have been able to accomplish if only she'd had the opportunity to study more than the few family portraits that hung in Pennington House's gallery? The idea of more such talent going to waste made him gnash his teeth.

Adler, though, would hardly be moved by such idealism. So Benedict must shape his argument to best appeal to the feelings of his audience. "Without a patron willing to sell or donate a substantial number of works of art to serve as a basis for such a collection, though, I fear our country will long lag behind our Continental brethren."

"And fat old Georgie won't give his own collection for the good of his people, will he, the selfish bastard."

"The king feels that allowing the British Institution to borrow several of his paintings each year for its spring show is the epitome of royal selflessness. Or so Sir Charles implies."

Adler snorted. "Old George wouldn't recognize selflessness if it bit him on the arse."

"But your collection contains far more Old Masters than does the king's," Benedict reminded. A bit of flattery never hurt.

"Yes, it does, doesn't it? You'd think a connoisseur with a personal income exceeding the national revenue of a third-rate power would have chosen more wisely, rather than spending so much on contemporary artists. Ah, but there is no accounting for taste, is there?"

Benedict himself far preferred the more modern works in King George's collection to Adler's almost slavish devotion to the Old Masters. But for a national museum, one needed paintings from the past as well as the present.

"And how many of my paintings does the fat old king think to cozen me out of?" Adler asked.

"Sir Charles did not specify any particular number."

"You do know that I cannot offer them all," Adler warned. "I must hold some back for Polyhymnia's dowry. Especially if I'm to catch a nobleman for her. Or even the son of a nobleman—"

"Certainly, sir," Benedict interrupted. The wealthy merchant had been hinting at a possible match between Benedict and Polly almost since they had first met in Italy almost a year ago. Luckily for Benedict, Polly reserved all her passion for her art, with none left for him. And all *his* passion—well, it was not for Polly, nor for any other young lady he'd yet to meet.

"Sir Charles did say other gentlemen may be hatching similar plans to yours. Offering to sell or gift their own art collections for the sake of establishing an art museum for the glory of England."

Adler sat straighter in his chair. "Who?"

"I've heard talk of Lord Leicester, as well as Sir George Beaumont."

Adler dismissed Benedict's words with a sharp snap of the hand. "Leicester's no competition; his collection contains only British works. Beaumont, though, he might present a problem. Is he in earnest?"

"Rumor has it he is interested, but wary, as he feels the British Museum does not have the space to display the collection whole."

The merchant's fingers drummed on his desk. "What if I offered to sell not only a selection of pictures, but also this house? Once Polyhymnia is married, I'll have little use for such a large London residence. Parliament would be hard pressed to turn down such an offer, don't you agree?"

Benedict leaned forward, catching his breath at the grandeur of the gesture. He could picture it, the wide rooms cleared of furniture, every wall hung with the glories Adler had amassed during his fifty years of traveling and collecting. No one demanding money, or tickets, or even one's name at the entrance, only handing out catalogs or guidebooks to the collection with a welcoming smile. Proctors stationed here and there, not to turn people away, but to supply the interested with information about the works, and to ensure the paintings were not harmed. And artists' easels scattered all about each room, eager students attempting to learn from their predecessors by imitating their techniques.

Adler's house was rather dark, not ideal for displaying art, but if they could put in a skylight or two . . .

"Well, Pennington?"

Shaking off his dream, Benedict turned his attention back to Adler. "That would be an amazingly generous offer, sir. Far more so than Leicester's, or even Beaumont's, especially if the paintings you offered were of equal worth."

Adler nodded. "I'll get the entire collection valued, then decide which—if any—pictures to offer. Mr. Young should know —"

A knock on the library door interrupted the most promising conversation Benedict had ever held about his dreams for a British national art museum.

"Are you ready for us?" Adler asked before the approaching footman could get in a word.

"Not quite yet, sir. This note just arrived for you, from Lady Milne."

Lady Milne? Benedict frowned. Adler had never mentioned an acquaintance with Dulcie's mother.

Adler cracked the seal and quickly scanned the note's contents. Then, with a crisp nod, he set it down on the desk and folded his hands atop it.

"Do you know anything of Milne's son, Pennington?" Adler asked.

Benedict caught back a painful laugh. Did he know anything of Clair?

Only that he was a golden-haired, golden-tongued risk-taker. A charming, enthusiastic lover of beauty in all its forms.

And to his everlasting embarrassment and regret, a selfish,

unfeeling abandoner, one who would forsake a friend without the least scrap of remorse.

Oh, he knew all about Viscount Dulcie. Too much, and too little, but nothing he could share without revealing secrets of his own.

"He's Milne's eldest child, and only son," he offered instead. "A true connoisseur of the arts. You and he should have much in common."

Adler smiled. "Lady Milne offers to introduce us so Lord Dulcie may act as guide to my granddaughter and myself during a proposed visit to the spring exhibition at the British Institution."

"Are you not already a member?"

"Assuredly. Yet the son of an earl, and one with an interest in art—well, such a connection is nothing to sneer at. Especially when one has a granddaughter to settle."

Benedict shifted in his seat. "I have heard it said that Dulcie will be soon engaged." And to Benedict's own sister, no less. Dulcie as his brother-in-law, rather than as his— Well, the mere prospect of it left a bitter taste in his mouth.

"Ah, but young men's hearts are ever so fickle, are they not? Particularly when the details of dowries come to the fore." Adler reached for his pen and inkwell, a self-satisfied smile curving into the rounds of his ruddy cheeks. "I shall accept. And have Polyhymnia offer to give him a tour of my own collection as a thank you."

Benedict frowned. Once Dulcie had raised his toploftical quizzing glass to the glories of Adler's collection, would he drop Sibilla Pennington in favor of Polly Adler, flitting like a careless butterfly from one flower to the next? As much as Benedict would rejoice over ridding his family of Dulcie's pall, he wouldn't wish him on anyone else he called friend, either. Especially since Dulcie would likely exert his charms on Polly only until he gained her dowry of Old Masters, then abandon her to move on to another self-indulgent pursuit.

"Mr. Adler, I think I should inform y—"

"We'll talk more of this matter after I've had the collection valued. We'll leave the Carracci unhung until then." Adler had already moved on, not even looking up from the sheet of foolscap over which his pen moved with sharp, decisive strokes. "Bid you good-day, Pennington."

Pinching his lips tight, Benedict bowed, then followed the footman from the room.

As they reached the gallery, Benedict paused to lift the corner of the drape from the as yet unhung painting. Yes, the handsome viscount might resemble Carracci's Saint John, but the small bowl of water the saint held would never be enough to purify such a sybaritic soul.

Would Adler truly trade his collection for a title for his granddaughter? Did he not realize that if Dulcie got hold of it, the preening peacock would only hide it away, or use it for his own self-aggrandizement, boasting of his own disinterest when he deigned to show it to a handful of select friends and acquaintances? And then what would become of the plans for a national gallery?

Even worse, Dulcie would be hurting Sibilla, and Polly, too, to achieve his self-interested ends.

The muscles of Benedict's entire frame pulled tight. No, he could not allow any man, no matter how captivating, to hurt the only two women for whom he had a care.

Nor to steal away an art collection that by all rights should belong to the nation.

Especially if that man were Sinclair Milne.

CHAPTER 2

DULCIE HUMMED AS HE STRODE the pavements of early morning Mayfair, an amusing little ditty he'd heard at the theater the night before, about a young carpenter torn away from his lady love by a cruel press gang. Been quite distraught, the poor lad had, when he'd finally returned, only to discover another chap warming his girl's bed.

Shaking his head, he tapped his walking stick against the iron railings fronting a Mount Street townhouse in time to his humming. Gullible fellow, that carpenter. Far better to keep one's distance from emotional entanglements, particularly those of a romantic sort.

After doffing his hat to a passing milkmaid and grinning at her reddening cheeks, Dulcie broke out into full-throated song:

"Oh! Sally Brown, oh! Sally Brown,
How could you *sarve* me so?
I've met with many a *breeze* before,
But never such a *blow*."

Now, if only Peregrine Sayre would finally declare himself to Sibilla Pennington and her family, Dulcie, too, would be as free as the young carpenter. Teasing Per with his sham courtship of the chit had proven vastly amusing, but it was more than time for Dulcie to move on to other challenges. Alas, Per had proven surprisingly behindhand in his own wooing, in spite all of Dulcie's prodding and maneuvering. Still, he'd stand Per in better stead than the carpenter's lover had stood him, keeping up the deception until his friend finally took the bit between his teeth and claimed *la Pennington* for himself. Hadn't he even risen at this ungodly early hour to attend a meeting with his father and Lord Saybrook to discuss marriage settlements, just to preserve the ruse? If Per and Sibilla did not name their firstborn Sinclair, well, he'd certainly have something to say about it.

With a jaunty whistle, Dulcie crossed Mount Street and made his way down Berkeley Square. But as he drew closer to Pennington House, raised voices began to drown out his own tune. Housemaids arguing over who would have the privilege of delivering the morning paper to the master? Footmen come to fisticuffs over the smiles of a passing wench? Saybrook should keep his domestics in better order.

Even worse, the front door to the townhouse stood wide open, with not a servant in sight. Dulcie poked in his head. "Lord Saybrook? Father?"

No one answered.

Down the passageway, he could just make out a group of liveried servants all clustered about a doorway. The entrance to the room from which the clamor spilled, no doubt.

Dulcie closed the street door behind him, then stepped past an open-mouthed scullery maid and elbowed his way between two footmen juggling for best position outside Pennington House's morning room. Today, though, the room seemed better suited to a theater than a fashionable home, a theater featuring a Restoration-era comedy on the bill. Theo Pennington, Viscount Saybrook, stood pressed against an armchair, being harangued by his great aunt and by another, older man, each trying to shout down the other. The remains of a broken vase—thrown by one of the disputants, or knocked over during the fracas?—lay scattered about the lush Turkey carpet. And there, his own father, edging carefully away from the feuding trio, backing towards a sofa far too delicate to hold his hefty bulk. A sofa by which stood Sibilla Pennington and Peregrine Sayre, their hands tightly entwined.

Dulcie smiled. If they were openly billing and cooing in front of her family, then Per must have formally paid Sibilla his addresses.

He stepped closer to the happy couple, eager to offer his congratulations and to discover the cause of the current to-do.

"Better not let Dulcie catch you in it, unless you don't mind being the butt of his witticisms for the next fortnight or two," he heard his father say as he reached his side.

"Don't let Dulcie catch you in what?" he asked. "Would be a fair treat, it would, to catch someone else out for a change, rather than always being caught out myself."

"Ah, but it's you who have been caught, or will be, if Saybrook and I have anything to say about it." His father's lips lifted in a satisfied smile. "In parson's mousetrap, that is. So glad you saw fit to attend the discussion of the settlements."

"The settlements?" Per asked, his voice ripe with belligerence. "What settlements?"

Dulcie raised an eyebrow. Was he the only one who noticed how closely Per and Sibilla stood? How Per's hand tightened on hers at the earl's words?

"Why, the marriage settlements, of course," his father said. "Saybrook may be a bit of an inebriate, but he's no fool. Won't be giving his sister to Dulcie here without wrapping up the financials, all right and tight!"

Beside him, Sibilla Pennington gave a startled squeak.

"Ah, I do beg your pardon, Miss Pennington," his father said, blinking. "Didn't see you there, my girl. Fancy-dress party, did Saybrook say?"

Yes, now that he looked more closely, Sibilla and Per, as well as her great aunt, all appeared to be in no little sartorial disarray.

31

As he lowered his quizzing glass from Sibilla's outlandish dress, he caught the expression of alarm she flung at him, but he only shrugged. He'd already done enough to push her and Per together. Besides, it would be far more amusing to watch them try to get out of whatever tangle they were currently in than to meddle in it himself.

Before he could find a comfortable chair from which to observe the melee, another commotion rose, this one from out in the passageway. Dulcie's breath caught at the sight of Benedict Pennington, his dark hair gloriously ruffled, his tall figure encased in a smock spattered with paint, stalking into the room.

"What in hell is going on in here? This racket's like to raise the dead! How can I concentrate on my art with such a clamor?"

Dulcie started. Benedict had always been such a shy, quiet creature. Where had this demanding, belligerent man come from?

A voluptuous woman, one obviously naked beneath her loosely tied dressing robe, trailed behind Benedict, her unbound hair hiding most of her face. Dulcie crossed his arms over his chest. Now that he was grown to manhood, did Benedict's ardor lay in another direction?

He pushed himself away from the wall against which he'd leaned, both eyebrows rising. "Art, is it? Or perhaps we distract you from a more . . . passionate endeavor?"

Benedict scowled, his nostrils flaring. But then, following the direction of Dulcie's gaze, he caught sight of the woman who had followed him. "Damnation, Sally! I told you to stay put!"

Benedict's face turned an utterly charming shade of crimson. Always prone to blushing, young Benedict had been, especially when the boys at school debated the relative merits of female bodily charms. At the time he'd assumed it was because the boy had not found such bodies as compelling as the others did. But perhaps it had only been inexperience.

"But Benedict! Up all night we've been, and me insides

32

growling' like anything!" the blowsy woman protested. "Can't a girl 'ave a bite to eat?"

"Yes, yes, I'll call for some tea, just go back to the studio!"

Benedict tried to lead the woman towards the door, but she snuck under his arm and strolled back into the room. "Must be a bite 'o something 'ere, wot wif a crowd like this . . ."

As the woman looped her hair behind her ears, Dulcie's stomach dropped. Lined and drooping, that face, yes, but still, the same bright eyes, the same cheeky smile. No, it couldn't be —

"Lord Sin!" the woman cried, throwing herself at him.

Reflexively, Dulcie's arms rose to catch the rounded bundle before she could bowl him completely over. Sally—not Brown, as in the song, but Goodman, if his memory served—his one sorry attempt to take a woman as mistress. What was she doing here, at Pennington House? And calling him by that ridiculous pet name for all to hear?

"Sal?" he said, squeaking like an out-of-tune fiddle. He cleared his throat and deepened his voice into its usual drawl. "Is it truly you? I thought you'd returned home to marry your village smithy?"

"Yes, and many a 'appy year we 'ad of it, Sinny, which was more than you'dve given a girl such as me."

Dulcie felt his own blush rising as Sal slapped him playfully on the back. No, he'd never really been able to muster the ardor to please any woman, not even one as bounteously endowed as the younger Sal had been.

"But then the poor fellow up and died on me, and it t'warn't any good," Sal continued, clearly aggrieved. "Not with none of the blokes back home with more than a few pennies to their names! Come back to town, I did, 'oping to make me fortune. Been modeling for Mr. Pennington, 'ere, but 'ard work, that is!"

Dulcie turned a wary eye to Benedict. He'd been painting female nudes? How unexpected.

33

Now even his ears began to turn red. Jerking his eyes from Dulcie's, he stepped toward his model. "Ha! Rather be back out on the streets, would you, then, Sal?"

But Sal ignored her employer, turning instead to run a seductive hand down Dulcie's cheek. "Wouldn't want ter set me up again, now, would you, Sinny, like you done afore? Right easy job of it I 'ad then, eh?"

Benedict stumbled back a step, a pained, vulnerable expression passing over his face. But then something in him seemed to harden. With a snarl, he pulled Dulcie free of Sal and shoved him to the wall. "Set her up again? Do you mean to tell me you once kept Sal as a mistress?"

Dulcie swallowed, inexplicably aroused by the feel of Benedict Pennington's now taller, broader frame pushing against his own. He'd always taken the role of *erastes*, the dominant partner, during his trysts with men, never *eromenos*. Why should being manhandled suddenly set his senses aquiver?

"How could you lie about a thing like that, you false cur? How could you?" Benedict whispered, his expression pained.

Lie? He shook away the unwonted physical response and racked his brain. As far as he could remember, he'd never said a word to Benedict Pennington about keeping, or not keeping, a wench. What could the fellow mean by it?

Before the man could shove him straight through the wall, his sister laid a hand on his arm. "Benedict, please! I thank you for your care of me, but there's no need to take on so. You'll hurt the poor man! And it no longer matters. About the mistress, I mean."

Dulcie gave his head a rapid shake. Yes, Sibilla Pennington had vowed never to marry a man who had kept a mistress, hadn't she? But somehow, he did not think that her brother's agitation over the matter stemmed from Dulcie's minor lack of candor about his past peccadilloes. Had the boy been nursing his calf-love for Dulcie all these years, even unto manhood? With his tousled hair and his breath sawing in and out, he looked as if he'd been rutting with Dulcie rather than on the verge of pummeling him.

Although with some men, the two were not all that different. Would they be, with Benedict?

He restrained a shudder as Benedict's heavy hands slowly slipped from his body. With deliberate care, Dulcie brushed away the wrinkles in his coat and fluffed up his crumpled cravat, paying no attention to the squawking of Sal as she turned and rushed towards Lord Saybrook and the others. He was still far more intrigued by the glowering Benedict, who shoved his body between Dulcie and his sister.

"Well, it seems as if your quest for an eligible *parti* is doomed to failure," Benedict said, still staring poignards at Dulcie. "Even Dulcie, whom we had thought to be a veritable paragon of virtue, at least as far as the voluptuary arts were concerned, has paid for the companionship of a female. No political man, no man in all of London, it would seem, can claim never to have sheltered a mistress."

"I can," Lord Milne exclaimed. "I've never kept a woman! Other than Lady Milne, of course."

Thank the heavens for his father, always a half-step behind in any conversation. "Yes, Pater, but that's nothing to the point. You've already married, and I don't imagine Mother would take kindly to talk of divorce. Miss Pennington needs a bachelor without a mistress, a personage so rare in our times that his price must be far above not just rubies, but sapphires, diamonds, and even gold."

"What does it matter whether a man has a mistress or no?" Per asked.

Dulcie's eyes lit. Forget allowing the fellow to do this for himself. It was time to finish this, once and for all, and free himself from Benedict Pennington's too-disturbing gaze.

He laid a friendly arm along Per's shoulder. "Because Miss

Pennington has vowed to marry only a man interested in politics and *un*interested in keeping a mistress. To be proven by his having never even once adopted the practice so common to those of us of the male persuasion. I fear the poor girl is doomed to a long, lonely spinsterhood. I, for one, have never heard tell of such a rare beast."

Dulcie hurrahed under his breath as Per shrugged free of his arm and took Sibilla's hand in his own. "I have never kept a mistress," he said, gazing with besotted ardor into the chit's eyes.

"Louder," he whispered, giving his friend a hard nudge.

"I am a man without a mistress!" Per shouted.

Praise the heavens! Or praise St. Raphael, patron saint of courtship, although he doubted Per and Sibilla had remained as chaste as the saint would have wished. But at least the two seemed finally to have admitted to each other, as well as to her family, that they were going to wed.

As much as he enjoyed being the center of attention, such a day rightly belonged to Sibilla and Per, not to him. And now that he was no longer required to pay homage to anyone in the Pennington family, he was free to turn his attentions to other important matters—such as to Polly Adler and her grandfather's collection of art.

Besides, the strange combination of anger and vulnerability on Benedict Pennington's face was making his entire scalp prickle.

After one last quick glance at Benedict, Dulcie beat a hasty retreat.

"Dulcie, Father wishes to speak with you."

Dulcie paused by the front door of Milne House and slapped

his gloves against his thigh. Damnation! Did anyone have as bothersome a sister as he? Wilhelmina, arms crossed and foot tapping, stood by the door of their father's library, a chiding expression more suitable to an aged spinster than a lady of five and twenty marring her countenance.

"Tut, tut, Mina," he said with a warning shake of his head. "Making up tales? You know quite well Father has no such wish to speak with me."

In fact, he and his father had been deliberately avoiding one another, ever since that delicious—or disastrous, depending on one's point of view—scene at Pennington House more than a week ago. Father so hated going to the trouble of chastising him, especially knowing how little Dulcie was wont to listen. And Dulcie, for all his heedless ways, truly did not enjoy disappointing his father. He'd much rather contemplate the memory of Benedict Pennington pushing his body to the wall. But the ghost who had once seemed to appear around every corner had been markedly absent from Dulcie's typical haunts of late.

"Perhaps he does not," his sister agreed. "But Father will do his duty as head of this family. Besides, he promised Mama."

Dulcie gave an exaggerated sigh and threw his gloves onto the console-table by the door. Lord Milne may be a powerful voice in the House of Lords, but in this house, his lady would always have the last word.

"Very well, Mina. But I'll not have you listening outside the door."

His sister sniffed. "As if I would ever stoop to such dishonorable machinations. Besides, Mama and I have already discussed the most suitable ladies, now that Miss Pennington has chosen another." With a toss of her blonde head, Mina flounced down the passageway.

Heaving a real sigh this time, Dulcie pushed open the library door.

"Oh, Dulcie. Yes, come in, come in, and close the door behind you, if you will."

Dulcie pasted on his most affable smile. "Father, is it true that Sir Peregrine has resigned? Do you require my help in finding a suitable replacement?"

"What?" Lord Milne asked, patting the piles of books and papers about him as if the solution to taming his recalcitrant heir might be found among them. Poor soul, he looked rather lost without his trusted secretary to put the right note in his hand at just the right time.

"A new secretary, Father. Now that Sir Peregrine is to marry, and accept the patronage of Lord Saybrook?"

"Yes, indeed. Ha. As if any intimate of yours would deign to take employment. But no, that is not what I wish to speak with you about. Please, take a seat."

Dulcie dropped into a chair in front of his father's broad desk and swung his booted foot. "I believe Sir Peregrine and Miss Pennington will be very happy together, do you not?"

"Oh, yes, yes indeed. But do you bear him no ill will? Stealing away the very chit you yourself had been courting!"

"My *amor propre* does still reel from the blow. Yet who am I to stand in the way of the course of true passion? If only I, too, might experience the rapture of the first kiss of love."

"Rapture is all well and good, but what is more important in a wife is her connections," his father said, completing missing his Byronic allusion. "As well as her ability to give you heirs. Your mother has told me of several likely young ladies—devil take it, where is that list?"

His father's casual mention of heirs knotted Dulcie's stomach. Seeing his putative mistress again after so many years had served as yet another reminder of his inability to bed a woman. How hard he'd tried, and how embarrassingly he'd failed, to summon any desire for the buxom Sal. Or for any other woman of his acquaintance. Lattimer Leverett may be able to sport with lord and lady alike, but Dulcie's ardor remained painfully dormant in the presence of the female form.

He still felt a foolish pang, every time he was reminded he'd never sire an heir. Mina would in all likelihood marry and amply provide his parents with grandchildren to indulge, but neither she nor her male children could assume the earldom. And his father had no other heirs besides Dulcie. After Dulcie's death, the title would become extinct, unless the King chose to bestow it upon some other deserving soul.

But a leopard cannot change his spots, and Dulcie could not change his proclivities, even had he so wished. Besides, he'd have a far more valuable legacy to gift to the world than any heir of his body: the innovative artworks he had collected, and would continue to collect, for the remainder of his time on God's good earth.

And if he could succeed in his goal of being named a Director of the British Institution, he'd use every bit of his charm to persuade its stick-in-the-mud members to bestow their patronage not just on artists who followed slavishly in the footsteps of the Old Masters, but those who chose to create more modern, experimental works. Now *that* would be a legacy well worth bragging of.

At long last, his father finally pulled a sheet of paper from his piles. "What say you to the eldest Miss Davenport-Devenport?"

"If she's anything like her brother, I say no thank you." Dulcie leaned back in his chair and wiggled his toes. He'd still not broken in these new boots entirely to his satisfaction.

"Lady Constance Wingfield? She'd be glad to wed a lively sprig like you after nursing a sickly husband all those years. Your mother tells me she'll be out of mourning next month."

"A saintly martyr?" Dulcie shuddered. "Far too good for the likes of me."

"What think you of Miss Fishclyffe?"

"The Fish? Who still believes the Oldenburg bonnet the height of fashion? And who never met a ruffle she didn't like?" Dulcie sniffed. "I think not."

"Now, you cannot find fault with every young lady in the *ton*," Lord Milne said, swatting at the paper with a frustrated hand. He gazed over his glasses with narrowed eyes. "Unless your head has been turned in a far less suitable direction. Must I remind you of your promise after that horrid Copeland affair, that you'd never again allow another man to tempt you to effeminate familiarities?"

Dulcie gritted his teeth. Lord Milne must be in dead earnest to openly refer to that dreadful incident. Dulcie's days—and especially his nights—with Tom Copeland, a stableboy he'd met while at Oxford, had been some of the most satisfying of his entire life. Yet in the end, what he'd thought had been a mutual *affaire de coeur* had proven markedly one-sided. Dulcie cringed to remember with what open ardor he had declared his passion to the young man, while Copeland, the opportunist, had only been using Dulcie as a means to a lucrative end.

He could still see his father's face as Copeland's uncle accosted him, flinging crude accusations of how Dulcie had corrupted his innocent nephew. No, Dulcie would never lay his feelings so open to another lover again, not after his father had been forced to pay such an outrageous sum to keep Copeland's uncle quiet.

And not after witnessing such an excruciating expression of dismay, disappointment, and disgust on his father's face every time he looked at Dulcie in the days and weeks that followed. Changing his proclivities might not be in his power, but discretion with his lovers surely was.

Dulcie tugged on his shirt cuff. "Who else is on the list?"

Lord Milne nodded. "Raikes's girl? Or Fry's? No, what say you to Adler's? Does he not own one of the finest art collections in all of London? You and he would be able to natter on about collecting, even if you had little to say to his granddaughter herself."

"Miss Adler? Miss Polyhymnia Adler?" Dulcie sat up in his chair. In all the chaos of his broken non-engagement with Sibilla Pennington, he'd done nothing to help forward his bet with Leverett. Well, well. How very interesting!

"Yes, I believe that is the girl's name. Have you been introduced?"

"We've not yet met, but I believe I caught a glimpse of her at Colnaghi's a fortnight or so back. Yes, I'd be more than happy to make Miss Adler's acquaintance."

Lord Milne folded his hands together and set them on his desk, leaning forward with far more eagerness than Dulcie had expected. "Excellent. For we've already send Adler an invitation to the British Institution's spring exhibition, and offered your services as guide. Just in case Miss Pennington, in the end, found your charms a bit too—er, petticoated?—for her tastes. Your mother's idea, you know."

Dulcie forced himself to smile, even as he flinched inside. "Mama's idea. Of course. And when is our meeting with the Adlers to take place?"

"In early May, soon after the exhibition opens. We must find a mutually suitable date."

"I am entirely at your service, sir."

Especially if beginning to court Miss Adler might throw him in the way of Benedict Pennington once more.

CHAPTER 3

BENEDICT STARED UP AT THE pair of carved stone lyres, each set within a beribboned wreath that flanked the fan-light over the entrance of the British Institution. Inside, no doubt, he'd find Dulcie tuning the lyre of his oh-so-charming voice, not to deeds of fame and notes of fire, as Byron would have it, but to a pitch best designed to resonate with an unsuspecting Polly Adler.

Oh, Benedict had tried to warn her, with hints growing less and less subtle as the day for her visit to the exhibition with Dulcie grew ever nearer, that she'd do well not to put too much faith in anything the viscount said. He'd told her about Dulcie's insincere courting of his sister, and even some part of the scene of chaos at Pennington House last week, caused in large part, he suspected, not by Sibilla or her new fiancé but by Dulcie and his behind-the-scenes manipulations. He'd been careful to avoid mentioning his own sudden burst of rage at the revelation that Dulcie had once kept a mistress, or his own uncharacteristically violent reaction. How could he explain it to Polly, when he could barely even explain it to himself? Besides, hearing how he'd almost shaken the teeth from the knave would only awaken the kindly girl's sympathy.

Instead, he'd been forced to hint at Dulcie's heartlessness during their mutual school days, although he'd not confided any of the more damning details. But Polly, tolerant to a fault, had just laughed. "I am only the more eager to meet a man who can stir the reticent Mr. Pennington into such a swither," she'd teased with her eager smile.

And so today he found himself at number 52 Pall Mall, standing uneasily between the two Horse Guards acting as sentinels at the British Institution's entrance, poised to insinuate himself into a gathering to which he'd received no invitation. At least Dulcie had chosen a public venue for his first meeting with Polly, rather than his father's London residence. Or a somewhat public venue. He pulled the ticket that his brother Kit, who had a far wider London acquaintance than did Benedict, had managed to wrangle for him from his waistcoat pocket.

After handing his hat to the attendant, and a shilling for a catalogue to the money-taker, he strode across the vestibule and mounted the steps to the Gallery. A gaudy chaos of the fashionable bustled about, gazing as much at one another, alas, as they did at the Italian, Spanish, Flemish, and Dutch paintings adorning the gallery's walls, temporarily borrowed from the collections of the nation's most prestigious connoisseurs. Many argued that the masses could have no appreciation for the fine arts, but few in this modish set seemed intent on aesthetic edification, either.

Benedict examined the crowd more closely but could not see any sign of his quarry. Nor, thank heavens, of Dulcie's boon companion, the odious Lattimer Leverett, a man he'd do more than cross to the other side of the pavement to avoid. Polly's grandfather, though, stood at the west end of the room, in front of what looked to be a quite fine Guercino. But Adler had his back turned to the masterpiece, his head lowered in close conversation with Dulcie's father, Lord Milne.

Damnation. Adler must have already abandoned his granddaughter to Dulcie's ingratiating charms.

Adler gestured him over before Benedict could make his way into one of the other two rooms of the gallery in search of the pair.

"Lord Milne, have you an acquaintance with Mr. Pennington?" Adler asked as Benedict arrived by his side. "If not, may I have the pleasure of introducing you?"

Milne, no doubt remembering the ridiculous scene to which they had both recently been a party less than a fortnight before, caught back a laugh. "Mr. Pennington and I were on the cusp of being far more than acquainted, sir. But once again Dulcie managed to let an eligible young lady slip through his fingers. I console myself that at least Sir Peregrine Sayre is a deserving young man."

"I am sorry to hear it, my lord. But take heart; the season is far from over. And as you see about you today, many a young lady of breeding and character remains as yet unmatched." Adler's eyes traveled the room, as if weighing the merits and faults of each such young lady present, setting them in the scale against all that his own granddaughter, and he, had to offer. "If you are set on Lord Dulcie making an eligible match before the fall, you will certainly have little difficulty finding a suitable lady. And a dutiful son will always respect the authority of the head of his family."

"As you say," the earl replied, his words of agreement at odds with a wry grimace he couldn't quite repress. Poor Lord Milne. Dulcie's lack of respect for authority had endeared him to many an admiring schoolboy during his days at Harrow, but it could hardly please a father.

"What think you of the exhibition?" Benedict asked, redirecting the conversation. "Are there any works which you particularly admire?"

Adler glanced down at the catalog in his hand, then shrugged. "I've seen better by most of the artists listed."

"That large one of the foreign king and the ghostly hand seems quite popular," Milne said, gesturing towards an open archway. "Over in the North Room."

Adler sniffed. "*Belshazzar's Feast*? Yes, the unknowledgeable will flock to a Rembrandt, even one of his lesser works."

"My son did seem quite eager to show it to Miss Adler."

Polly's grandfather smiled. "So he might impress her by expounding on its faults?"

"Ah, yes, Dulcie does love to flaunt his knowledge to all the world, and to the ladies in particular."

"My granddaughter will be in raptures with anyone who will speak with intelligence to her about art. A wise choice, having them meet at this Exhibition. Rumor has it that Dulcie may be named a Director of the Institution before long."

"The North Room, did you say?" Benedict interrupted as the two older men shared a companionable laugh. Between them, they'd have Polly and Dulcie betrothed—and the best of Adler's paintings installed in Dulcie's home rather than held aside for a national gallery—before he could even blink. "I confess I am eager to see the *Belshazzar* myself. If you will excuse me, gentlemen?"

Benedict bowed, then made his way through an open archway to the next gallery. A crowd of viewers was indeed clustered in front of the large Rembrandt, but Polly and Dulcie were not among them. Instead, he found them before one of the few paintings of a woman in this room—one of the Catholic saints, no doubt. Polly had always been drawn to such works whenever they encountered one during their many visits to churches and galleries on the Continent.

Polly's eyes were fixed on the painting, but Benedict's turned almost as if by instinct to the man gesticulating with animation beside her. The coltish adolescent body that had strode with such confidence onto the playing fields of Harrow had grown broader, stronger, yet retained all its lithe elegance. Almost preternatural, it was, the grace with which Clair moved, the glow of vitality which suffused his every expression. And his golden curls, more suited to a cherub than to an Englishman, paired with those impish blue eyes glinting in unholy humor—

one could never tell whether angel or devil would take the lead on any particular day. That taunting ambiguity, its glorious unpredictability, had once been Benedict's ideal of male perfection.

A boyish habit, this staring at Clair. But for the life of him, he could not seem to stop it. Even knowing how easily the devil could drive him, the sheer vitality of the man still took his breath away.

". . . both a princess and a scholar, and a powerful orator," Dulcie said as Benedict moved close enough to catch hold of their conversation. "Had the effrontery to lecture the emperor Maxentius about his barbarous treatment of the Christians to his very face."

"Yes, and when the emperor called fifty of his best philosophers to reason her out of her religious beliefs, it is said she outdebated them all," Polly answered. "Several even converted after hearing her speak."

"How fortunate I am to be in the company of a lady as learned as Saint Catherine herself." Dulcie reinforced his compliment with a particularly winsome smile.

"You are too kind, my lord," Polly demurred.

"Miss Adler has made a particular study of the virgin martyrs, and can regale you with all the most pertinent details of their lives," Benedict said as he joined them before the painting. "Good day to you, Miss Adler. Lord Dulcie."

"Mr. Pennington." Polly's eyes glinted with amusement. "You did not tell me you intended to visit the Exhibition today."

"Perhaps he wished to escape the uproar at Pennington House," Dulcie said. "You did hear that his sister has recently become engaged to my friend Sir Peregrine Sayre?"

"Indeed, I have," Polly replied with a smile in Benedict's direction.

"I did once think to secure Miss Pennington's affections myself," Dulcie said, then gave a deep sigh. "But alas, the lady preferred sober Sir Peregrine to my more insouciant self. I do hope you will take pity on me, Miss Adler, and offer the balm of your consolation to my bruised heart."

Yes, he would make himself out to be the wounded party, wouldn't he? But surely Polly was too intelligent to be taken in by such dramatics.

"From what I understand, the paintings on these walls would offer you far better consolation than any mere human could," she said with a chuckle.

Benedict's hackles settled at Polly's cheerful taunt. No, she hadn't yet been taken in by Lord Dulcie's polished charms.

"Oh, Mr. Pennington, do you not agree that she is sublime?" Polly asked as she turned her attention back to the depiction of the saint. "How rapt she is in her inspiration. The red of her lips, and the flush of her cheeks, fired with such spiritual passion."

"Fired? Or fevered?" Dulcie asked. "You must admit, her poor face does look a bit bloated."

But Polly took no offense, kind girl that she was. "Yes, perhaps not the best execution there. Yet I cannot help but admire the way he's captured her sorrow, as well as her passion. See, in those deep, dark eyes? She knows her time on the earth is soon to end."

Benedict's jaw clenched. After only an hour's acquaintance, Polly would share such intimate insights with Dulcie? Benedict was of a far more reticent nature than the viscount, but still, it had taken weeks of traveling with Polly and her grandfather before she and Benedict had become so at ease with one another.

"Perhaps Saint Catherine should have accepted the emperor's offer of marriage," Dulcie said with a far too charming grin.

"And given up her beliefs?" Benedict scoffed, even knowing Dulcie had likely only said it to provoke. He'd always taken delight in extending any argument by adopting the role of devil's advocate. "How craven."

Dulcie raised an eyebrow. "Few beliefs are worth losing one's head for."

"Few beliefs, and even fewer people?"

"Very few people indeed," he answered, not responding to the sarcasm in Benedict's tone. The slightest of smiles played about his sensuous lips, as if he took pleasure rather than offense at the implied insult in Benedict's words.

Before he could move closer to the man, Polly stepped between them, glancing from one to the other with a frown. "Condemn herself to the control of such a cruel, arrogant husband? I do not believe a woman as educated and intelligent as Catherine would have ever done such a thing."

Benedict clenched his fists. "No. Being subject to another's control is irksome in the extreme."

"But you did not always feel so, did you, Mr. Pennington? In fact, I recall a certain schoolfellow taking boyish pride in completing the tasks set him by his fagmaster."

Dulcie's taunt sent a pulse throbbing at Benedict's temple. "I soon learned, though, that a master rarely appreciates such pride, or such effort. Far better to be one's own commander than subject oneself to the whims and caprices of another."

"Oh, on that we all may surely agree," Polly said, laying a hand atop his arm. "But will we also share the same opinion of Guercino's St. Catherine? In the South Room, was it not?"

With a tug on his arm, she pulled him free of the flow of people carefully circulating the room, examining each picture in the order in which they were listed in the exhibition catalog.

"Please, stop, before you cause a scene," she whispered to Benedict, her face a mixture of confusion and concern. "I've never seen you behave with such discourtesy. And to a man so pleasant and amusing, too."

Benedict shook his head. He'd managed not to lay hands on Dulcie this time, but only just. How could he keep letting the man goad him so?

"Polyhymnia, my dear," Adler called as Polly pulled him

back into the middle gallery. Adler glanced at Benedict with a tinge of displeasure. "Have you finished looking at the pictures yet? And what have you done with Lord Dulcie?"

"She has merely demonstrated her desire to please by granting his wish to review the pictures completely out of order." Dulcie, clearly not put off by Polly's abrupt departure nor by Benedict's rudeness, offered an engaging smile as he joined their small circle. "I wished to compare how the followers of Carracci each attempted to capture the passion of Saint Catherine."

"But perhaps you would enjoy seeing a painting by the master himself, rather than one of his followers? My new Carracci has just been hung in our gallery."

"Such an invitation does me honor. And if Miss Adler would agree to serve as guide . . ." Dulcie bowed in Polly's direction, a ray of sun from the skylight above dancing chiaroscuro over his golden head.

"It would give me the greatest pleasure," Polly said with a reproving glance in Benedict's direction.

A plague upon him for the veriest fool. He'd meant to protect Polly from being taken in by Dulcie's winning ways, but his own boorish behavior had led to precisely the opposite result.

"That older gentleman standing by the door is the Marquess of Stafford, one of the two current presidents of the British Institution, and a devoted collector," Dulcie whispered to Polly as they made their way towards the exit. "Have you visited his gallery at Cleveland House? He welcomes the public on Wednesday afternoons, but I'm certain he'll grant me a private viewing. Shall I introduce you?"

His blue eyes flicked to Benedict, a small, but decidedly satisfied smile playing about his lips.

Yes, Dulcie had certainly won this first battle in the chess match for Polly's dowry. But he would never win the war. Selfishness would never win out over the higher good. Benedict would stake his life on it.

"Viscount Dulcie to see you, miss."

A bracing whiff of pine, tinged with just a hint of licorice, assaulted Dulcie's nose as he crossed the threshold of the small room to which Adler's footman had led him. Turpentine? The lady had said something about dabbling in oils rather than the more usual feminine medium of watercolor. And the room certainly looked to be the studio of a serious artist, with its haphazard pile of stretched canvases leaning against the far wall, its bench littered with pencils and charcoal, bottles of oils and animal bladders of paints, and its two large easels propped opposite one another by the north-facing windows, poised to catch the best of the morning light.

But it was not an artist, but an heiress, who was the object of his quest today. And there, turning away from the easel closest to the door, she was: one Polyhymnia Adler, the key to perhaps the most highly regarded collection of Old Masters paintings in all of England.

"My lord, how kind of you to call," the lady said as she gave him a perfunctory curtsy and the slightest of frowns. "Is today the day we set for you to visit with grandfather's paintings?"

He bowed. "Say rather to visit with one who can teach me to appreciate those paintings as well as she does herself."

He topped his compliment with the most winsome of smiles, drawing not only an answering smile but also a blush from his quarry. Easily charmed, or just embarrassed to be caught in such a state of dishabille? That drab smock covering her from neck to toe did little to enhance her tall, ungainly figure, nor did the messy streaks of paint smeared across its bodice add anything to the decidedly modest charms that lay beneath it. Odd, that the footman hadn't asked him to wait while he informed his mistress of a gentleman's arrival and allowed her time to repair her appearance. Dulcie would certainly never hire a servant who would place him in such an embarrassing predicament. Pennington must care more for Mr. Adler's paintings than any of his granddaughter's sartorial skills.

And speak of the devil. There he stood by the second easel, Miss Adler's reputed swain, just as Dulcie had predicted. But the man was proving a lax guardian, too caught in his own work to pay any heed to the entrance of a potential rival. Heavens, between Adler's clear desire to snare a lordling for son-in-law, the lady's seemingly sororal, rather than amorous, feelings for the fellow, and Pennington's own natural diffidence and reserve, manipulating Miss Adler and Mr. Pennington into wedded bliss would certainly present a challenge. If, in fact, Dulcie chose to pursue that course . . .

"My grandfather, or Mr. Pennington, would be a far better guide than I could ever be," Miss Adler said as she swirled her brush in a jar of turpentine. "Mr. Pennington, we have a visitor."

The sound of her raised voice brought Pennington's dark head up with a start. He gazed about him in confusion, as if he needed a moment to recollect just where he was, and with whom.

"A caller, Miss Adler? I'm sorry, I must have forgotten. . ."

So different, that voice was, from the soft, piping tones of the twelve-year-old schoolboy of his memories. Yet at the same time it sounded so familiar, that air of distracted surprise, as if the speaker had just been jolted awake from the most absorbing of reveries. He'd always been such a one for daydreams, young Pennington had. Was he still now, even at what—seven or eight and twenty?

Dulcie took a step farther into the room, so that Pennington might see him more clearly. As Benedict's eyes shifted from his own canvas to Dulcie's face, his charmingly absent-minded smile transformed into a frown, then an outright glower. Good, the pup had grown teeth. Dulcie did not find the idea at all unappealing.

Last week, at the British Institution, he'd suspected his potential rival might have caught word of the wager between himself and Leverett. But now, watching his brown eyes narrow, distrust playing across those wonderfully mobile features, Dulcie was certain of it. No one forgot Sinclair Milne, not even a man so prone to becoming lost in the wanderings of his own mind as Benedict Pennington. He was here for a reason, and that reason was to keep Dulcie away from Miss Adler, even if he was not yet confident enough to declare his own intentions to the lady.

Which would present the greater challenge—to help the incipient courtship to its logical conclusion? Or to steal the lady out from underneath her own watchdog's nose?

"Have I come at an inconvenient time, Miss Adler?" he asked. "Your grandfather assured me that you would be free any morning I cared to call."

"Not at all, my lord," Miss Adler said, even as she cast a longing gaze back towards her easel. "Mr. Pennington, would you mind terribly if we postponed our lesson until this afternoon?"

"Pennington is your teacher? And what is the lesson for today? Perspective? How to transfer a drawing to the canvas? Which brush to use to achieve the effect you desire?" Dulcie strolled over to the paired easels, careful to keep his coat from brushing against wet canvas. Fulsome, if unspecific, praise poised on the tip of his tongue; he could find something flattering to say about any work of art, no matter how unaccomplished.

Yet when he caught sight of the picture taking form on her canvas, the glib words caught in his throat. She'd chosen to paint a half-length portrait of her instructor. But it was a portrait unlike any he'd ever seen. The chit was not attempting to portray

Pennington in dignified repose, or positioned in echo of a classical sculpture or Old Master painting, as a more accomplished portraitist surely would have done. Nor had she constrained herself to the idealized flattery common to the commissioned portraits of the titled and wealthy. No, mere physical attractiveness did not take the place of personal characterization here. Pennington's flaws—his overly-full lips, the minor lack of symmetry in the curves of his cheeks, the small scar on his chin from when he'd tripped on the playing fields at Harrow and cut himself on a sharp stone—drew the viewer's attention far more than any finer points. No, Miss Adler's portrait would never be featured in a collection devoted to ideal male beauty.

And yet there was something compelling, something vital in her depiction, in spite of the many flaws she portrayed in her sitter, not to mention the obvious flaws in her technique. Something about the dreamy intensity of the eyes, the conviction in the set of those lips, reminded him of what had first drawn him to Pennington as a boy, something that he'd seen little of in the grown man he'd encountered over the past few months. Yet it had been there, had it not, in the aggression and anger he had let burst forth that day at Saybrook's? Had someone as unpromising as Miss Adler been able to draw him out from the aloof air he now commonly draped about him? Perhaps nudging their courtship along would not prove quite as difficult as he'd initially thought.

"Why Miss Adler! I had no idea such recklessness hid behind that quiet exterior of yours. Whatever led you to paint such an unconventional thing?" Dulcie could readily imagine the sneers of condemnation that Leverett and other British Institution connoisseurs would heap upon such an unpolished work. But there was something so right, so quintessentially *Benedict* about it that he could not help but be impressed.

"My lesson for today is one I often practice—tell the truth in your work." Miss Adler gave a quiet smile. "I wonder who has made a better job of it, Mr. Pennington or myself?"

"Ah, a competition, is it? And I am to be judge. Come, Pennington, let us see what you've done."

Pennington's scowl turned from Dulcie to the canvas in front of him. "We needn't waste Lord Dulcie's time on such frivolities. It was only meant to be an exercise."

"Exercise or no, the lady has issued a challenge. Have you not yet learned that denying a gentlewoman her fondest wish is no way to win her favor?"

"Mr. Pennington has no need to win my favor," Miss Adler said as she laid a hand on the man's arm. "The kindnesses he has done me stand in the hundreds, if not the thousands."

"Ah, but now you make me quite desperate to catch him up." And to wish that it was his own hand, rather than hers, upon Pennington's sleeve. Had that once-scrawny boy grown into the promise of his frame?

"And you think to curry her favor by feigning a preference for her work?" Pennington's waspish tones interrupted his reverie. "I assure you, my lord, dissembling will not impress."

"I'm sure his lordship intends no such thing," Miss Adler said, brow furrowing at Pennington's rudeness.

"Indeed," Dulcie agreed, laying his palm flat across his heart. "I promise to be the very soul of honesty. Not a word of false flattery will fall from these lips."

Pennington's dark eyes narrowed. "An unusual course for you, I believe."

"Benedict!" Miss Adler chastised. "Lord Dulcie is reputed to be one of the finest judges of artistic skill in all the city."

Dulcie swept out a casual hand. "But if Mr. Pennington fears having his own work judged against your own . . ."

Miss Adler shot a questioning look at Pennington, who threw up his hands in reply. "Oh, let the damned fellow see. He's not likely to give us any peace until he does."

With one last scowl at his canvas, Pennington gave ground. Dulcie quickly moved to take his place in front of the second easel. Heaven help him if it turned out to be a naked Sally Goodman. He'd already seen enough of those charms to last a lifetime.

Pennington, too, had brushed in a quick portrait, not of Sal, nor of a gentleman, but of a lady. Unsurprising, that the teacher's portrait showed far more technical expertise than that of his student. "A confident line, a minute attention to coloration and tone. And a clear understanding of the conventions of deportment and expression," Dulcie opined as he raised his quizzing glass to inspect the painting more closely. "But true to nature? I could not say, without knowing the model upon which it is based."

Beside him, Miss Adler laughed. "I told you, didn't I, Benedict? No one will see me behind all those foolish props and draperies."

"Ah, it is Miss Adler embodying her namesake, complete with scroll and lyre? How charming a muse you make." Dulcie blinked at an unexpected feeling of disappointment. Somehow, despite its technical proficiency, something about Pennington's work struck him as decidedly lacking.

"Charming! Why, you didn't even realize it was meant to be Polly," Pennington scoffed.

Dulcie bowed his head in acknowledgment. It was true; if one did not know her full given name, one might take the painting for any tall, handsome brown-haired young lady rigged up as the classical muse of poetry and dance. Pennington had captured little of the warmth or sensitivity, and none of the unconventionality, that characterized the Polly Adler he was coming to know. If truth were the goal of this aesthetic exercise, Miss Adler undoubtedly took the laurels.

"But is it not the portraitist's task to present his subject in the most complimentary light possible?" he offered instead of the false praise the man would surely see right through.

"Complimentary? Insipid is closer to the mark." Pennington crossed his arms with a groan.

"Miss Adler, insipid? Really, Pennington, to insult a lady so. And to her very face!"

The lady laughed. "Benedict referred to his painting, my lord, not to me, as well you know."

But Pennington did not share in the joke. He only shut his eyes and tapped his head back against the wall. "Nothing I've done since returning to England is worth the least damn, Polly. And you know it."

"Because you've stopped taking risks." Miss Adler gave his arm a squeeze. "You're thinking too much about the rules, about the shoulds instead of the what ifs. Paint what inspires you, Benedict, not what you think, or how you think, you should."

Ah, she was allowed to call him Benedict. Just as he had, once.

Dulcie shook his head at the memory. No, this was a promising moment of intimacy between potential mates. Should he leave them alone?

A knock on the studio door made choosing irrelevant.

"Miss Adler, your grandfather invites you and your visitor downstairs for tea," announced the footman who had led him up the stairs a few moments before.

The lady glanced back at her easel once again, then gave a great sigh. "Of course he does. Well, we'd best get on with it. Grandfather does not like to be kept waiting."

Pennington straightened from his slouch with a grimace. "Perhaps I should take my leave, then, Polly."

"No, please. Keep grandfather from quizzing Lord Dulcie too impertinently while I change into something more suitable for receiving company. You know how cross he'll be if I bring the scent of turpentine into the room."

Ah, good to know that the elder gentleman was not entirely

happy with his granddaughter's artistic pursuits. Might that lack of enthusiasm also extend to Pennington as a suitor?

"Yes, my good sir, do stay. I'm quite curious to hear your thoughts on Mr. Adler's collection."

Pennington gave a wary nod. "As you wish."

"Miss Adler, we will await your return with bated breath. Come along, Pennington." He ushered the lady from the room, then followed the servant without looking back to see if Benedict would follow. He hadn't felt that prickling at the back of his neck since his schooldays, the one that rose whenever young Pennington had dogged his footsteps. But he felt it now, a frisson of sparks that began at his nape and then nipped down his spine, settling with unexpected heat in his groin.

Dulcie grinned. Who knew what might happen if he brought his considerable charms to bear not only on Polly Adler, but on Benedict Pennington, too?

CHAPTER 4

BENEDICT SCRAMBLED TO FOLLOW DULCIE and his perfectly groomed curls down the steep staircase of the Pall Mall townhouse. Dreams of those curls, and the smile that had so often lit the face below them, had gotten Benedict through many a homesick hour during those long, lonely first weeks at school. The adolescent viscount had seemed the epitome of a proper young gentleman to Benedict's dazzled eyes, lithe and fleet-footed on the playing field, personable and capable and confident in the classroom, as easy with his fellow students as with his teachers, no matter the person's interests or temperament. How he had admired that young man, longed to be him, longed to be *liked* by him.

And then, one day, Dulcie caught him staring, and with a knowing smile, asked him his name . . .

Benedict shook his head. If one only required a physical model of the well-bred gentleman, the thirty-two-year-old viscount still might serve. That broad but elegant back, the slender, tensile frame, the crop of gilt curls that called to Benedict almost as powerfully as did his paintbrush, urging him to twine his fingers through their luxurious twists and turns.

But the lofty ideals he'd once assumed Dulcie had shared, nay, had exemplified, no, those were there no longer.

Perhaps they never had been. Perhaps, foolish boy, Benedict had simply imagined them, made them up out of whole cloth.

Every morning this week, he'd drawn out his work with Polly, disappointment vying with relief when the time for morning calls passed with no sign of Lord Dulcie. He should have been glad that the fellow had finally made good on his promise to call, and that he'd been here to stand watch over Polly. But he'd hardly expected to have his own work paraded in front of the damned fellow. Frustrating enough to be faced with his own artistic shortcomings; even worse to have them thrust in front of a true connoisseur. Especially a man whose opinions he had once taken so much to heart.

And still did, if the painful tightness in his throat at Dulcie's tepid commentary on his work was any indication. He shouldn't care, especially if, as rumor had it, the viscount was not only interested in winning Adler's collection by wooing Polly, but had had the presumption to agree to a wager about it with that bastard Leverett. But he'd never been one to hide from his own feelings, no matter how illogical or inconvenient they might prove, even if he was slow to share them with others. Something deep within him still respected Dulcie's aesthetic judgment, even if he could no longer admire his morals.

"My Lord Dulcie! Come to see the pictures, have you?" Adler strode across the drawing room to give his guest a formal bow. "And Pennington, too. But where is Polly?"

"We were in the midst of a lesson when the viscount arrived," he explained as the older man ushered them into the drawing room. "I'm certain she'll be down momentarily."

But Adler paid him little heed, focusing all of his attention on his guest. "Sit here, will you, in the most comfortable chair. Will you take refreshment while we wait, my lord? Or would you prefer to step into the gallery first?"

To see such fawning behavior in the usually businesslike Adler would be comical, if only his plan to snare Dulcie for his granddaughter did not depend on handing over some of the best works in his collection to the rogue.

"If I were a true gentleman, I would insist we wait for Miss Adler to return. But will you excuse my impatience if I admit I would prefer the gallery?" Dulcie's winning smile had charmed many a man even more assertive than Julius Adler. "Your granddaughter may view any of your paintings at any time she wishes, but my opportunities are far more fleeting."

"Just now, perhaps," Benedict said as he stepped between the two men. "But not so rare in future. Mr. Adler is to donate a portion of his collection to the nation, to form the basis of a national gallery."

"Are you indeed, sir?" Dulcie's eyebrows rose high over his bright blue eyes. "How public-spirited of you. I'm afraid that were I in your position, I would be hard-pressed to be so selfless."

"Now, now, Pennington, nothing has been positively decided on that front, as you well know," Adler said, his genial tone at odds with the sharpness of the look he cut at Benedict. "And I would not deserve the name of grandfather if I did not retain some of the pictures for Polyhymnia, for when she sets up her own household. Come, my lord, let me show you some of my favorites."

Benedict followed the pair into the long gallery, intending to keep his eyes, and ears, attuned to his companions. Yet his breath could not help but catch at the sheer abundance of artistry on display on Adler's walls. When he'd last been in this room, he'd been distracted by the chore of hanging a picture, by Adler's impatience and Polly's indecisiveness and frustration. But today, Adler's now-familiar stories of how he had acquired this Titian and that Rubens lapping at the edges of his attention, he gradually slipped into his own mind, transfixed by the wonders before him. The ideals of virtue and beauty he had once foolishly thought to find in a mere human being hung embodied, here on these walls. He gave himself over to it, losing himself in their transcendent glories.

Dulcie's voice broke Benedict's silent worship. "And you think to open your gallery to the public, sir? Can such a wide audience be trusted to show proper respect to such works?"

Benedict fumed. Why should Dulcie, or even Benedict, be allowed to experience such sublime beauty when so many others, men and women far more worthy than he, might never be given the chance? What a loss, never to see the textures of paint on canvas, nor the subtleties of color and tint and shade. To have to be content with mere engravings, if one wished for a glimpse at all.

How many weary people passed in the street below each day, entirely unaware that such splendor, such sublimity, lay just beyond the door? The world would be a far better place if people could break free of the mundane details of their everyday lives, even for a few brief moments, to ponder such transcendent beauty. These paintings should not be the province of only the privileged few, but open to any pilgrim who wished to worship at their altar.

"How dangerous you look!" Clair whispered in his ear, jerking him from castles he was building in the air. "A knight on crusade, no, a holy martyr, fired by the passion and purity of true devotion—that is how I would paint you, if only I had the skill."

How long had he been standing there, captive to his own frustrations?

He blinked, too aware of the warm body standing by his side.

"You favor the new Carracci? Saint John in the wilderness is a sight to inspire," Dulcie continued when Benedict remained silent. Damn, his attention would fix on that painting, even when his thoughts drifted elsewhere. He took a deep breath, his upper arm brushing for an instant against Dulcie's shoulder. A trick of the mind, to still expect that Dulcie would be the taller. But if he turned to face him, he would have to look down, not up, to meet those clear blue eyes, snapping with intelligence and laughter.

Dulcie laced a hand through Benedict's arm and turned him to the opposite wall. "But my attention is drawn to Ganymede and his eagle. Was not the story told in one of the passages you once translated for me, Zeus abducting the most beautiful of mortals to be his cup-bearer in Olympus?"

And to be something more to the god, too, at least according to the passage in Xenophon young Dulcie had set him. Benedict's toes curled in his boots.

"I am surprised Mr. Adler allows it to be displayed where his innocent granddaughter may see it. But perhaps he is not as familiar with all of the versions of the myth as we are. Or he assumes Miss Adler's ignorance." Dulcie strolled farther down the gallery, stopping before Adler's Poussin. "I wonder how he explains the meaning of this bacchanalian scene to the poor girl."

Yes, that particular picture, with its whirling satyrs and naked men, its fleshy nymphs and fat Silenus too cup-shot to stand, was licentious enough to give even a collector like Adler pause. Yet it was one of the most accomplished, and most dazzling, works in the entire gallery. He was glad he had encouraged the man to purchase it, despite Adler's doubts.

"You have no thoughts, Mr. Pennington?" One side of Dulcie's mouth rose, always a dangerous sign. "I suppose I must ask Miss Adler herself, then."

"Clair, no," Benedict said, but it was too late. Polly must have come downstairs while he had been lost in his own musings.

Clair's eyes sparkled—damnation, had Benedict truly spoken that old pet name aloud?—as he waved to Polly, encouraging her to join them rather than linger by the door waiting for her grandfather, who stood discussing some matter with a servant. "Come, Miss Adler, we must have your opinion."

"My opinion of what, my lord?" she asked as she joined them.

"Of depicting vice in art," Dulcie answered, his voice heavy with affected concern. He gestured to the painting. "Are you not afraid of being condemned by the moralists for hanging such a scene on your walls?"

Polly frowned. "The Poussin? Grandfather says it is one of the master's finest works."

"But it depicts the most outrageous of bacchanals. No pious orgy that! Who can view such mad-headed, tipsy revelry without wanting to emulate it? Should not our finest artwork promote virtue, rather than vice?"

"Certainly! But no man of discernment would scorn to display a scene taken directly from the mythology of the Greeks."

"Ah, it is its classical subject which excuses it," Dulcie said, nodding in apparent agreement.

"Not just its subject, but its execution," Benedict interjected, unable to keep silent even though he knew Dulcie was only teasing. "Have ever you seen such prodigious draftsmanship? Such high-wrought expression? It would be a crime to condemn such mastery."

Dulcie raised an eyebrow. "Does the purity of the drawing, then, make amends for the impurity of its subject?"

"Yes," Polly said before Benedict could answer. "The same subject, badly executed, would hardly be endured."

"Indifferent pictures, like dull people, must be absolutely moral!" Dulcie exclaimed. "And those persons of more gallantry than discretion, who think that to have an indecent daub hanging up in one corner of the room is proof of a liberality of taste and a considerable progress in virtue, quite mistake the matter."

Dulcie and Polly's shared laughter drew the attention of her grandfather, who smiled, no doubt pleased by the pair's growing accord.

"And when will a painting by your granddaughter adorn

these walls, Mr. Adler?" Dulcie asked.

"A painting by Polyhymnia? Amongst the Old Masters?" Adler looked taken aback. "I doubt any woman, particularly one gently bred, will ever be numbered amongst the true geniuses of the art."

Benedict cringed inwardly at Adler's lack of sensitivity. "If ladies are never given the opportunity to practice and study, as men are, then I would have to agree with you, sir."

"I wonder if Miss Adler might consider the opportunity of painting a portrait?" Dulcie asked. "I have been considering having my own likeness taken, in anticipation of sharing it in the not too distant future with a—well, the least said on that front, the better. I had thought to engage Northcote, or perhaps Beechy, but after viewing Miss Adler's work, I am taken with the idea of a portrait painted by a lady."

Damn, but the man knew how to flatter. After viewing her work on Benedict's portrait, any sensible man would flee from the prospect of having Polly's critical eye limn his likeness. But Polly's shoulders, which had drooped so at her grandfather's comments, suddenly straightened, and she clasped her hands to her chest.

"What a charming thought. So gallant you are, my lord," Mr. Adler said before Polly could offer her own assent. "But here is a better idea. Why not have Pennington undertake the task? Sitting for one's portrait is tedious at the best of times, but Polyhymnia could read to you, or engage you in diverting conversation, while Pennington sketched and daubed. Yes, far more proper, a far better idea."

Adler knew his granddaughter well enough that he realized she'd be far more intent on her own art than on being pleasing to Dulcie if she were to paint him. And he no doubt thought he was doing Benedict a favor, by suggesting he take on the commission in Polly's place. But the thought of sitting for hours gazing at the mere shell of beauty that was Sinclair Milne—no.

Benedict would never undertake such a thing, even if doing so would cause Polly no hurt.

"Sir, while it would be a privilege to take the viscount's likeness, I hardly think—"

"No need to think, Pennington," Adler interrupted, intent on arranging things to his own liking, as was his wont. "Just to paint. You could use Polly's room, bring in any materials, take as much time as you like."

When they had traveled together on the continent, Benedict had valued Adler's ability to organize and to plan, and been more than content to leave all the mundane details of tickets and timetables to the older man. But he was beginning to understand how Polly could find her grandfather's need to control more than a little frustrating.

But when he turned to Polly for support, the girl was smiling, not frowning. "What a wonderful idea, grandfather. But you cannot ask Mr. Pennington to bring his materials back and forth between his house and ours each time the viscount comes to sit."

"Bah, he needn't do any such thing. John the footman can do any carting required."

"But Grandfather, you cannot imagine the trouble it would cause Mr. Pennington, asking him to move his things."

"And an artist needs to be free to create whenever the inspiration overtakes him," Dulcie added. "In the middle of the night, at the first blush of dawn, even, if he is not the most pious of men, on the Sabbath. If his best brush, or the precise pigment he needs, are not immediately to hand—well, I would never wish such frustrations on an artist I admired."

"You wouldn't?" Adler said, clearly caught between his desire to please Dulcie and his wish to keep any meetings between the man and his granddaughter under his own roof.

"No indeed. Just imagine the portrait that might result, if the poor painter took out his frustrations on canvas."

"Yes, grandfather, I think it far better for me, rather than for Mr. Pennington's things, to be the one to travel back and forth. You would not mind calling at Pennington House, my lord, while the necessary sittings are required?" she asked Dulcie.

"No, not at all," he answered with a grin. "Though Miss Pennington is betrothed to another, she and I are still on cordial terms."

"Well, then." Adler's brow furrowed. "But would it not be an imposition on your brother, or his household, Mr. Pennington?"

"Oh, Saybrook won't mind," Dulcie answered before Benedict could even open his mouth. "The more the merrier with him. And besides, I've practically the run of the place myself already."

"Then it is all but settled, except for the day we shall begin," Polly said with a clap of her hands. "What say you to Friday?"

Benedict blinked. But the moment to protest seemed already behind him. Dulcie and Polly were engrossed, fair curls bent to chestnut knot, planning and scheming, with Adler interjecting the occasional offer of a carriage, servants, and supplies.

What in heaven's name was Polly up to?

And why did she wish Benedict to play chaperone while she did it?

Benedict threw down his charcoal and glared at the face he'd just roughed out. His father, drawn from memory with quick, flowing lines, smiled back, even though in Benedict's rendering he looked more like a mocking ghost than a human being. Laughing at Benedict's feeble efforts to capture his likeness, no doubt. The late Viscount Saybrook, the epitome of sociability, had never understood how a son of his could prefer being alone with his pencils and sketches rather than engaging in the rough and tumble of the political wrangling he so thrived on himself.

With a grunt, Benedict yanked the sheet from the easel he had set up in his attic studio and crumpled it into a ball. Trying to draw from memory rather than from a model hadn't helped him shake off the damned pall that had shrouded his creativity ever since he'd returned to England. Perhaps he should take himself back to Paris after his sister's wedding, or maybe even to Rome. He'd thought he'd learned all he could from studying the glories of classical antiquity and the great masterpieces of the Renaissance one encountered every day in that ancient city, thought he'd been ready to move forward into something fresh, something new. But perhaps he needed to go back to the beginning, back to the roots, to recapture the inspiration London had snuffed right out of him.

Or perhaps he only needed to escape this infernal English rain. Who could create anything of beauty in such a dismal climate? With a curse, he kicked the crumpled ball of his drawing towards the far too large pile of half-finished canvasses leaning on the studio's back wall.

"Foot-ball, Pennington? I don't recall you being particularly fond of the playing fields when we were at school," drawled a voice behind him.

By the holy poker of hell! Benedict closed his eyes and rubbed the back of his neck, stilling the small hairs that had stood on end at the sound of that familiar voice. Bad enough to have demons of the imaginary sort haunting his only sanctuary; now he had to suffer its invasion by one in the flesh, one that he'd been stupid enough to invite in himself.

Benedict turned, taking in the sight of Sinclair Milne as he leaned against the door frame in a pose of studied casualness, one clearly meant to draw the eye. Immaculately turned out in a dark green coat, full-length trousers, and an elaborately knotted cravat that must have taken his valet hours to perfect. Though the peacock couldn't quite bring himself to completely follow Brummell's austere sartorial dictates; feathered paisleys of a rich green and coppery-gold danced across the breadth of his showy silk waistcoat. Benedict laughed under his breath. Hardly surprising that Dulcie should wear a garment that would require the use of king's yellow, a pigment known for its dangerous fumes and offensive smell, to reproduce on canvas with any degree of accuracy.

Benedict's muscles tightened. Dulcie stood by himself in that doorway, no footman or Miss Adler beside him. As a boy, Benedict had seized any opportunity he could to catch the popular Dulcie away from their fellow schoolmates, but since returning to England, he'd made sure never to allow himself to be with the man alone. How had he made his way up to the Pennington House attics without anyone to guide him?

"Dulcie. Was not Miss Adler to accompany you today?" he asked, shaking out the stiffness in his drawing hand as if this heightened awareness of Dulcie might be shaken off along with it.

"Oh, she did," Dulcie replied as he pushed off from the door frame and made his way into Benedict's studio with a practiced smile. "But we met with your sister on your doorstep, and were asked to admire her betrothal gift for Sir Peregrine: a miniature of her lovely self, painted on my recommendation by Mr. Heaphy." He picked up a paintbrush and twirled it between nimble fingers. "I did wonder when she requested my advice why she did not ask you to undertake the commission."

Benedict shrugged. "Miniature work is of little interest to me." But Dulcie's offhand comment stung. Sibilla had never once broached the subject of a portrait with him. He and his sister had never been close—Benedict had been sent off to school when she had been barely out of leading strings, and then had spent her adolescent years traveling on the Continent—but she must know he'd have been more than happy to attempt her likeness.

Or perhaps she didn't. He hadn't been at all happy to be dragged in by their eldest brother Theo to help in the search for a suitable mate for their sister. Benedict's complaints had often sounded bitter, even to his own ear. To his mind, any mate besides Viscount Dulcie would have done. But Sibilla had been far more fastidious, and far less tolerant of Benedict's warnings than he had liked.

"You do know some of these pigments are poisonous, don't you?" he asked as he reached for the brush in Dulcie's hand. His entire body tingled, just as it always had whenever his schoolboy fingers had accidentally brushed against Clair. At twelve, innocent and untutored, he'd not understood why he should respond with such ardency to the older boy, why even the most glancing touch should fill him with such painful longing. But his travels on the Continent had introduced him to more than new ideas about art, and he now knew well the passions of both spirit and flesh. His mind might no longer be infatuated with Dulcie, but his wayward body still flamed to life in his presence, damn it.

"I didn't touch any of the paints," Dulcie said, one corner of his mouth lifting as it used to when he was amused by some silly behavior of one of his peers. "And that brush was clean. Would you be sorry if I were to die a bitter death at the hands of your paint-box, Mr. Pennington?"

Benedict yanked the brush from Dulcie's hand and threw it back down on the table. "I'd be sorrier to be thrown into gaol for murdering a mere dandy. Now tell me, what has Sibilla's miniature to do with Miss Adler's disappearance?"

"Yes, sir!" Dulcie set his hands behind his back, as if he were reciting lines for the schoolmaster. "Miss Pennington was not entirely happy with the miniature, sir, but could not quite explain why. And so Miss Adler asked to see it, and soon they were deep in conversation about its merits, or lack thereof."

But Dulcie could never keep still for long. Benedict watched as one of his hands reached out to skim over the bladders of paint, then the palette knife on the table, taking care not to touch. "Miss Adler has very few female acquaintances in London, I believe, and I did not like to interrupt the beginnings of a burgeoning friendship. So I informed her that I would just toddle up here myself, so as not to keep you waiting, and she might follow whenever she liked."

Benedict frowned. Of course he had known Polly was lonely. After their connection had deepened from teacher and student to peer and peer, she'd told him about the close friendships she had with many of the other girls at her convent school, and how heartbroken she had been to leave them behind. But he had few acquaintances of, and even less comfort with, the opposite sex, especially here in London. Assuming he could do nothing but offer his own self in friendship to ease Polly's solitude, he'd completely disregarded his very own sister.

And here, after knowing Polly for only a fortnight, was Dulcie, not only sensing her desire for female companionship, but introducing her to a potential friend as soon as the first opportunity presented itself. Even though it took her from his own side, giving him less time to press his suit. Why?

Because he knew it would make his own life easier, if his future spouse could content herself with female friendships while he kept company with other men?

Or because a hint of that kindness that had once led him to befriend a lonely, homesick schoolboy still lurked somewhere below the polished surface of the perfectly turned-out dandy?

While Benedict debated the question in silence, Dulcie prowled about the studio, his eyes alight with interest. "How shall we begin this first sitting? Have you a book of poses you wish me to consider, or some of your own finished paintings as examples?"

"There are no portraits here," Benedict said, intercepting him before his inquisitive hands could reach for canvases leaning against the back wall. If Dulcie had not been impressed by his portrait of Polly, he'd find even less to praise in these abandoned projects.

"Prefer historical work, do you? Then perhaps you should paint me as an allegorical figure, or hero of ancient myth. Do you not think I would make an excellent Paris, surrounded by Hera, Athena, and Aphrodite, all awaiting my judgement of which was the fairest?"

Benedict's imagination flared, less from the thought of painting three naked goddesses than in trying to capture Paris in that moment of indecision. But Dulcie would hardly make a likely model for such a painting; he had always been far more decisive than Benedict ever could bring himself to be. Hadn't he decided to pursue Adler's paintings by wooing Polly mere days after first hearing of the connection between them?

"And what would you ask for reward, in return for granting the apple to Aphrodite?" Benedict asked, his tone sharpening. "Miss Adler's hand in marriage?"

"What makes you think I would follow Paris's example?" Dulcie said. He had always been a dab hand at turning a conversation away from any questions too inconvenient to answer. "A poor decision he made, choosing female beauty over power or wisdom for himself."

Benedict frowned. "But you never used to be interested in power for its own sake. And your judgment was always sound. If not beauty, then, what is it that you do want, Clair?"

"Oh, I did not say I scorned all beauty. Just that I prefer my beauty not be embodied in a female."

"Ah. You prefer the masculine form? Mr. George Norton's, perhaps?"

Dulcie stepped up behind him and laid a hand on his shoulder. "A comely boy, is he not? But the beauty of youth fades so quickly, here and gone before you can barely blink an eye.

No, what I truly want—" Benedict's pulse fluttered in his throat as Dulcie leaned over to whisper in his ear—"is the beauty of the ages. The beauty of the world's greatest works of art."

Benedict shook free of the viscount's hand, turning on him with a scowl. "The beauties of Mr. Adler's collection, in fact?"

Dulcie laughed, then draped himself over the small chaise-longue by the window. "So protective! But in truth, I'm hardly interested in winning the title of most voracious art collector."

"Then what?"

"Why, to be regarded as the finest art connoisseur of the age, by both my peers and by posterity." Dulcie laughed and waved a hand as if the admission were another joke. But his refusal to meet Benedict's eyes suggested he had revealed something meaningful, something important.

Benedict forced back his frustration at Dulcie's false coquetry, recognizing the opening the man had just given him. If he could use Dulcie's desires to win him to the cause, rather than act against its interests, perhaps he could protect Polly and forward the museum plans, too.

"If you wish to be remembered after your death, you would do better to undertake something that will make the world a better place."

Dulcie raised an eyebrow. "Such as a national museum of art, open to all ranks and degrees of men?"

"Yes. The founders of such a museum are far more likely to be remembered by posterity than any gentleman connoisseur, no matter the skill with which he makes his artistic pronouncements, or how many gentlemen he persuades to agree with them."

"Ah, but our definitions of posterity might not quite be the same, I fear. I wish to be remembered by the educated, the genteel, not by the rabble at large."

"But if the ranks of the educated were to increase, think how many more there would be to admire you. And how better to increase those ranks than by introducing them to the finest genteel culture has to offer: the works of the greatest masters of art."

Dulcie barked out a laugh. "Are you truly stooping to appeal to my basest desires? You must want this museum quite badly."

Benedict paced in front of the chaise, waving his hands. "I have no patience for those who argue that culture is best advanced by supporting great private collections, walled off from the masses. Art is meant to inspire virtue, and national spirit, in the populace. How can it do so if only a handful of privileged men are allowed to view the greatest works the world's premier artists have produced?"

Dulcie swung his legs down from the chaise and spread his arms wide over its back. "Ah, there's the Benedict Pennington I remember, fired by the need to do good for others. Always so filled with compassion for the downtrodden, going quietly about trying to lessen their woes. Do you remember that long treatise you wrote to the headmaster, expounding on the dangers of abuse inherent in the fagging system? Even though you may have idolized your own fag-master"—Dulcie paused to give Benedict a knowing smile—"you could not help but protest at the way some of the other senior boys took undue advantage of their power of the younger. How I admired you for it!"

Dulcie smoothed a hand over the seat of the chaise, almost as if inviting Benedict to sit with him as they reminisced about days gone by. But the memory of the egregious behavior of some of the fag-masters—of one boy in particular—and the way Dulcie had left him to that boy's dubious mercies made Benedict recoil.

"Am I to understand, then, that you do not wish to become an advocate for the museum? That you will instead do all in your power to secure Mr. Adler's paintings for your own private ends?" he asked, his voice harsh with disappointment.

Dulcie gazed up at Benedict for a long moment, a smile

playing about his narrow lips. "I am only resolved to act in a manner which will, in my own opinion, constitute my own happiness."

"And what would constitute your happiness, my lord? I confess, I have often wondered," Polly Adler's voice asked.

Benedict's attention jerked to the doorway, to where Polly stood beside his sister, Sibilla, both with slightly puzzled expressions on their faces.

"To escort Miss Adler to tomorrow's meeting of the Society of Arts," Dulcie said with a flourishing bow in that lady's direction. "I confess, I am quite eager to hear who has won this year's medals for original oil paintings. Did you know that one of our friends has entered her work for consideration?"

Benedict's eyes darted to Polly, whose face flushed with pleasure and embarrassment at Dulcie's declaration. How the hell had Dulcie known such a thing, when Polly had not even told Benedict she'd taken such a step?

"Oh, how I wish I could join you, Miss Adler!" Sibilla's unruly curls bounced with excitement as she turned to offer her congratulations to Polly. "But I'm promised to Sir Peregrine tomorrow. May I call on you later this week, so you may tell me all about it?"

"Thank you, Miss Pennington. I would be honored," Polly answered with a shy smile. "But Mr. Pennington, you will accompany Lord Dulcie and myself?"

Benedict could not resist the hesitancy, nor the apology, in Polly's voice. "I would be equally honored."

He would also be damned if he allowed Dulcie to spend any more time alone with Polly, not if he could prevent it.

CHAPTER 5

"Excuse me, that's a good fellow. If you will just step one pace to this side I believe we might just squeeze through. . . Ah, yes, a million pardons, my good woman, I did not mean any insult to that finest of bonnets. . . An award for a new kind of rat trap, you don't say! Now, if you will excuse us. . ."

Dulcie used equal parts charm and elbow to guide himself and Miss Adler through the throng assembled in the spacious Hall of the Drury Lane Theatre for the annual meeting of the Society for the Encouragement of Arts, Manufactures and Commerce. A far different crowd here this afternoon than when he typically frequented the theater. While the honorary premiums for polite arts were reserved for the nobility and gentry, the bulk of the Society's prizes were awarded for agricultural and industrial innovations, hardly the province of the *ton*. What else should one expect, though, from a Society which continued to consider artists as mere craftsmen, on par with the inventors of an improved ribbon loom, or a more cunning trap for vermin? Yet the public had taken such an increased interested in the Society that its annual meeting had been moved from its own building to a local tavern, and now to this spacious theater.

He'd far rather spend his time at the Royal Academy Exhibition, or even at the exhibition of the painters in water colours at the Egyptian Hall, than amongst such a crush. What other sacrifices would he be forced to make in pursuit of Miss Adler's dowry?

Or in pursuit of Benedict Pennington?

Yes, that instinctual attraction was still there between them, that strange spiritual chemistry that had flared during those few brief months they'd been together at school. The younger Benedict's strong feelings and deeply held beliefs had often tempted adolescent Dulcie to delve below the surface of gaiety and charm he typically showed the world, even though he knew that revealing such vulnerability never profited in the long run. But yesterday, alone with the adult Benedict for the first time, he'd had to fight hard to keep his prattle charmingly superficial.

Because even though Benedict was no longer an eager-eyed boy, he still had a way of making Dulcie reveal more of himself than he ever intended. Witness Dulcie mentioning his desire to be a respected arbiter of aesthetic taste. He'd spoken flippantly, yes, but still, he'd said it, given voice to his most ardent desire. And then the fellow had had the cheek to make him feel a twinge of guilt at the selfishness of that wish with his avid devotion to a far more public-spirited cause.

Toying with Benedict Pennington, no matter how his senses leaped to inconvenient awareness in that gentleman's presence, would not be the safest course of action, not for either of them.

But Dulcie's angel of righteousness never did speak as compellingly as his angel of iniquity. . .

Dulcie glanced behind them, to make sure Benedict had not fallen behind. But the other man still stood by the theatre's entrance, engaged in conversation with Sir Charles Long, one of the original founders of the British Institution and a trusted advisor to the King. Some wags said that when it came to choosing which artists to patronize, George IV saw only through Long's spectacles. Benedict must have been hoping to persuade the King, through Long, to support his national gallery plan.

"Dulcie. Well met, sir!"

Dulcie quashed his annoyance and donned a practiced smile as he turned to greet his unwelcome interlocutor. "Leverett. And Mr. George Norton. What an unexpected pleasure. I did not know you were interested in matters commercial and industrial."

Young Norton blushed and bowed. "Lord Dulcie."

"Certainly we've no interest in the bulk of the awards," Leverett said, skipping the niceties. "But Norton and I, we've made a few wagers on who will win the Gold Medal in each category of the Polite Arts, and who must settle for the Isis. Would you care to place a bet of your own?"

Mr. Norton, better-mannered than his companion, turned to Miss Adler. "Will the lady whom you accompany permit an introduction, my lord?"

"Yes, Dulcie, please introduce us," Leverett seconded with a knowing smile. He'd maneuvered George Norton into attending this meeting, no doubt, suspecting Dulcie would invite Polly Adler to attend. And hoping to pour poisonous gossip about him in her ear. Dulcie silently applauded. Leverett always proved a worthy rival. But his own budding friendship with Miss Adler wasn't likely to be overset by any spoke Leverett could toss in its wheels.

He raised a questioning eyebrow to Polly, who gave a brief nod.

"Miss Adler, may I present Mr. Lattimer Leverett and Mr. George Norton? Both are avid patrons of the arts, as well as fellow members of the British Institution. Leverett, Norton, Miss Polyhymnia Adler. Granddaughter of Julius Adler, of Pall Mall. She is one of the artists competing for a prize today."

George Norton bowed. "I applaud your bravery, Miss Adler. I would never have the courage to show my own poor artistic attempts to the public."

"Miss Adler," Leverett said as took her hand in his. Ingratiating dog. She'd not invited such familiarity. "I know your grandfather by reputation, naturally, but I have never had the privilege of viewing his renowned collection. What a joy it must be, to live and breathe amidst such treasures!"

"A joy, yes, indeed," Miss Adler said as she drew her gloved hand from Leverett's. Not one for idle chit-chat, was she? Especially not with an encroaching stranger.

Dulcie's angel of iniquity prodded. "A joy you may soon have yourself, sir, if the gods smile upon you."

Leverett leaned forward, his nostrils flaring. "Indeed? You have the run of Adler's collection already, do you?"

His rival rarely showed his rapacity so openly. How it must gall him, knowing Dulcie had access to a collection of such quality when he did not.

"Oh, I would hardly call it that," Dulcie said with an easy smile. "No, I speak of a quite different opportunity. Did you know Miss Adler's grandfather is considering donating his collection, or at least part of it, to our fair country? To serve as the basis for a national gallery of art?"

Leverett grimaced. "Surely you jest, Dulcie. What intelligent collector would turn his life's work over to the state?"

"One who believes that the general taste of the public will be improved by having models of real excellence in painting constantly before them," Benedict said, nodding to Norton and Leverett as he joined their small group.

"The general public? Do you mean such a gallery would be open to anyone, just like the British Museum?" Norton, poor boy, looked a bit sick at the idea. And Leverett, why, he seemed almost on the verge of an apoplexy. What fun!

Dulcie waved his hand to the crowds about them. "To the higher orders, to the middling classes, why, to any milkmaid or stableboy who wishes to visit! Even to fellows as unworthy as you and I, Leverett."

Norton frowned—trying to make sense of a scheme that everything in his upbringing told him was irrational? "But why would a milkmaid or a stableboy be interested in viewing a painting? I could understand opening such a gallery to our own artists, so they might study the techniques of their betters. But —"

"I doubt even constant study of the Old Masters could improve the English school of art," Leverett interrupted. "I would never disgrace my collection by hanging the work of a native upon my walls."

"You are wrong," Benedict said, waving a hand in clear dismissal. "Since my travels on the Continent, where I was exposed to artists, nay, entire schools of art, that I would never have seen had I remained at home, my approach to painting has changed entirely. But many of England's artists never have the chance to study abroad, and thus lack the opportunity to become acquainted with what is really fine in art."

"And it is not only our artists who would benefit from a gallery in the heart of London," Dulcie added with a sly glance at Leverett. "Think of all the foreign visitors such a collection would draw! And those visitors would add to the prosperity and riches of our metropolis, would they not?"

"London is crowded enough without dirty foreigners cluttering up our streets, don't you agree, Norton?" Leverett interposed.

"I had not considered that, Dulcie," Benedict said, ignoring Leverett completely. Oh, how that would grate! "But the gallery in Dresden, and the Pitti palace, yes, even the Louvre, they all draw more people to their cities than would ordinarily visit, don't they?"

The respect in Benedict's eyes, a respect he hadn't seen since their schooldays, fired Dulcie's brain. "Indeed. And you've overlooked perhaps the most important advantage. Such a gallery will lead to an improvement in the general taste of the public. By visiting such an institution, by gazing on the admirable models contained within its walls, those who never had the chance before to see the best that the world's artists have created will now have a just and proper standard of excellence before them."

Benedict leaned towards him. "And that will in turn increase the number of patrons of art—"

"And render them more competent judges of what constitutes truly fine productions—" Dulcie interrupted.

"And thus encourage improvement in our own native British artists," Benedict concluded with a satisfied nod.

Lord, he'd forgotten how Benedict's enthusiasm could set his own thoughts spinning. The sheer, uncomplicated joy of two minds sparking one off the other, Benedict's rich imagination inspiring his own more rational brain to plumb possibilities neither would have reached by themselves.

If they were still boys, he'd have grabbed Benedict and wrestled, releasing this bubbling energy their collaboration bred in mock-fighting before it could grow into something different, something he hadn't been quite sure he was ready to acknowledge then, or even name.

But they were not boys, not any longer.

"And what think you of your grandfather's plan to donate such riches to the nation, Miss Adler?" Leverett's words were directed at Polly, but his eyes were fixed on Dulcie and Benedict. "Are you not concerned that you will be deprived of a property you—or your future husband—might otherwise expect to inherit?"

Damn him for a fool. He'd simply intended to goad Leverett, not allow pleasure in sparring with Benedict to overtake good sense. Bandying about justifications for a national gallery with the man would hardly convince Leverett of his indifference. And now Leverett was taking his spite at being ignored out on Polly.

"I would miss living and breathing amongst those paintings, as you so eloquently describe it," she answered, neatly sidestepping Leverett's jab. "But if the new institution stipulates that ladies as well as gentleman will be granted access, I believe I might be persuaded."

"But truly, Miss Adler, do you not think a public of the sort which could entrusted with art ought to be restricted to—"

A gong ringing from inside the theatre interrupted Norton's protest.

"I believe that signal means the meeting is about to begin," Dulcie said, winging an arm to Polly. "Miss Adler? The family box is on the second tier."

Leverett laid a heavy hand on Dulcie's arm. "A word, first, sir, if you please."

"Stay, Dulcie. I'll escort Miss Adler." Benedict took her hand and placed it on his own sleeve. "Good day, gentlemen."

Dulcie kept his eyes on the pair as they skirted the rotunda and turned up the grand Prince's staircase, feigning indifference to whatever his rival might have to say. But Leverett did not wait, moving close beside him to whisper in his ear.

"Are you certain you wish to continue with our friendly wager? It seems you now have not one, but two, rivals for Miss Adler's dowry."

"Ah, but if Adler donates his paintings to the nation, then he cannot give them to Mr. Pennington." He nodded at a passing acquaintance, bowed to another as the crowd scrambled towards the auditorium.

"But nor can he give them to you," Leverett replied, his grip tightening on Dulcie's sleeve. "Our bet is not just that Pennington will lose, but that you will defeat him. I could almost wish you success if your victory simultaneously scuttles Pennington's ridiculous plan to allow the vulgar masses to gape and gawk at works which they have not the taste nor understanding to appreciate. What a mawkish, mollyish sentimentalist."

Dulcie stared down at Leverett's encroaching hand, his eyebrows raised. He was no molly, no matter what Leverett might insinuate about Benedict.

Understanding the silent message, Leverett took a step back. But the fellow still had not finished.

"Don't underestimate Pennington's wiles, Dulcie. He may appear to go along with Adler's mad scheme, but in the end, he'll show his true colors. He's as concerned with his own welfare and advantage as either you or I. Or young Norton here." He threw a companionable arm about the boy's shoulder, just as Dulcie had back at the print shop. "Don't you agree, my dear?"

Norton's eyes flicked between the two older men, indecision written clearly across his round face. Leverett had spoken in such a low voice that he had no idea what the man wished him to agree to.

Dulcie put the poor boy out of his misery. "Thank you for your concern, sir. But I have no thought of reneging on our wager."

"Then shall we add spice to the pot? Put a time limit, say, on your wooing?" Leverett smirked. "What would you say to an additional five hundred pounds if you can win her dowry by Michaelmas?"

"I would say you're in danger of losing not only your wager, but also your wits."

"Oh, but you haven't yet heard what I demand of you if you should have the misfortune to lose. I'm a magnanimous fellow, so I'll allow you your choice: at the British Institution's next meeting, you must inform Stafford that you wish me, rather than yourself, to be given a seat on the Board of Directors, acknowledging me to be your superior in artistic taste and judgement. Or you must denounce Benedict Pennington as the talentless hack he so obviously is."

Dulcie, responding more to the challenge in Leverett's voice than to the meaning of his words, immediately thrust out his hand. He would never allow that man to get the better of him, or show him up in front of another gentleman. "Agreed."

Leverett smiled as he took Dulcie's hand. "Come, George,

we'll bid Lord Dulcie good-day. I'd rather be as far from his box as possible when Miss Adler learns she's not even won a silver for her poor attempt at a Waterloo scene. As if a mere lady could do such historical work any justice. But her loss will give Dulcie an opportunity, no doubt, to offer comfort to the poor girl. Never say I am not a fair competitor, my lord."

"But how do you know she has not won. . ." Norton's voice faded as the two made their way through the rotunda and through the doors to the pit.

Dulcie frowned as the details of the wager slowly infiltrated his conscious brain. Why, no matter the outcome, Leverett had ensured he would be forced to repudiate Benedict Pennington in some way. That is, unless he swallowed his pride and gave the man what he truly wanted: a seat on the British Institution's Board.

Well, he'd been many a situation tighter than this one, and always managed to wriggle his way free. He'd find a way to come out the winner yet.

No one would ever get the better of Sinclair Milne.

Taking the stairs two at a time, he searched his pockets for a handkerchief with which to dry Polly Adler's soon-to-be-shed tears.

"Good morning, oh loveliest of mothers in all the land." Dulcie bent down and placed a light kiss on Lady Milne's cheek, then snatched a buttered roll from her plate. "And how will you be spending your last day in our fair city?"

"My heavens, Dulcie!" Lady Milne blinked down at the table, as if surprised to find her plate empty. "Awake in time for breakfast?"

Dulcie's sister Wilhelmina, seated beside his mother in the dining room, gave an exaggerated sigh. "We will be doing what we always do when it is time to remove to the country, which you would know if you ever paid attention to anyone but yourself. Packing, packing, and more packing. And then instructing the servants on how best to keep you and father in line until Parliament is dissolved."

"Are you certain you will not come with us, my dear?" Lady Milne asked, patting at the air beside her. But Dulcie had already moved on to inspect the offerings on the buffet. "I can never understand why you would want to remain here in the city when Hampshire is so much more pleasant in the heat of the summer."

He snorted silently. No, his mother would certainly not understand the attractions of a city—certain parks at night, taverns and public houses with private back rooms for the hire, even bog houses (if one could tolerate the stink)—for a man of Dulcie's proclivities.

He reached across the table and snatched his sister's cup, then took his usual seat opposite her. "Chocolate, Mina? Are you not afraid of coming out in spots?"

"Are not you?" she answered as he tipped the cup to his mouth. "You're the one a-courting, not me."

"And that is precisely why Dulcie must remain in London," Lord Milne said, shaking his head and pointing his knife at his son from his seat at the head of the table. "Only a fool would leave as likely a prospect as Adler's granddaughter to go traipsing about the countryside. Must secure her, Dulcie, the sooner the better. I want to meet the future fifth Earl Milne before I shuffle off this mortal coil."

The fifth? Dulcie frowned at the too-familiar heaviness in his chest. His father was the third earl, and he himself would be the fourth. But each would be more likely to spot a chicken with teeth than to witness the birth of a fifth.

Dulcie shook his head. Why dwell on such unpleasant thoughts? And on such a beautiful morning!

"Oh, Father, you're only upset because Miss Pennington's choice of husband is depriving you of a valued secretary," Dulcie teased, even as he picked to pieces the remainder of his stolen roll. "High time that Sir Peregrine fledged the Milne nest and began a political career of his own."

"Not before he explains all his duties and methods to his replacement," Lord Milne declared. "Won't have my affairs muddled by an uninformed clerk."

As if any poor clerk could put Father's affairs into any more of a muddle than the man himself. Still, Per had been a damned good secretary, as well as a pithy writer. Dulcie had even trusted him to document and catalog each new addition to his own art collection. Who would he ask to do so in the future?

Benedict Pennington?

"Have you chosen a new secretary?" Wilhelmina asked, her focus sharpening on their father. Poor Mina, still unmarried at five-and-twenty. If Father had not thought Sir Peregrine, a baronet, worthy of his only daughter, Per's replacement was not likely to prove proper suitor material either.

But if the new fellow proved attractive, perhaps Dulcie might indulge? Per had not proven susceptible to his charms, silly boy, but his replacement just might. Father had a rule about not dallying with dependents, but a secretary was not precisely a servant. And Lord knows he could use a good flirt to distract him from plaguing thoughts of a certain viscount's son. Especially since said viscount's son was supposed to be arriving this morning with Miss Adler for Dulcie's next portrait sitting.

"A new man?" Lord Milne answered. "Yes, Sayre is to bring him by today. That is, if he can tear himself away from his lady love for a morning."

"I can indeed, my lord. At least for long enough to deliver an invitation to our wedding breakfast. I do hope you all will be able to attend."

Peregrine Sayre stood in the doorway, an uncharacteristic smile on his narrow face. Yes, Per's betrothal to Sibilla Pennington certainly had done wonders for the fellow's typically dour spirits. Dulcie silently congratulated himself again for being the making of that match.

Lady Milne smiled as she held out a hand for the proffered invitation, patting at the table about her with the other. Poor dear, forever forgetting where she had left her spectacles. Dulcie plucked them from where they perched atop her head and slid them over her nose.

"What a good boy. Thank you, my dear. But who is this you've brought with you, Sir Peregrine?"

"Did you not hear, it is Father's new secretary, Mama," Mina said. But when Per stepped farther into the breakfast room, it was not a stranger who followed.

"You all remember my soon-to-be brother-in-law, Mr. Benedict Pennington?" Per asked.

Benedict, hands full with paintbox and sketch books, gave Lady Milne a clumsily endearing bow. His dark, wary eyes flicked over to Dulcie, then skittered away.

Dulcie straightened in his seat and shot a glance down the table. Surely Father would not recall the name of the writer of that long-ago letter?

"The son of a viscount for a secretary, Father?" Dulcie shook his head in mock sorrow. "Surely you can do better than that! Are there no sons of dukes with an interest in politics and pockets to let?"

"Pennington?" Lord Milne asked, ignoring Dulcie's attempt at distraction. "Thought you said the fellow's name was Cummings, Sayre?"

Dulcie settled back in his seat. Praise heavens Father had a memory little better than a sieve.

Per nodded, well used to needing to explain the obvious to

Lord Milne. "Yes, but Mr. Cummings is yet to arrive, my lord. Benedict accompanied me from Pennington House, as he has some business with Dulcie?" Per turned to Dulcie, one eyebrow raised.

"Yes, business of the most pressing kind." Dulcie swallowed down a last bite of roll then jumped to his feet before his friend could interrogate him further. "Did I tell you, mother, I'm to have my portrait painted? As a gift to my future betrothed, whoever she may be. And Mr. Pennington here is to undertake the task."

Mina laughed. "Dulcie? Able to sit still for long enough to have his likeness taken? When the Thames stops flowing, perhaps."

Benedict's head dipped in acknowledgment. "Your brother is proving a difficult subject to capture, Lady Wilhelmina."

"Yes, my first sitting proved particularly unfruitful, did it not, Pennington?" Dulcie said, patting him on the back with sympathy. An appealingly broad back, its strong muscles shifting under his fingers. What might it feel like, without these layers of clothing between them?

"My fault, of course," Dulcie continued, removing his palm from the tempting expanse of Benedict's shoulder. "All the tools of the artist's trade in Pennington's studio fascinated me, and I could not seem to hold one position for any length of time. Miss Adler suggested I might be less distracted in my native milieu, as it were, and thus Pennington has come to me today, rather than I to him. But was Miss Adler not to accompany you?"

"She sent a note saying she would meet us here." But Benedict's frown suggested some doubt about the matter.

"But I do not understand," Lady Milne asked. "What is Miss Adler to do with your portrait?"

Dulcie could not help but smile. A changeling he must be, left here by a sly fairy to be forever teased by parents too slow to keep up with his own quick wit. Still, mother was a dear.

He bent down to place another kiss upon her soft, powdered cheek. "Miss Adler is to keep me occupied while Mr. Pennington goes about his work."

Lord Milne seemed as puzzled as his wife. "Curious way to go about wooing a chit."

"Really, Dulcie?" Mina crossed her arms. "You expect us to entertain in the midst of all our packing?"

"If today is inconvenient," Benedict began, "I can certainly return another time—"

"Don't be silly," Dulcie said as he chivvied him back towards the door. "We will be in no one's way upstairs. I am in desperate need of advice: shall I don the same waistcoat I wore during our last sitting? Or will blue be more flattering? Mama, please have Miss Adler sent upstairs when she arrives, will you?"

They climbed the wide staircase together, leaving the clatter of the breakfast room behind. Half-way up, Dulcie jumped a bit ahead, to give Benedict the chance to admire the snug fit of his frock coat, the fabric of his pantaloons clinging to his calves. It was always delicious to have the eyes of another fixed upon one, but knowing the eyes behind him belonged to Benedict Pennington—well, that made the warmth radiate not just through his chest, but to the farthest reaches of his fingers and toes.

Dulcie stopped to glance into the drawing room, then his mother's sitting room, but both were filled with maids folding gowns and packing shoes and jewels and other female frippery into trunks. Father and Per would be nattering away in the library, and they'd have to dodge footmen hauling boxes in the front hall. No, his bedchamber it would have to be.

"The light here should not be too bad if you are only making sketches. Should I change my frock coat? Put on a more colorful waistcoat?"

"Not necessary. A feel for the line, the form and the shape, that's all I'm after today. But before we begin, I wish—"

He paused, his hands playing with the metal clasps on his paint box.

"You wish?"

Benedict looked up, his brown eyes wide, unguarded. "I wish to thank you for defending the idea of a national art museum to your friends. And to apologize for my assumptions about your interest in Miss Adler. No one who comforted a lady with such kindness after her disappointment in not winning a prize for her painting could be intent on wooing her only for her dowry. And no one who spoke with such insight about the benefits of a national gallery could truly want to keep Mr. Adler's collection solely for his own private use."

Dulcie pressed his lips tight to keep from smiling. Benedict had clearly not outgrown his boyish penchant for idealizing his fellow man. Nor, it seemed, had Dulcie outgrown the pleasure of being the subject of such idealization. His words in favor of the museum project had been said more on a whim than in earnest, but he need not disillusion the fellow, not just yet. Hanging, taut, in that delightful tension between the poles of multiple possibilities was too delicious to give up just yet.

"Your thanks, and your apology, are both accepted, sir."

"I doubt your arguments will change the minds of men deeply entrenched in their own aristocratic privilege," Benedict continued, opening his paint box and drawing out a stick of charcoal. "But younger men might find your reasoning persuasive. May I use your arguments when I speak with Sir Charles Long, and other gentlemen I need to convince of the worth of the project?"

"Of course you may. But come, we should not waste the morning nattering on about a museum when we have far more important tasks to address. Have you decided yet how you wish me to pose?"

Benedict shook his head. "I would think you would have your own opinion on the matter. A sitter usually does."

"Oh, I know the traditional pose for the male figure of rank. Stand tall, face front or three-quarter turned, pull your shoulders back, but do not round them, place one foot gracefully behind the other, thus"—Dulcie illustrated each directive as he uttered it —"and for all that's holy, never, ever smile."

"Yes, just so," Benedict said, a slight smile turning up the corners of his full lips. "Now hold still so I may put it down on paper."

"But may I—"

"And keep silent. I cannot capture your expression if you insist on jabbering away like a sailor's parrot."

Dulcie tried, he really did. Head erect. Back straight. Lips lightly joined, one arm bent at the elbow. Eyes fixed on the wall opposite, and not on the man crouched on the floor in front of him. But even the lowering clouds and rocky shoreline of the unfashionable Constable landscape he had purchased against all advice and hung in his bedchamber could not hold his attention for long. Not with this strange restlessness that seemed abuzz inside him, as if he had swallowed a swarm of bees. Having all eyes upon him was not usually an unfamiliar, nor an unwelcome, experience. But somehow when those eyes belonged to Benedict Pennington, it was a different matter altogether.

But damn him, the fellow rebuffed every attempt he made to engage him in conversation, no matter how witty. And only spoke to him to demand he shift into yet another traditional portrait stance, each one stiffer than the last.

Attempting to stave off ennui, Dulcie began to tease, quirking an eyebrow here, wrinkling a nose there, even whistling a bawdy tune he'd heard the comely Miss Noel, she of the sly wicked eyes, sing last night at Vauxhall Gardens. But instead of laughing at Dulcie's antics, Benedict only scowled more fiercely, ripping each study he completed off his sketching pad and balling it up before tossing it to the floor.

After each "Stand still, damn you!" from Benedict's lips, Dulcie would try to stop fidgeting. But his good intentions would only last for so long. Finally, after what seemed like hours of posing, Dulcie could stand it no longer. With a groan, he bent from the waist and sent his arms flying, like a jack just sprung from its box. He let his torso bounce once, twice, a third time before finally allowing it to come to a floppy stop.

When Benedict remained silent, he peeked up from under the ringlets falling over his forehead, greeting him with his most insouciant smile.

Benedict's nostrils flared, a bull on the verge of rampage. Why should the thought excite him so?

"Stand up, will you?" Benedict bit out. "I agreed to paint a portrait of a gentleman, not a clown."

Dulcie's body followed the sharp command, even as his tongue resisted it. "Cannot a gentleman be amusing?"

"Certainly. But is that how you wish to present yourself to your future wife, and to the world? As a jester, a mere joke?" He wiped a hand across his brow, leaving a smudge of charcoal by his eye.

"Not to a wife, no. But to the world? Perhaps it is unwise of me, but I could wish for something more memorable to leave to posterity than yet another depiction of genteel male deportment."

Benedict huffed. "But each person should have that expression which men of his rank generally exhibit. The joy or the grief of a character of dignity is not to be expressed in the same manner as a similar passion in a vulgar face."

"How disappointing," Dulcie tutted. "Are you a parrot, then, repeating the tired dictums of another? Sir Joshua Reynolds's words, are they not? From his fourth *Discourse*, if I am not mistaken."

"You disagree with Sir Joshua? A portrait of a man of dignity and power is not memorable enough for you?"

Dulcie laughed without humor. "Is that all you see in me now? A man of dignity and power? It seems your travels have blinded, rather than opened, your eyes."

Benedict tossed his charcoal and sketch-book on a chair. "If all you show to the world is your polished surface, is it any wonder if that surface is all that others see? All they think to reflect back at you?"

"What, first you abuse me for not embodying the proper dignity of my station, and now you take me to task for not displaying my depths as carelessly as a drunkard spews his guts on the pavement? You might wish to make up your mind about what you want from me before you berate me for not giving it to you."

Benedict stepped closer, crowding him back against the bedpost. "What I want? What I want is what I've always wanted."

Dulcie's breath caught as Benedict reached out and touched him. Long, tapered fingers skimmed over the bones of his face, his brows, his ears. Almost as if Benedict could capture his features through touch rather than through sight.

His throat tightened as a thumb, rough, calloused, traced the bow of his lip.

Even through closed eyes, he could feel Benedict's tousled head lower to his, curls and breath whispering in his ear. "I want to see you. *You*, Clair, not the charmingly frivolous Viscount Dulcie you parade before the rest of the world. It's been so long —"

A staccato rap on the door sent Dulcie jerking to the other side of the bedchamber before he had the chance to shape his lips into any coherent response to Benedict's provocative words.

"Miss Adler has arrived, my lord," the ill-timed footman announced. "She awaits in the drawing room."

Dulcie pulled at his cuffs and pasted on his easy social smile, willing the tension in his muscles to ease. It was not like him to become so flustered by a simple touch, a few tempting words.

"Polly, my dear girl," he said as he entered the drawing room and held out his hands in welcome. "You arrive just in time to save me from the tyranny of this cruel martinet you call friend. Can you imagine, he's had me standing at attention for more than an hour and has refused to converse with me the entire time?"

"I am so sorry, my lord!" Polly said with an apologetic frown. "I know how difficult it is to remain still for so long, especially for an active gentleman such as yourself. And have you been playing with Mr. Pennington's charcoal pencil? You've a smudge on your cheek—here, take my handkerchief—there, right below your left eye."

Dulcie's gaze flew to Benedict, who had followed him into the drawing room. But all his frowning attention was fixed on the handkerchief in his hand, scrubbing away at his own telltale smudges.

"Now, do you have a book you'd like me to read to you while Mr. Pennington makes his sketches? Or shall I tell you about my frustrations with the chairmen of the Society of Arts' committee on Polite Arts? They utterly refused to explain why no premiums were given for original oil paintings of historical subjects this year, even though others besides myself submitted such works."

"Because history painting is at the pinnacle of the Academic hierarchy, and thus they believe only men of rank should be allowed to paint historical subjects," Benedict said with a scowl.

"Is that why you were late? Bearding the lions in their dens, were you?" Dulcie asked.

"In grandfather's, rather. But all to no purpose. I might have been a child for all the consideration they gave me. Lord, how I wish I'd been born a man!" Polly murmured.

Dulcie gave her shoulder a comforting squeeze, but she just shrugged him aside.

"*Confessions of an Opium Eater?*" she asked, reading the title of the book her restless hands had plucked from a nearby table.

"That does not sound very entertaining."

"Oh, just a little moral tract of my sister's," Dulcie said, pulling that scandalous volume from her hands and setting it down again out of her reach. What else could he use to distract her? "I believe this month's *Ackermann's Repository* is about here somewhere. You shall read to me about the other exhibitions in town, and we can decide which we should visit next."

"No need to keep Dulcie entertained, Polly." Benedict shoved his handkerchief into a pocket. "I've done enough here today."

Oh, hardly enough. Not after offering such a tantalizing invitation. Not that Dulcie would be so foolish to give any man, especially one as perceptive as Benedict Pennington, unfettered access to the inmost parts of his being.

But if he might persuade him to settle for a few tiny glimpses —well, such a trade might be entirely worth the risk.

CHAPTER 6

THE CLANKING OF SILVER AGAINST plate, the cheery prognostications for the future happiness of the newly wedded couple, the sheer inanity of the chatter of a dining room filled with well-fed members of the English nobility—Benedict could only stand the celebratory bustle of his sister's wedding feast for so long. Nor the unexpected longing that overtook him each time Sibilla smiled with surprised delight upon her bridegroom, each time Sir Peregrine patted his wife's hand or clasped hers in his. Even if Benedict ever found himself in love, found a person to whom he wished to pledge his troth, a man of his inclinations would never have the chance to stand up and declare his vows in front of his friends and family as his sister just had.

With this Ring I thee wed, with my Body I thee worship, and with all my worldly Goods I thee endow: In the Name of the Father, and of the Son, and of the Holy Ghost. Amen.

He rubbed the tight muscles in his jaw. He'd never be allowed to express his joy in joining with the mate of his soul, not with the openness and freedom Sibilla and her new husband took entirely for granted. Not in church, nor in the midst of Pennington House's ballroom.

Benedict's head jerked as an amused laugh pealed out from across the room. No such unfulfillable longings seemed to plague Lord Dulcie, who had stood beside Sir Peregrine during the long wedding ceremony with nary a wistful sigh. And here, amongst company, he was in his element, drawing the attention of everyone within earshot with his amusing stories and scandalous gossip. Was it a blessing or a curse, to take such pleasure in the way things were, rather than rail and regret over what they should be?

But perhaps Dulcie did not long for anything different. Whenever Benedict saw him, he was always surrounded by a coterie of young men, rather than one special companion. Rumor among a certain set had it that each season, Dulcie made a particular friend of one or another young fellow new to town each year, but the same rumors also insisted that his attentions were as fleeting as a rainbow amongst the clouds. Was young George Norton, the son of the gentleman whom Benedict's father had supported for a seat in Parliament, currently vying for the right to spend a few brief hours basking in Dulcie's reflected glory? He certainly hung on the viscount's every word.

Not that Benedict gave a tinker's curse for whom Dulcie deigned to bestow his favors on.

"A toast! A toast! Every married man shall toast his wife!" Theo, Lord Saybrook, thrust his nearly empty wineglass towards his new brother-in-law. He'd declared to anyone who would listen that he was celebrating finally having the responsibility for their troublesome younger sister taken off his hands. More likely, though, he was drowning his guilt at being talked into declaring that their youngest brother, Kit, who had just wed an entirely unsuitable Irishwoman, not be invited to this morning's festivities. Damn Uncle Christopher for his stupid, pointless prejudices.

Benedict wrapped a piece of the wedding cake in a napkin—he'd promised to take one to Kit and his Fianna—then slipped it, and himself, out of the noisy ballroom. Uncle Christopher could be the one to make sure that Theo did not make a drunken fool of himself today.

His footsteps took him not up to his studio—too many

reminders of his creative frustrations awaited there—but to the small drawing room at the back of the townhouse, the chamber that had once been his mother's favorite retreat. In it her own paintings, the landscapes of familiar views from the Saybrook estate and the exquisitely detailed watercolors of humble Lincolnshire flora, were kept in bound folios, not deemed grand enough for public display.

He picked up a volume and flipped through its pages, trying to shake off this damned melancholy.

With what patience and skill his mother had taught him to hold a black-lead pencil, to shape perfectly straight lines and full, rounded curves. To take his time and to erase his mistakes with his Indian rubber when his ambitions outran his ability. How he'd burst with pride when she'd declared his watercolor of the cathedral in Lincoln, the last painting he'd completed before being sent away to school, worthy of being framed and hung, when she would not even frame her own far more accomplished works. To look again at her paintings, to remember her soft, kind voice, the stroke of her gentle hand over his brow whenever he'd toss his brush down in frustration—it soothed him, even on a day like today, when restlessness and impatience pricked at him like a burr under a horse's saddle.

"Your sister's work? How did I not know she painted, as well as yourself?"

Benedict closed his eyes, willing away the awareness the soft-spoken words uttered behind him sent skittering down his spine. Why should he be surprised that Dulcie had followed him, after he'd given him such an ill-advised glimpse of his own longing during their last sketching session?

But should he really throw all the blame on Dulcie? Had not his own instincts, betraying good sense, urged him to leave the festivities, hoping that Dulcie—no, that *Clair*—might follow?

"They are not Sibilla's," he said, his voice low. "These were done by my mother."

Dulcie sat on the sofa beside him and tugged on the folio so that it sat half on Benedict's lap, half on his own. Benedict's breath caught at the closeness of Dulcie's thigh, the brush of his arm against his side as he turned each page. But the viscount's attention remained focused not on Benedict, but on the contents of the folio, examining each of the paintings with the eyes not of a loving child, but of an intelligent, opinionated critic.

Would Mother's heart have beaten as quickly under the appraisal as Benedict's did?

She had liked him, that golden, laughing boy he'd described in the letters he'd written to her from school, and encouraged her shy son to pursue a friendship with him. If she had still been alive, would she have helped him find that boy again, draw him out from where he hid, safe behind the varnish of his social smile? Or would she have counseled Benedict to forget him? Assured him that boy no longer existed?

"Quite accomplished she was, your mother," Dulcie said when he had finished examining the final painting—Benedict's favorite, a scene of a flower-strewn meadow on the Saybrook estate. "Such a dreamy, almost ethereal quality to them, as if she were painting her own visions rather than actual topological views. Did she ever submit her work to the Royal Academy exhibition?"

Benedict ran his fingers round the tinted border surrounding the painting. How lovely it would look, mounted in a simple gold frame. "I believe several of her friends urged her to do so. But she never valued her own talents highly enough to accept their praise. And my father thought it ill-suited of a viscountess to subject herself to such public display."

"Did you believe so, too?"

"I hardly think the opinion of a mere boy would have changed his mind."

Dulcie turned back to studying the picture. "Ah, yes, you had the misfortune to lose your mother at a young age, I believe?"

"When I was but fourteen." Two years after he'd lost Clair. Each time, he'd thought he'd lose himself as well, his grief had been so potent, so overwhelming.

"A pity. She had a talent that many a professional would envy."

Benedict closed the folio and slid it from Dulcie's lap, careful not to allow his fingers to touch the other man's thighs. "She would have been even better if she'd had the chance to see the works of Poussin, or Claude, or any of the old Dutch masters of landscape."

Dulcie shifted to face Benedict. "But as the wife of a peer, surely she had the chance to visit many a private collection?"

"A few, yes. But during a social visit, one is hardly allowed the chance to contemplate one painting before being rushed on to the next."

"Especially if its owner is prouder of himself for purchasing it than of the merits of the art itself," Dulcie said with a grin.

"Yes! If you wish to understand on an instinctual level a painting's composition, its use of line and shadow, the play of light and color, you must spend time with it, examine it in detail. Which you could do, if the country's best paintings were not all held in private collections. Gather them in one place, a place open to any who wish to view them, and watch how England's art would flower."

Dulcie waved a careless hand. "There are other museums, on the Continent."

"But my mother never had the opportunity to travel abroad, to study the great works of the past. How many other talented young artists are lost to the world, or never reach their full potential, for lack of the opportunities enjoyed by the wealthy, or the privileges granted the male sex?"

"How impassioned you become when you speak of your museum scheme!" Dulcie gave a lazy smile, one that belied the sudden tension in the air between them. "Eyes frowning, brows lowering, that teasing sulkiness about your full lips—why, it's almost as if you were speaking of a lover, rather than a plan to make the world a better place."

Benedict shot to his feet. "Is that why you followed me? In search of a lover?"

"Bold words, Mr. Pennington. And if I answer with equal boldness, and say that I am?" Dulcie rose with far more grace from the settee than Benedict was sure he had.

"Is not Mr. George Norton already filling that role?"

"Not yet, although I have considered him. Teaching untutored youths in the ways of the flesh is a particularly piquant pleasure. But the more I see of you, the more I find myself unaccountably curious to know what it would be like to play with a more experienced man."

"You take a risk, revealing such things to me."

"No more of a risk than you once took. Sending that impassioned letter to me when you were a mere schoolboy."

"My letter." The blood rushed to Benedict's face. "You did receive it, then. I was never certain."

"Well, in a manner of speaking. My father opened it, then read certain parts to me aloud."

"Your father?" Benedict's stomach fell. He'd pictured Dulcie reading his letter a million times—laughing, sneering, sharing it with his friends, shredding it into tiny pieces and feeding it to the pigs. But that it might have been intercepted by a parent—that he'd never once imagined. "Lord, Clair. I'm so terribly sorry."

"Yes, as was I when my father informed me that I would not be returning to school again." A wry smile crossed Dulcie's face. "And when he forbid me to write back to you. I did so wish to tell you how accomplished I found your translations of Xenophon."

"Accomplished?"

"Yes, accomplished. From what my father shared with me,

your translations were not only remarkably accurate, they were rendered in quite elegant prose."

"The accuracy and elegance of my prose—is that what you remember about that letter?"

Dulcie crossed his arms and perched on the arm of the settee. "Well, Father did mention something about certain amorous wishes you expressed towards my person. But he did not deign to share any of the more salacious details. Perhaps you'd like to tell me of them now?"

Benedict felt his flush spread to his ears. "I'm no longer a child, smitten by calf-love for the most popular boy at school."

"No, you are certainly no child." Dulcie's eyes roamed with shocking directness up and down Benedict's body. "And I am no longer a boy who must heed his father's orders. If I wish to write to you, or to sit in front of you half-garbed while you take my likeness, or to grab what I imagine is your eager and lively prick and frot you until you spend in my hand—why, who is there to object?"

"No one," Benedict whispered.

"No one," Dulcie echoed, then reached up to pull Benedict's head down to his.

God, he was kissing Dulcie, pressing his lips to Dulcie's, nudging his mouth open and shoving his tongue deep inside it. No, not Dulcie, but *Clair*, the boy he'd worshipped from afar for so long, the boy still there beneath the man he'd spent months warily circling.

Whenever he'd dreamed of this moment, he'd imagined gentleness, something transcendent, even spiritual. Yet this kiss was crass and lewd, all tongues and teeth and *need*. Not just on Clair's part, but on his own, his body thrumming with the sheer necessity of his desire. He wanted to bite Clair, devour him, suck him down like sweet honey from the comb.

Punish him for staying hidden for so long.

"God, Pen," Clair whispered, his voice low, yearning. "I've

missed you so."

With a groan at the sound of that old pet name, Benedict pushed him to the wall and shoved a leg between his. Yes, there it was, Clair's cock rising against his thigh, twitching under the pressure. Slim and elegant and proud, he'd imagined it, just like the man to whom it belonged. God, would he have the chance to actually see if he was right? The thought was almost enough to make him spend there and then.

He grabbed Clair's waist, forcing him to hold still as his own hips pressed and released, pressed and released. Clair clutched at Benedict's arms, as if trying to stop himself from falling.

A loud thump jerked him from Clair's hold. His mother's portfolio lay on the floor beside them, jostled from its perch on the table by the intensity of their rutting.

Clair gulped in a deep breath, then swiped a thumb over the swell of Benedict's lip. "Well, well. It seems someone has learned a few things about kissing in the years we've spent apart. Alas, this is neither the time nor the place to discover how far your studies have progressed. Perhaps, after Friday's meeting. . ."

Benedict blinked, struggling to shake free from the daze of arousal. "What meeting?"

Clair laid a silencing finger over his lips. "No questions. It's a surprise I've arranged, particularly for you. Be ready; I'll fetch you in my carriage at half past five."

He grabbed Benedict's neck and pulled him down for one last lingering kiss, leaving him open-mouthed as he made for the door.

"And bring your sketching pad and charcoals. And your best arguments in favor of establishing that museum you're so intent upon. I've some people I think might be interested in hearing them."

With a wink and a grin, Clair sauntered from the room.

"Gentlemen, I give you tonight's topic: Shakespeare's *A Midsummer Night's Dream*. The scene: Bottom's transformation from weaver to ass. Before we begin to sketch, Viscount Dulcie, our guest this evening and an amateur thespian of some renown, will read aloud Bottom's lines, as well as those of his fellow rude mechanicals, to help inspire our pencils. Lord Dulcie, if you would?"

Dulcie rose from his comfortable seat and accepted the proffered folio from John Chalon, tonight's host of the Society for the Study of Epic and Pastoral Design. More familiarly known as the Evening Sketching Society, the group of eight professional painters gathered each week during the London season at one or another's lodgings to draw, paint, and critique each other's work on a subject set by the night's host. They weren't the most innovative, but still, they were men well worth Benedict's acquaintance. It would be wise to persuade practicing artists, as well as the connoisseur set, of the value of his museum plan if he wished it to move forward.

Dulcie had originally intended to ask Polly Adler to accompany him when he'd received his unexpected invitation from John Chalon and his brother Alfred to be a guest at this week's Society meeting. But not even Lattimer Leverett's taunts that he'd been lax in forwarding his courtship of the girl could sway him from his new plan. Lord, the memory of the heady haze of pleasure in Benedict Pennington's eyes after their surprisingly carnal kiss at his sister's wedding breakfast earlier in the week! What he wouldn't do to bring that look back to the man's eyes again.

Including extending to him this coveted invitation.

The eyes of most of the artists were fixed on him as he

cleared his throat and began to read from the play. But the only pair he cared about were dark and intense, thick brows brooding like thunderheads over their shadowed depths. Benedict gazed not at Dulcie, though, but down at his two elegant hands, clasped tightly atop his knees. Hands that had only a few days before held Dulcie's hips tight against the wall, squeezing and caressing with a strength he'd never imagined the schoolboy of his memories would one day possess.

"*This is to make an ass of me, to fight me if they could,*" Dulcie read in the swaggering voice he'd adopted for Bottom. Yes, there, a slight lifting of Benedict's lips, although his eyes still remained downcast. He continued, his entire performance aimed at Benedict, then gave a sweeping, exaggerated bow when he reached scene's end. The entire company cheered and applauded; one fellow even threw out a provocative whistle. Not Benedict, alas. But he'd make him laugh before it was over, or his name wasn't Sinclair Milne.

"A capital performance, my lord." John Chalon accepted the folio from Dulcie and laid it on the table beside them. "Now, gentlemen, you have two hours to do what you will to depict the moment of Bottom's transformation. We will reconvene at ten o'clock for supper, after which we will offer our critiques of each other's work."

Dulcie had been mistaken in telling Benedict that he'd need to bring sketch pad and pencils to the meeting. Whichever artist played host for the week, it seemed, provided not only refreshments—bread, cheese, and plenty of beer—but also all drawing materials any member or guest might require. Dulcie helped the younger Mr. Chalon distribute the paper and pencils, India ink and sepia, hoping he'd not be equally mistaken in believing such a gathering might help Benedict shake free of whatever aesthetic malaise he'd been suffering under.

It took far longer for Benedict to begin to draw than it did the professional painters, although Dulcie could not help but admire the ferocity of his scowl. Dulcie forced himself to roam the room, watching the other men at work, some tossing aside their initial efforts, others, more satisfied, going on to embellish with ink and wash their first ideas.

By the time he returned to the corner where Benedict had set up his small easel, the artist's imagination had seemed to catch, his frustration giving way to intense concentration and a hand that flew across the page. He'd taken a seat somewhat apart from the rest of the group, preferring a semblance of solitude rather than the chatter in which the other artists indulged.

Dulcie stepped closer, trying to catch a glimpse of his efforts.

Benedict frowned without looking up. "Move away, Dulcie. I don't wish anyone to look yet."

"But I am not just anyone, am I? Please? Just a quick glance?"

"Move away, I say. I can't concentrate with you hanging over my shoulder."

"Far be it from me to discompose the genius at his work," Dulcie said, allowing just a hint of pique to creep into his voice. But Benedict paid him no heed, already engrossed again by his pencil and paper.

What a rude, gruff fellow. Too bad Dulcie should find such heedlessness to the opinions of others so damned appealing.

"Here, Dulcie. Come and tell us of all the doings at the British Institution," called out Mr. Bone, one of the younger artists in the room. "You know how we love to hear about the faults and foibles of the connoisseur set."

Dulcie smiled. No men, even ones with lofty artistic pretensions, could resist a good gossip.

The hours passed with remarkable speed, even though Dulcie himself never took up a pencil or pen. Instead, he carefully guided the conversation from gossip to the more serious topic of public support for the arts, a topic that spilled over into the supper hour. During the earlier, working part of the evening, Benedict had remained silent, fixed on his own work, but at table, Dulcie's introduction of the idea of a national art gallery gradually drew him out of his shell. By its conclusion, Benedict's passionate championing of the scheme had even Mr. Cristall, the oldest and most doubting member of the Sketching Society, nodding in agreement.

Benedict's quicksilver smile as both Chalon brothers vowed to speak in favor of his scheme to other professionals of their acquaintance—now, that was a sight well worth committing to canvas.

Dulcie rubbed his hands together as the table was cleared and John Chalon set up a standing easel at its head. He would relish this last portion of the meeting, when the evening's paintings and sketches would be placed, one by one, on the easel at the head of the table for all members of the group to review and comment on. The Society's members had a reputation for being far more candid with each other than any professional critic. Dulcie loved a good insult, especially when given under the guise of being helpful. And he was never shy about voicing his own opinion of a work of art.

But no matter how many times he tried to draw Benedict into this part of the conversation, his companion seemed far more comfortable listening to criticism than in giving it.

"Thank you, Lord Dulcie, for your insightful comments," Mr. Chalon acknowledged. "But what of our other guest? Mr. Pennington, what do you make of Mr. Stump's composition? Has he captured the spirit of Shakespeare's scene?"

Would Chalon's direct question draw Benedict out? Dulcie moved to the edge of his seat, eager to hear his answer.

"Spirit?" Benedict asked haltingly. "I am not certain I—I do not understand the question. Does not the spirit of the scene depend upon the actors who embody it, as much as the lines they speak?"

"Yes, perhaps so," Chalon conceded. "Shall you give us your

opinion of the technique, then? What have you to say about the balance of the composition, or the depiction of bodies in motion?"

Benedict gave an apologetic shrug. "I'm afraid I am far more interested in emotion than technique."

"How do you mean, sir?" asked Mr. Stump.

"It is what is in here"—Benedict pounded a fist to his chest —"rather than what is in here"—tapping fingers against his temple—"that draws my attention when I first view a work of art. Your sketch, Mr. Chalon, and that of Mr. Leslie, and yours, too, Mr. Bone—when I look upon them, I feel the terror of the mechanicals, their dismay at the sight of their friend and leader so awfully transformed. Bottom is at the center of these two pictures, and the mechanicals in this one, but Bottom's outstretched arms in Mr. Chalon's and Mr. Leslie's, as well as the way you've both drawn the mechanicals leaning away from the creature—I feel he is more a figure of fear, than of comedy in these. If your aim was to evoke that feeling in your viewers, I would give the laurels to Mr. Chalon, for his Bottom is a touch more menacing than Mr. Bone's, with his body reaching out towards the other men. I also find the expressions on the faces of his compatriots more fearful."

"How unusual. You speak as if you are a viewer, rather than a fellow practitioner," John Chalon said, his eyebrows rising.

Benedict shrugged, his eyes skittering away from Chalon's. "I would never presume to tell a professional how to go about his business. I can only tell him how his drawing makes me feel."

Dulcie shook his head. Here they all were, arguing about the length of a line or a position of a tree, and Benedict cut through all their petty squabbles, right to the heart of the matter. Dulcie could always find fancy words to explain his preferences, but when it came right down to it, wasn't it how strongly a work made him feel that made him eager to add it to his collection, or to champion its creator to his fellow connoisseurs?

"What else, I wonder, is going on inside that fascinating mind of yours, Pennington?" Chalon nodded towards the sketching pad which Benedict had laid on the carpet beside his chair. "I confess, I am curious to see what you have done, working away off in that corner by yourself."

"I did not anticipate such an honor, sir," Benedict said with a worried glance towards Dulcie.

"Come, come. No honor to suffer the slings and arrows of their outrageous criticisms, surely!" Dulcie urged. "Give it over, if you please."

Benedict rubbed his ear, then pulled a page from his sketchbook and handed it to Chalon.

A sudden laugh, just as quickly suppressed, drew Dulcie's attention away from the curious, and quite unexpected, smile lifting up the corners of Benedict's lips. Some of the artists gazed back and forth between Benedict's drawing and Dulcie, while others chuckled and exchanged knowing grins. What the devil had Benedict drawn?

Pulling out his quizzing glass, he stepped in for a closer look. There, braying at a low-hanging moon, lay Shakespeare's Bottom the weaver, his head magically transformed into that of a donkey. But instead of the humble clothing appropriate to an ancient peasant, Benedict's Bottom wore the fancy waistcoat and tight-fitting frock coat of a nineteenth century gentleman, garments remarkably similar to the ones currently adorning Dulcie's figure.

The laughter nearly burst from his chest.

"You think me worthy of the lovely Titania, do you, sir?" he asked Benedict. "I had no idea I ranked so highly in your esteem."

"Ah, he doesn't acknowledge your knavery, Pennington," Mr. Leslie said with a chuckle. "No one can make an ass of Lord Dulcie."

"Still, best keep him away from the ladies, sir, or they'll be declaring their love for him on first view, just as Titania did," quipped the younger Mr. Chalon.

"Methinks they should have little reason for that!" exclaimed Dulcie, raising his eyebrows at Benedict.

"And yet, to say the truth, reason and love keep little company together now-a-days," Benedict answered, capping the Shakespeare line, a game in which they had often indulged while at school. His eyes caught on Dulcie's for a brief moment, then shied away.

"Come, sirs," John Chalon exclaimed. "We are not here to recite lines from the bard, but to comment on the art they inspire. Now, what do you make of the composition of Pennington's scene? Bottom, alone, without Titania or the other denizens of her forest?"

The conversation continued until the clock on Chalon's mantel struck midnight, the signal for the breaking up of the meeting. As the other artists gathered their belongings and bid their hosts good-night, Benedict moved to reclaim his drawing.

"I'm afraid not, Pennington," Mr. Chalon remonstrated, pulling the paper from Benedict's grasp. "Did not Lord Dulcie tell you, all sketches done of an evening remain the property of him at whose house they were made?"

Benedict frowned. "You do not sell them, do you, sir?"

"Oh, heavens no. But perhaps someday we all will be famous enough that this new national art gallery you speak of will welcome their donation," Mr. Chalon said with a smile. "I hope, Mr. Pennington, if you are still here in London in the autumn, you will join us when we next meet?"

Benedict's smile was almost wider than Dulcie's. "I would be honored, sir. And perhaps we might discuss then your ideas for suitable members to sit on a committee of superintendence for the proposed gallery?"

"The composition of that group is likely to be decided by the politicians rather than the artists, I fear. But I'd be happy to offer some names that you might put into the ear of your brother Lord Saybrook, or of any other political fellows of your acquaintance."

"Lord Dulcie might be the best man to make such arrangements. I understand he might soon be named a Director of the British Institution. All the political men who take an interest in the arts are to be found there."

"Indeed," Chalon said with a wry twist of his lips. "The nobs are always ready to instruct us in our own business. You proved a quite refreshing exception this evening. Bid you good-night for the nonce, Pennington. Lord Dulcie."

"I wonder what Miss Adler would have made of such an evening," Dulcie said as they gathered their hats and gloves from the Chalons' manservant then made their way down to the street. "She complains she has no one with whom she can discuss art, other than you and myself."

Benedict nodded, but his attention seemed focused on something else, some vision that only he could see. Without warning, he grabbed Dulcie's hand and pulled him down the pavement in the direction of Mayfair.

"Ah, in a rush to be alone with me, are you?" Dulcie chuckled as Benedict yanked his arm nearly out of its socket.

"Yes. Back to Pennington House, now!"

"Pennington House? Would you not rather—?"

"No. Pennington House."

"But is not your brother in residence?"

"No, he's gone down to Lincolnshire. And my sister and Sir Peregrine are off on their wedding journey."

"But what of your sister's chaperone? Has she, too, returned to her own abode?"

"Yes. Now hurry!"

Dulcie yanked Benedict to a halt. "Such desperation is flattering, Pen, but if you do not slow down, I'll not have breath enough to speak. Not to mention any other activities you may be contemplating."

Benedict's eyes smoldered down at his. "You'll not need to speak, not with what I have in mind for you."

A delicious shiver ran down Dulcie's spine. Was his plan to seduce Benedict Pennington already bearing fruit?

"Then by all means, let us throw decorum to the winds."

Heart pounding, spirits flying, Dulcie took off at a run.

CHAPTER 7

"Sit. No, lie down." Benedict pushed Clair back on the chaise-longue in his attic studio, then took a step back to consider. "No, not on your back, not as if you were sleeping. Turn onto your side, facing me. Yes, just like that."

"Why, Mr. Pennington," Clair drawled. "How very demanding you are tonight. But why are you leaving me here to languish on my own?"

Benedict rushed about the studio, gathering the materials he needed to begin painting. As he'd worked on an entirely different drawing at the Sketching Society, this other, far more compelling image had risen like a ghost in his mind. The first sketch had started as a joke, voluble Lord Dulcie in the guise of Shakespeare's Bottom, a way to make fun of Clair, or perhaps poke a hole in that seemingly endless reserve of charm with which he kept the world at one remove. But as Benedict had shifted from drawing the ass's head to sketching in the man's lean, strong body standing amidst Titania's fairy bower, the memory of a quite different leafy covert near the grounds of Harrow had popped into his mind. A shady recess which had served as his own personal retreat from the hue and cry of the busy school, a place of silence and secrets, of dreams and desires. A place he'd longed to share with that laughing golden boy who had so occupied his thoughts, but which he'd never quite had the courage to reveal.

That is how he should paint Clair, he'd realized. Not standing, carefully and artfully posed, or sitting in a heavy chair, the symbols of his rank and privilege scattered about him like any other aristocrat or figure of authority. But lounging at his ease, out of doors yet hidden within that shady bower. Hatless, rumpled, cheeks flushed from true love's kiss. Stripped entirely bare. Not physically, but emotionally. Stripped down to his very essence.

Benedict's fingers nearly ached with the need to capture that vision on canvas.

"No, don't get up!" he nearly shouted as Clair, ever impatient, began to rise. Benedict abandoned the easel he'd been moving to push him back down onto the sofa. "Stay right there."

"Sit! Stay! What am I, your lapdog?"

Benedict laughed and shook his head. How could Clair not see it? "Not my dog, you ridiculous man. Don't you see—you're my muse."

Clair's fingers ghosted over adorably pursed lips, petulance transforming into surprise, then gratification. "Your muse? A gentleman as muse?"

"Of course, a gentleman. Now sit back and prop yourself up on your elbow. Yes, lean it on the arm of the chaise-longue. Tip your head into your hand, cross one foot over the other, ah yes, that's it. Now stay."

Clair snorted. "I may be the first male muse in history, but I warn you I am no puppy. I will *not* be begging you for your favors, no matter how elegantly you pose me."

Benedict propped a primed canvas onto the easel, then grabbed a handful of brushes and his walnut-wood palette. Painting directly on canvas, without first sketching in the lines, rarely served. But something inside him told him the risk was worth taking tonight.

"I'm almost ready. Just let me squeeze out some colors."

"Paint? You plan to *paint* this evening? After spending the last four hours sketching?" Clair pouted. "This is decidedly *not* how I imagined this night proceeding."

Benedict shook his head. He far preferred to work in silence, but if he wished Clair to maintain his pose, he'd best keep him talking. "Is it not? Then why don't you tell me what you did imagine."

"Is that a challenge, Pen?"

"Take it as you will," Benedict said. Flake white, India red, black. Then mix the shade tints.

Benedict turned back to the subject of his portrait to see Clair stretching out on the chaise, the muscles of his legs rippling beneath his clinging pantaloons. Yes, there, the line of that calf, the curve of that thigh. He grabbed a brush and slashed bold strokes directly onto the canvas, blocking in the background.

"Now that I've your attention once again, let me tell you precisely what I imagined," Clair said. He could talk as much as he liked, as long as the rest of his body remained still.

"I imagined we would go to a tavern I know, one not too far away, but not close enough that we'd run into anyone familiar." Clair's voice dropped low and smoky, as if he were actually sitting in that tap-room.

"Yes? And would we have a drink there?"

"I imagined buying you a glass of wine, or brandy."

"Not ale?"

Clair shuddered. "Certainly not. Ale is for gulping, not for savoring. And I'd want to watch."

Benedict's brow furrowed as he dabbed in the darkest shades on the canvas. "Watch? Watch what?"

"Watch you drink it. You'd do it slowly, savoring the taste of it on your tongue. Your cravat, sloppily tied as always, would dip, revealing the line of your throat as you swallowed."

Had he got the tones quite right? Benedict squinted, looking at the shades rather than the lines.

"And then I imagined you watching me do the same. The glass against my lips. The fire in my eyes."

Reaching for a dry brush, Benedict almost missed the sight of Clair kicking off one shoe, then the other.

"Then, I imagined you would divest me of my slipper, like so."

Benedict frowned. "Stay still, if you please."

But Clair ignored him, sliding his stocking-clad toes down his own calf. Benedict's arm stilled, his breath catching.

"And then, I would slide that foot about the muscles of your lower leg. Those poor muscles, so taut from the strain of drawing and painting for hours on end."

Oh! Benedict's eyes widened. Was *that* the kind of evening Clair had anticipated? Suddenly, the vision of a reclining, embowered Clair shifted, replaced by this compelling creature of flesh and bone on the chaise before him. Yes, that was how he should paint him. Not some orderly, detached likeness, but tumultuous, seductive, all the emotions he typically held in check bubbling to the surface. Intense. Wild.

Clair's eyelids lowered, his smile turning feral. "Ah, Pen, I believe you finally begin to understand. And would you like to hear what I next imagined?"

Benedict lowered his paintbrush and gave a silent nod.

"Out of sight under the table, I imagined pushing your legs wide and teasing your inner thigh with my toes. Perfectly respectable from above, filthily lewd out of sight below."

Benedict jerked his eyes back to the canvas and cleared his throat. "Please move the tail of your coat; it is blocking the line of your upper leg."

Clair flicked the offending coattail over his hip, then moved his hand to toy with the ends of his cravat. "I'd let you drink enough to heighten your senses, and bring a flush of color to those sublimely rounded cheeks. But not enough to make you stupid with it."

Clair's fingers curled around the end of his neckcloth and yanked the intricate knot free. "Because I'd want you to be aware of everything, Pen. Everything I did to you. Everything I was thinking to do to you next. I'd want you quivering with awareness, poised on the pinhead of suspense, wondering if I'd move the arch of my foot to cover your straining prick, or tickle your taut stones with my toes. Wondering if I'd dare to bring you off right there, make you spend in your small clothes in front of an entire roomful of other men."

Good God. Benedict clenched against the stirrings in his groin, hoping the easel blocked Clair's view. The curves of Clair's body on the canvas, the line of his trousers, the spill of his cravat over his waistcoat—did any of it come close to capturing the depths of his allure?

"And would you?" he finally choked out.

Clair grinned. "Oh, I'd make you wonder for a while. But I wouldn't be so cruel. No, before you began to shudder in your seat, I'd draw my foot slowly back down your thigh, down your calf, and slip it back into its own shoe." But instead of putting on his own shoe, Clair pulled at his neckcloth, dragging the fabric slowly from around his neck. "And then I'd toss a coin to the barkeep for the room in the back, the one that can be paid for by the hour."

Benedict stepped away from the easel. "And you'd invite me to go with you, into that room?"

"Invite you? My dear boy, by that time you'd be begging me to take you." After dropping the cravat to the carpet, Clair flicked open the single button at the collar of his shirt. The linen gaped, revealing a smooth clavicle, a hint of warm skin.

"And what do you imagine we'd do, in that room in the back?" Benedict dropped his paintbrush. He'd never be able to capture the subtle details of the face, not without his finest brush. Not with Clair distracting him, enticing him, with every carefully chosen word.

"Oh, the possibilities then!" Clair's fingers traced a line down his throat, then slipped inside his gaping shirt, circling, what? His pectoral muscle? His nipple? Whichever it was, it had Clair's hips hitching forward. Benedict jerked his eyes back to the easel, but the sight was already replacing the vision in his head, the vision he'd been so eager to commit to canvas.

"Perhaps I'd lie down on a table—no comfortable chaise-longue in a tavern, alas—and array myself for your delectation. Or flick open the falls of my trousers, and tempt you with the hint of what lies behind them."

Benedict ground his teeth as Clair's hand did just that, slipping the buttons out of their holes, tracing over the bulge hardly hidden by the thin fabric of his smalls.

With a curse, Benedict took a step towards temptation.

"Yes, Pen. That's right. Forget about that fellow on your canvas and come frig me."

"Come frig me, or you'll be blacking the boots of every boy in the sixth form. Now, Pennington! Dulcie says I'm to have charge of you since he's gone."

The sick feeling in his stomach stopped Benedict in his tracks. He'd long ago outgrown the fear those words had once inspired, the hot mixture of powerlessness and curiosity and shame. Yet their ghost still served as a warning, a reminder that the Clair whom he'd once idealized could flit away just as quickly, and as carelessly, as he could entice.

Would the adult Clair prove just as fickle?

"And is that all you want of me?" Benedict asked, stepping back behind the easel. "A drink, and a quick frig?"

Dulcie rose from the chaise, all languid grace. "I doubt I'd be satisfied by a quick frig. No, Benedict Pennington, I intend to take my time with you."

"But for how long? And would I be the only lover with whom you'd be engaging in such dalliance, for however long this lasted?"

117

Clair smiled as he trailed a hand across Benedict's shoulder. "Ah, it seems I am not the only one with a vivid imagination. Does that give you pause, thinking of me with my hand around another man's cock?"

"Jealous?" Benedict shook his head. "Why should one be jealous, if a lover is faithful and constant?"

"Faithful? Constant?" Clair's laugh held a hint of mockery. "First I'm an ass, then a dog, and now you want me to play the ostrich or an ape, a creature so constant that it mates for life? Next you'll be demanding I give over my courting of Miss Adler for you."

"You still plan to court Polly?" Benedict nearly choked in disbelief. "After bringing me to the Sketching Society tonight, and supporting the plan for a National Gallery?"

"What has one to do with the other? Besides, just because I gave you the opportunity to speak to a few painters about your plans does not mean that I support the project myself. I simply took pity on your creative difficulties, and thought that visiting with fellow artists might push you beyond them." Clair buttoned his shirt and picked up his cravat, then strolled towards Benedict's easel. After examining the unfinished painting for several moments, he stepped back and waved a hand in dismissal. "But if this is any indication, the visit does not seem to have helped. Perhaps you should return to rudimentary still life studies if the more elevated genres are beyond your grasp."

Still life studies? The lowest genre in the hierarchy of painting? "If you thought so little of my skills, I wonder you bothered to invite me to the Sketching Society at all."

"Well, the odds in favor of my gaining Miss Adler's hand, along with her grandfather's paintings, just seemed so high, it hardly seemed sporting not to offer you some sort of a leg up."

Benedict ground his teeth. "Sporting? Is it sporting to entice a man to fuck you, when all the while you intend to do him wrong?"

"I've never kept my intentions hidden," Clair answered as he retied his cravat and jerked at his cuffs. "You misinterpreted them. You are welcome to take them, and me, as you will. Or not."

Benedict's hands fisted. "Not."

Clair tipped his head, as if not quite convinced by the single word. "You will, of course, inform me if you change your mind. But one thing you should know before making a final decision. I never allow any man to fuck me. Not even one as comely as you, Benedict Pennington."

And with that, Clair turned his back and strode from the room.

Benedict threw his palette at the arrogant fellow's retreating figure with a barely suppressed curse. But he was too late; the paint-smeared palette bounced harmlessly against the closing door, then clattered to the floor.

Shaking, he grabbed for a cloth and began to scrub at the smears of paint threatening to stain the boards.

If only he could so easily erase the memory of the man who had, once again, left him behind without a backward glance.

"All the modern conveniences, sirs, what you can't get in most parts of the city, not without setting down a pretty penny for 'em," declared the portly man sitting in the carriage across from Dulcie and Sir Peregrine. Dulcie had hoped accompanying his friend to inspect a property Per was considering leasing would be a welcome distraction from the painful memories of Benedict Pennington that kept popping into his brain at the most inopportune moments. The infinitesimal widening of his eyes as Dulcie's words of allurement first broke through his abstraction.

The tightening of his lips as Dulcie sang him deeper into the seduction. The way he'd ignored his paint-filled brush as it dropped from fingertips to spatter against the floor, so eager to touch something warmer, something pulsing with life.

The smart of his unexpectedly stinging rejection . . .

Dulcie sighed. If only Benedict had left him with just a frustrated cock-stand, he could have offered up a prayer to St. John the Long-Suffering to be relieved of unwanted lust. But no, Dulcie found himself saddled not just with sensuous appetites, but with all these ridiculous *feelings*, too. Longing, and loss, and even, heaven forfend, a touch of shame. He, the imperturbable Lord Dulcie, feeling ashamed? Perish the thought!

No, this jaunt with Sir Peregrine might take his mind off of Polly Adler, who had left London for her grandfather's estate in Kent for the summer. But it was doing little to help him banish Benedict from his brain.

"And pray, Mr. Faulke, what constitutes the most modern of conveniences in the burgeoning district of St. John's Wood?" Dulcie inquired with a smile. He'd shake himself free of this uncharacteristic ill-humor yet.

"Do you not feel the smoothness of our ride?" Faulke tapped a finger against his nose. "Macadam roads, all throughout the district. Good-looking, quick to install, and above all, the quietest ride you're like to get on any road in London."

"Indeed!" Dulcie exchanged an exaggerated wide-eyed look with Per. "And is that all?"

"All? No, indeed, sir, far from it! Have *you* clean water piped right to your house, and sewers to take it all away again?"

Dulcie shook his head in mock sorrow. "No, sir. I cannot say that I do."

"Buy a villa here and you will. Water any time you wish! No need to pay out extra to lay pipes, like the nobs in Mayfair do; pipes here are already laid. And no need to pay servants to haul your water up and down the stairs. Now, that's a real savings, that is."

Per's eyes twinkled. "And I understand that Mr. Eyre, the owner of the land, has also laid in good drainage?"

"The best drainage!" Faulke enthused as the carriage slowed. "Your cellar won't never flood in a rainstorm, not in St. John's Wood. And you've your own garden, too, much grander than anything you'll find in the dirt of town. Your very own country estate, only steps from the city!"

Dulcie raised his eyebrows at Sir Peregrine, who had in fact just returned from his very own country estate, where he'd taken his new bride on their wedding trip. But Mr. Faulke was too caught up in his own enthusiasm with his investment to pay much heed to their amusement. When the carriage rolled to a stop, he opened the door and jumped down to the amazing macadam pavement, waving an eager hand.

"Not the most fashionable London address for a rising young politician, Per," Dulcie said, laying a hand on his friend's arm. "Why do you not purchase in Mayfair?"

Per frowned. "Mayfair is too crowded, and too expensive. Besides, I don't want my children to be brought up amidst the smog and noise of the city, and Sibilla will not stand to be left alone in the country for months at a time. St. John's Wood seems a good compromise."

"Children already?" Dulcie teased. "Been quite busy on that wedding trip, have you?"

But Per only laughed as he followed Faulke from the carriage. It seems marriage—or perhaps the sexual congress that must be its chief attraction for an upstandingly moral fellow such as Per—had done wonders for his friend's previously somber temperament.

No townhouses greeted his eyes as Dulcie alighted from the carriage, as they would have in the center of London. No, only a single detached villa, set snug in a garden which shielded it from the prying eyes of neighbors, a privacy one could never find in

121

the city proper.

If he'd brought Benedict here, rather than accosting him in his own brother's townhouse, might he have proved more amenable to Dulcie's advances?

Puffed up with obvious pride, Mr. Faulke showed them about the small house as if he were giving a tour of Blenheim Palace. Yet by the time Faulke finally finished extolling every minute virtue of the property, Dulcie had lost interest in baiting the fellow. The outside of the villa may have smelled of clean country air, but inside it still reeked of fresh paint. Just as Benedict's studio had. It seemed to mock him, that odor, reminding him not only of his missteps there, but of the failure of his plan to not seek out Benedict again, to wait for the man to come to him of his own accord. Because Dulcie had passed nearly a fortnight without even a sighting of the cursed fellow.

Dulcie took out his pocket watch from his waistcoat and clicked open the case. If they left here soon, he'd have time to stop at Pennington House before he had to return home to dress for the theater.

"I hope I have answered any questions you might have to your satisfaction, and that you're pleased with the property?" Faulke said with a quick glance at Dulcie's watch.

"Yes, thank you, Mr. Faulke," Per answered. "I confess I am quite pleased with what you have shown me today."

Faulke rubbed his hands together. "Then come back to my office, and we can discuss the finer points of the lease."

Per shook his head. "I'm afraid that I'm not quite prepared to do that, sir. Not without having my wife examine the property herself first."

Dulcie shook his head. "No, no, mustn't make the missus unhappy! Especially a newly-wed such as yourself."

"Indeed, sir," Faulke agreed. "But I would be remiss in my duty unless I told you that the leases are being snapped up right quick. Might want to place a deposit—completely refundable, of course, if your lady was to prove reluctant—to secure your interest in the best property still available."

A pained look crossed Per's face. "I thank you again for your consideration, sir. But I think I must take my chances. May we drop you back at your offices on our way back to town?"

"Ah, I thank you kindly for your offer, sir, but I've another appointment soon, just down the road a piece."

"Then we will bid you good-day for now. I will send word when my wife and myself will both be available to view your properties."

After making their good-byes to Mr. Faulke, they climbed into the carriage and settled in for the ride back to town. Dulcie propped his boots up on the seat opposite, leaned back, and gave his friend a curious look.

"Letting the fellow down easy, were you? Or was there some reason you decided not to just come out and tell him you're no longer interested?"

"Oh, I'm still interested. Even more so than I was before I had seen the villa. But I'm not in a position at the moment to put down a deposit."

"Whyever not? Surely the expenses of campaigning for a seat in Parliament don't require the entirety of what I know for certain was your wife's bountiful dowry."

Per scowled. "How do you know the size of Sibilla's dowry?"

"Surely you haven't forgotten that my father and Lord Saybrook were actually on the verge of signing papers for my own betrothal to her before you stole the girl out from under my nose?"

But instead of laughing, Per only sighed. "No. I hadn't forgotten. But Saybrook's run into a bit of difficulty with the funds."

"What?" Dulcie sat up in his seat. "Has the fool gambled away his own sister's dowry? Is that why he's fled town?"

Per shook his head. "More a question of miscommunication,

or perhaps poor management, I think. Or I hope. I understand from Sibilla that her father's man of business left soon after Lord Saybrook's death, and her brother has never replaced him. Theo's gone to Lincolnshire to try and sort it all out."

"And in the meantime, you've not collected a farthing of the money you were promised?"

"Oh, it's not as bad as all that. The bank held enough funds to cover part of Sibilla's dowry, just not all. But I know from working with your father how expensive it can be to fund an election."

"But Saybrook should be the one paying for that, not you!"

"Yes. But if he can't find the funds for his sister's dowry, he'll hardly be able to pay for an election, either. So I don't wish to commit any of my own funds without first knowing if Saybrook himself will be able to help."

How dare Saybrook put Per in such a precarious position. Dulcie's anger burned on his friend's behalf. "And does your dear lady wife know anything of this?"

Again, Per shook his head. "Theo asked me to keep it from her while he inquired into the business himself."

Dulcie snorted, but Per held up a hand before he could offer a protest. "Now, don't you go putting your nose into things that don't concern you, Dulcie. Theo's in Lincolnshire, not London. And he must have asked his brother for help, for Benedict left for the country soon after Theo, even before Sibilla and I returned to town."

"Benedict? In Lincolnshire?" So that's why he'd not caught hide nor hair of the man all this time. Had Benedict really left London to help his brother? Or had he fled in reaction to their last meeting, too afraid he'd succumb to Dulcie's temptations if he remained?

"Yes," Per said, rubbing a finger over the bridge of his nose. "And Sib and I will be heading north soon, too, to begin the actual work of campaigning. So you see, there is no need for you to harangue poor Saybrook on my behalf."

Dulcie sat back in his seat, his arms carelessly crossing his chest. "When, precisely, do you intend to depart?"

"On Friday, I believe."

Dulcie tapped a finger against his lips. "Well, I'll have to cancel an appointment with my boot maker. And I'll have to let Leverett play host to the connoisseur set at the British Institution next week. But no matter. I can be ready."

Per's eyes widened. "You intend to come to Lincolnshire with us? When you've not even been given an invitation?"

"Even if I weren't the particular friend of both his sister and his sister's husband, do you not think the name Lord Dulcie invitation enough?"

"Well, if you're brazen enough to invite yourself, I doubt anyone would be equally brazen to turn you away. And lord knows I could use all the help I can get in campaigning."

"Of course. And I can speak from first-hand knowledge of your moral, upstanding character, as you turned me down flat when I tried to entice you into my bed."

"Good thing I know you well enough to know you're only teasing, or I'd bar every toll road into Lincolnshire to keep you out."

Dulcie waved a careless hand. "As if such a paltry thing would keep me away."

"In truth, Dulcie, I'd welcome your company as I campaign, for speaking to strangers is not my forte as it is yours." Per reached out to lay a hand on Dulcie's arm. "But please, promise me you will not upbraid Saybrook about these financial matters. Surely by the time we arrive, he will have straightened out his account books. His steward, thank heavens, is a hardworking, experienced fellow, Sibilla tells me."

"Well, if I must," Dulcie said with a pout. "But just say the word, and I shall sharpen the edge of my tongue against Saybrook's thick skull."

"That would hardly endear you to Sibilla. But she will be more than happy to have you employ your considerable talents in charming the electors of the county on my behalf."

"Then charm I will."

Although he'd keep a bit of his vaunted charm in store for a certain fascinating, if reluctant artist.

CHAPTER 8

BENEDICT THREW HIS CHARCOAL IN the dirt and kicked it away in disgust. Portraits, nudes, landscapes, figures in landscapes—nothing he attempted came anything close to the sublime, or even the beautiful. Dull, bland, tediously mundane, each and every one. Perhaps he *should* turn his hand to ovine portraiture, as Miss Atherton, the daughter of the steward of the Saybrook estate, had sarcastically suggested when he'd arrived in Lincolnshire earlier in the week. Animal painting, even when the animal in question was as lowly as a sheep, was still a step up the hierarchy of genres than were the still lives to which Dulcie had rudely suggested he turn his hand.

Unlike the self-contained Dulcie, young Harriot Atherton had once mooned after him like a calf after its mother, praising his every drawing as if he were an adolescent Rembrandt. But of late she seemed to have turned her affections towards his elder brother, a happy development to Benedict's way of thinking. Her father's once-sharp wits seemed to be on the wane, a dangerous situation for a young, unmarried lady. Especially happy if Theo shared her feelings, as Benedict had begun to suspect his brother might. He'd welcome anything—or anyone—who could curb Theo's unfortunate habit towards drunkenness and debauchery, a habit into which he had fallen after their father's death more than a year before. That Harriot was the daughter of a steward, rather than a gentleman of leisure, Benedict cared not a jot. High sticklers might worry over the rank of the women his brothers married, but as long as those females made Kit and Theo happy, he'd be satisfied, too.

Benedict rubbed the back of his neck as he walked the lane back towards Saybrook House. If only he had someone who could help him curb his own bad habit—yearning after the elusive Lord Dulcie. Though he'd denied it to Theo, his flight from London had been motivated largely by that frustrating, infuriating man. Or at least by his own unfortunate attraction to him. Benedict's desire to draw and paint, a desire which had once so dominated every waking moment, had been displaced by this decidedly unhealthy obsession with Lord Milne's heir.

Why was Clair kind one moment, cutting the next? Why entice him only to then turn around and push him away?

During his years on the Continent, Benedict had welcomed only a handful of men into his bed, and even fewer into his heart. Quiet, cautious, he demanded more than just physical attraction before he would open himself up to another. Strong emotional or intellectual attachment must always come first. And as such attachment took time to build, his liaisons tended to develop slowly, from acquaintance to liking, liking to friendship, and only then from friendship to physical passion. He could not be happy with a man who was willing to share his body, but not his mind and his heart. He needed a lover who would trust him with his fondest dreams and his most horrifying nightmares, not just with the secret of his unconventional sexual desires.

This attraction to Clair, though, was nothing like the slow-building affection that had drawn him to each of his past lovers. Clair confided none of his deepest wishes, nothing of his terrors or fears, and yet Benedict's senses flared to immediate awareness as soon as the man walked into the room. The two of them together would be as sublimely explosive as a long-dormant volcano, of that Benedict had no doubt. Yet to be a marionette at the mercy of Clair's puppeteering, jerked about by the strings of his whims—no, he could never be content with such a relationship, no matter how eagerly his body yearned for Clair's elegant form.

Far better to retreat than to allow himself to succumb to the temptations of comely but callous Lord Dulcie. True, he'd had to leave without having first secured the government's promise to purchase the most esteemed paintings from Julius Adler's collection, or Adler's promise not to include said paintings in his granddaughter's dowry. But little government work would take place during the summer months, and Adler had taken Polly down to his country seat in Kent. Before they left, Benedict had made Polly promise to write to him immediately if her grandfather extended Dulcie an invitation to visit. She, and the paintings, should be safe enough until London's Little Season began in the autumn.

And perhaps by then, Dulcie's fickle attentions would have turned to another object besides Benedict.

The rattle of carriage wheels and pound of hoofbeats against the wooden bridge behind him shook him free of that surprisingly melancholy thought. Sibilla and her new husband, no doubt, coming to Lincolnshire to begin campaigning for the seat in Parliament Theo had promised Sir Peregrine. Funny that out of all of their father's children, it was the daughter, not the sons, who enjoyed the political wrangling he had so loved. Benedict wouldn't have stood for Parliament, not for love or money.

He stepped to the sward, making way for the carriage to pass. Not just one, nor two, but three, then a fourth, churned up the dust of the dry summer lane, making it impossible for him to see who sat within them. Still, he supposed he should make an effort to go and greet whoever they might be.

By the time he had made his way back to the entrance of Saybrook House, the occupants of the carriages had already alighted. His sister and her husband, just as he had surmised.

"Benedict!" His sister turned her cheek for a kiss, which he obligingly gave. "But where is Theo? Do not tell me he is still abed? I had hoped he would keep to country hours now he is away from London."

"Sir Peregrine, welcome to Saybrook House." Benedict offered his hand to his brother-in-law before answering his sister's question. "No, Theo is not still abed, Sibilla. Mr. Atherton —the family steward," Benedict added for Sir Peregrine's benefit —"suffered a sort of a fit yesterday, and Theo is much occupied with him." And with comforting said steward's daughter, no doubt.

"Oh, poor Mr. Atherton! I must call on him, and his daughter, and offer my help," his sister said. "And if he is incapacitated for any length of time, Theo will surely need advice on how best to run the estate. You see, we have arrived just in time, Per."

A sharp bark cut off any reply his brother-in-law may have made. One of the estate's many sheepdogs seemed to be trying to herd the passel of servants scurrying to unload the boxes and trunks.

"Three carriages just for baggage?" Benedict raised an eyebrow. "Sir Peregrine must have been a very generous husband during your wedding trip, Sibilla."

"Oh, Per and I could have made do with a single carriage. But our companion insisted on bringing his entire wardrobe."

"Companion?"

"Why, yes, Mr. Pennington," a familiar voice drawled. "I have taken it upon myself to come along with Sir Peregrine and his lady, to persuade the electors of the county of the worth of his candidacy. And one must always put one's best sartorial foot forward, especially when amongst strangers."

Sinclair Milne, his smile replete with secrets, gave Benedict an elegant bow.

130

Lord Saybrook, Dulcie's host, drank down the last of his wine, set his glass on the dining room table, then rose from his seat at its head. "Are we ready to join the ladies?"

No doubt Saybrook was. His infatuation with the oddly named daughter of his steward—what man in his right mind would allow his daughter to be called Harry?—shone as obvious as the sun on a cloudless day. Although the steward was rumored to be somewhat out of his wits, if the gossip of the servants was to be believed. As for Sir Peregrine, the besotted fellow, he always seemed eager to leave male companionship behind if his new bride was anywhere about.

But Dulcie himself had other plans.

"I wonder if first I might prevail upon your brother to take me on a tour of the picture gallery?" he asked Saybrook as the other men moved towards the door. The taunts he and Benedict had exchanged before dinner had whetted his appetite for more. But during the meal, Benedict had sunk back into his more usual reticence and made no further attempts to antagonize him. Although the glares he occasionally shot across the table proved his silence was not due to indifference. Surely by now he must have gotten over his pique at Dulcie's refusal to espouse everlasting devotion before they engaged in any carnal sport. No, his pique must be due to another cause entirely—the length of time Dulcie had taken to track him down and follow, no doubt.

"The sun's likely to set before you even have a chance for a cursory inspection, Dulcie," Saybrook said as he shot a look—of concern? How odd—towards his brother. "Would you not prefer to wait until tomorrow?"

Dulcie clapped a companionable hand on Saybrook's back.

"But I fear we may be in for a storm, and no true connoisseur would dream of viewing a painting when clouds or rain obstruct the natural light. No, I'll settle for a glimpse of the Lawrence portrait this evening, and make a more detailed inspection of the rest of your collection on the next fair day we are not busy with campaigning. Convey our apologies to the ladies, if you will, Saybrook?"

Dulcie left the room, not even glancing behind him to see if Benedict would follow. Rare was any lure he baited ignored by his intended prey.

And yes, before a minute had passed, Benedict Pennington caught up to him on the staircase. But he didn't pause, just strode right past without stopping to see if Dulcie followed *him*. Ah, playing who would be leader, and who would be follower, was he? The best kind of game, while it lasted.

He grinned, following meekly in Benedict's wake. Let him have his head for the nonce; Dulcie would take the reins soon enough. Besides, the pleasure of watching his trim form take those stairs two at once, the tails of his coat flapping enticingly over the globes of his taut arse, more than made up for any momentary frustration.

At the top of the staircase, Benedict opened a door and swung his arm, inviting Dulcie to precede him. Ah, yes. Here were other enticing beauties to admire. The last rays of the setting sun slanted through the windows of the long gallery, glinting off the matching gilt frames which embraced each painting displayed on its walls. Not as large a collection as Beaumont's, or Lord Leicester's, and not as fine as Adler's, by any means. Few family picture galleries, designed primarily to preserve family history rather than to celebrate the finest works of art, could boast as much. Yet, scattered between the ancestral portraits of often indifferent production, Dulcie spied more than a few works even he would not scorn to praise.

He stood in the middle of the room, letting the heady

mixture of contentment and joy that always came to him in the midst of pictures of the first excellence rise within him. Unlike the more unruly passions, one never need hide one's love for truly fine works of art.

"Is that a Velásquez, wedged in between those horrible portraits of your sixteenth-century forebears? And a Teniers, too? And just look at the chiaroscuro in this nativity at night—I don't recognize the artist, but it is breathtaking. How the babe glows!"

Dulcie flitted about the room, drinking in all its pleasures with an appetite as great as Lord Saybrook's for his after-dinner port.

"Why did you never tell me your home held such treasures?" he demanded after twice making circuit of the entire gallery. But his purported guide made no answer. No, Benedict stood silent, gaze fixed on the painting that held pride of place above the gallery's fireplace. Lawrence's painting of his mother.

"It is very fine," Dulcie offered as he stepped to Benedict's side. "I've always admired the flowing elegance of his female portraits."

"Yes, the public creature of fashion and society is there, in her pose and dress. Yet I see the more private sensibilities of her heart, too, in the way he has rendered her face."

"Lawrence captures the brilliancy of expressions in his sitters as no artist before him," Dulcie offered. Aesthetic commentary was far safer than any more personal comment, surely.

"It helps me remember her gentleness, her deep well of composure," Benedict replied, too caught in his own feelings to respond to Dulcie's attempt to shift the conversation onto more impersonal grounds. "But at the same time, he's captured her dreaminess. A propensity for reverie and contemplation that only a few ever really saw in her."

One that Dulcie saw in Benedict. Was that what attracted him? That almost otherworldly air of abstraction he often fell into, as if he could see things, beautiful, wondrous things, far beyond the ken of ordinary man?

"The line has bred true in temperament, if not in coloring," he said, his eyes flitting between the tight blond curls and curving brows of the canvas and the dark, tousled locks and straight slashing eyebrows of the man beside him.

Benedict smiled. "People were always surprised by that. Theo and Sibilla, and even Kit to an extent, all looked far more like her than I. Yet she and I shared something none of the others did."

"A private, yet deep devotion to the people you value."

Wherever had that thought come from? And how had it escaped his lips?

Benedict seemed to find the comment as surprising as Dulcie did, and far from welcome. He took a step back from the painting and frowned, his dark eyes narrowing as they turned to Dulcie.

"Although I tend to be far more direct than my gentle mother could ever bring herself to be. And so I will ask you, Lord Dulcie: why have you come here?"

Ah, a direct challenge. But if Benedict chose directness, Dulcie need not follow. "Why, just as I told your brother. I wished to admire this lovely portrait."

Benedict crossed his arms over his chest. "No, not here to the picture gallery. Here, to Lincolnshire, to my brother's estate."

"Again, as I informed your brother, I am here to help my friend. Although your brother assured Sir Peregrine this election would be his for the taking, we cannot be sure that another candidate will not enter the fray."

"Yet of all the rumors and gossip I've heard of you since my return from the Continent, none has hinted you've the least interest in politicking. You've never stood for Parliament yourself, nor have you ever canvassed the electorate on behalf of any candidate your father has supported. So you'll forgive me if I find your assertion a bit hard to believe."

Dulcie leaned against the mantle, a self-satisfied smile creeping over his face. "Been listening to rumors and gossip about me, have you? And here I thought you completely without interest in my humble self."

"You know all too well I've an interest in you," Benedict growled, his hands fisting by his sides. "Damn it, Clair, I left London to get away from you!"

"To get away from me? Or to hide from your own desires? Do you find it distasteful, or," Dulcie whispered, "sinful, what your body wants from mine?"

"I've never hidden from my own desires, Dulcie. Did I not spell them out clearly enough when we were schoolboys?"

"But we are no longer boys. I had assumed you as experienced as myself in these matters, but perhaps I was mistaken. Did you not wish me to give chase, when you ran?"

"No!" Benedict turned his back, hands fisting in his hair. He paced the length of the room once, then again. Then, in a voice so quiet Dulcie could barely hear: "Yes."

"Yet now that I've run you to ground, you still hesitate." He placed a hand on Benedict's shoulder, surprised to feel him shudder. "Is it a game, Benedict? Do you wish to increase my fascination by suspense, according to the usual practice of elegant females?"

Benedict shrugged free of his touch. "I am not interested in games, Clair! What I want— What I *don't* want is some furtive jerking of cocks behind a tavern, or a quick swive in the back room, then off again on our separate ways."

Dulcie's forehead furrowed. What, precisely, was Benedict after? "My dear boy, I told you I would take my time with you. Although I would be lying if I told you the other holds no appeal."

Benedict began to pace, completely ignoring the winning smile with which Dulcie had charmed many another wary lover in the past. "No! You misunderstand me. What I want is someone with whom I can be honest, and who will be honest with me in turn. Someone who will share not just his body, but his thoughts and dreams, as I share mine with him."

The muscles in Dulcie's legs tightened, as if readying to dash from the room. "Ah, I see. You want me not only to commit myself solely to you, but to bare my very soul while I do it." As if he'd ever act the impetuous, lovelorn fool again.

But Benedict did not laugh at the sarcasm in his voice. "Yes," he said, the softness of the word belying the conviction that lay beneath it.

"You ask too much, Mr. Pennington."

"I ask only for what I need."

"You ask for what I cannot give."

Benedict's eyes lowered for a moment, before rising once again to meet his. "Then I can't, Clair, no matter how much my body wishes it. Not if you're unwilling to share yourself with me. Share all of you, not just the superficial, insubstantial parts you show the rest of the world. I've had the other, and it won't do for me. It just won't."

The last glint of sunlight slid from the room, shrouding Benedict's face in shadow. Praise the heavens for small favors. The intensity of the yearning in those dark brown eyes nearly brought Dulcie to his knees.

Instead, he took a step back. "And what you need will not suit me."

"Then I fear there is nothing further to be said on the matter."

"Indeed." Dulcie nodded, then turned towards the stairway.

But his own composure broke for an instant, sending him whirling back to stare at Benedict's bowed head. "Achieving the ideal may be possible in painting, but I fear you will doom yourself to disappointment if you expect to find perfection in the mundane world about you. But no matter. Your decision is made, and I will importune you no longer."

Small consolation, that, getting in the last word.

Shrugging off an unfamiliar tightness in his chest, Dulcie left the room.

CHAPTER 9

"And will you be joining us in the canvassing today, Mr. Pennington?"

For more than a month now, Dulcie had posed the very same question to Benedict Pennington, each morning as breakfast came to a close. The bulk of the Saybrook House party —Dulcie, Sir Peregrine and his wife, Lord Saybrook, and even occasionally Miss Atherton, when she was not otherwise occupied with planning for a forthcoming village fête—would set off soon after the meal, intent on wooing the electorate of Lincolnshire. Dulcie had taken to electioneering like a duck to the water, even though he'd shaken more hands, cajoled more snotty-nosed children, and drunk more cups of watery tea and ale than any friend, even one as deserving as Per, had any right to expect. Whether through rational discourse, ribald jokes and winsome charm, or promises of Saybrook's future patronage, Dulcie knew just what each man needed to hear to convince him that in the upcoming special election, Sir Peregrine should be his candidate of choice.

Some ridiculous part of him longed for Benedict to witness each small triumph.

But each and every morning, the infuriating man only gave the same answer to his query: "No, not today. I've other business to attend to."

If that other business had included continuing to paint

Dulcie, he might have been content. But Benedict had steadfastly refused any and all attempts to persuade him to take up the portrait again. Instead, he spent hours and days and weeks penning letters about his damned museum plan to the denizens of the *ton*, scattered for the summer to their sundry country estates.

At least Benedict hadn't chosen to leave Lincolnshire altogether and visit them in person. A lack of action which on most days gave Dulcie heart.

But this morning, Dulcie's tone had shifted from pleasant inquiry to mocking taunt. He'd smiled to see clenching hands and flattened lips accompany Benedict's refusal. Damn him if he was the only one to feel out of sorts at their impasse.

Pennington's eyes flicked to him for the merest instant before he offered his sister the brittlest of bows and then stalked from the room.

Dulcie stared at Benedict's fast-disappearing form. Even in a rumpled, poorly cut coat, the man's shoulders appeared to frustrating advantage. And why should Dulcie feel a tug of tenderness at the sight of his dark hair curling against his neckcloth, locks far too long for any man with a claim to fashion?

Dulcie gave a small tug on the cuff of his shirt. "Lord, he must have got up backside first, as your charming countrymen are wont to say."

"I don't know why you keep asking him," Sir Peregrine said mildly. "You know by now what his answer will be."

"And there's no cause to call attention to his shyness," Lord Saybrook added, setting his teacup down on its saucer with a distinct *clink*. "Not everyone needs be as gregarious as you."

"Or as overprotecting as you," Dulcie drawled, wiping his fingers with fastidious care on his napkin before folding it neatly and placing it on the table. "From your reaction, one would think I'd insulted your brother, rather than made a simple civil inquiry."

Saybrook pushed back his chair and threw his own napkin down by his plate. "With you, the two are often one in the same, are they not?"

"Dulcie." Per shot him a cautioning glare. "Might I have a word before we leave for Carringham?"

Damnation. Someone was calling undue attention, but not to Benedict. No, with his own behavior, he pointed all too clearly to himself, to his own continuing fascination with Saybrook's middle brother. Who would have imagined it, Lord Dulcie moldering away in dull Lincolnshire for all this time, on the mere chance that Benedict would repent of his foolish refusal to engage in a casual liaison! Why could the man not see the perfect opportunity in which they found themselves, one combining daily proximity with the distraction of so many of the household's other occupants? When else would they find such a situation, with inhabitants and staff alike too caught up in electioneering and preparing for the village fair, to pay the least notice to a discreet dalliance taking place right under their noses?

But Benedict had proven even more stubborn as an adult as he had been as a boy. Damn a man with principles! Tossing himself off at night while dreaming of Benedict's full lips or rough hand engulfing his cock was all well and good, but after he spent, Dulcie found himself still unsatisfied, inexplicably longing for the warmth of another body in the bed beside him, the unpredictability and comfort of another's touch.

And not just any touch, either, damn it all to hell and back. He'd been on the receiving end of more than one suggestive look since coming to Lincolnshire, yet he'd not been the least tempted to send any of his own in return. Surely Benedict must have noticed his self-restraint. How much longer could he expect Dulcie to wait?

"Only *a* word?" Dulcie asked as he nodded his acquiescence

to Sir Peregrine. "For you, my friend, a dozen at the very least."

Dulcie offered Saybrook a smile before he followed Per down the passageway and into the library.

"What troubles you, Per?" he asked, throwing himself into a chair by the hearth. He'd take better care now, turn the conversation to his friend and thus avoid any embarrassing discussion of his own overly revealing behavior. "Do you grow weary of smiling and cajoling the voters of Lincolnshire, along with all their kith and kin?"

"I fear that I am more similar to Mr. Benedict Pennington than to you, Dulcie," his friend said with a wry smile. "But I understand the necessity of canvassing, especially in this county where I am hardly known. And why should I complain, when I have you and Sibilla, as well as Lord Saybrook, to engage even the most disinterested of voters?"

"I am rather good at it, aren't I? A pity I have not the least interest in standing for elected office myself." He crossed a booted ankle over his knee and settled back into his chair. "Marital difficulties, then? Problems satisfying your lady in the bedchamber?"

Per sat up straighter in his seat. "As if I would consult you about such a thing."

"I may not enjoy bedding them myself, but I am well-versed in what the ladies wish for from their lovers. You'd be surprised by what even a gentlewoman will confide to a sympathetic ear."

"No!" A blush spread over his reticent friend's cheeks. "It's not that, not precisely."

Dulcie sat forward in his seat and clasped his hands between his knees. "But some problem between you and Lady Sayre? Are you and she at odds over the election? Disagreeing about the best methods for canvassing, or the amount of time it is taking away from your personal concerns?"

"Not methods, no . . ." Per gaze's flitted over everything in the room but Dulcie.

"Come, come, spit it out, man. How can I help if I've no idea what the problem is?"

"It's the expense, damn it!" Per jumped from his chair and paced before the library windows. "I didn't realize how much all this electioneering would cost. And every day, Sibilla urges me to spend even more."

"But is not Saybrook paying for such things?"

His friend still couldn't meet his eyes. "I've not had the heart to ask him. Since he has not yet paid me the remainder of Sib's dowry."

Dulcie rose from his own seat, annoyance warring with amusement. "Can I believe my ears? Did noble Sir Peregrine actually tell me a falsehood? For I distinctly remember you saying, soon after we arrived in Lincolnshire, was it not, that it had all been taken care of."

"Not a falsehood. Just a little white lie." When Dulcie raised a doubting eyebrow, Per burst out, "Because I knew you'd only just harass poor Saybrook about it if I told you the truth! I wanted to give him time to get his finances into order, to consult with his steward and retrench, before I pressed him further."

"Consult with his steward? You refer to Mr. Atherton, who has been confined to his bed for the past month?"

Per rubbed the back of his neck. "Yes. I had no idea the fellow's illness would last so long. Theo's at his wit's end, trying to run the estate without Atherton to consult, and I'm loathe to add to his burden. But Sib doesn't understand why I'm reluctant to lay out any further funds for the election. How can I, though, without knowing whether I'll need to make up her missing dowry from my own accounts or no?"

"You never told her?" Dulcie's voice rose in incredulity.

"No." Per hung his head. "You know how unhappy she was with Theo after their father's death, because of his carousing and not taking up his proper role in the House of Lords. I did not wish to give her a new reason to find her brother lacking."

"You've kept such a secret from your wife, all this time? No wonder the hair at your temples is turning gray."

At Per's weak smile, Dulcie slapped his hands against his knees. "So, what do you wish me to do? Take Saybrook aside and tell him how little I appreciate his taking advantage of my friends? Spread gossip about his finances so far and wide he'll never be able to catch an heiress to repair them? Challenge him to a duel? I am entirely at your disposal, my friend."

"Dulcie, don't be so melodramatic. I only wish you to ask about a bit, see if you can find out the cause of Saybrook's financial difficulties."

"Ah, you wish me to be your spy, do you?" Few gentlemen would be honored by such a request, but Dulcie had never been one to stick to the letter of anyone else's laws.

Per shrugged. "You are much better at ferreting out information than I am."

"Too true." Dulcie rubbed his hands together in anticipation. "It will be my pleasure."

"Your pleasure to do what, Dulcie?

Per's blush rose again at the interruption of his lady wife. Sibilla Sayre, a handful of papers clutched to her chest, strode into the room, purpose in every step.

"To continue to aid you and your noble husband in the canvassing, of course," Dulcie answered. "I find it strangely satisfying, persuading the voters of another man's integrity and worth. Much easier than having to do the same for myself."

Sibilla sniffed. "What you find satisfying is having all eyes on you. But this morning I've need of Miss Atherton's skills, not yours. She's the only one who can reconcile these conflicting poll lists. I sent Theo up to find her, but that was nearly half an hour ago. I don't suppose you've seen them?"

"I believe I might know where the missing lady is to be found. I'll fetch her for you, shall I?" Dulcie bowed and strolled from the room. Miss Atherton, he knew, usually spent the early hours of the morning with her ill father. And Theo Pennington typically met her in the passageway, waiting for her to leave her father's bedchamber.

Bounding up the staircase, Dulcie suppressed a cheerful whistle. Not wise to give warning to those he planned to spy upon.

He stuck his head around the corner of the family wing, where Mr. Atherton was being nursed. Yes, there they were, Saybrook and Miss Atherton, just outside her father's door. The two stood far closer than any simple acquaintances should. Was Saybrook morally lax enough to seduce the daughter of his employee? Or, fool that he was, did he have a more lasting alliance in mind?

The little minx stepped closer to Saybrook and slipped a hand under his cravat. Yes, far more than friends, these two. Had she or her father swindled Saybrook out of his funds? And was she cozening Saybrook now to distract him from their perfidy?

"Harry, I'm trying to have a care for your reputation. Can you not do the same?" Saybrook asked in a strained voice.

"Must I?" Miss Atherton's question hovered in the silent hall as her fingers wandered under Saybrook's linen.

"Yes." But he let out a deep groan of pleasure all the same. Dulcie could not help but imagine his own fingers, wandering across the expanse of another Pennington's chest, making another Pennington moan with longing.

Thankfully, Saybrook's hand tightened around Miss Atherton's and pulled it free of his garments before Dulcie's imagination could grow too heated.

"Yes, you must," Saybrook chided. "Unless you're prepared to walk to the rectory and ask Mr. Strickland to read the banns."

Dulcie took this as his cue to interrupt. "Read the banns? Who is foolish enough to trade freedom for the dubious pleasures of a leg-shackle?" he asked as he strolled down the passageway towards them, swinging his quizzing glass by its ribbon. His question left them room enough to deny their relationship if they wished.

Miss Atherton jerked away from Saybrook, her face flushing even redder than Per's had. Saybrook frowned and stepped in front of her. Playing the chivalrous beau, was he?

"Why, for two of my tenants," Saybrook boldly lied. "Have you met Farmer Croft and his Daisy?"

Miss Atherton choked back a sudden snort of laughter. Some joke to which he was not party, no doubt.

No need to force the issue. Dulcie had found out enough for his purposes.

He raised his quizzing glass and turned down his lips into a most disapproving frown. "Your sister sends you up here to bring Miss Atherton down as soon as possible, and instead you dally to discuss the domestic concerns of a shepherdess and her swain? Have you forgotten there is an election to be won? Come, Miss Atherton, leave this lazy fellow to his own business. We have an emergency on our hands, and only you can help."

"Whatever is the matter?" she asked.

Lord Dulcie placed her hand on his arm, a move that made Saybrook grimace. Oh, yes, the fellow was clearly smitten.

"Sibilla has been asking for you since sunrise, my dear," he said as he guided her down the staircase, Saybrook trailing in their wake. "It seems during their trip to Gainsborough yesterday she and Per were given a different poll list, one that includes far more electors on it than the one from which they have been working. *Quel catastrophe!* She needs you immediately, to tell her which men still reside in the county and which control votes in need of courting."

"I'll be happy to help," Miss Atherton answered. Affable girl.

When they reached the library, Sibilla pulled a booklet from her pile of papers and waved it in Miss Atherton's face. "Fifty more names. *Fifty!* How could that agent's original polling list have been so wrong? You must tell us, Miss Atherton, which voters still live in the district. I have marked each one missing from our first list with a check mark."

The three began to confer over their lists. But all Dulcie's attention was taken by the other occupant of the room. For Benedict Pennington now sat in the chair Dulcie had abandoned, booted foot tapping the carpet. Odd to see him without a pencil or a stick of charcoal clutched between those long, tapered fingers, or a sketching pad behind which he might shield his face. Even with that heavy lock of hair falling over his eyes, their absence made him look strangely unguarded.

If he had been any other man, Dulcie would have pounced upon that vulnerability, turning it to his own use. But the thought of manipulating Benedict to find out about his brother's finances made his throat grow tight.

In fact, he had the strangest urge to apologize for treating him with such flippant disregard at breakfast. A man shouldn't need to protect himself from the petty taunting of a thwarted lover, especially in his own home.

Dulcie turned on his heel and strode towards the stables. This curfuffle over the polling lists would likely prevent their setting out to canvas for some hours, giving him more than enough time for a canter over the Saybrook downs and fields. Yes, a bruising ride would surely rid him of this ridiculous streak of sentimentality that increasingly plagued him at the sight of the bent head and lowered eyes of Benedict Pennington.

And how does your portrait of Lord Dulcie progress? When I extended an invitation to come to us at Westcombe Abbey, he very prettily declined, explaining you could not complete the picture without his presence, which I do not understand in the least. Is your method so

different from that of men who make portraiture their profession? Why, even the great Sir Joshua required only three sittings to take my likeness!

Far better if you both to come down to Kent and put any finishing touches on the work here. Write to me at your earliest convenience and inform me when we should expect you.

By attending to this letter you, sir, will greatly oblige,
Julius Adler

A hot summer breeze lifted the curtains of his bedchamber and ruffled the letter in Benedict's hand. Of course Dulcie would use Benedict as excuse to fob off Adler. He could not but wonder, though, why Dulcie need evade Adler's invitation at all. After their painful conversation the night Dulcie had arrived at Saybrook House, he'd expected the viscount to pack up all his belongings and decamp to Adler's Kent estate, or at least go back to town, with the news that no portrait from Benedict Pennington would be forthcoming. Yet for more than a month, now, Dulcie had ignored his courtship of Polly Adler, choosing to remain in Lincolnshire instead. To canvass electors on behalf of Sir Peregrine, he claimed. And perhaps to taunt Benedict with all he had lost after he'd turned down the chance to become Dulcie's temporary lover?

He'd expected Dulcie to find the repetitive nature of electioneering far too tiresome and abandon it within a week. But to his shock, the viscount had not rushed off to find some more entertaining occupation. Nor a more stimulating companion to share his bed. Not that first week, and not any time during the weeks that had followed.

And all the while, he had pointedly ignored Benedict. Oh, he was civil enough, asking him every day if he would accompany them on their canvassing expeditions. But all his witty sallies, all his energetic charms, those were gifted to Theo, or Sibilla, or Sir Peregrine. Even Miss Atherton, a lady whom he had just met, came in for her due share of Dulcie's attentions. But for Benedict, he had nary a smile.

For which Benedict was, he must keep reminding himself, deeply grateful.

But Dulcie's eyes—why could he not rid himself of the feeling that those eyes turned to him whenever they were in the same room, even though he could never catch the man in the act of staring?

Benedict glanced at his pocket watch. Yes, enough time had passed that the rest of the company should be well on their way to whatever town they were intent on canvassing this morning. He had letters of his own to write, letters that he preferred to compose in solitude.

When he pushed open the heavy library door however, his sister and her new husband stood within, whispering over a newspaper.

"Excuse me. I thought you would have left the house by now." Should he return to his room, or proceed with his own business?

Benedict gave Sibilla and Sir Peregrine a brief nod before taking a seat behind the desk and picking up his pen.

He'd spent far more time in the library over the last month than he ever had before his father's death, writing letter after letter to men of influence, expounding upon the benefits a national art gallery would bestow upon the country. If he were as silver-tongued as Dulcie, he might have made his way from one summer house party to another, championing his plan to each gentleman directly. But he knew his own strengths and weaknesses far too well to set about such a scheme. No, he was far more persuasive on paper than in person, as the growing letters of support stacked in the drawer of this very desk proved. Perhaps by the time Parliament convened again in the spring, he would have gathered enough support to urge Sir Charles Long or

148

another member of the Commons who believed as strongly as he did that the public should have access to art to put forth a resolution for the establishment of a national picture gallery.

Still, the pen felt far less comfortable in his hand than a pencil or paintbrush. The sketches he'd been making of the laborers about his brother's estate had excited him like no other work he'd done since returning to England—with the exception of that one night painting Dulcie's likeness back in London. But he'd left that unfinished canvas behind, unwilling to tempt himself. All color and frivolity and movement that painting had been, with nothing of the formality or grandeur required of an aristocratic portrait. No beauty at all, at least not in the eyes of one who embraced the classical ideals. His friend Géricault might have liked it, but Dulcie's cutting assessment reflected the opinion of the most of the rest of the world; no artistic academy in England or on the Continent would have found such a thing worthy of praise. And Adler—Benedict shuddered, imagining the deprecations that would have sprung from that confident man's lips.

Yet his hands still longed to pick up a brush and attack it once again, to create on canvas something only he seemed to see. Something in Dulcie that the simplicity of the true style could never hope to convey.

Theo's bitter cursing jerked Benedict from his musings. He'd been so lost in his own mind, he hadn't even heard his brother —or Dulcie and Harry—enter the room. Or the footman, who had obviously just delivered bad news of some sort to his brother.

"What is it, Theo?" Sibilla asked, her eyes fixed on the letter he held out to her husband. "Per?"

"I'm afraid we have more to worry about than a few overlooked voters, Sib," Sir Peregrine said as he handed the letter to Sibilla. "The ever-equivocating Mr. Norton has broken his promise to your brother. For he finds he cannot allow a 'seditious demagogue' such as myself to stand unopposed."

Benedict grimaced. Henry Norton, the current holder of the Parliament seat for which Per was standing, had never been a man of much intellect, although he had always been loyal to their father. Theo had no such influence over the fellow, although he had persuaded him to step aside for a candidate of the new Lord Saybrook's choosing. Did he truly think Theo would stand for his writing such inflammatory words about their brother-in-law?

"Demagogue? I'd be surprised if the fellow even knew what the word means," he said, rising to stand beside his brother.

"It's the seditious part that irks me," Dulcie concurred, taking up a stance beside the chair Benedict had just abandoned. "Why, I'd be as like to swim the Channel in nothing but my smalls as Per would be to do anything so ill-bred as fomenting rebellion."

Sibilla picked up the letter and read aloud. *"As your object is to bring into contempt the Sovereign, the Clergy, and all the noble, moral, and worthy part of society, I fear I cannot allow you to stand unopposed. My son, therefore, will contest this election, with my full support."*

Benedict's eyes narrowed. Young George Norton, standing for Parliament? That boy who had lounged about Colnaghi's print shop, espousing his devotion to the arts, and gazing with cow-eyes at Dulcie? And who turned to Lattimer Leverett after Dulcie had begun to pursue Polly Adler?

Damnation! Had Leverett, a dyed-in-the-wool Tory, played a role in persuading Norton to stand against the more liberal Sir Peregrine?

"Well, we won't let a man who spouts such drivel to best us," his sister proclaimed as she tossed the elder Norton's letter on the desk. "Now, Per, do you see the wisdom of employing more agents to canvass each town?"

Her husband ran a hand through his dark hair. "But Sib, the expense—"

"Hang the expense. I'm not as proficient with accounting as is Miss Atherton, but even I know that my dowry is large enough to pay for what we need."

"Your dowry will be kept for our children," his brother-in-law said, taking his wife by the hands.

"I had thought," Dulcie interrupted, staring through his quizzing glass at Theo, "that a man's patron discharged all debts incurred during an election. At least, that is how my father always conducts the matter."

Benedict's hands fisted. Was Dulcie insulting Theo? Not just to his face, but in front of his siblings, too?

"I will take responsibility for any additional expenses," Theo answered. "It was I, after all, who assured Per that the seat would not be contested. Why, I'd never be invited to another dinner if word got about that I forced my brother-in-law into penury. Now go, Sib, and hire all the canvassers and whomever else you require."

Sibilla rushed over and embraced him. "You are the best of brothers, Theo, no matter what father may have—" She stepped back, biting her lip. "No matter what anyone might say. The very best, Theo."

"Do not let Benedict or Kit hear you say such a blasphemous thing," Theo said, tossing a small smile at Benedict. But one that distinctly lacked all of Theo's usual easy good humor. "Now, off with you, before Mr. Norton and his son have a chance to spread disloyalty and disaffection like dung across the fields."

"Wait until you see the cards we're having printed, to leave behind if a voter is not at home!" their sister crowed before pulling her husband from the room.

Theo left immediately after, but turned in the opposite direction from the one taken by Sibilla. Harry, worry lining her features, quickly followed.

Leaving Dulcie alone with Benedict.

"Why did you not remain in town, Dulcie?" Benedict

grimaced at the anger in his tone, but he could not seem to banish it. "If you had stayed, you might have prevented this."

"Prevented what?"

Dulcie's blinking innocence only made Benedict's frustration rage more fiercely. "Prevented George Norton from entering the race for this Parliament seat."

Dulcie's head jerked back, his eyes widening. "I? What have I to do with young Norton?"

"Oh, I saw the way he admired you, how he hung upon your every word. Art, not politics, that is where his real interests lie. And you might have encouraged that, counseled him against this mad plan to challenge Saybrook interests."

"Perhaps." Dulcie leaned on the desk and crossed his arms. "But how was I to know his father would insist he enter this contest?"

"His father? Or Lattimer Leverett? Leverett, who, no matter how much he avows his love for art, loves his own aristocratic privilege more. Can you tell me it wasn't Leverett, as much as Norton's own father, who persuaded him to the Tory side?"

"Your reasoning, Mr. Pennington, leaves something to be desired. Is it influence over George Norton that you attribute to me? Or some supernatural power to read Mr. Leverett's mind?"

Benedict ground his teeth. No, he wasn't always the most rational person when his emotions ran high. "Over Mr. Norton. Even if you did not want him for yourself, you might have warned him away from Leverett."

"Are you still speaking of Mr. Norton?" Dulcie asked, his voice full of genial curiosity. "Or are you perhaps speaking of yourself?"

Benedict jerked backwards, the question as painful as a slap in the face. He should have remembered that attacking never cowed Dulcie. It only incited him to fight back all the more fiercely.

Trying to catch his breath, Benedict strode over to the

windows. But Dulcie only followed, then grabbed his arm, turning him so they stood face to face.

"You *were* speaking of yourself. How curious. What, precisely, do you think I should have warned you against? That he was a braggart and a bully? I thought everyone in the entire school knew that."

Benedict struggled to find the words. "After you left—when you didn't come back to school, he told me—"

Dulcie frowned. "Told you what?"

"He said you'd given me to him. You'd written to tell him so —"

"I wrote to ask him to look after all the boys under my care," Dulcie interrupted. "Not to give them away, as if they were baubles or toys. And I made no specific mention of you."

Was that supposed to comfort him? Benedict jerked free of Dulcie's hand. "How was I to know? You never wrote to me."

Dulcie scowled. "My father would not permit it. Not after he read your letter. He even made me show him the note I wrote to Leverett before he franked it, to make sure it contained no covert messages to you."

"And you could not figure out a way to circumvent that?" Benedict choked out a laugh he hoped sounded more harsh than heartbroken. "Viscount Dulcie, cock of the school? No, if you'd truly wanted to, you could have sent me word."

Dulcie took a step closer, a muscle twitching at his temple. "And what would you have had me write? Should I have exposed you to the same shame, the same punishment, as you did me? Should I have rhapsodized over my desires for the male figure, as you so foolishly did in your letter? Espoused everlasting love for a twelve-year-old boy?"

Benedict hung his head. For weeks after the start of the new term, a term without the warmth of Dulcie's friendship in which to bask, Benedict's younger self had yearned for such a missive. If not a declaration as open as his own had been, at least some token of Dulcie's continuing friendship and esteem, a sign that his rash letter had not estranged them completely. And after Leverett began to command him to do more than black his boots and clean his room, Benedict had become desperate for word from the boy he'd so idolized. Not just an acknowledgment of what they had been to one another, which had begun to seem a trick of his imagination, but a desperately needed dispensation from his new fagmaster's stomach-turning demands.

Did you not hear me, Pennington? I said, Dulcie's given you to me. How disappointed he'll be to hear you've refused to honor his wishes.

Still, at seven and twenty, he could not but acknowledge the wisdom of Dulcie's words. Lord Milne had pulled his son from school to separate him from a witlessly besotted boy. Benedict shuddered to think what his own father might have done if he had intercepted such a note addressed to one of his sons.

"Come, Benedict," Dulcie said, giving him a playful punch on the arm before scooting around the desk and tipping back in the chair behind it. "What good does it do to brangle over things long past? Especially now, with an election to contest? What we need is a plan. First, we must find out just what the Nortons are up to, and how we may best circumvent them. Give me a paper and a pen, and I will write to my political acquaintances in town and find out all there is to know of the matter."

"And will you write to George Norton, too?" Benedict asked. "I would not discount your influence over the boy, even if he has taken to following about Leverett in your absence."

"Yes, I will write to young Norton. Not to express my surprise and disappointment at his jump into the political pond, but to tempt him back to his true interests, by describing my latest artistic acquisitions. Far more effective to influence a person by appealing to what excites him, rather than berating him for something over which he may have little control. And then, my dear Benedict, if my fingers have not grown numb from penning so many missives, I will take up my pen once again and write to Lattimer Leverett, to chastise him for his bald lie to your younger self."

"No." Benedict paled at the thought. That first term, serving as Leverett's fag, he'd indulged in feverish dreams of a valiant Viscount Dulcie, returned to Harrow to pluck him from Leverett's malignant grasp. But after waiting for months in vain, he'd finally realized he'd have to be the one to stand up to Leverett if he ever hoped to be free of him.

Benedict had always hated conflict, but ever since that day, he'd understood the necessity of confronting and resisting any attempt to use rank or power to cow or intimidate.

No, Dulcie need never know what violations Lattimer Leveret had committed, all under the cover of Dulcie's name.

Benedict pushed the inkwell aside. "As you say, there is no need to dwell on the past."

"As you wish." Dulcie picked up a penknife and began sharpening a quill. "Still, silly boy, you should have known better than to believe I would ever have 'given you' to Leverett. No true appreciation for the finer things—or the finer people— in life, none at all. I shudder to think he might someday have the raising of a child."

Benedict swallowed back his rising bile. Especially if that child were a boy.

CHAPTER 10

Harriot Atherton—Dulcie simply refused to call the poor girl "Harry"—took a few hesitant steps towards the library, then glanced back at him with a frown. "Are you certain, my lord?"

"Yes, yes," Dulcie assured her, then made a shooing gesture down the hall with the fencing foil he held in his hand. "Did you not yourself tell me he has been the most helpful of all the family in preparing for the upcoming village fête?"

"Yes, but to participate in such a public display?"

Almost pretty, she was, when her brow furrowed in concern. He could understand why Saybrook had taken such a fancy to her, although *he* would never align himself with a person whose father had lost his wits and misplaced hundreds of pounds of the rents from his estates, as Dulcie had recently discovered. But then Saybrook never had been accounted a man whose own wits would set the Thames on fire.

Did Benedict know of his brother's financial problems? Ferreting out the truth about Saybrook's missing funds had taken even Dulcie several days, and a fair bit of work—abundant winks and smiles at the housemaids, multiple chats about the high costs of keeping good horseflesh in fettle with the grooms, and even a few rounds of ale at the Oldfield Inn's taproom on the half-holiday of a footman or two. Even so, he'd not discovered the full story until he'd finally finagled an hour alone in the house this morning, and paid a visit to Miss Atherton's "injured" father during one of the steward's more lucid moments. Saybrook really should begin to search for a new steward; poor Mr. Atherton seemed unlikely to recover his wits any time soon.

Dulcie longed to preen over the success of his discoveries with Per, but Sir Peregrine and his wife were off canvassing in the eastern reaches of Lincolnshire and would probably not return until after dark. Neither could he discuss young Norton's challenge, for he hadn't yet heard back from any of the political gentleman to whom he'd written earlier in the week. Waiting for the dark, waiting for the post, waiting for Benedict to stop ignoring him—impatience rode him like a hag. He needed some physical outlet, some challenge to distract his body from all the possibilities whirring around his mind.

Challenging Benedict to a swordfight would be just the thing.

Miss Atherton gave a discreet cough, then knocked upon the library door, even though it already stood ajar. If Saybrook did end up marrying such an unlikely chit, he'd have to teach her that a viscountess did *not* move about her own house with all the timidity of a church mouse.

"Mr. Pennington, I wonder if we might beg your assistance?" she asked as Benedict appeared at the library door.

Something inside Dulcie settled into place at the sight of him. The infuriating fellow had been avoiding him like the plague ever since their argument over young Norton and Leverett. Well, he'd kept his distance from Benedict for more than a month, waiting in vain for him to admit how foolish it was to moon after some ideal, unrealizable vision of an imaginary future lover rather than to embrace the actual man who wanted him now. He wasn't about to let Benedict employ the same tactics on him, even if there was far more to that story about Leverett than Benedict had let on. Benedict's emotions had seemed in danger of getting the better of him, and Dulcie had saved him the embarrassment by not pressing him for more details. He'd have to remember to find out the truth from Leverett once they were both back in town.

"Of course, Harry," Benedict agreed, obviously not having yet caught sight of Dulcie leaning against the wall beside the door. "Bunting to be pulled out of the attics? Tea urns to be dusted and polished?"

"Nothing as domestic as all that," she said with a diffident glance towards Dulcie. "Lord Dulcie is persuaded that a display of swordsmanship by the gentry would be a fitting conclusion to the festivities of the Oldfield fête, and has kindly offered himself up as participant. I did express some doubts as to the safety of such a display—"

"Indeed." Benedict stepped into the passageway to search out Dulcie, and then to fix him with a chastising glare. "But I'll warrant the viscount offered to demonstrate its harmlessness if you could but find him a partner with whom to spar."

Miss Atherton sighed with relief. "However did you know?"

Benedict did not roll his eyes, although Dulcie could see he was sorely tempted. But annoyance was only a small step away from liking, was it not?

"A lucky guess, no doubt. And where does my lord wish this demonstration to take place? Saybook House hardly features a *salle d'armes.*"

Dulcie pushed himself off from the wall and gestured towards the back of the house. "If it were rainy, the picture gallery would do. But on such a lovely day, I think the rear gardens a far better choice. I've spied a suitably flat patch of walkway just beyond the rose bushes. And before you protest that you have no foil, I assure you that I always pack extras whenever I travel."

"Of course you do. Why else would you need an entire carriage for your baggage? Thank you, sir, but I prefer a weapon from the Saybrook armory."

"Very well. Come, Miss Atherton, let me show you the precise spot I have in mind."

Dulcie took the lady's hand and tucked it into his elbow, then led her outside, keeping up a lively patter all the while, all about the transformation of fencing from an art of war to a sport, and the benefits to health, poise, and grace that it developed in a gentleman. He had no need to look over his shoulder to see if Benedict followed. The fellow was too kind to disappoint Miss Atherton, the companion of his childhood, or to leave her stranded with Dulcie for any length of time.

He smiled when footsteps sounded on the wooden floor behind them.

"You see, this is a practice foil, covered with a leather button at the tip so that no harm can come from it," he explained as they stepped out into the sunshine. "Even if one did have the sad misfortune to run into it by accident."

"My sword has no such button," Benedict declared, holding out the weapon he had retrieved for Dulcie's inspection. Sharp steel, with an open brass guard and a wire-wrapped grip. Not the weapon of one unskilled in the art. "Perhaps you should reconsider?"

"How kind of you to worry, sir. But I doubt you'll be able to come close to pricking me." Dulcie pointed his own weapon towards the side of the pathway. "And if you stand just so, Miss Atherton, you will be well out of the reach of our thrusts. Mr. Pennington, you may take your stand on the walk opposite."

"What if I'd never even trained with a foil?" Benedict asked as he moved into position opposite Dulcie. "I could kill you simply through ignorance."

"Are the stories Leverett wrote to me from Harrow untrue, then? That you returned to school Michaelmas term with your own weapon, and threatened to run through anyone foolish enough to torment you?"

Benedict's eyes narrowed. "You corresponded with Leverett

159

after you left?"

"I did. And he was not at all pleased to have a fag with more skill at the sword than he himself ever had, I assure you. I wish I had been there to see you mock him with Hamlet's famous lines: *I'll be your foil, Laertes. In mine ignorance / Your skill shall, like a star i' th' darkest night, / Stick fiery off indeed.*"

Why should his praise of Benedict's skill bring such a scowl to the man's face?

He must have been staring for some time, for Miss Atherton finally interrupted with an awkward clearing of her throat. "How do you go about beginning such a match?"

"Ah, yes, the opening." Dulcie pulled his eyes from Benedict's and took up his position on the walkway. "We begin thus, with our feet placed in a lineal manner. Some argue that it is better that the weight of the body should rest wholly on the left leg, but I am of the opinion that is incorrect, for a body resting on *both* legs must be more firmly planted than if it rested only on *one*. Do you not agree, Mr. Pennington?"

Benedict frowned, but nodded.

"This is what we call *En garde*," Dulcie continued, raising his empty left hand behind him and his right, sword held lightly, in front. "Then we ask if both combatants are ready: *Pret*. And then: *Allez!*"

At school, Benedict had never enjoyed the rough and tumble of physical competition. Yet the adult Benedict fenced with even more skill than Leverett—jealous, no doubt, of the younger boy —had attributed to him. It took most of Dulcie's attention, and much of his breath, to maintain his defenses. Benedict's face glowed with the exertion, and his own blood sang in his veins. Damnation, why had he not thought to challenge Benedict before?

Between quick breaths and fleeting grimaces, he called out the simpler parades for Miss Atherton's edification. All the while, his opponent kept remarkably silent, saving his breath not to

160

cool his porridge but to drive Dulcie back whenever he ventured an assault.

"You see, Miss Atherton, the true art of sword defense depends, in great measure"—Dulcie paused to parry Benedict's latest thrust at the last possible moment—"on judgment in deceiving the adversary's motions, and in *not* being deceived by his."

A gloved hand batted Dulcie's sword to the side before he had a chance to riposte. "Judgment?" Theo Pennington fumed. "Neither of you show very much of it, waving weapons about in the presence of a lady. Could you not have chosen some less violent manner of settling your disagreement?"

"Disagreement?" Dulcie exclaimed. "Why, I would never presume to take issue with the upstanding Mr. Benedict Pennington. No, we took up these weapons—foils only, you see, so no danger of harming even a fly—to show Miss Atherton how a display of swordsmanship might add to the festivities at the upcoming fête. Do you not agree, Saybrook, that yon peasants would thrill to witness such a sight?"

"Less so than at the sight of your waistcoat, Dulcie," Benedict answered, tossing his foil to the grass and swiping a sleeve over his damp brow.

"Indeed." Dulcie slid a complacent hand over the silk of his gaudy garment, wishing instead it could sweep over Benedict's temples and thread through his damp curls. "Your people will hardly be able to talk of anything else for weeks, of that I have no doubt. Now do say you agree, Miss Atherton, and allot us time to display."

The lady picked up Benedict's discarded weapon and swished it experimentally through the air. "Such a performance would be wonderful, of course, my lord. But the contests at the fête, they are usually for the villagers themselves. And not between gentlemen they hardly know," she added with an apologetic frown.

"But that is even better!" Dulcie said, clapping a hand to his thigh as an idea began to form in his brain. "They know the new Lord Saybrook, do they not? Or, at least, you wish them to know him better, and regard him in a more positive light. So, rather than cross swords with the younger Mr. Pennington here, I will make Lord Saybrook my opponent. And when he defeats me in glorious combat, why, he'll be a veritable hero in their eyes."

Dulcie knelt before Theo and held out his sword before him in a mocking display of medieval fealty.

"You're an accomplished swordsman, Theo?" Miss Atherton asked as she held out the abandoned foil to Saybrook. "Why did you never say?"

"Oh, Saybrook's skills do not matter," Dulcie interrupted, pounding a fist against his chest. "Because I will *allow* him to win. The locals need never know." He winked at Miss Atherton's shocked expression.

"And you would do such a thing out of the kindness of your heart?" Benedict scoffed.

"Certainly not," Dulcie replied as he rose to his feet. "Sentimentality is the realm of the foolish. Saybrook must first do something for me."

Benedict's brother snorted. "What, promise you my firstborn son?"

"Ha! As if I'd ever want any get of yours. No, you will order this stubborn brother of yours to accept my commission for a portrait."

"A portrait?" Miss Atherton asked. "Of whom?"

Benedict shook his head. "Of his preening, coxcomb self. I've told you and told you, Dulcie, I've given over painting the human figure. Landscapes are my focus now."

"And what of all those doughty shepherds you've been sketching? Are they too lowly to count as human?"

"Dulcie, you are impossible." Benedict threw his hands up before turning his back on them all and stomping towards the house.

Miss Atherton's brow wrinkled. "Why should the idea of a commission so upset him?"

"Because he is a stubborn, petulant child?" Dulcie asked. "And look, he's stormed off without even retrieving his foil. Would you be so kind, Miss Atherton, as to return it to him before he regrets its loss?"

"Certainly, my lord." The girl dashed off a quick curtsey before following in Benedict's wake, the sword tucked carefully by her side.

"You wish to employ Benedict to paint you? After you've teased him so unmercifully about his clear lack of talent?" Saybrook asked.

Was that regret, that strange feeling zinging through his chest? "The boy should know by now that I don't always mean every cutting word that falls from my lips."

"I think an apology from you would go farther in changing his mind than anything I could say to him."

How ironic that Saybrook should choose *this* moment to play sanctimonious elder, a role for which his drinking and carousing in the past hardly qualified him. Although he hadn't appeared cup-shot in company of late, at least not since Dulcie had come to Lincolnshire.

"But he won't listen to me." Dulcie did not stoop to outright pleading, but he did add just a touch of entreaty to his voice. "Not anymore."

But Saybrook seemed uninclined to pity. "Take care of the problem yourself, Dulcie. I am not the kind of brother to order about my own siblings."

"Oh, but I think you will," Dulcie said as he dropped a heavy hand on Saybrook's shoulder. "Because if you do not, a little bird just might whisper in your sister's ear that part of her dowry has not yet been turned over to her spouse."

Saybrook's face snapped to Dulcie's, his expression a comical mix of surprise and dismay. "How do you know of that?"

"I didn't, not for certain. Not until your oh-so-revealing face told me so." No need to divulge his actual methods to the fellow. "Good thing you never play cards, Saybrook, for your expressions give all away."

Saybrook's eyes narrowed. "A little bird will tell her? Say rather a sly, scheming snake."

Dulcie laughed, not taking the least offense. He'd been called far worse, and by men far grander than Saybrook. "The tale will be as unwelcome to Lady Sayre whatever form the bearer takes. Would you have her hear it now, when you've only just managed to earn back her respect?"

Saybrook grimaced, but remained silent.

"I did not think so," Dulcie said, answering his own question. "Now, do this one little thing for me, Saybrook, and I promise to give a performance your people will never forget."

"What, we have to go through this damned pretense of a sword fight as well?"

"Why, certainly. I wouldn't want anyone to say I am in your debt." Dulcie whipped his foil to the *en guard* position, then slashed it down with a flourish. "Bid you good day, my lord."

Yes, he would have his portrait, and Benedict too.

"Another dram, my lord?"

Dulcie lowered his glass and gazed about the Saybrook library, which earlier this Sunday morning had been filled with the gentlemen of Lincolnshire, gathered to raise a glass in celebration of the new Lord Saybrook's birthday. But now, the room stood nearly empty, the visitors trickling out in dribs and drabs, either to return to their homes or to attend the fair taking place in neighboring Oldfield Village later in the day.

"No, thank you Parsons. I've need of a clear head this afternoon at the fête. I do hope Saybrook has relieved the staff of its duties for the rest of the day, so you may all attend the festivities."

"Indeed he has, my lord. A sad day it would be, to miss the Oldfield Village Fair." Parsons nodded, then moved away to gather the abandoned glasses that littered the scattered tables and fireplace mantel.

The plan to formally present Saybrook to his tenantry with a birthday celebration before the village fête had struck Dulcie as deliciously feudal. But Saybrook and his people had managed to pull it off without anyone, including the head of the family himself, appearing ridiculously out-of-fashion. Why, Saybrook had looked almost as comfortable taking the center of the stage as Dulcie would have been, if his father had ever thought to host such an event for his own son and tenants.

At twenty-one, though, when such events usually took place, Dulcie had decidedly not been in Lord Milne's good graces. His father had hoped sending him to Oxford would cure him of his juvenile attraction to members of his own sex, yet temptation existed at university too, even as the privacy afforded a collegian made it all the easier to turn temptation into act. The sins Dulcie had only dreamed about at Harrow proved wickedly easy to indulge in at Oxford. And after his father had intercepted yet another note, this one not from a besotted boy but from the affronted uncle of an actual lover, a man who crudely demanded not Dulcie's affection but Lord Milne's money in exchange for his silence on the matter, he'd hardly been inclined to hold a coming-of-age ceremony for his disappointment of a son.

Since the excruciating shame of that day, Dulcie had never again been tempted to allow passion to take the reins over reason. Oh, he indulged his carnal urges, yes, but never with the same carelessness or abandon of his university days. And rarely with the same fellow for more than a fortnight or two. No incriminating love notes to betray him that way, and little risk of the wrong person noticing him paying undue attentions to any one man—safety in anonymity and perpetual variety, that was Dulcie's creed.

Today, he saved his deepest passion for his favorite paintings. No one could feel shame at expressing regard for a Poussin or a Rembrandt. A lesson he would have taught George Norton, if this whole business with Benedict and Polly Adler had not disrupted his plans. *Yes, young George, I am looking at you*, his smile of recognition informed the gentleman, who stood by his father by the far library windows. Norton, the hen-hearted boy, had not answered his letter, but it seemed neither he nor his father wished to openly acknowledge the rift between their family and Benedict's by failing to attend this party for the Saybrook heir. George had stuck to his father's side like a barnacle on a boat bottom all morning, though, giving Dulcie little opportunity to cut him off from the herd of his fellow Lincolnshire gentlemen and give him an earnest talking-to. And now that the room had emptied, the clock striking noon, it seemed Saybrook himself might beat him to the effort.

Would Benedict's brother have the stomach for it, though, to pull a wavering supporter into line? Dulcie would pay good money to observe such a scene. Slipping into the passageway, he shooed away a maid, then sent Parsons to his bedchamber on a made-up errand, giving the combatants the privacy they needed.

And removing any witnesses who might remark on his own lingering presence just outside the library door.

Dulcie's lips pursed as Saybrook fumbled the start of the negotiations, beginner mistakes a more experienced Dulcie would never have made. But when George Norton insulted their sister, Benedict's brother rose nobly to the occasion, giving the thoughtless cub a witty set-down that had even Dulcie chuckling. And then, before he could whisper "Jack

Robinson," Saybrook had proposed a deal that not only had the Nortons agreeing to cease their political challenge, but also had them purchasing a piece of Saybrook property they had long coveted, a purchase that would go a long way towards filling the inconvenient gap in Saybrook's coffers.

Dulcie grinned. Yes, Saybrook was finally leaving his careless, wastrel ways behind him, prodded in no small part by a certain shrewd viscount of their acquaintance.

A quiet cough behind him pulled him away from the door. "Your weapon, my lord," Parsons said, holding out his foil on two flat palms.

"You are a gem, Parsons." Dulcie took the sword in hand. "And remember, two of the clock on the Oldfield village green, if you've an interest in witnessing the most thrilling martial display in Lincolnshire since the Battle of Winceby."

That is, if Saybrook's triumphs with the Nortons did not embolden him to reject Dulcie's extortionate challenge.

"Very good, my lord." Parsons bobbed, then returned to clearing the detritus of the morning's gathering.

Dulcie poked his head around the library door, then tapped the tip of his foil against the doorframe. "Forgive me for interrupting. But you've a promise of your own to keep, Saybrook. And I am certain you would not wish to disappoint your dear, dear sister, would you?"

Saybrook's jaw clenched in annoyance. What fun!

"I'll be with you in a moment, Dulcie. Mr. Norton, George, will we see you both at the fête this afternoon?"

"Yes, my lord. My wife would never forgive me if we did not visit Mrs. Hawley's booth before she sells out of her famed gingerbread," Mr. Norton said.

"Then I will wish you good morning. Parsons will see you to the door."

Dulcie gave the younger Norton a wink as he brushed past him in the doorway. Unfortunate, that the boy's blushes were so much less attractive than Benedict's.

"Dulcie, a word."

Dulcie turned to Benedict's brother with a sly smile. "Do not tell me you've misplaced your sword, Saybrook? Or forgotten the time of our match? Two of the clock, it is to be—all you must needs do is listen for the church bells to ring once, then again. Quite easy, really. So easy, even a simpleton could manage."

"I am not a simpleton, Dulcie, despite any belief you may have to the contrary. A simpleton would give in to extortion, thinking to escape further harm, not realizing that taking one step back in fear will only lead a bully to demand another, and another."

"Ah, you've let today's adulation go to your head, haven't you?" Dulcie swung the foil in a mocking circle about that head, but his opponent stood his ground. "Not wise, Saybrook, to think you can renege on our agreement without consequence."

"If you tax your memory, I believe it will tell you I never agreed to this damned duel, or to persuade my brother to paint your charming visage. If you want Benedict to paint your bloody portrait, then you will have to persuade him yourself."

"Ah, feeling your oats, are you, Saybrook? But will you be so sanguine after your sister hears of your mismanagement of her dowry?" Dulcie tauntingly flicked the tip of the sword against Saybrook's waistcoat. "For I cannot, in all good conscience, promise to hold my tongue much longer."

Saybrook not only shoved the rapier away, he then grabbed it in one hand and pulled, sending Dulcie nearly sprawling.

"Please, do not trouble your delicate conscience, my lord," Benedict's brother said. "I will save you the distasteful task of telling my sister. Tonight, after the fête."

If Saybrook had not just brought Dulcie to his knees, he might have kissed him for taking yet another spot of work from his already crowded plate. He rose, brushing an imaginary speck of dust off his trousers. "Ah, the affable lion finally rears rampant. Forgive me for doubting the Saybrook coat of arms still accurately reflected the character of the family."

"Threaten me, or any member of family again, Dulcie, and you'll soon find out how sharp are the claws and teeth behind my affable front."

Saybrook held out the sword, hilt forward, to his opponent. Dulcie stared at it, then at him, for a long, considering moment. Then, with a quicksilver smile, he grasped the hilt and, with a sharp snap of his wrist, flourished it in acknowledgement.

One crisp bow later, and he was backing from the room. Some might have called it manipulation, what he'd done to Saybrook, but Dulcie preferred to consider it skillful management. Lord knows he'd not done it for Saybrook, but for Per, and Sibilla. And for Benedict, too; if Saybrook finally grew comfortable in and accepted his responsibilities as head of his family, Benedict would have to spend far less time worrying about his brother.

Leaving him more time to worry over Dulcie.

"My lord! Might I have a word?" George Norton stood by the foot of the staircase, his chin nearly buried in the folds of his neckcloth.

Dulcie raised an eyebrow. "With me? The known associate of a seditious demagogue?"

Norton grimaced. "Words written in the heat of the moment, and regretted almost before the ink had dried on the paper. Would you accept my apology? And extend them to your friend, Sir Peregrine?"

Though it would be fun to torment the pup, Dulcie could afford to be magnanimous. He gave the boy a brief nod. "Certainly. It would have been a trying waste of your talents, such a fine judge of artistic merit forced to toil away over Whitehall's tedious writs and dispatches."

"Yes. But my father wished me to follow in his footsteps, and Mr. Leverett thought—"

"I will speak no ill of any man's father. But in future, you'd be wise not to allow the unworthy to influence you against your own better judgment."

"Do you not hold Mr. Leverett in high regard?"

The dismay on Benedict's face when he'd forced himself to speak of Leverett as fag-master—no, Dulcie would not soon forget it. "I admire his taste in art, but of his morals—well, perhaps the least said on that front, the better."

Norton nodded. "I did so prefer you, my lord—what I mean to say, is, your knowledge of the Fine Arts far surpasses Mr. Leverett's. I would have been—I still could be—your loyal acolyte, if you would deign to teach me all you know." He clutched Dulcie's hand, the one not holding a sword, and squeezed.

Dulcie clucked under his breath. Clearly, that "all" encompassed far more than a few lessons in *les beaux arts*. Best to let the poor boy down gently.

But when he spied a scowling Benedict lurking by the door to the drawing room, he couldn't resist tormenting the stubborn man. Resting his sword against the wall, he took both of Norton's hands in his own and raised them to his lips. "You are too kind, sir. Perhaps now that you are relieved from the burden of canvassing, you might find an hour or two to spare me? I'm expecting some new sketches from Paris that I'm certain will spark your interest."

The slam of a door told Dulcie his performance had hit its intended target.

But now he had a starry-eyed Norton to deal with. Ah, was a schemer's work never done?

Dulcie took Norton's arm and directed him towards the front of the house. At Dulcie's nod, the footman pulled the door wide. "But I fear we have kept your dear father waiting. I will never forgive myself if I cause you to miss Mrs. Hawley's gingerbread!"

"But, my lord—" George Norton stuttered.

"Perhaps after the canvassing is concluded, I will have the time to show you my new acquisitions. Will you be long in the country? Or shall I find you in London come the autumn?"

"George?" The elder Mr. Norton stood by an open carriage, impatience writ large on his face. "Come along, now, before your mother grows worried we've overturned in the lane."

Dulcie whistled as he picked up his foil and raced up the stairs. Even if Saybrook refused to participate in a display of swordsmanship at the fête, he'd wager he could goad Benedict into taking part.

But first, he needed to change into the garments he'd been collecting all week for the occasion.

And dig up Benedict's sword.

CHAPTER 11

BENEDICT STOMPED ABOUT THE OLDFIELD Village green, the joy and pleasure of the fairs' attendees irritatingly at odds with his own temper. He should have been happy after witnessing the successes of his eldest brother this morning. Despite his lack of self-confidence, Theo had made a more than creditable showing at his birthday celebration, when he'd been formally introduced to the Saybrook tenants as their new lord. He'd listened with patience and attention to the speeches a handful of men had been elected to make in his honor, and had even given a charmingly modest—and thankfully brief—speech in return. Theo had always pretended not to care that their father had thought him so ill-suited to the viscountcy, but Benedict knew how much doing a creditable job truly mattered to him.

Theo's successes, then, should have had him brimming over with pride. But seeing Clair preen and posture in front of George Norton—the very man throwing a spanner into the works of his own friend's Parliamentary bid—had banished all his better feelings.

He shook his head. What right did he have to feel jealous of the attentions Clair paid young Norton? Or the attentions he paid any man? Benedict had been the one to reject Clair, not the other way round.

Stopping by the round-about that had been constructed especially for the fair, Benedict pulled out his sketching pad and

172

stroked short, quick lines across the page. Drawing always helped him calm his churning emotions, giving him the inner quiet in which to sort through his own feelings. Had it been the right thing to do, rejecting Dulcie's offer of a casual liaison? He sketched the barker with his blue striped coat and cracking whip. He'd told himself over and over that the unexpected feeling of emptiness and of loss that had followed his rejection of Dulcie would pass, or at the very least would lessen over time. But it had been more than a month, now, and his yearning for the man had not abated in the least.

His hand shifted, sketching the small boys perched upon the sawdust-filled horses, some holding tight to their hats, others waving them in the air in enthusiastic display. He'd been little older than the tallest one when he'd first met and began dreaming about Sinclair Milne. Had he kissed the man only once? It seemed like a thousand times, so often had he relived that moment as he fell into an uneasy sleep each night.

He drew the tiny girl peeping out from behind her brother from the window of the round-about's child-sized coach next, braids flying, narrow face giddy with delight. When was the last time he had felt anywhere near as happy as that child? Not since Dulcie had begun to deliberately ignore him. Not since Dulcie had kissed him.

And then, the shock of watching him flirt with George Norton, the explosive anger that had him nearly bursting out of his skin—well, that had been an unpleasant, if salutary, experience. Some might be able to wish their own feelings away, *will* them away, by the sheer strength of their minds. But not Benedict. As this damned yearning for Clair showed, suppressing his feelings only made them more insistent.

Benedict's charcoal limned the boys pushing the wheel of the round-about, their arms straining, their feet flying. He would offer to take a turn, as he often had as an adolescent, but even the thrill of speed and motion seemed to dull in light of his current frustrations. If he didn't take care, this unrequited longing for Clair might just suck him down into a boggy, smothering melancholy.

But if his feelings would not leave, Benedict certainly could. Leave Saybrook House.

Leave Clair.

His hand flew to finish his sketch as the round-about slowly came to a halt. When he was a child, he'd always protested the inevitable end to the ride, and immediately jumped back into line again to take another turn. But these children seemed almost eager to leave, laughing as they slipped from their perches and pointed towards some tumult behind him.

Benedict bit back a laugh as the cause of the uproar hove into view. A Barbary corsair, swaggering about the Oldfield village green? Or at least a fair imitation of one, for those who had never seen a real member of the Ottoman navy. Where had Clair got them, those baggy trousers and richly embroidered vest, and that ridiculous hat—obviously meant to suggest a fez —wrapped about with a brightly striped scarf? Not to mention that absurdly curling mustache, made from hair a far darker shade than his own. What a thrill he was giving the villagers, most of whom had never traveled more than ten miles from Oldfield, and had never come close to meeting an actual pirate.

But would he truly ruin the entire illusion by pulling out his oh-so English quizzing glass to examine the pies and tarts on offer in Mrs. Hawley's booth?

Yes, he would. Benedict pressed his lips tightly together, trying to contain his pleasure as be-costumed Clair swaggered over to Miss Atherton and Parson Strickland. The fellow should have looked ridiculous, strutting about with all the grandiosity of Byron's Corsair. But Benedict's breath still caught at the mere sight of him.

He couldn't help but edge closer as Strickland rushed away —goaded by Clair, no doubt, off to fix some ridiculous problem he had made up of whole cloth.

"Were not you supposed to be helping Lady Sayre and her husband in the canvassing?" Harry asked Clair.

"Not until after my fencing match. Two of the clock, you told me." Clair held out his pocket watch. "And it is nearly that now."

"Yes, but where is your opponent?"

"Oh, I'm sure Saybrook will be here any moment. He promised to meet me on the field of combat."

Saybrook? Had Clair actually convinced Theo to participate in his silly display?

Whipping out his fencing foil—nothing like the wickedly curved saber of a true corsair—from a scabbard by his side, Clair stepped into the middle of the village green and shouted.

"Where is he, the miserable cur? Yes, I speak of Lord Saybrook, who has impugned the honor of my country, my family, even my own lord! Saybrook, I defy thee to single combat to the last extremity!"

The children who had gathered to stare at Dulcie's outrageous costume now edged even closer, mouths agape at the prospect of a real sword fight in the midst of their annual fair.

"One of the actors from the troupe, drumming up attendance for the show this afternoon," said a woman in the crowd with a complacent nod.

"Yes, but to call for the lord to take part? Overbold, that is," an older farmer protested.

"Oh, our Saybrook's a prime 'un," a young fellow insisted. "Won't rub him the wrong way."

Benedict searched the crowd for his brother, but could find nary a glimpse. Serve Clair right if Theo left him here to bellow to nobody but the wind.

But if Theo had intended to leave Clair in the lurch, what was Benedict's own sword doing there, leaning on the side of Mrs. Hawley's booth? Had Theo, who had no weapon of his own, borrowed Benedict's, then forgotten it? Or had Dulcie brought it, sure that his taunts would draw out his opponent?

Benedict strode over and picked up the foil before an overly curious village child could injure himself on it. The foil still did not have a protective leather cap.

The crowd grew restless as the minutes ticked past with no sign of Theo. But Clair, always happy to be the center of attention, escalated his verbal taunts. "Do you disregard my challenge, Lord Saybrook? It is true you hold a higher place than I, but your dignity does not privilege you to do me an injury. As soon as ever you do me an injury, you make myself your equal, and as you are my equal I challenge you!"

A hand grabbed Benedict's sleeve. Harry Atherton, worry wrinkling her brow. "Where is he?" she asked.

"I've no idea. And he's without his foil, too," Benedict said, snapping the weapon in question through the air.

"More of such conversation would infect my brain!" Dulcie shouted. "Shall such a man insult me so, and still walk free? Fie upon it, I say. Fie!"

"Could something have happened to him?" Harry whispered.

Benedict shook his head, the answer suddenly obvious. "No. He just loses track of the time."

"You'd think he might be punctual at least once in his life," Sibilla huffed as she and her husband joined them. "But he refuses to carry father's watch."

Before he could open his mouth to upbraid his sister for insulting the head of their family, hands on his back shoved him into the center of the village green.

"Noble Sir Benedict will defend the honor of the Saybrook name from this scurrilous attack," he heard Harry yell as he stumbled onto the grass in front of Clair.

He set a hand to the ground to keep himself from toppling over. As he caught his balance, he looked up to see Clair examining him through his jeweled quizzing glass, a wicked smile lighting his face.

"Ah, at long last! A scion of the Saybrook line, here to answer for the sins of his family." He lowered his quizzing glass and raised his sword. "*En garde*, sir!"

"Really, Dulcie?" Benedict asked as he pushed himself to standing. "Must we engage in such a ridiculous display?"

"Did you not promise to meet me on this field of combat, and to put on a display your people would not long forget? And did your brother not promise to aid me when it seemed you would go back on your word?"

"What? I never promised you any such thing, Dulcie, as you well know. And I very much doubt Theo did, either."

Clair's eyes flashed, then he turned to the crowd and shook his sword. "Call me a liar? Thy tongue outvenoms all the worms of Nile! I demand satisfaction!"

All the worms of Nile? Benedict struggled to hold back a laugh. Only Clair would hurl Shakespearean insults in the midst of a challenge to a duel.

But the villagers, it would seem, were not as familiar with the words of the Bard as was Benedict. The circle around them tightened, as if some of them might soon set upon Clair themselves if Benedict did not come to the defense of the honor of his family.

"Have at it, now!"

"Dunna let him insult ye so, sir!"

"You can take 'im, sure you can!"

Clair raised his sword once again. "Come, now, Mr. Pennington. Would you show yourself a coward in front of your own people?"

It wasn't the insulting goad that propelled Benedict forward. No, it was the invitation in Clair's eyes, an invitation that promised far more than a simple clash of swords.

"I'm not afraid of you," he said, raising his own foil as he culled his memory for an appropriate verbal riposte. "Thou rankest compound of villainous smell that ever offended nostril."

Clair's grin widened. "A duel of wits, is it to be, as well as of swords? *Pret! Allez,* thou damned and luxurious mountain goat!"

Benedict's foil parried the sudden thrust of Clair's with a clang. "Thou lump of foul deformity!" he shouted as he pushed free, then flicked the quizzing glass from Clair's free hand with the tip of his foil.

The crowd cheered as the jeweled trinket tumbled to the ground. But Benedict barely heard it, the blood drummed so loud in his ears.

Clair circled about Benedict, making quick, sharp jabs with the point of his foil, none close enough to prick, just enough to make his opponent dance. "Thou cream-faced loon."

Benedict dodged out of reach. "Thou sodden-witted lord! Thou hast no more brain than I have in mine elbows."

Clair feinted, panting. "Ah, but thy face is not worth sunburning."

"The tartness of thy face would sour ripe grapes."

"Thou clay-brained guts!"

"Thou knotty-pated fool!"

The crowd roared ever louder with each verbal attack. How many more insults from Shakespeare could he dredge up from his memory? Clair, damn him, had always triumphed at every game of cap a quotation at school.

Benedict lunged at an opening, but pulled back at the rasp of a ripping seam. His shirt? Or his trousers?

"Would thou wouldst burst!" Clair crowed.

"Would thou wert clean enough to spit upon!" Benedict answered, forcing Clair's back to the side Mrs. Hawley's pastry booth. Their swords entangled, their faces only inches apart. The musk of Clair's sweat made his nostrils flair.

"You're supposed to allow me to win," he muttered in a voice too low to be heard by the crowd.

"Ah, but that was my agreement with Saybrook. And only if he would convince you to paint my portrait. Otherwise, I promised to inform your sister of how he's failed to pay over a good portion of her dowry to Sir Peregrine." With a sudden shove, Clair sent him reeling back.

Benedict shook the hair out of his eyes. "What did you say?"

"I said, your eldest brother has failed in his fiduciary responsibilities to my friend," Clair whispered as he once again circled Benedict. "Not only did he promise him an uncontested seat in Parliament, which he has failed to do, but he's also failed to pay Per the full amount due to him upon his marriage to your sister."

Bloody hell. His brother, the estate, in financial difficulties? And Theo hadn't thought to confide his troubles to his own brother.

How long had Clair known?

"Ah, weren't aware of that, were you? No, Sir Peregrine is too kind to embarrass your brother by revealing such a thing to you. Or even to his own wife." Clair's hand was a blur, his sword flicking and teasing, but never quite engaging with Benedict's. "But someone has to look out for his interests, if he will not."

Damnation. Was Clair threatening to spill Theo's secrets to Sibilla? Now, when she'd finally started to forgive their elder brother for not embracing a political life, as she and their father before her had always dreamed he would?

"You will hold your tongue," he snarled, circling Clair in his turn.

But Clair only smiled. "Will you be wiser than your brother, I wonder, and accept my generous offer? My silence, as well as my ignominious defeat in this duel—"

"If I complete your portrait?" Benedict's voice cracked in disbelief. What a manipulative bastard.

Clair flicked his sword, teasing at the end of Benedict's cravat. "As you promised you would."

Rage hazed Benedict's brain. With a sudden thrust, the tip of his foil slipped under Clair's guard. The tip unprotected by a leather button.

A thin line of blood seeped into the fine linen of his opponent's sleeve.

Clair's eyes blew wide as his weapon slipped from his suddenly shaking hand.

"Done." Benedict swept his sword up and down in acknowledgement, his pulse pounding in his head. Then, before the urge to wound more than Dulcie's pride conquered good sense, he strode off the field in search of his brother.

Dulcie sat heavily on his bed and swore as he struggled to wrap a length of linen about the cut on his upper arm. One of Saybrook House's footmen, eyes wide with barely contained curiosity, had offered to send for a surgeon when a bloody Dulcie returned, alone, from the village fair, but Dulcie had shooed him away. Benedict's foil hadn't gone that deep. Besides, the idea of stitches, or even worse, being bled by leeches to stave off possible inflammation, turned his stomach.

Still, even a glancing cut stung like the very devil.

He grunted as he pressed his arm against the side of his chest, trying to keep the end of the bandage from slipping. Yes, the wound stung, but not as badly as that look on Benedict's face had, when he'd demanded Dulcie hold his tongue. He'd never seen such pain in another's eyes. At least not eyes fixed on him.

Had Benedict really believed he'd babble away his brother's secrets? How could he have not known that Dulcie was only provoking him? His earlier challenge to Benedict's brother, to fight or have Dulcie tell Sibilla all—he'd only made it to push the poor fellow into shaking off his insecurities and showing his true strength. And to help Per, too, because the strain of keeping such a secret from his wife was daily chipping away at the peace and happiness his friend had finally found. A week of standing aside and watching *that* without stepping in to help was a month too long.

And it had worked like a charm, just as Dulcie planned. Dulcie's taunts had finally led Saybrook to stand up for himself as a proper nobleman should. Why, Benedict should be falling to his knees in gratitude, not looking at him as if he were a slug he wished to crush beneath his boot.

Dulcie dabbed a bit of honey he'd wrangled from the kitchens onto the cut, then whipped the linen about his upper arm. Thank the gods the damned thing had finally stopped bleeding. He'd already ruined one good shirt today.

But when he raised his arm up and down, testing his mobility, a red stain seeped through the layers of bandage. Damnation. He hated to rely on his valet to tie his cravat. Brookings never could get it to drape to Dulcie's liking.

A light tap on the door made him grimace. "Go away, Brookings! I told you I'd call when I've need of you!"

But when the door opened, it revealed not his servant, but Benedict Pennington, a small package tucked under one arm.

Dulcie stilled, too aware that his shirt, ripped, bloodied, lay on the floor by his feet. He'd often preened and strutted in a far greater state of dishabille in front of other men. Why, then, should he feel so naked under Benedict's gaze?

Those dark eyes slowly roamed his bare chest, tracing the trail of hair down his stomach, then moved even lower—

Benedict's head jerked up, his gaze skittering to Dulcie's, then away, finally settling on the bandage flapping against Dulcie's upper arm. With a scowl, he set down his package on a chair and strode to Dulcie's side.

"Why isn't a surgeon attending to this?" he asked as he ripped the end of the linen and tied it off in a neat knot. "Or your valet, at least?"

"I'm quite capable of taking care of a minor scratch."

"A wound still bleeding after four hours can hardly be accounted minor. I will have Randall summon a surgeon."

Whenever Dulcie had suffered any small injury as a child, he'd always enjoyed being the center of solicitous female attention—his mother's, his sister's, the housekeeper's, the cook's, even a kitchen maid's—gentle hands and soft words soothing his temper and pride just as their poultices and dressings soothed his physical hurts. Yet today, some unfamiliar feeling urged him to turn away, to lick his wound in private.

Shame? Why, when it was Benedict who had injured him, not the other way round?

Dulcie pulled free from Benedict's hand and reached for the clean shirt he'd laid on the bed. "You do think highly of your swordsmanship, don't you? But I assure you, it is only a scratch. It stopped bleeding some time ago."

"Is that rouge on that bandage, then? Hope to make us all pity you by a false display?"

"What need have I of pity, when I can charm you all with such ease?" Dulcie answered, struggling not to wince as he lifted the shirt over his head and sent it coursing down over his shoulders. Better to stain another shirt than to stand here another second under Benedict's unwavering gaze.

"All except you, of course," he said as Benedict remained silent. "Why are you here? Come to lord it over your vanquished foe?"

Benedict took a deep breath, then looked him directly in the eyes. "I've come to apologize. I should not have let my feelings get the better of me, no matter how provoking your behavior."

"Provoking? And what, precisely, did I do to provoke that simmering temper?" he asked as he struggled with the button on the cuff of his sleeve.

"You threatened my family."

Dulcie swallowed against the surprising lump in his throat.

"And you thought I would make good on such a threat? Your brother did, when he finally agreed to tell Sibilla himself about her missing dowry money rather than have me do it. But I expected better of you."

Benedict's forehead wrinkled. "But you threatened—"

"I made no threat. I only offered."

"You're splitting hairs. I distinctly remember you offering silence in exchange for a portrait."

"But I never said I'd tell if you didn't give it to me. Am I responsible for the inferences you make?"

"Yes! For you clearly intended for me to infer the opposite. Your entire scheme depended upon it."

The stiffness of Benedict's posture, the flatness of his lip, his rough, noisy breathing—yes, he truly did believe Dulcie capable of hurting his sister, all for his own gain. Of course, Dulcie had wanted Benedict to think—only for an instant—that he might let Saybrook's secret slip, and act to avoid the minuscule possibility. But at the same time, it cut him, cut him far deeper than Benedict's sword had, realizing Benedict could not see the truth behind the manipulation, the man behind the act.

"Perhaps. But I didn't think you'd actually believe me capable of it." Dulcie sat down heavily on the bed and shook his head. "Do you not know me at all?"

Benedict's expressive hands carved frustration in the air. "How can I know you, Clair, when you hide everything you are?"

Dulcie tried to hold Benedict's gaze, but even that small attempt to open himself to another seemed beyond him. His instinct for self-preservation ran fathoms deep.

But it suddenly mattered, that Benedict see he was more than what he showed the rest of the world. It mattered more than he could comfortably stand.

If he wanted Benedict to see him, though, he'd have to lower his guard, far more than he ever had with any man.

How, though?

As he searched the room for an answer, his eyes caught on the package Benedict had laid on the chair. Dulcie jumped up from the bed and snatched it up from its precarious perch atop the cushion. If it contained what he hoped it did, perhaps it might serve as a bridge, a way for him to begin to step across the chasm he'd created between his own feelings and the rest of the world. A way to show Benedict who he was, by showing him what he loved.

He ripped off the brown paper to reveal a small portfolio, its boards covered with marbled paper. He ran a hand over its surface, then took a deep, calming breath.

"Open it," he said, as he thrust out the portfolio towards Benedict.

CHAPTER 12

BENEDICT TOOK A STEP BACK, away from Clair and whatever the hell he held in his hand. Did he think offering some sort of gift would appease Benedict? Had he not heard a single word Benedict said?

"It's for you, Dulcie, not for me." He snatched his hands behind his back, clutching them tight against the curve of his spine. "Arrived yesterday, Randall tells me, but with all the to-do with the fête and Theo's birthday, it was overlooked."

"No matter. Better, even, since everyone else is still in the village. It's not something I wish to share with anyone. Anyone except you."

Benedict frowned. If Clair had uttered such words on any other day, he'd assume the portfolio held some titillatingly scandalous erotic print. But the tone in which he'd said them—cautious, halting, even a bit fearful—suggested something entirely different.

He took a step closer, curiosity overcoming anger. "What is it?"

"A drawing, by an artist named Géricault. I've longed for something by him ever since I saw his *Raft of the Medusa* on display at the Egyptian Hall two years ago."

Hearing the name of the young French painter sent a tumult of memories cascading through Benedict's mind. He'd spent a few electric, if confusing, months in Europe in Théodore

Géricault's company, caught between fascination and dismay at the artist's decidedly unconventional painting style.

"You admire *The Raft?*" he asked as Clair eagerly unwound the cord that kept the portfolio closed. His breath caught as Clair opened the folder to reveal a pen and ink sketch—an early, smaller scale drawing of what would later become the larger-than-life-sized painting of the aftermath of the infamous wreck of the French naval frigate *Méduse.* A raft of the shipwreck's survivors, the dead entwined with the dying, the still living in torment, starving, naked, a few grotesque souls even cannibalizing the flesh of others.

Outrageous.

Appalling.

Riveting.

Beside him, Dulcie shivered. "Admire is not quite the right word. That pile of corpses, the anguish of the survivors—so excruciating, yet so utterly compelling. I confess I nearly ran mad when I first laid eyes on it."

"But I thought—are you not a devotee of the classical style? What of the dictates of the academies, that insist only ideal beauty, not mundane reality, is worthy of the name of art?"

"Mundane reality?" Dulcie flung a hand towards the sketch. "You call such a terrifying depiction mundane?"

"No, indeed. Yet how can such a hideous subject be suitable for painting? Is not art supposed to elevate, rather than repel?"

"Perhaps. But while Géricault breaks the rules, there is something in his work that is not so easy to dismiss. Lord, Benedict, it makes even *me* feel, hardhearted creature that I am."

Benedict gazed down at the sketch once again. Yes, that is what had drawn him to Géricault's work, too, the artist's ability to make his viewer *feel*, even to the point of being overwhelmed by the power of the emotion evoked. For a few short months, Benedict had even tried to create something similar himself, filling pages and pages with sketches of the ghastly things pulled from his own dreams and night terrors. Yet so many of France's art critics had been disgusted by *The Raft*, denouncing it with such vehemence after it had been shown at the Paris Salon that poor Géricault had fallen into a deep melancholy. Benedict himself soon gave over his own poor attempts at something not constrained by the classical ideals of harmony, simplicity, and proportion endorsed by all the academies in England and on the Continent.

Clair stroked a trembling finger against the edge of the sketch. "It is the most beautiful work I'll ever own," he whispered.

If a wild wolf had dropped to its back and exposed its vulnerable underbelly to him, Benedict couldn't have been more surprised. The reverence of Clair's words, the elation crinkling his eyes—Benedict had never seen such raw, open emotion from him before, at least not since Harrow. Had Clair known how Géricault's provocative work would crack open the shiny shell of his composure? How could he have not? Why, the body next to him fairly thrummed with barely-contained feeling.

Benedict swallowed, his throat thick with yearning. If Clair ever gazed at a lover the way he was staring at that sketch . . .

"I, too, once admired Géricault's work," Benedict finally said, his eyes fixed on the portfolio.

"Once? Not any longer?"

"I don't rightly know. I haven't looked at the sketches he gave me in some years."

Clair's eyes blew wide. "What? Géricault *gave* you some of his sketches?"

"I spent some time with him in Paris, and did him a small service." Accompanying the painter to the Salpêtrière where he had been commissioned to paint portraits of the mad, watching as he struggled to capture the essence of each subject's particular mania even as he fought to keep hold of his own sanity—a small, but harrowing, service. One he'd not wish to repeat anytime soon. "He offered me a few of his sketches in thanks."

Clair clutched both hands against his ribcage, as if to keep his own longing from spilling right out of his chest. "Please tell me you haven't sold them off, or misplaced them. Or that you've left them behind in London."

"I believe I had them sent here when I returned from the Continent."

"Then what are we waiting for?" Dulcie grabbed Benedict's hand and yanked him towards them door. "Show them to me now, this instant!"

They spent the waning twilight ransacking the family apartments, searching for the folio in which Benedict remembered storing the sketches in question. It hadn't been in the room Benedict had slept in since his return to Lincolnshire, nor had it been in any of the empty guest chambers. Dulcie would have barged in on poor Mr. Atherton, still recuperating from his fit earlier in the summer in the one remaining guest chamber, if Parsons had not suddenly remembered carrying a portfolio to the attics earlier in the year. In the end, though, the stray folio finally turned up in his mother's sitting room. Its pastel yellow and blue walls, the elegant symmetry of its plaster relief, and the intricate rococo Chippendale furniture served as an incongruous setting for the macabre work of the French artist. But Clair, too impatient to wait, jerked on the string to the folio's closure as soon as Benedict had pulled it from where it had been shoved amongst his mother's own unframed paintings.

"Lord, Benedict!" Clair flipped quickly through the contents of the portfolio, then returned to the top of the stack and fanned out the first group of sketches across the table so that they could be viewed simultaneously. "How could he?"

"I know," Benedict said, staring down at the severed arms and legs and other body parts carefully arranged in sickening parodies of still lives. "Most painters study anatomy by drawing living nudes, but during the time I knew him, Géricault was obsessed with collecting and drawing severed heads and limbs."

"I hardly know whether to fall to my knees in veneration or to vomit."

"If you think these are appalling, you should have seen the finished paintings. So realistic, yet so devoid of life. I thought perhaps he made them in protest of the death penalty, especially the guillotine."

Clair shuddered. "I can barely stand to look at them. But I can't look away, either."

"That is his gift, I think. Confronting you with what you would rather not see."

Benedict gathered the still lives and placed them back in the folio, then pulled out another stack, less horrific, perhaps, but still shocking nonetheless. Subjects from the myths of the Greeks, yet rendered with none of the polite decorum dictated by academic classicism. No, there was nothing moralizing in that pen and ink sketch of a satyr attacking a nymph, nothing civilizing in the two crayon drawings of naked couples sinuously entwined, copulating with abandon. Violence, sensuous exaltation, perhaps even death, yes.

But were they beautiful? Were they *art*? Part of Benedict's soul cried out *yes*. But Géricault's own despair, his retreat to a clinic to be treated for melancholia after his *Raft* had been denounced, had made Benedict doubt. Especially when coupled with the confident pronouncements of Julius Adler, made soon after their first meeting that same year, that Géricault's work had been painted solely to please the vultures, that any mother would cast off a son who would stoop to depicting such depths of depravity as the mad painter had.

What would his own mother, kind, gentle woman that she was, have thought of them? Gone, now, for more than a decade, she would never be able to say.

"But surely these are not by the same hand," Clair said as he pulled two drawings from the folio and laid them beside the others.

Benedict snatched them away. "No, they are not."

Clair's eyes fixed on his hands, clutching the drawings to his chest. "Yours?"

Benedict glanced away, then nodded.

"My God. How could you be content to paint such insipid portraits when you have something as powerful as *that* within you?" Clair whispered, gently pulling the sketches from his fingers. His hand smoothed out the two drawings of male nudes with something almost akin to awe.

Benedict had drawn the men in balanced poses inspired by Greek and Roman sculpture, yet deviating from the perfect symmetry demanded by classical art. Each muscle precisely articulated, the tendons and sinews clear, each body expressive with barely-contained energy. Ideal beauty was all well and good, but these were bodies that moved, that strained and toiled, that spat and stank and sweated. Bodies that lusted, and acted on that lust.

The slap of Clair's hand against the table jerked Benedict from his mental absorption. High color flushed over his face as he stabbed a finger at the drawings. "This, Benedict. This is how you must paint me."

Benedict's shock made the words tangle in his throat. "What?" he finally managed to squeeze out. "A nude for your wife-to-be? Dulcie, really!"

"No, of course not a nude. But something more vital, more alive, than you've done before. Something like you've captured in these life drawings. And not for Miss Adler, or for any other young miss. You will do it for me. And you will do it for yourself."

Almost frightening in its intensity, that look of determination in Clair's blue eyes. As if he were a captain urging his team onto the cricket pitch, or a commander sending his men into battle.

Shaking his head in disbelief, Benedict backed away from

190

the table. "No."

But Clair stalked after him, his eyes fixed on Benedict's. "Yes. You must and you will."

"No," Benedict said, one hand grabbing hold of the doorframe. He would not allow the man to send him fleeing him from the room, as if he were a hound and Benedict a fearful beast of the chase. "If I won't even paint your engagement portrait for Julius Adler, what makes you think I'll take up my brush for you?"

"Because it would be a sin to keep such passion from the world. A far greater sin than any of my halfhearted threats against your family could ever be."

Benedict choked out a laugh. "Is that meant to be an apology, Dulcie?"

Clair's shrug, half elegance, half abashment, pulled at something soft deep inside Benedict. "Of a sort. But you'll never get me to say the actual words, not if you refuse this commission."

His fingers twitched, imagining the feel of the brush in his hand, the way he might wield it to capture that infuriating combination of vulnerability and insouciance of the breathtakingly open Clair hiding behind the mask of Lord Dulcie. Imagining the colors and the strokes that would capture the flex of the man's arm, the curl of his hair against his nape, the well of feeling that hid behind the charm . . .

He'd intended to leave Lincolnshire after the fête, meant to remove himself from the torment of a Sinclair Milne always at hand but forever out of reach. It would be wrong to remain here, everything inside him longing for Clair but unable to touch him in body or in spirit. Far better to leave and dream of what might have been than stay and struggle in silent anguish.

But what if those dreams—or some semblance of them—had a chance of becoming reality? If, instead of longing in vain for an ideal lover who could never truly exist, Benedict made a determined effort to coax out the actual man? If, while he sketched and painted his unconventional portrait, he also talked with Clair, enticed him with questions and ideas that also pushed beyond convention? Might such an effort give Benedict a chance to slip behind the hard shell of Clair's self-protection and make the man *feel*, just as Géricault's drawings had?

"You will pose for me, without protest?" Benedict asked after a long silence.

Clair's back immediately straightened. "I will."

"And allow me to paint you how I wish, the way I see you, without critique or comment?

"If you paint me in the same style as those sketches, then yes."

Benedict took a step closer. "And you will explicitly apologize for your ill-considered threats against my family, even if you never intended to carry them out?"

"I will, and I do." Clair offered up the courtliest of bows, sweeping an invisible courtier's hat from his head to the floor. "Mr. Pennington, please accept my deepest apologies for trying to manipulate you by implying I would defame your brother and your sister. Even though you should have known I would never have caused anyone you held dear intentional harm."

Benedict wanted to shake his head at the unrepentant coda to that charming apology, but instead, he nodded. "Then I accept your commission. But it will have to wait until we return to London, as I don't have the tools or the paints I would need here."

A smile wider than the Thames radiated from Clair's face. "Then I will order my valet to pack my things immediately. How early can you be ready to set forth?"

The vibrant pinks and subtle oranges of a midsummer dawn skimmed London's rooftops, limning the windows of Benedict's attic studio with stunning light. But even the unusually vibrant sunrise couldn't fix his attention for long this morning. Though he and Clair had arrived in town well after midnight, he'd still woken before the sun, the itch of inspiration tingling in his fingers, fizzing in his brain.

They must be here, the other sketches he'd made after he'd first met Théodore Géricault, the ones he'd done in a fever of excitement at the prospect of tossing aside all the academic rules that he'd once struggled so hard to assimilate. He wanted to see them again, those drawings he'd hidden away in embarrassment after being befriended by Julius Adler and his granddaughter, but this time through Clair's eyes. Or rather, through his own eyes, eyes newly opened by Clair's praise of his unconventional work.

He knelt in front of the cabinet in which he'd stored his old, unworthy productions and began rummaging through its contents. Tepid landscapes and tired portraits soon littered the floor, work hardly worth the paper they'd been painted on, never mind a framed place on the wall. Why had he held so tightly to such insipid stuff? They would have better been tossed onto the fire.

As he pulled one last stack from the cabinet, he touched the smooth surface of a leather-bound book. Not the sketch-book for which he'd been searching, no, but one far older, one he'd thought he'd lost. His fingers skimmed over the worn cover, tracing his initials in gold embossed letters. A gift from his mother, when he'd first left home for school. She must have sensed how afraid he was to leave her and Lincolnshire, for all he'd kept his fears bottled up inside. With a grave face, she'd handed him this book, telling him how lucky he was to have the chance to go to school and study with a true artist, as she herself had never had. He must take full advantage of his opportunity, and make her proud.

Little had his mother known that drawing masters at boy's schools were far more interested in teaching their students the practical uses of drawing—recording geographical features and architectural landmarks while traveling or on military campaign—than inspiring any true appreciation of, or skill in, the higher beauties of art.

He flipped open the book, past those early lessons in line and perspective and balance, to the sketches he'd begun to make on his own time. At first, drawings of the woods and fields about Harrow, and then, as he'd become more comfortable at the school, sketches of the people around him. And then, images of one boy in particular.

His breath caught at these early sketches of Lord Dulcie, taken from a distance, inspired by hero worship of the most painful kind. And then later, more casual poses, after the older boy had befriended him, Dulcie transforming right on these pages into his far more beloved Clair. His hand, twirling a leaf between nimble fingers. The fall of his hair as he bent over a book. The crinkle of his eyes, the upturn of his brow as he joked and laughed away all of Benedict's so very earnest worries.

Awkward, yes, and unskilled, these sketches, but still, there was something vital and alive here, something important, something *real*. Something none of the more formal sketches he'd made of the adult Dulcie had come even close to capturing.

If he could but marry this, this intimate knowledge of Clair, with a painting technique that strove not to create rational order out of vibrant chaos, not to depict him as a hero, but as a *man*—

Expectation, heady and potent, ripped through Benedict's body. After scrambling to his feet, he kicked aside the bland drawings on the floor and reached for his pencil.

Only the rattle of china and the smell of toasted bread woke him from his absorption. How long had he been sketching?

Several hours, if the position of the sun and the cramp in his fingers were any indication.

"Hungry?"

Benedict started, almost dropping his pencil. Clair, immaculately turned out in spite of the early hour, shouldered open the door of the studio, a tray replete with breads, butter, preserves, and a pot of steaming tea in hand.

"The staff tells me you've had nothing to eat all morning. You cannot create art if you starve yourself."

The corners of Benedict's mouth lifted. He still could hardly believe Clair had agreed to stay with him instead of at his father's London house. Even if Parliament had adjourned earlier in the week, and Lord Milne had decamped for his country estate, Clair might have slept at Milne House, walking to Berkeley Square each day to pose. But all Benedict had to do was mention how it would be a pity to inconvenience two sets of servants rather than one before Clair jumped back onto his horse and rode the short distance from Mount Street to Berkeley Square alongside him.

He could only pray the thought of no longer living in the same household had made Clair as lonely as it had Benedict.

And that now that he and Clair were here together, alone, he'd be able to coax him out of hiding. Show him that he was in safe hands.

Clair shoved away paint pots and brushes, making space on the table for the tray. "Cream, no sugar?" he asked as he picked up the teapot.

"Yes, thank you."

Benedict smiled in bemusement as a surprisingly adept Clair readied his tea.

"And what, sir, do you find so amusing?" Clair asked as he handed the saucer to Benedict.

He waved a hand towards the teapot. "Your unexpected domesticity. It's almost as if we were back at school—"

"But with the roles reversed," Clair interrupted, reading his mind. With a flourish, he set a plate of toast beside Benedict's saucer. "You the master, and I the dutiful fag, bringing you your morning fare."

Benedict chuckled. "High and mighty Viscount Dulcie, reduced to servile running and fetching? Impossible!"

"Ah, but I was not always a high and mighty sixth former! Remember, I was sent away to school at a far younger age than you. And I served my turn as fag, just as you did, and to fellows far less genial than myself, I assure you."

Benedict's cup rattled in the saucer. He'd never even imagined—

"Did they bully you?" he asked, hands fisting on the table. "Force you to do things you did not wish to do?"

Clair shrugged as he readied his own cup. "What son of a nobleman *wishes* to black boots, or dig melted wax out of candlesticks? Silly, tedious work, most of it. But adolescent boys do enjoy lording it over one another, especially if they realize that in future, the situation is likely to be reversed."

His concern must have been evident on his face, because Clair reached out and squeezed his arm. "No, I was never bullied. It takes more than a few unkind words to intimidate me."

Benedict's pounding heart gradually slowed. No, even as a child, Viscount Dulcie would never have tolerated such treatment.

If only he himself as a schoolboy had had a fraction of the self-assurance Clair took for granted—

Shaking off his melancholy, Benedict shoved a bite of toast in his mouth. He was supposed to be drawing Clair out, not wallowing in his own hurt feelings.

Still, he needed a few moments to gather himself again. He sat, eating in silence, as Clair entertained him with gossip from the morning's newspaper. Usually, he preferred a quiet breakfast, but today, Clair's prattle washed over him, as comforting as water warmed for the bath.

Clair set the tray outside the door, then returned, rubbing his hands together in expectation. "Now we are ready to get started. Where do you want me?"

"First you need to tell me what size portrait you wish. Full-length? Kit-Cat? A bust only?"

Clair shook his head, golden curls flying in vehemence. "Come now, Benedict. You know this is not to be one of those society portraits made only to demonstrate my rank and position. It is to be a work of art, and as such, not only its composition and style, but also its size, is to be entirely at the discretion of the artist."

"Well, then. A few standing poses to start. There, over by the window."

Benedict typically preferred not to talk while he sketched, but today, his companion would only fill the silence if he remained mute. And besides, he'd never coax Clair into revealing more of himself if he made no effort.

He took a deep breath. "Did Sir Peregrine take it very ill, your leaving Lincolnshire so abruptly? He is always the polite brother-in-law to me, but I can well imagine him reading you the riot act for your abandonment."

Clair shook his head. "With the Nortons no longer bent on contesting the election, Per should have no difficulties winning the electors to his side. And when I told him Saybrook had something difficult to confess to him and his lady wife about his finances, something he'd be far more comfortable discussing without my presence in the house, he could protest my leaving no longer."

"Sinclair Milne, considering the feelings of others. How unexpected," he teased.

"As if I would ever let another's feelings take precedence over my own," Clair said with a exaggerated shudder. "I simply wished to avoid playing witness to the vulgar display of sentiment that was likely to ensue upon your brother's confession. You did say you spoke with him before we left, and that he would keep his promise to tell Sibilla?"

Benedict nodded.

"No need, then, for me to witness your sister's dressing-down of your brother, Saybrook's abject apologizing, Miss Atherton's rushing in to defend him and to take the blame all on herself, all inevitably followed by tears and forgiveness all round. Not to mention the weeping when Saybrook finally announces his betrothal to Miss Atherton. More tears of happiness than of chagrin, then, I warrant. Still, I take pains to avoid such scenes at all cost."

"Oh, without doubt. And living with your parents and your sister when you are in town, rather than taking rooms, of course allows you to avoid family scenes of your own. Because everyone knows that Lord and Lady Milne are as devoid of feeling as a doorknob."

Even Clair could not keep a straight face at the thought of his voluble father and sentimental mother being labeled unfeeling. Yes, amusement shading into affection, if he might just capture that expression—

"Hold that, Clair," he ordered as his hand moved rapidly over the page. "Do you always reside at Milne House when in town?"

"Yes, and not because of lack of funds, which is what some gossips enjoy implying." Clair blew at a wayward curl that had fallen over his forehead. Again Benedict scrambled to capture the fleeting expression on paper.

"If I've blunt enough to purchase fine artwork, I certainly have enough to rent a set of rooms," Clair continued. "Or even to purchase a town house of my own. But unlike so many young men of fashion these days, I am inordinately fond of my parents. And since I am the only son, my father prefers to keep me close at hand."

"But you did take rooms once, did you not? When you set up Sally Goodman as mistress?" he asked, striving to keep his voice from betraying his own strong feelings at the memory. "Move to the left, please. And turn your torso to the side, your arms extended."

Clair obliged, but then glanced over his shoulder with an exaggerated scowl. "Please, do not remind me of that embarrassing episode. 'Lord Sin,' she liked to call me, as if I debauched her at every opportunity."

"You did not?"

Clair snorted with an elegance one rarely associated with the act. "Even the most pious of parsons could not have taken exception to the tepid embraces in which we two engaged."

His eyes suddenly narrowed, as if he just realized Benedict's words were meant to draw him out. "But what of you? Have you ever lain with a woman?" he asked, attempting to turn the conversation away from himself.

Benedict paused before raising his eyes to Clair's. "Yes. I have."

"And did you enjoy the experience?"

He could see Clair wished him to say no. But he wouldn't lie. "Yes. Yes, I did."

Although not nearly as much as when he'd shared his bed with a man. Not that he need confide that detail to Clair. Not just yet.

Benedict's words silenced Clair for a moment. "Lucky man," he said at last, then shrugged, half sheepishness, half pride. "I, for one, never have."

"Never? Then why did you do it? Set Sal up as your mistress?"

Clair snorted again. "Thought it would please my father. Or at least distract him from other, more salacious gossip that I had not yet learned to avoid. But it was simply too embarrassing. I'm far more careful now than I was when I first came up to town."

A sympathetic shudder raced over Benedict's frame. He'd always taken care to keep word of his unconventional appetites from reaching his family, especially his father. Viscount Saybrook already looked him askance for his devotion to art and his lack of interest in politics; what would he have said if he discovered his middle son committing the sin of Sodom? He hadn't ever really taken a male lover until he'd gone to the Continent. But Clair, despite his cosmopolitan interests, had never left England.

"Turn to the right, please, and reach towards the ceiling with your left hand. Now, tip your head back towards me."

Benedict set down his pencil, exchanging it for a stick of charcoal. "Is that why you've never married? Because of your antipathy to the fairer sex?" He kept his eyes carefully fixed on his sketch.

"Oh, I enjoy the company of females, do not mistake me. I've simply never been able to maintain a cock-stand in the face of an amorous one. Makes the prospect of siring an heir rather unlikely, does it not? For all my father wishes to see me wed?"

Clair's lips twisted in wry amusement. But Benedict couldn't bring himself to laugh. Even though he had no real objections to bedding a woman, he'd always prayed hard for Theo's good health and safety, not wishing the obligation of carrying forth the family line to fall to him. Shouldering such a burden when one was a family's sole male heir, and was entirely unaroused by the sight of a woman's body—no, he could not laugh at Clair, not for that.

"But does not living with your family make it difficult for you to conduct your, ah— your, *affaires de coeur*?" Benedict asked to divert the conversation away from the difficult topic.

"My *affaires*, as you so delicately put it, rarely involve *mon coeur*," Clair proclaimed, as if he were proud of the fact.

"Your *affaires du corps*, then, if there are only bodies, and no hearts, involved."

"A private room at the back of a discreet tavern, or even a dark path in a park, does admirably for such things. Or if I take on a protégé, as I sometimes do, I will hire a room for the month or two we are together. But I never spend much time there."

"An expeditious lover, are you? But speed, I find, is not always to be admired. Some of my happiest hours have been spent lingering in bed, taking my time in bringing pleasure to a partner, and receiving my own pleasure in turn."

Clair's eyes darkened. "If I ever found myself in your bed, Pen, I assure you, expediency would be the last thing on my mind."

"A pity, then, you're not likely to wind up there." He closed his sketchbook with a snap, willing his blush to recede. "Shall we move to the park before the light fades? And perhaps bring your horse? I'd like to try a few sketches of you astride." A quick ride would be a much-needed physical outlet for all the feelings they'd edged up against during this morning's conversation.

"There's something—someone—else I'd rather be astride than Eligius, noble steed that he may be," Clair said with a suggestive smile.

But Benedict only raised his eyebrows.

"As you will," Clair said with a gusty sigh of disappointment.

Benedict smiled and gestured to the door.

"Did you know that Eligius of Noyon is the patron saint of horses?" Clair asked as he followed Benedict down the staircase. "Seems he willed his prancer to a fellow priest after his death, but the new bishop stole it for himself. The poor beast sickened, though, and only recovered when it was returned to its rightful owner. Some also say the saint removed a horse's leg to shoe it, then magically attached it without harm, although I'm disinclined to give much credence to that particular yarn."

Benedict allowed Clair to slip back into the safety of his prattling without interruption. Let the fellow lull himself into thinking himself master of the situation. Benedict knew better.

Sitting for one's portrait often led to an unusual intimacy between subject and painter, an intimacy of which Benedict was prepared to take due advantage in the coming days.

He would show Clair how the pleasures of companionship, of fondness and affection, could be just as fine as those of sexual congress. Better, even, if one were willing to share those feelings Benedict knew were bubbling just under Clair's surface.

Only then would he accept Clair's invitation into his bed.

CHAPTER 13

"*Je n'y crois pas!* Can that be you, Dulcie?"

The city streets had been largely empty this rainy summer morning as Dulcie and Benedict made their way across Mayfair to Soho Square, to the shop of one J. Newman, colourman to artists. Oil paint, apparently, did not keep for long, and Benedict required fresh tints before he could embark upon his new, experimental portrait. At the first sign of rain, Dulcie had hidden away all the spare umbrellas from Pennington House's cloakroom, so that during their walk, he and Benedict would have to huddle close together under a single silk mushroom. And Dulcie had been quite enjoying the experience, his own arm snugging tight against Benedict's back, Benedict's fingers cupping the ball of his shoulder. Who was that rude fellow, calling out his name and interrupting such a pleasant, if damp, outing?

Ducking his head, Dulcie pushed Benedict along the pavement. But the splash of boots in puddles behind them warned him that the interruption to their companionable solitude was not to be avoided.

Benedict's arm dropped from his shoulder, and his hip nudged Dulcie further away. Dulcie let his own arm fall between them.

Ridiculous, to feel so bereft at the loss.

"Dulcie, it is you! And Pennington, good day to you both!"

Jean Melheux, a fellow member of the British Institution, jogged up to their side, panting. He bent over for a moment and huffed to catch his breath, then added, "Good heavens, man, what are you still doing in town? Why, the Glorious Twelfth has already come and gone! You'll miss the best of the grouse."

"The Twelfth? Already? Impossible!"

Dulcie looked to Benedict for confirmation, but his companion only raised an eyebrow. "Yes, it's Tuesday, the twentieth. We've been in town for more than a fortnight."

How odd. He usually spent the early weeks of August on his father's estate, preparing for the autumn shooting season by reviewing his invitations to house parties, writing his acceptances or regrets, and ensuring his fowling pieces and his wardrobe were all in order. How had the Glorious Twelfth, the opening day of the bird hunting season, passed without his notice?

His rational brain supplied the surprising answer: he'd been taking such absorbing pleasure in the company of Benedict Pennington that nothing else had mattered. Even with the majority of the ton having decamped for the countryside, he and Benedict had found more than enough to occupy a fortnight's stay in town. Posing and sketching, of course, each morning, while the light was best. Long walks, or riding about town on horseback each afternoon, Benedict taking him to visit sights in, and denizens of, the city he'd never before encountered. The Turf Coffeehouse, where a purported specimen of a mermaid was proudly displayed; an exhibition of military antiquities on Pall Mall, twenty-five full suits of armor including the set worn in secret by Bonaparte under his vest ("just like our dandies and their stays!" Dulcie had exclaimed); and Astley's Amphitheatre, where they cheered along with the lusty crowd at the reenactment of the battle of Waterloo, complete with cavalry advances, bugle calls, and cannon fire. He'd even enjoyed paying a call on Benedict's sharp-tongued uncle, a former military officer, and charming the silly but kind great aunt who saw to the disabled man's needs. And the several visits they'd paid to Benedict's younger brother, the one all of society had decided to shun both for his radical political views and for his recent marriage to a deliciously outspoken Irishwoman—why, those had been out and out entertaining.

And the evenings—well, if the evenings had not yet yielded all the carnal delights of which his slumbering brain insisted on dreaming, they were still ripe with the promise of something tantalizing, something he could not help but pursue. Heavens knew he was always happy being the center of attention, but somehow Benedict's attention seemed different, more focused, more *intense*, especially at night, when the dark shadows and flickering candlelight shrouded them in even more of an air of privacy than in Benedict's studio. That attention wasn't easily distracted, not even by Dulcie's expert innuendos and flirts. Though each evening he set off to disarm his companion, it was he who most often found himself won over, giving serious answers to Benedict's provocative questions, questions so unconventional that no other man would ever have presumed to ask them, let alone expect a response. Would he rather there be no heaven, or no hell? Did he look forward to inheriting the earldom, or did the idea of his father's death kill all pleasure in the prospect? Were the social ranks preordained by God, or a self-serving myth crafted by the privileged? What would he say if he ever met a ghost?

"Lord Dulcie?" Melheux's voice interrupted his reverie. "Are you quite well?"

Damnation. Dulcie gave his head a rough shake. What had come over him, to allow a conversation to lag so uncivilly?

"The twentieth, indeed. Why, then, do you remain in town, Melheux?" he asked. Most gentleman of his acquaintance were more than happy to have the conversation turn to themselves and their own doings, easily giving over any line of questioning that Dulcie wished to evade. Indeed, only the ringing of the midday bells at St. George's, which reminded Melheux of his own pending appointment with the gunmaker which had brought him temporarily back to town, stopped his self-absorbed chatter.

"I dare say we'll see you at Devenport's come September, eh, Dulcie? Perhaps with Miss Adler in tow? Wouldn't want Leverett to get the best of you there, would you?" Melheux said with an exaggerated wink in Benedict's direction. He tipped his hat. "Bid you good day, my lord. Pennington."

"St. Cajetan help me," Dulcie whispered under his breath as he watched Melheux dodge the raindrops. He'd all but forgotten that ridiculous bet with Lattimer Leverett.

"St. Cajetan?" Benedict asked as Dulcie grasped his arm and set a brisk pace towards Soho Square.

"The patron saint of gamblers." And before Benedict could ask him why he had need of Cajetan's intervention, Dulcie quickly added, "They say people asked him for favors, and bet him a rosary that he wouldn't be able to fulfill them, which seems a bit unlikely for a pious fellow, don't you think? More likely he just gave loans to men foolish enough to sell their souls to moneylenders and their usurious interest rates. They do say he came from a very wealthy family."

"How is it that you know so much about even the most obscure Catholic saints?" Benedict asked. "You are Church of England, are you not?"

Thank heavens for Benedict's intellectual curiosity. Nicodemus must be his patron saint. "Of course. Blame my beloved aunt, who gifted me with Butler's *Lives of the Saints* at my twelfth birthday in the vain hope their exemplary behavior would somehow rub off on me. Now, is this the shop you had in mind? It hardly looks promising."

Dulcie had expected to see a paint box or two, or at least a few watercolor cakes, scattered between brushes and palettes, pastels and drawing charcoal, in the window of the colourman's shop. Or at the very least a selection of the art instruction books the fellow had on offer. But apparently Mr. J. Newman's small shop did not cater to the amateur artist. All Dulcie could spy were a few small glass bottles in various shapes and sizes, filled with colored liquids—representations of the colors they stocked within?

A dark-skinned shopkeeper with a paint-stained apron bustled over to greet them. "Mr. Pennington! We did not expect to see you again until the autumn," he said, a pleasant lilt to his voice. "Miss Adler told us you had left town. But how may we assist you?"

Benedict and the colourman soon became engrossed in a discussion of which colors should be blended with linseed oil and which with walnut, Benedict waving with animation in the stuffy shop air. He'd always been drawn to the quiet but intense passion at the heart of Benedict Pennington, even when he'd been a mere stripling. Dulcie leaned over the counter, chin in hand, and gazed hungrily at the sight, the animation on Benedict's face, his bright eyes, those mobile, expressive features.

A movement from the other side of the shop pulled him from his abstraction. How long had he been staring?

He didn't care if all the merchants and apprentices in Mayfair knew of his infatuation. But Benedict might not like to be the subject of such gossip, especially in a shop he obviously visited with some frequency. With a shrug, Dulcie stepped away and prowled the room.

Palettes, easels, and stretched and primed canvases crowded the small room, with little space for would-be purchasers to browse or linger. And the smell— No, decidedly not a place for amateurs, but rather for those, like Benedict, who knew precisely what they wanted, and could instruct the owner to bring it directly. He shuddered at the thought of a genteel lady such as Polly Adler visiting such a shop. Was this where she'd scurried off to whilst pretending to sit with him as Benedict sketched his likeness?

An old-fashioned muller and slab, which looked as if it was actually put to good use grinding the pigments that colored the paints, rather than just serving as a prop to lend historical ambience to the proceedings, stood on a table towards the back of the shop. As Dulcie picked up the muller, testing its weight in his hand, another fellow—the colourman's apprentice?—hurried over, pulling at his forelock in a gratingly subservient manner.

"Begging your pardon, sir, but the pigment's more 'n like to stain those fine gloves of your'n," he said as he lifted the stone muller from Dulcie's suddenly nerveless fingers.

Dulcie froze. He'd not heard that voice in more than a decade.

But as the other main raised his eyes to his, he schooled his features into a semblance of impassivity.

"Copeland."

"My lord." The fellow nodded once again, this time with far less subservience. The war between fear and defiance in his expression made Dulcie's stomach turn.

"But I thought—did my father misunderstand?—you were to have left the country."

The fellow's eyes—eyes that had once gazed at him with adoration and lust—narrowed. "Come back again, haven't I? No crime in that."

"Not in that, no."

Copeland said nothing, just crossed his arms. Letting the words hang there above them both, more precarious than the sword of Damocles. Though whether he or the apprentice was the one the sword would cleave was still to be determined.

Dulcie leaned against the counter, using his greater height to loom over the smaller man. "Your uncle will not write to my father again." A pronouncement, not a question, despite the roiling of his gut.

208

The other man shrugged. "Dead now, isn't he?"

"So you'd be a fool to call attention to yourself, then, wouldn't you?"

"Indeed, my lord."

How much of that blasted letter sent to his father—a letter far more damning than anything Benedict had ever written—had been Copeland's doing? And how much his uncle's? Dulcie had never been certain.

Do you regret it? The foolish words were on the tip of his tongue, but were forced back inside by the weight of the hand that fell on his shoulder.

He smiled up at Benedict, praying his companion hadn't felt the start that shook his frame at the unexpected touch.

"Finished, are you?" Dulcie chirped, his voice sounding hollow even to his own ears. It took real effort to turn his back to Copeland, but he forced his body to obey. Still, he could not quite bring his eyes to meet Benedict's. "I am more than ready to leave. The stink here is even worse than in your studio."

"Good day to you, sirs," the shopkeeper called to their retreating backs. "I'll have those packages sent to Berkley Square immediately."

"Good day, Lord Dulcie," Copeland added.

Dulcie halted, just for the merest instant. Then, before he could betray himself with a glance over his shoulder, he dashed out again into the rain.

Saint Epipodius, patron of bachelors and victims of betrayal, pray for me.

Though Dulcie's charm, taste, and sartorial style had all received many a compliment, no one had ever praised him for his ability to sit still. During church services, his mother always had to squeeze his hand to keep him from pinching his sister, or twirling his hat in his lap, or dancing his restless fingers against his hymnal or the back of the family pew. School had been little better; though he could speak when called upon, his restless elbows and tapping feet still managed to frustrate his instructors almost as often as his quick wit disarmed them. As an adult, he'd soon learned to avoid prosing scientific lectures, plodding musical performances, and lengthy political orations unless he knew the room in which they were being held included space at the back through which he might pace without unduly annoying the other attendees. And to soothe his restless spirit by indulging his carnal appetites. Something he'd not had the opportunity to do for more than a month, now, thank you, Mr. Benedict Pennington, so very much.

Perhaps that was why the drawing room felt so stifling tonight, despite being one of Pennington House's most spacious chambers.

Visions of a younger Tom Copeland, arse teasingly on display as he bent to lift a bale of hay, biceps flexing as he raised a glass in the pub, muscular body gloriously naked as he sprawled in abandon across the bedsheets in Dulcie's Oxford chambers, washed through his mind. Dulcie shook, sloughing off the unwelcome memories as instinctually as a dog shakes the rain from his coat.

Since coming to London, he and Benedict had spent almost every evening out—attending the opera, calling in at the Athenaeum and the Alfred Clubs, even dining with the few gentlemen still in town who might be persuaded to support Benedict's museum plan. But tonight, provoking man, Benedict had declared he required a quiet evening at home. He sat across from Dulcie, completely engrossed in a new book on the nomenclature of colors he'd purchased this afternoon at the colourman's shop. The only sound in the room was the occasional turn of a page. And the tap of Dulcie's toe against the fireboard that nestled inside the bricks of the unlit hearth.

"Inviting the bats and mice to join us?" Benedict asked, nodding at the fireboard, which Dulcie's tapping had kicked out of place. Any vermin that wished to climb down the chimney could now easily escape into the room.

Dulcie snorted. "London is so thin of company in summer, I just might welcome such lowly visitors. But I'd never be so rude as to issue invitations to another man's house."

"Then stop taking out your frustrations on that poor fireboard."

Dulcie placed a hand on his jiggling boot. Frustrations? What frustrations? Benedict didn't know what he was talking about.

"Besides," Benedict continued, his voice deceptively mild, "I've more than a little affection for it, as it was painted by my mother."

Damnation. Dulcie knew in how much esteem Benedict held the late Lady Saybrook. He scrambled from his chair and shifted the abused fireboard back into place, then scrubbed a handkerchief at the smear of polish his boot had inadvertently left behind. "My apologies, Benedict. A most exquisite fireboard, to be sure. The *non plus ultra* of fireboards. Come, shall we carry it in state over to the British Institution, and set it on display for all to admire?"

Benedict smiled. "The fireboard thanks you kindly for the honor, but prefers to remain quietly at home."

As did Benedict, damn it. Fitting action to pronouncement, he took up his book again, paying no more attention to Dulcie than he would to a cat who just happened to occupy the same room.

"Ah, but we need not follow the timid fireboard's example," Dulcie replied, striding over and grabbing Benedict's book out of his hand. "Shall we visit Brooks's? Or go and see *Gil Blas* again?

Set aside this dull tome and pluck the day with me. Or the evening, as it were."

Benedict reached out a hand for the purloined volume. "If you tire of my company, Clair, you're more than welcome to venture out on your own."

"But I don't want to go by myself," Dulcie said. How appalling, that hint of a whine in his voice. But still, he could not seem to temper it. "I want you to come with me. Please say you will? I'll make certain it's worth your while."

Benedict cocked a single eyebrow, a most fetching look on that expressive face. "Reduced to begging, are you? Who could have imagined the great Lord Dulcie brought so low?"

To his surprise, Dulcie could. On his knees at Benedict's feet, running his palms up the thick muscles of those luscious thighs, begging to be allowed to undo the buttons of his falls—lord, how his cock stiffened at the mere thought. The perfect way to distract himself from other, less welcome ghosts, if only Benedict were not so damned determined that each and every sexual act be filled to the brim with some deep meaning . . .

His companion must have caught something in Dulcie's expression that betrayed his longing, for he blushed, then turned quickly back to his book.

No distraction, then, damn it to hell and back. Dulcie jumped up from his chair and began to pace. His boots thudded softly on the carpet. Thud, thud, thud.

The clock in the front entryway chimed the hour.

Benedict flipped another page.

Finally, Dulcie could stand the quiet no longer. "Did you— Your father, or one of your brothers, or— No, what I mean to ask is, has anyone in your family ever been told, or discovered on his own, of your, your . . . ?"

Bloody hell. How ridiculous, the way those questions staggered out of his mouth, as clumsy as an intoxicate reeling home after one too many at the local public house. He pressed his thumbs against his temple. What had compelled him to even broach such a painful topic? And with Benedict, of all people?

The thump of a book on the table told him he had finally caught his companion's attention. He risked a glance at Benedict's face.

The sympathy he found there nearly set him reeling.

"Does anyone in my family know that I enjoy the company of men, as well as of women, in bedsport?" Benedict folded his hands in his lap. "Is that what you wish to know, Clair?"

Dulcie sank into a chair and cradled his head in his hands. "Yes," he mumbled between his fingers.

"The topic has never been mentioned to me by any of my relations. At least not directly. Theo has taken of late to sharing certain bawdy stories from the ancients with me, which makes me think he might have some suspicion. But he does nothing more than hint obliquely. He's not one for stirring up a hornet's nest."

As are you. Dulcie heard the words in his head, though Benedict was too polite to utter them aloud.

"So no one ever caught you kissing a stableboy? Or a comely Saybrook footman?" *Or a certain fag-master at school?*

"In *flagrante de licto*? No." Benedict sat forward in his chair, leaning closer to Dulcie. "Is that what it felt like, when your father confronted you about that ill-advised letter I sent you so long ago? To be caught in the very act?"

"No," Dulcie said, hands clenching in his lap. "Father proved surprisingly forgiving, at least that first time."

Benedict's hand moved to rest lightly on one of Dulcie's. "It happened again?"

Dulcie's mouth twisted. "Yes."

"With that man in Newman's shop today? His employee, the one with whom you were so engrossed?"

"Engrossed? With Copeland?" Dulcie sprang from his chair and strode to the hearth, wishing it held a fire. An unnatural chill had descended on him. "What did he say to you? Did he threaten you?"

"No, Clair!" A soothing hand came to rest against his turned back. "No. He did not even speak to me. But you've been as skittish as an unbroken horse ever since we returned from Mr. Newman's shop. I knew something must have upset you, upset you deeply. I thought it might have been something Melheux said, until you began asking me those unexpected questions. And then I remembered how that man stared at you as you rushed from the shop."

Bitterness knotted Dulcie's stomach. "What, with gloating and disdain? He wrote to my father, you know, or at least, his uncle did. Threatened to reveal to all the world how Lord Milne's depraved son had debauched his innocent nephew. Unless, of course, the earl made him just restitution."

Dulcie stared down at his white-knuckled hands, clenching the edge of the mantelpiece. He could hardly bear to remember the disappointment on his father's face that day. An expression that appeared all too often in the ensuing years, whenever the dubious exploits of his painfully wayward son were thrown in his face.

"I doubt Copeland participated willingly in such a scheme," Benedict said as his hands came to rest on Dulcie's shoulders. "Mr. Newman confided to me that his new apprentice had his life blighted by an early lost love."

"And you imagine me in such a role?" Dulcie gave a hollow laugh.

Benedict gave him a shake. "Well, if he did know what his uncle was about, I'm certain he long since regrets it. All I saw in his face was longing, and the deepest of sorrows. As if he were a grieving Achilles, and you his beloved Patroclos, lost to him forever."

Behind him, Benedict took a deep breath. "The way I must have looked, when I heard you were never to return to school.

214

The way I did look, all these months since my return to London, whenever I caught sight of you."

Dulcie spun and had to catch his breath at the naked emotion on Benedict's face. Longing, yes, tempered by sorrow— for all the years that they had lost? But also something shockingly expectant, vulnerably open. Something that declared he was willing to risk the sting of rejection, because the anticipated reward would be so very great.

The most frightening feeling of all.

Hope.

"Lord, how did you find the courage to say such a thing to me?" he whispered, stroking a thumb down the whiskers curving from Benedict's ear to his cheek. "You shame me by your willingness to show such vulnerability to my careless, hard-hearted self."

Benedict shuddered under his touch. But his words did not waver. "You are not unfeeling. You're simply afraid. As am I. But if you put yourself in my hands, Clair, I promise with all that I am that you'll be safe with me."

Lacing his hand behind Dulcie's neck, Benedict bent his head. "Let me?" he whispered.

Blood pounding in his brain, Dulcie nodded.

Then his head nearly exploded as Benedict's lips ignited against his.

CHAPTER 14

LORD, WHAT FOOLS THEY'D BEEN, allowing fear to keep them apart for nearly three months. Three long months since their lips had last met. And their hands, and their skin—

Dulcie unwound the cravat looped around Benedict's neck and tossed it beside the chaise longue, entranced by the achingly vulnerable dip between Benedict's collarbones peeking out from behind the single button of his shirt. What was that spot called? Benedict, who had studied anatomy as part of his artistic training, would surely know. He'd have to remember to ask him. Later. Much later. With a growl, he flicked open the single button, then lowered his head to trail his tongue over the shadowed depths of that skin.

At Benedict's moan of approval, Dulcie buried his nose in that divot as his fingers threaded through the waves of his hair, chasing the scent that had haunted him for months—a mixture of charcoal, the bitter orange of bergamot, and the musky tang of Benedict's sweat. He wanted to wallow in it now like a hippopotamus in the waters of the Nile, steeping until he'd never be free of its scent. If only a perfumer might bottle it for him, so he could keep it close after Benedict left him—

Hands on his arse pulled him tight against a hard thigh, forcing his brain away from the melancholy thought. The feel of Benedict's fingers, kneading the muscles of his own bottom. Benedict's lips, trembling as they gently nuzzled the cord of his throat. Benedict's cock, taut but mobile, twitching with life beside his own.

"I want to see you," Benedict whispered, his voice vibrating, husky and deep, in his ear. "Please."

Benedict's attentive artist's eyes, focused solely on him—how the thought sent the blood rushing to his cock. He pulled free of Benedict's arms to whip his linen over his head, then stood, hands on hips, allowing the other man to look his fill.

Benedict's face—the intent tilt of his lips, those dark, dark eyes that gazed at him, unblinking—Dulcie could almost blush under the fixed attention of such a gaze.

"Like what you see?" he asked, hoping Benedict did not hear the slight quaver behind the teasing tone. He added a seductive smile for good measure.

But Benedict would not hide what he felt. "Yes," he whispered, nothing remotely humorous in his tone, only bemusement, and wonder, and perhaps, even a touch of awe. "I could gaze at the perfection of that torso for days."

A man could grow used to listening to such a voice murmuring his praises.

Or begging to be their recipient.

Dulcie arched his back and cocked a hip. "Like to see more, would you?"

"Lord, yes." Benedict's hands fisted at his sides, as if he had to restrain himself from crossing the line from sight to touch. Enjoyed the tension of drawing out his own pleasure, did he? Dulcie would have to remember that when he had Benedict's prick in his hand.

"Please, Clair."

With a languorous smile, Dulcie leaned back on the chaise. Reaching down, he slowly drew off boots, then breeches, then smalls, taking as much time as he could at each task, his eyes fixed not on his garments but on Benedict's face. Watching as his eyes darkened, narrowed, listening as his breath caught when

Dulcie's prick came springing free. Was this how Bathsheba felt when King David's eyes chanced on her during her bath?

Dulcie drew in a deep breath and raised his arms over his head. Pointing his toes, drawing his muscles taut, he stretched his body over the chaise, nearly growling in satisfaction as Benedict's eyes traced up and down his length. How could he have not realized how thrilling it would be, to be completely exposed while his would-be lover remained fully dressed?

How long, though, could Benedict stand only to look?

"Drawing me in your mind, are you? I warrant your art would prove more successful if you used your other senses to trace my lines and sinews. Touch, perhaps?"

Dulcie turned on his side, then ran a hand along his own flank in open invitation.

Benedict dropped to his knees beside the chaise, reaching out a trembling hand. "God, Clair, how I want you. Need you. Tell me it's the same for you."

The vulnerability in Benedict's voice nearly made Dulcie flinch. Could he ever give himself completely over to Benedict the way he sensed Benedict was poised to give himself? Not just his body, but his mind, his very soul?

But what was the alternative? Allowing Benedict to prove him a coward?

Or, even worse, losing him entirely?

No.

Even so, it proved surprisingly difficult to utter a few simple words. His voice came out far softer than he intended when he finally said, "I need you, Pen. Please, come lie here with me."

Before he had even finished the words, Benedict curled his hands around Dulcie's neck and drew his head to his ear. "How brave you are, Clair. You steal the very breath from my lips."

And then those lips were on his again, his tongue probing, delving, devouring the overly sensitive flesh of Dulcie's mouth. After long, drugging moments, those lips shifted to Dulcie's neck, to nuzzle and nip with lips and teeth as hands wandered his bare skin, raising the tiny hairs all along Dulcie's body. Searching out all the spots that made him jerk, and moan, and tremble.

He pulled Benedict down atop him, too impatient to remove even his waistcoat. Its buttons rubbed his chest, raising his nipples to painful nubs. But he didn't mind, for Benedict soon moved to soothe each with a wicked, wicked tongue. Then Dulcie nearly arched right off the chaise—God, had the fellow had the temerity to bite him?

Dulcie groaned. He could not take much more of such devoted attention, not without crying in need. No, going slow would have to wait for another day. Reaching between them, he flicked at the buttons of Benedict's fall, fingers searching out the root of Benedict's desire.

He couldn't see it, not with all Benedict's clothes in the way, but he could feel it, hot and slick against his hand, the smooth head thrusting out from beneath the wrinkling foreskin.

"Yes, Clair, yes," Benedict whispered, his hips arching in need. "Touch me, make me spend."

"Make *us* spend," Dulcie answered, bringing his own hard length close against Benedict's. He clutched his fingers tight around them both, sliding and squeezing until he found a rhythm that made them both groan.

"Want you, Clair. So much."

Benedict's hands grasping his shoulders, the musk of his sweat and his imminent mettle, the heat of his cock rubbing, rubbing—Dulcie thought he might drown in the flood of sensations.

And then Benedict's entire body heaved, his breath catching for an instant as the cock in Dulcie's hand grew even harder. Benedict's head flew high, his face radiant as he chased his release.

"Pen," Dulcie cried as his lover shuddered and spurted

against their stomachs.

His hand slippery with Benedict's ejaculate, Dulcie squeezed once, again, and then yes, his balls tightening, his back arching, he, too, reached for the bliss—

Merciful heavens. Dulcie closed his eyes, panting, waiting for his senses to drift back into his body. Such relief, to finally spend with another, after so many months alone. He'd certainly never felt such pleasure from his own hand, such shuddering, overwhelming waves of bodily satisfaction.

And had he ever felt such peace in the aftermath? Even with waistcoat buttons digging painfully into his chest, and the chaise's bolster cushion about to slide out from under his arse, he had no desire to get up and rush off to the next good thing. Because this thing, this *person* right here in his arms, was a very, very good thing indeed.

He laughed as he ruffled his fingers through Benedict's dark hair, luxuriating in the softness of its waves. The poor boy would soon get a crick in his neck, lying with his cheek pressed to Dulcie's chest that way. And his fine linen shirt, damp, no doubt, and reeking of their combined spend...

"Did I satisfy you, sir?" Dulcie whispered, greedy for Benedict's praise.

Benedict raised his head from Dulcie's chest, his eyes glassy, a peculiar smile flitting about his lips. "It's not how I imagined it. Not at all."

"What?" Dulcie exclaimed before he could hide his dismay. But he quickly assumed a teasing tone. "Did you not take pleasure in the act? I am mortified!"

Benedict reached out a hand and drew it across Dulcie's cheek. "No, Clair, no. It's only that I don't think I've ever even imagined such a physically pleasurable sensation in my entire life. Or felt such a welling of emotion in my heart. This, you—it means the world to me, don't you see?"

Something in Dulcie's chest gave a small quiver. Whenever

any other man had begun to prattle on about his finer feelings, Dulcie had always shrugged them off, stifled by the demands they made on him, the expectation that they must be returned in kind. Oh, Dulcie could always find some sweet words to mumble in response, but he only used them to get what *he* wanted from the other, not to reveal anything deep or true of his own self. But somehow, the earnestness of Benedict's declaration did not fill him with indifference or disgust, but with something far different. A tentative, unfamiliar lightness at his very core.

Lord help him, was he actually developing a sentimental streak at the ripe old age of three-and-thirty? If he began spilling his budget, burbling endearments to this man in his arms, now that would truly be mortifying!

He closed his eyes, abashed by the intensity shining in Benedict's.

But instead of pressing him to say something equally revealing, Benedict just laid his head back on Dulcie's chest. "What saint did you invoke, to bring such a cataclysm about? I'll have to remember to pray to him myself next time."

"Next time? There will be a next time, then?" Dulcie asked, hating the way his jaw clenched with uncertainty.

The muscles of Benedict's face shaped into a smile against his bare chest. "I'd like that, if you would."

"Yes. Yes, I would."

His entire body softened in relief. Benedict, who was lying half atop him still, must have noticed. But he didn't laugh, or even mention Dulcie's ridiculous reaction. He only hummed a tuneless lullaby as he combed soothing fingers through the sparse curls on Dulcie's chest.

He remembered, then, whenever something important or upsetting happened when they were at school, Benedict had always needed time and space to come to terms with it. Usually by himself, alone in the quiet of his own mind. He still obviously had the same need as an adult. But that he felt safe enough with Dulcie to retreat to that space while lying in his arms—it said far more about his feelings than any sentimental words would ever reveal.

Dulcie had almost fallen asleep when Benedict finally spoke. "I know you don't like it, Clair. To talk about what you feel, I mean. But as long as you don't hide from me, or pretend to be someone you're not, I don't need any fine speeches or florid pronouncements. Just never disparage my own feelings, even if you can't understand them. Because I feel so much, so much for you, Clair. And I think I would die if you ever ridiculed me because of it."

With a shaking hand, Dulcie stroked down the back of the vulnerable head burrowing into his neck. "I'll try," he said, shocked by the earnestness of his own words. "I'll try my damnedest not to hide from you. Or to hurt you."

Benedict's hand stroked his side whiskers in silent acknowledgment.

"Promise me the same?" he whispered across Benedict's curls.

"I swear."

Dulcie sighed, and slipped back into sleep.

"Have you heard Henry Bone's opened his rooms for an exhibition of those Elizabethan enamel miniatures he's been working on all these years?"

"Haughty Queen Bess, and her lovely cousin Mary Stuart, and the courtiers who swanned about each of them—lord, you wouldn't catch me kowtowing to a mere female, not even if she were the queen."

"But will you kowtow to Bone's genius? I hear that's the real price of admission."

Benedict let the hum of Clair's chatter with his fellow members of the British Institution eddy over him, a comforting background to his own far more enjoyable musings. He would have far preferred lazing in bed all day with his new lover, as he and Clair had done every day now for nearly a week, than rushing out into company. But he wasn't so foolish as to imagine he could keep Clair forever to himself. Not if he wished his new lover to remain content.

Benedict might prefer to spend time alone, or closeted with one special person, but Clair, for whom sociability was as necessary as water, would soon grow restless if he did not venture out into company. Clair might claim to prefer being alone with Benedict, but he'd not protested overmuch when Benedict had suggested a visit to the British Institution this morning. Benedict himself hardly expected catching up on the gossip of the few men of Clair's artistic set who still remained in town would do anything to advance the cause of a national art museum, or Clair's own quest to be named a Director of the Institution's Board, but the suggestion had been more than enough excuse to persuade Clair. Socializing might not be Benedict's greatest enjoyment, but he'd do almost anything to make his lover happy. Even spending time in this stuffy room surrounded by men who thought their wealth and lineage made their aesthetic judgments more sound than those of an actual artist.

But even if he'd chosen to accompany Clair here, he needn't participate in the conversation between Clair, George Norton, Sir Charles Long, and several other of Clair's fellow art connoisseurs. He could still retreat to the privacy of his own mind, daydreaming of lips and hands and nose and tongue exploring every inch of Clair's elegant body, discovering each spot that drove him mad with longing. Of visiting each spot, one after another, over and over, until his lusty angel's flashing blue eyes tipped back into his head and he shouted with exultation as he spent in Benedict's arms.

Indeed, a part of Benedict could hardly believe the past week hadn't all been just a dream, fever-visions inspired by his long-unrequited want for a Clair forever out of reach. Yet whenever his sense of reality faltered, he only had to glance at his lover to be reassured. Others might not be able to see it, but Benedict saw well-deep contentment in the contained animation of Clair's face, the greater ease with which he held his body. Hard not to take pride in bringing such peace to the ever-restless Clair.

A bustle from the library door, though, too soon shattered Benedict's own contentment.

"Leverett!" George Norton jumped to his feet. "I thought you were still out of the country!"

Benedict's entire body stiffened as Lattimer Leverett strolled into the British Institution library. Norton, he saw, looked as little pleased by the sight of the new arrival as did Benedict. Had the young man, too, discovered how cruel the fellow could be?

Benedict held back a grimace as Leverett jerked off his gloves and tossed them with little care to a footman. "Don't be so womanish, Norton. I told you I'd only remain in Antwerp until the end of the sale."

"The sale of Monsieur Stier's pictures? Oh, how I envy you," Clair exclaimed as he gestured to Leverett to join them. "So many van Dycks and Rubens, all in one room!"

Clair couldn't cut the fellow dead, not in a club they both belonged to. But it still stung, his overly warm greeting. Why did his lover have to be so welcoming, especially after Benedict had hinted at how poorly Leverett had once treated him?

But perhaps he'd forgotten their conversation back in Lincolnshire. Clair did tend to live in the moment.

"Please tell me it was an Englishman who purchased Rubens' famed *Chapeau de Puille*," Clair said with a glance in Benedict's direction. "I'd love to see that work on British soil."

In a soon-to-be established national art museum, perhaps? In spite of his unease in Leverett's presence, Benedict couldn't help smiling at the idea. Clair might focus on the present, rather than the past or the future, but he did not forget Benedict's new place in that suddenly brighter now.

"One Mr. Smith, reportedly of London, was the purchaser," Leverett answered as he pulled a chair close to Clair's. "But it is rumored he bought it on speculation, and will now dispose of it to the best bidder in any country."

"I heard that it had been purchased on behalf of Mrs. Coutts, and was immediately shipped to London," Benedict said, sitting up straighter in his seat. Foolish, that urge to jump up and push Leverett from his chair to take up guard beside Clair.

"A woman? I believe you are mistaken." Leverett's cold eyes rested for a quick moment on Benedict, then shifted away to the older man beside him. "But what news from the King, Sir Charles? Has he accepted Lord Leicester's offer of his paintings to serve as the foundation for an English art museum?"

"Leicester made a formal offer?" Dulcie exclaimed. "But his collection only includes paintings by Englishmen."

"Yes, he did offer," Sir Charles answered. "But Liverpool and I persuaded His Majesty to refuse. Despite what certain Royal Academicians may argue, a gallery need not exclude foreign painters to be truly national."

"And it need not include such eccentric works as Hogarth's modern moral subjects, or Mr. Turner's quasi-historical landscapes, either, even if they were created by Englishmen," Leverett said with a delicate shudder. "If we must attempt to improve the taste of the public by means of a government-funded art museum, it should at least cultivate a proper appreciation for the highest genres."

"And will you, in turn, develop an appreciation for the low?" Clair asked, crossing a leg over his knee. "Visit the waxworks in Fleet Street, or the Panoramas in Leicester Square, and learn what you can from them?"

"Is that how you've been spending your time of late, Dulcie? Mixing with the masses?" He cast a dubious glance at Benedict, then gave an audible sniff, as if Benedict's social standing were far lower than his own. "Instead of summering in the country as is your usual wont? And here I thought you intended to make good on your promise to finally take on a leg-shackle."

"A leg-shackle?" Clair's swinging foot suddenly went still.

"Yes, a leg-shackle," Leverett continued, with a smile that did not reach his eyes. "Did you not wager, in front of nearly every gentleman here today, that you'd steal Adler's granddaughter and her dowry right out from under Pennington's very nose? And Norton, did he not vow only a few days later that he would wed and bed her before Michaelmas?"

What a look of triumph on Leverett's face! The damned blackguard obviously expected his revelation to upset Benedict.

As did everyone else in the room, if the evidence of their quick glances in his direction were any indication. Even Clair's blue eyes jerked to his for an instant before immediately shying away.

But discovering that Clair had been flitting about Polly Adler not because he wished to scuttle Benedict's museum plan, or to steal Adler's paintings for himself, but simply because he'd been goaded into a bet—the revelation nearly made him smile. How like the silly scoundrel, to accept such a ridiculous wager. And then, if Benedict had the right of it, to forget all about it as he hared off to Lincolnshire in pursuit not of Polly Adler, but of Benedict.

He stifled the affectionate laugh that burbled up inside him.

With Michaelmas only a month away, Clair had little to no chance of winning such an ill-considered wager. Not that Benedict believed he had any real intention of trying now, even if he had been at all in earnest when the bet was first made.

He only hoped the sum Clair had wagered would not put

too big a dent in his finances. He'd not enjoy begging his father for additional funds.

When Benedict roused from his internal musings, he found Leverett staring at him with narrowed eyes, waiting with eagerness for some angry outburst. But Benedict would not give the lout the satisfaction. He leaned back in his chair, trying to match Clair's nonchalant air.

"Sir Charles, have you heard anything from Beaumont?" George Norton, kind boy, attempted to divert the conversation. "Is it true he has secured Michelangelo's exquisite group in marble of the *Virgin*—"

"But instead of courting the chit, Dulcie's here, whiling away the summer in town," Leverett continued, raising his voice over Norton's. "Unless he has already secured her hand, and is keeping their agreement a secret, so as to draw out the suspense? Or perhaps to give himself the chance to conduct another clandestine romance with a pretty chit in the interim?"

"A clandestine romance! How exciting you make life sound, Leverett." Dulcie flicked at the cuff of his sleeve with admirable indifference, though a slight tightening of his lips told Benedict his temper was on the rise. "Tell me, with whom do you suspect me of trysting? Sarah Siddons? Angelica Catalini? The Princess Sophia?"

The men in the room gasped. Damn it, Clair must be truly furious, to bandy about the name of the king's sister so.

"No lady quite so exalted, I'm afraid," Leverett said, with a cruel smile in Benedict's direction.

This was getting out of hand. Could he not put a stop to it? Perhaps, if he took a page out of Dulcie's book and put on a good show—

Rising from his chair, he allowed both scorn and hurt to play over his features. "You must excuse me, Lord Dulcie. I have no wish to distract you from either your courtship of Miss Adler or any other romantic partner. Or to interfere with your wager with

227

this gentleman. Bid you good day, sirs."

After making his stiffest bow, Benedict strode from the room.

There. Rousting Benedict from the field should make Leverett pull back his claws.

Benedict fetched his gloves and hat from the British Institution's footman, then set off down Pall Mall, an unfamiliar spring in his step. He wouldn't like to make a practice of it, but pretending to feel something he did not could be quite entertaining. No wonder Clair found it so endlessly amusing.

Before he'd even reached Piccadilly, the pound of booted feet on pavement and the hoarse shout of his name drew him up short. He turned and spied Clair, hair charmingly wind-blown, racing up St. James' Street in his wake.

"Benedict, stop." Clair huffed as he struggled to catch his breath. "Polly— Leverett— you must know I have not the least intention of— Not after we—"

"Clair, this is hardly the place," Benedict said, suppressing his smile as he cast his eyes towards the bow-front window of White's Club. Had his attempts to stop Leverett's taunts had the unintended consequence of making Clair worry?

"But Pen, you must understand—"

Benedict pulled Clair down an alley, where they would be out of view of the bustling London crowds. "You utterly ridiculous man," he said, then pushed him against a rough wall and pressed his lips to his.

Benedict kissed him until Clair finally begin to relax in his arms.

"You're not upset with me, then?" Clair asked, the blue of his eyes nearly swallowed by his desire-blasted pupils.

Benedict took a step back and searched for his best schoolmaster voice. "Did you begin courting Polly because you wanted Adler's paintings?

Clair shook his head.

"Or because you wished to prevent Adler from donating

them to a national museum?"

"Certainly not!"

"And do you still intend to court Polly?"

This brought a scowl to Clair's handsome face. "How could you even think such a thing?"

Benedict raised his eyebrows. "Do you? A simple 'yes' or 'no' will do."

"Of course not," Clair answered with a petulant toss of his head. "I never really intended to in the first place, in spite of my father's urging. But Leverett would goad me so."

"Well, I must say, I don't think very highly of your good sense, entering into a wager with Leverett, of all people. And I don't believe Polly will enjoy discovering she's the subject of gossip among the artistic set."

"But still, you're not so very angry with me?" Clair wheedled, laying a hand on Benedict's arm.

Benedict laughed. "How could I be angry, when you're the one who accepted that wager, then unthinkingly did everything in your power to lose it? The bet wasn't your idea, was it?"

Clair shook his head again, sending his golden curls flying. "Leverett's, entirely. Your return to London distracted me, which annoyed him for some reason I cannot begin to fathom."

Benedict, though, was beginning to suspect. "And he thought such a wager would set us at odds. But you, you preening peacock, accepted it because you wanted some excuse to draw my attention, to throw yourself into my path."

Clair's mouth opened in quick denial, but after a moment's consideration, drifted closed. And then, a corner turned up in charmingly rueful admission. "How can you see so clearly inside me? Better than I can even see myself?"

Benedict shrugged, his eyes fixed on his boots. "Anyone who looked closely would see."

Clair shook his head. "No. No one else sees what you do, Pen. No one has your eyes, or your way of viewing the world.

I've never met anyone quite like you. I only hope you won't run screaming when you finally see down to the depths of my rather muddy soul."

It almost blinded him, the sheer wonder blazing across Clair's face. Benedict swallowed against the rise of feeling that threatened to steal all of his words.

"That's a risk you'll just have to take, won't you, my lord?" he finally managed to say.

"Indeed. A risk only a fool would refuse, knowing the rewards to be reaped by the victor." Clair's glove hand reached out and grazed Benedict's cheek. "Now, shall we return to Pennington House, so I may claim my prize?"

Benedict could only bite his lip and nod.

As they strolled back up St. James, and then across Piccadilly, to the sounds of Clair's jaunty whistle, Benedict made a silent vow. Each and every time he paid homage to Clair's body, he'd make it more inventive, more intense, more memorable than the last.

Anything to keep that look of near-reverence in his lover's eyes.

CHAPTER 15

MID-MORNING SUN BLAZED THROUGH the windows of Benedict's studio, dancing like diadems over the curls atop Clair's head. And the ones on his bare chest, too. Benedict sighed, longing to swirl his fingers through that small patch on Clair's sternum as his lover reclined, breeched and booted but shirtless, on the settee like a true Sybarite. But since the night they'd become lovers, he'd had the devil of a time convincing Clair to devote any of their hours alone to anything but bedsport—or wallsport, tablesport, or sport in locations Benedict had never before associated with frigging, frotting, or tossing another off. Clair claimed Benedict was the one with imagination, but Clair's sensual inventiveness had nearly driven him to distraction this past week.

Benedict's mind had always been far more important to him than his body. With other lovers, the sexual act had been a pleasure, yes, even occasionally a joy, but not a craving that drove him all his waking hours. He could go months, years even, without sating that particular hunger. But lord, with Clair, neither of them could seem to allow even a moment to pass without touching, an hour without kissing, a day without making the other shudder and spend.

Still, he couldn't allow this newly-awakened lust to divert him from his art. Especially not when he was this close to finishing Clair's portrait. Both of Clair's portraits.

Still, with his demon-angel lounging there, temptation incarnate . . .

"Is it true, what you said that night after we visited the Sketching Society?" Benedict took care to keep his eyes focused on his painting as he posed his question. "Or did you just say it to taunt me?"

"Everything I said that night was meant to taunt you," Clair answered with a knowing chuckle. "To which taunt in particular do you refer?"

"To your Parthian shot. I believe your precise words were, 'I never allow any man to fuck me. Not even one as comely as you, Benedict Pennington.'"

"Ah, that stung, did it? I'm very glad to hear it."

Benedict shook his head. How could a man swagger while lying down?

"But is it true?" Benedict continued, head bent to his palette, swirling red and white together to match the shade of Clair's flesh. "You don't take pleasure in playing at all fours?"

"Oh, I'd love to have you on all fours in front of me," Clair answered, languorously stretching his arms over his head. "But allowing a cock to be shoved in an orifice God never intended to be breached? I think not."

"Put your arms back down," Benedict ordered, forcing his eyes away from the tempting whorls of hair revealed by Clair's movement. "How can I finish if you keep shifting about?"

"But you don't really need me here to pose any longer, do you? More muse than model now, I am. And I believe this pose is more likely to inspire." With a sly smile, Clair settled his hands behind his neck and crossed a booted foot over the other. A position that drew even more attention to his slim chest, as he well knew.

"Perhaps one day you'll paint me without any clothing at all," he said, his eyes glinting with heat.

Benedict ducked his head to hide the blush he felt creeping

over his cheeks. Some day, indeed.

He set down his brush and palette and strode to the settee. With one hand, he batted Clair's foot down, then used the other to pull his arms back into the correct position.

"One would hardly guess you prefer taking the active role during the act, the way you incite me to manhandle you so."

"But I never said I prefer to take *any* role during the act," Clair exclaimed, jerking upright without his usual grace. "If, by 'the act,' you refer to fucking. When the mere sight of a lady's bower of bliss makes me shudder, what makes you think I'd find dipping my wick in some fellow's shithole any more appealing?"

Benedict took a step back, his eyes widening. Clair disdained buggery altogether? And he, quiet, contained Benedict Pennington, had more in the way of sexual experience than the adventurous Lord Dulcie?

At his lover's frown, Benedict kneeled on the rug beside him. "Is it that you've never attempted it? Or that you've tried, and know that it gives you no pleasure?"

"Must we truly discuss this?"

Benedict arched his eyebrows.

Clair raised his own eyes to the ceiling as if begging the gods to have pity on his long-suffering self. But when Benedict remained determinedly silent in the face of his dramatics, he cursed quietly under his breath for a few moments, then turned his eyes back to Benedict's. No, his lover was no coward.

"Yes, Pen, certainly I've tried it. And from both ends, as it were. Neither gave me the least bit of pleasure." His hand skimmed Benedict's cheek. "Will it be a problem? If I can't share such a thing with you?"

Benedict's fingers covered Clair's and gave them a squeeze. "You must know I'd never ask you to do something you disliked."

"But, much to my own surprise, I find I wish to please *you*, Pen." Clair chuckled. "Almost as much as I wish to please myself.

And I surmise that inventive brain of yours has been dreaming of all sorts of salacious acts. Perhaps if there are a few that do not include playing at buggeranto, you'll share them with me?"

Benedict smiled. "Some day, perhaps," he said as he pushed up off the floor.

"What better time than the present?" Clair set both hands on Benedict's shoulders, guiding him back down.

Benedict's breath caught as his hands, searching for balance, lighted against Clair's well-muscled thighs. Even beneath the superfine of his breeches, Benedict could feel them flex and tense beneath his fingers.

"But the painting—"

"Damn the painting. It's been nearly a day since I've had your cock in my hand."

Said appendage leaped to attention at Clair's words, even as something in Benedict's chest tightened. He'd likely only be able to keep Clair's attention for a few short months at most, until Parliament convened again in the winter and the Season once again drew his lover into its social whirl. Perhaps even less than that, if Clair decided London in autumn grew tiresome, and accepted one of the many invitations he'd received to hunting and house parties in the countryside. After he left, Benedict would always have his art to console him. Better to make hay while the sun of this beautiful, infuriating man deigned to shine so brightly in his vicinity.

Gliding his hands with teasing slowness up Clair's thighs, Benedict said, "Well, the Bible does say that He becometh poor that dealeth with a slack hand: but the hand of the diligent maketh rich."

A bark of laughter split the air. "Diligent hand! And people say I am irreverent. . . "

Yes, there it was, that open, delighted smile Clair so seldom showed to the world. Benedict rubbed his cheek against Clair's thigh, breathing deep of his rising arousal.

"Will you reveal my secret? For I must admit, I revere nothing more than your transcendent body. So much so that I can't go another minute without worshiping you with my mouth."

"Your mouth?" Clair's cheeks pinked. "You wish to put my cock in your mouth?"

Benedict sat back on his heels. Had he managed to disconcert the broad-minded Lord Dulcie again? No, Clair's expression revealed more dismay than embarrassment.

"You don't enjoy that either?" Benedict asked, struggling to keep the disappointment from his voice. Frigging and frotting were nothing to sneer at, but pleasuring a partner with his mouth—even the thought of it sent an electric jolt from his sack to his spine.

Clair gave a delicate shudder. "Doesn't sound very sanitary, does it?"

"Would you ask that I clean my teeth first?" he asked, moving to rise. "I'd be happy to, if it would set your mind at ease."

"No!" The look of horror on Clair's face would have been comical, if only their situation weren't so fraught. Of what was he afraid?

Benedict laid a hand on his arm and squeezed.

Clair bowed his head and sighed. "My concern wasn't about you, but about myself."

Benedict settled back on his knees with a grunt. Clair worried that *Ben* would find him less appealing if they engaged in such an act?

"This from the man who spent a good part of the evening in the bath?" he joked, attempting to lighten the moment. "Why, has the world ever seen such an overly fastidious fellow?"

Clair's hands moved as if to tug on a shirt cuff, as he so often did when he wished to appear unperturbed. But when he found he wasn't wearing any linen, he frowned and crossed his arms over his chest.

"Pen, I've never even considered such a thing. At least, not with a man of equal rank," he said at last. "Would you not find it degrading to be used so?"

Benedict sat back on his heels, hiding his face behind a fall of hair. He knew many educated men, having read Latin or Greek texts in which such acts were viewed as debasing for both parties involved—*os impurum*, filthy, impure mouth—refused to allow mouth and cock to ever meet. Some obscenely comic verse even went so far as to suggest the act left one with breath so foul it was nearly toxic, a claim as false as it was ridiculous.

But Clair's concern was all for Benedict, not for himself. The realization sent a flood of joy coursing throughout his body.

He lifted his face so that his lover could see the truth of his words. "Not degrading, Clair. Exalting."

Clair's own eyes widened, his breath coming in short, sharp bursts. But he said not a word.

Benedict took heart from his unusual silence. Slowly, so as not to startle him, he slid his hand up to the buttons on Clair's breeches. "Please? May I?"

"Go to it, man," Clair said, his brash words belied by the trembling of his hands.

Benedict undid Clair's falls with eager, fumbling fingers, then paused to press his nose against his smalls. Yes, there was the lemon of the soap he favored, and there, a hint of saddle leather that a horseman could never quite wash away. And, there, beneath them both, the musk of Clair's arousal, briny, keen, electrifying.

With a sudden, sharp jerk, Benedict yanked breeches and smalls down until they hung over the tops of Clair's boots. Yes, those boots would have to go, otherwise, he'd not be able to fit his body between Clair's thighs, nor reach the nest of golden curls that held his prize. Hands on his lover's hips, he shoved Clair back onto the settee, then jerked off his boots and tossed them aside. Freeing one foot from breeches and smalls, he left both to hang off the other, too eager to get his lips on the loadstar of his lust to have a care for Lord Dulcie's fine tailoring.

A hand on each muscular thigh, he shoved Clair's legs wide. His lover grunted, an inelegant sound he'd never thought to hear escape the imperturbable Clair's lips.

During their previous trysts, he'd seemed to like it when Benedict took the more active part. Still, that need not mean he enjoyed being mauled like a ravening beast.

But no. Pupils blown-wide, nipples pebbled, cock straining against his lightly furred stomach—Clair's grunt had been one of pleasure, not of dismay.

Benedict nearly groaned himself at the sight of Clair laid so achingly bare. He kneed his way between those outstretched legs, then lowered his lips to the inside of a thigh, licking and nipping as the muscles tensed and rose beneath him.

The salty tang in his mouth, the rich smells in his nose—lord, he could spend hours, no, days rummaging the heavens between Clair's outstretched legs.

But his lover's cock, slim, elegant even when suffused with blood, could no longer be ignored. Grabbing hold of his hips, Benedict yanked Clair's body to the very edge of the settee.

His eyes fixed on Clair's, he lowered his mouth to take the tip between his lips.

The way Clair's neck arched at the first lick, the way his entire torso lifted at the first suck—no, not even Benedict's most arousing fantasies had prepared him for such a sight.

With a muted groan, he slid his mouth down the shaft. Rigid yet yielding, solid, and hot, and so very *alive*, all the vibrancy of Clair's personality distilled. He let his fingers stroke down, combing through the curls of hair atop Clair's thighs, then dragged them up again, raking across the smooth skin of his hips and the globes of his arse with his nails. Teasing his lips over Clair's length, he stopped just long enough to tongue the tip, then reeled him back in, slowly, so slowly, until the head lodged at the back of his throat. His lips stretched, throbbing with need, every nerve in his mouth afire.

He buried his nose in Clair's groin, breathing in his musk, and moaned as the muscles of Clair's abdomen jumped. His lover moaned, too, as Benedict pulled back once again and swirled his tongue about the salty tip. A breeze whispering through the curtains tickled the back of his neck, urging him forward once again. He gloried as Clair's breath caught, just as his cock lodged at the top of Benedict's throat. Lord, had he ever felt as connected to another human being as he did to Clair at this moment?

From the corner of his eye, he caught sight of Clair's hand, his fingers clenching and releasing, clenching and releasing, as if he desperately needed to grab hold of something, someone, but was too afraid to reach out and take what he needed.

Benedict grasped that hand, and then the other, moving both to the back of his own head. "Fuck my mouth, Clair," he whispered in a voice so husky he barely recognized it. "Let me drink you down."

With a feral moan, Clair's hands tightened, his hips lifting and falling, lifting and falling, filling Benedict's mouth, filling Benedict's soul.

He moaned his own pleasure as, with one final thrust, Clair flooded his mouth with seed. The sight of Clair's face, tight with rapture, sent Ben quickly tumbling in his wake, spending in his breeches like the greenest of lads.

They lay there together for long, quiet minutes, Benedict's head resting atop one of Clair's thighs, Clair's fingers tracing languid furrows through Benedict's hair.

So this must be what it felt like to fly with the seraphim, filled to overflowing with fire and exultation and joy.

The scrape of a door behind him yanked him from the warmth of his reverie. Damnation! Had he not told the servants to keep away?

By the time he had scrambled to his feet, though, whoever had had the temerity to interrupt them had disappeared.

"Clair? Who was it?" He swallowed, hard. Clair had been facing the door, his naked body on full display. Bloody hell. Had he soothed his lover over a past blackmailer only to lead him into the snare of another?

But Clair only shot him an unconcerned smile as he moved about the room collecting his abandoned garments. "Nobody to concern yourself over, dear boy. Just the housekeeper's cat. You see, even the beasts of the fields cannot wait to see my handsome portrait. Which you will never complete, not if I remain here distracting you so."

"But Clair—"

His lover stifled his protest with his own lips, capturing Benedict's mouth with a kiss of uncharacteristic tenderness. "Hush. I'm off to Milne House, to steal away a bottle of father's finest champagne. We will need something effervescent with which to celebrate, after you've put the finishing touches on the painting."

Before Benedict could say another word, Clair bent a knee to retrieve his rumpled cravat, then padded, barefoot, out the door.

The door that Benedict was certain he'd closed behind him earlier in the morning.

What cat could *pull* open a door?

On any other day, being asked to wait in the picture gallery of Julius Adler's London townhouse for Miss Adler to receive him would have struck Dulcie as a blessing. The chance to contemplate, uninterrupted, several of the world's finest paintings, and worship at the shrine of Art—was not that proper object for which civilized man was created?

Yet the events of earlier this morning—the unimaginable eroticism of what Benedict had done to his body; the unexpected emotional connection that had followed in its wake; the antipathy and pity in Polly Adler's eyes as she spied them entwined together on the settee in Benedict's studio—no, today not even the agony of Coreggio's Christ in the garden, nor the innocent voluptuous delight of a young Apollo learning to play on the pipes, could call forth the most intense desires of his soul.

Today, all those desires had but one focus: protecting Benedict Pennington from harm.

"Viscount Dulcie! How kind of you to call. I hope I did not keep you waiting overlong."

A smiling Polly Adler strode across the room and held out a welcoming hand. Whatever distaste she had felt at discovering Dulcie and Benedict together, Dulcie with not a stitch of clothing about him, she now kept carefully hidden.

Surely she was too innocent to understand what she had seen. Unless her continental travels had somehow opened her eyes to practices of which most Englishwomen would never speak?

"My dear Miss Adler!" he said as he bowed over her hand. The odor of oil and turpentine clung to it, just as it did to Benedict's. She still must be finding time to dabble with her oils, despite her grandfather's displeasure. "How sly you were, returning to town days before you originally planned. Why did you not send word? If I had but known, I would have sent all the flowers in Covent Garden Market to celebrate your homecoming. But I'm afraid you must settle for this humble songbook, which at least has the grace to share your name."

Dulcie handed over the copy of *Polyhymnia, or Select Airs* he had dashed over to the bookseller on Oxford Street to procure for her before tearing off to Adler's Pall Mall townhouse. A poor gift to one whose true passion lay in the visual, not the vocal, arts, but the just-published volume had been the best he could do on such short notice.

"Thank you, my lord." Color flushed her face, more from embarrassment than from pleasure at his gift. "I wonder if I might ask—"

"Your grandfather did mention he enjoys listening to you sing," Dulcie interrupted. Distract, divert, evade—his forte.

"Grandfather would prefer I do almost anything besides paint," she replied with a dampening frown.

"Still, perhaps it may contain one or two songs to your liking? I am available as a partner for duets, whenever you may find yourself in a musical frame of mind."

Miss Adler lowered her head to hide an amused smile. Yes, he teetered on the edge between charm and babble. Still, better to be regarded as a fribble than to be charged as a deviant. "Your instrument is in the drawing room, is it not? I am no virtuoso, but I dare say I can pick out a tune or two."

"Lord Dulcie." Miss Adler took a deep breath, then gestured towards a pair of chairs in the middle of the picture gallery. "I do not think you came here today to entice me into singing with you. You were worried, weren't you?"

"Worried that you had forgotten me during your weeks in Kent?" Even he felt the strain of the false smile in the muscles of his cheeks.

But Miss Adler did not smile in return. "I did wish to forget. But after what I saw this morning—"

"Yes, it was a particularly lovely morning. Far more temperate than one is accustomed to finding late summer—"

"Please, my lord. This is difficult enough for me as it is, without your continual interruptions. Oh!" Her hand flew to her mouth, as if she'd shocked herself with the rudeness of her words.

Perhaps it would be better to get it all out on the table. He waved a careless hand. "Pray excuse my incivility. You wished to say?"

"I wished to ask you—to enquire—no, to discuss with you —" The poor girl's face blushed as scarlet as an officer's regimentals.

Perhaps they could speak around the issue, without ever naming it directly. "I believe I can hazard a guess as to what you wish to discuss. You wish me to cease my courtship."

But instead of agreeing, she shook her head with such violence, a few pins fell from her coiffure. "No, no indeed, my lord. That is not what I wish. But I do have a . . . A counterproposal, if you will."

"A counterproposal? You intrigue me, dear girl." Was it to be blackmail, then? He could hardly imagine a genteel young woman stooping to such a thing.

But then, he'd not imagined Copeland could ever be persuaded to betray him either.

Dulcie waved a careless hand before lowering himself into the chair beside hers. "Please, do proceed."

Polly took a moment to gather herself before leaning forward, her elbows balancing on her knees in an almost masculine manner. "Let me begin by assuring you that I have no intention of revealing to anyone what I witnessed earlier today."

"A simple embrace between a painter and his model?" Dulcie crossed his legs and leaned back in his chair. "Hardly worth noting, to be certain."

Miss Adler's eyebrow rose even higher this time. "A simple embrace? With one party completely unclothed?"

"Yes, it is rather eccentric to model for one's portrait as naked as a needle." Dulcie relaxed into his chair and spread his hands wide. "But you should know by now I am not one to conform to convention."

"No, nor is Mr. Pennington. I simply did not realize that you both snubbed your nose at the same *particular* convention. A convention most would regard as sacrosanct."

Dulcie widened his eyes in theatrical display. "My dear girl! I know those of an artistic temperament are prone to flights of imagination, but surely—"

"Lord Dulcie. Do not treat me as if I were a child," Polly interrupted. "I may have been educated in a convent, but I am not as innocent as all that. I know *precisely* what I saw."

Dulcie waved a dismissive hand. "A bit of affection between friends."

"Say rather, an act for which you both could be hanged."

Dulcie's stomach churned. "What, do you imagine us conducting occult rituals in poor Benedict's studio? Sacrificing innocents on a pyre of canvas and turpentine?"

"Your caution, I see, will not allow you to give voice to the truth. So I fear I must speak plainly." Her eyes turned away from his, fixing on the hands turning restlessly in her lap. She took a deep breath, then another.

"You see, I am well aware that relations of the bodily sort can be engaged in by members of the same sex, as well as with those of the opposite. And that some gentlemen have a decided preference for such acts, and such unconventional partners."

Dulcie sprang to his feet. "My dear Miss Adler! You have entirely mistaken—"

"And not just gentlemen," she interrupted, her voice wavering. "Some ladies, too. Do you take my meaning, sir?"

Dulcie struggled to keep his jaw from dropping. What was he meant to infer from such a statement? That Polyhymnia Adler was of a Sapphic inclination? He sank back into his seat.

"If that is indeed true," he asked after a long pause, "why would you wish to discuss such things with me?"

Miss Adler leaned forward, a hand clasping his arm. "I have often thought it would be an event to be devoutly wished, for a woman of such a nature to meet with a similar man."

"Indeed? And will you share the reasoning behind such an odd wish?"

"Because then they might wed, and keep the eyes of the world from prying into their intimate affairs."

Ah, a glimmer of understanding at last lit his brain. "Leaving each free to pursue their own interests?"

A smile spread over her face. "You do take my meaning, my lord. I, for one, would wish for a husband not intent on burdening me with babes. One who would leave me free to pursue my art."

"You do not long for motherhood?"

"No. A child would only distract me from my art. But I understand that if I wish to secure a husband acceptable to my grandfather, I may have to be flexible upon this point. I would consent to do my duty if an heir were absolutely required. But nothing further."

"And in turn, you would not mind if your husband entertained himself with his own friends and pastimes?"

"I would not. Especially since we share a friend in common. You see, Benedict Pennington has been my champion these many months, helping me convince my grandfather to tolerate my 'dabbling' as he likes to call it. I would not wish any harm to come to him. And if I can promote his interests in any way, I will do so."

"You could marry Pennington." Dulcie suppressed the involuntary grimace that rose at the thought.

"I once thought to do so. But now that we've returned to England, grandfather is set on my marrying a nobleman, rather than just the brother of one. In fact, he is set upon my marrying you."

"A fate you hoped to evade, I take it, by your flight to the countryside earlier this summer?"

"Indeed. You can't imagine how angry Grandfather was, especially when you did not immediately follow us. Yet what I

244

saw this morning makes me inclined to appease him, rather than continue my protests. Do you not think we could rub along famously together, now that we have a right understanding of the wishes and desires of the other?"

Dulcie's mind raced, playing out all the possible repercussions. Miss Adler's proposal could solve several of his problems in one fell swoop. His father's insistence he wed; his reluctance to cheat a potential bride by withholding the secret of his true proclivities; even the need for an heir, if he could but bring himself to bed a wife when neither expected any satisfaction or pleasure from the act. Marrying Miss Adler would even take care of that ridiculous bet with Lattimer Leverett over Adler's paintings.

But the paintings . . . What would such a marriage do to Benedict's plans for a national museum?

"Ah, you've realized the one stumbling block, haven't you?" Miss Adler grasped his hand. "Mr. Pennington. He's not one for pretense, as are you and I."

"No, he's not. And he's likely to protest even further once he hears that many of the works of art he hoped your grandfather would donate to his museum scheme will now be a part of your dowry."

"Yes, but as Grandfather has got a bee in his bonnet about my marrying into the aristocracy, those paintings will be a part of my dowry in any case," Miss Adler said. "Is it not better that they go to a friend? A man who understands and sympathizes with his plans for a national museum, rather than to a gentleman with no artistic understanding, one who would likely only hoard his new riches rather than share them with the world? How Mr. Pennington would admire the man generous enough to donate such works for the public good, especially after being disappointed by my grandfather . . ."

Dulcie caught his breath. Benedict looking to him not only for his physical pleasure, but as the benefactor who made his most cherished dream come true? Ah, Polly Adler knew just where to thrust her sword. The possibility of such unadulterated admiration shining from his lover's eyes nearly made him shudder.

"You are not completely opposed to my plan, then, I take it?" Miss Adler asked, laying a hand on his arm. "If Mr. Pennington can be persuaded to accept it?"

Dulcie laughed in bemusement. "No, I am not opposed. But I'm not at all convinced that even my glib tongue can reconcile Mr. Pennington to such a course."

"Then allow me to broach the subject with him. He is far less likely to vent his spleen on a lady than on a lover. And I think I may be able to bring him to see reason, where someone for whom he cares deeply might not."

"He does care for you, Polly. Do not doubt it, not for an instant. If we wed, you will gain not just one champion, but two."

"But you will always be first in his heart. No one who had seen what I saw this morning could ever doubt that." A hint of melancholy tinged her smile before she visibly shook it off. "Nor that he will always be first in yours."

First in Benedict's heart? Dulcie laughed, shying away from the unfamiliar fluttering sensation in his chest. "But my dear girl, have you not heard? Viscount Dulcie has no heart."

Polly grinned. "Of course he doesn't. How foolish of me to even imagine such a thing. Now, do go and have a word with Grandfather before you leave. He's quite put out by your lack of attention. Happily for you, we had no copy of *Debrett's* in Kent for him to scour, searching for other suitors to replace your dilatory self."

With a light touch on his back, Polly pushed Dulcie towards the door. He tumbled out into the passageway, nearly dazed by his sudden turn of fortune. Was he indeed going to marry? And perhaps even provide his father with the heir for which he so longed?

And give his lover the foundation for a museum?

What had he done to have Fortuna, St. Anthony, and all seven of the Lucky Gods shining down on him today?

CHAPTER 16

"THANK YOU FOR COMING, MR. Pennington. Mr. Adler awaits us in the South Gallery. Do you know Mr. Agar-Ellis?"

Benedict bowed his head to Sir Charles Long, anticipating thrumming through his every nerve. Next to the King's most valued art advisor stood George Agar-Ellis, a leading proponent of government support of the arts in Parliament. His presence today in the vestibule of the British Institution suggested that Benedict's lofty dreams of a national museum might at long last be moving towards a concrete plan of implementation.

"Mr. Pennington." Agar-Ellis held out a hand. "A pleasure to meet the author of that impassioned letter I received earlier this summer. I couldn't agree more that there is a pressing need for a publicly funded museum devoted specifically to the visual arts."

"An equal pleasure, to meet such a vocal advocate of government support for art of all kinds," Benedict answered, grasping the other man's hand in his. An interesting face, long and narrow, but with a lively intelligence in those dark eyes. Had anyone ever painted him?

"I hope you will give me leave to use some of the arguments from your letter when I urge my fellow MPs to allocate funds for the establishment of such a museum," Agar-Ellis said. "We've just had word that the Austrian government has unexpectedly repaid a sizable war loan, funds which I will argue should be earmarked for this vitally important project."

"This vitally important project will go nowhere, however, without Mr. Adler's contribution," Sir Charles interrupted, waving an arm towards the staircase. "Shall we, gentlemen?"

The three linked galleries of the British Institution were far quieter now than they had been back in May, when the spring exhibition had been open to general visitors. The paintings borrowed from private collections for that show still hung on the walls, but since the beginning of September, only student artists had been allowed to view them. Benedict and his companions kept to the middle of the rooms, far away from the students with their easels and stools and canvasses, intent on studying and copying works they'd likely never again have the chance to view. That fellow standing atop a wobbly stool, attempting to get close enough to see the brushstrokes of a Poussin landscape hanging high up on the wall, had best watch out, or he'd be falling head-first right into the painting!

He would have liked to have stopped and listened in on the snippets of whispered conversation between the students, their heated discussions of line and color and technique, the occasional pointed debate on the merits of one painting over another. But it was a silent young lady over in the corner, her eyes moving between the Dolci Magdalene hanging midway up the wall and the canvas propped on her easel, who fixed his attention. How intently she stared, as if wrapt in her own world of color and light and shadow. If he were rude enough to pause by her side and speak, he doubted she'd take the least bit of notice.

Is that how he'd seemed to Clair these past few days, so caught up in his portrait—the one Clair knew about, as well as the one he'd painted as a surprise—that he lost all track of place and time? Whenever he was close to finishing a painting, especially one where he wasn't certain his skills could adequately capture the ambitions of his vision, he tended to sink deeply into his own brain, for hours, sometimes days, on end. If he seemed as distant, as otherworldly and inaccessible as this young lady did, why, it was no wonder Clair had largely left him to his own devices this past week.

He wished Clair were here now, though, to share the pleasure of this moment. He'd sent a note to Milne House, where Clair had stayed last night, requesting his company. But had been disappointed to receive no reply before he'd had to leave for this unexpected appointment.

When they entered the North Gallery, it was not Lord Dulcie who stood in conversation with Julius Adler and his granddaughter in the otherwise empty gallery. It was his father, Lord Milne.

Was that why Dulcie had begged off from returning to Saybrook House last night? Because his father had unexpectedly returned to town? But why would he not mention such a thing in his note?

"Ah, gentlemen, good-day, good-day!" Lord Milne, pleasant affability where his son was all liquid charm, bowed to their group. "I understand you and Adler here have important things to discuss this morning, so I will take myself off directly. But look for a card from Lady Milne, an invitation to a small party we are arranging for later in the week. Many a toast will ring out when we make that happy announcement, eh, Adler?"

Mr. Adler looked more put upon than pleased by the friendly elbow Lord Milne sent in his direction, although he quickly stifled his frown. "Indeed, my lord. My granddaughter and I look forward to receiving your invitation."

Benedict stepped over to greet Polly as her grandfather and Lord Milne said their good-byes. Her usual calm seemed to have deserted her, replaced by a strange mixture of excitement and worry. But before he could ask what troubled her, Sir Charles and Agar-Ellis gestured for him to join them around the table in the center of the gallery.

No students painted in this third room, although signs of

their presence—a lone paintbrush, a paint-smeared cloth— suggested the room had only recently been cleared. Specifically for their private discussion, and at Sir Charles' direction, no doubt. The Deputy Director of the British Institution had his privileges. . .

Benedict pulled out a chair for Polly, but she shook her head. "This is no meeting for me. But I do wish to have a word with you, after you've finished here. I'll wait for you in the vestibule below," she whispered, then smiled and stepped from the room.

Sir Charles cleared his throat. "Mr. Adler, may I introduce Mr. Agar-Ellis?"

"Lord Clifden's son, yes?" Adler said as he shook the younger man's hand. "A fine man, the viscount. And a fine family. Very fine."

"My new wife seems to agree with you, for which I praise the heavens each day," Agar-Ellis said with a smile that somehow managed to be both friendly and dampening. Benedict stifled his own grin. Rumors of Adler's eagerness to find a noble grandson-in-law must be spreading.

"Thank you for agreeing to meet with me today, sirs," Adler said as he pulled his own chair up to the table. "Mr. Pennington has acted on my behalf up until this point, but I believe things are now come to a stage where meeting in person must be the proper course."

"Indeed, Mr. Adler," Agar-Ellis agreed. "I've long admired your many philanthropic contributions to our country, and stand ready to help facilitate any worthy charitable endeavor. I have heard through certain channels"—he nodded in Sir Charles' and Benedict's directions—"that you are considering a donation that will enrich the entire nation for generations to come."

"Yes, Pennington was kind enough to express my interest in the creation of an art museum in London to Sir Charles here. One funded by the government, not by any private group."

"And open to the public," Benedict added. "None of this sending for tickets, or asking permission, or shutting it up half the days of the week."

"And located not in an unfrequented street, nor in a distant quarter of the town," Agar-Ellis added. "But in the very center of London."

"And accessible to all ranks and degrees of men," Benedict reiterated. "No fee required."

"Visitors must be decently dressed," Sir Charles insisted.

"Sirs, sirs, you put the cart before the horse!" Mr. Adler folded his hands on the table, waiting until he had the full attention of the other men in the room. "I did at one time think to offer a sizable portion of my collection to the country, for a sum far less than its current worth. And my London house as a site in which it, and other paintings acquired by the museum, might be displayed. But my circumstances have very recently changed, and I find that I am no longer in a position to make such an offer. I felt it only right to inform you of this myself, rather than asking Mr. Pennington to once again act as my intermediary."

Benedict looked at the other man in disbelief. What circumstances had changed? A financial setback of some sort? But Dulcie, a magnet for every scrap of ton gossip, had not said a word about Adler since they'd returned to London.

And the older man's calm demeanor did not suggest his changed circumstances related to any ruin or scandal . . .

The memory of the sneer on Lattimer Leverett's face, taunting Dulcie over his ill-considered wager— And Lord Milne, right here in this very room—

Benedict shifted in his seat to face the man beside him. "Am I to understand congratulations are in order, sir? Miss Adler will soon be wed?" *And her grandfather's best paintings given away as dowry?*

Adler smiled and shook his head. "Ah, Mr. Pennington, I will never understand how your mind so frequently jumps to such accurate conclusions. But I beg you, do not tell my granddaughter my too-revealing words gave away her secret. She so wished to inform you of the engagement herself."

Benedict leapt to his feet, his chair scraping as loud as a cannon against the uncarpeted floor. "She did tell me she wished to speak with me after our meeting. And as my services no longer seem needed here, I will go and find her directly. Excuse me, gentlemen."

Before Sir Charles or Mr. Agar-Ellis could even rise from their seats, Benedict had rushed through the arched doorway. His heart pounding, his palms sweating, he clattered blindly down the stairs, as if he could outrun the horrible, stabbing hurt.

Clair wouldn't . . . He couldn't . . .

But as soon as he saw the smile on Polly's face fade into a worried frown, he knew how wrong—yet how right—his intuition had been.

Polly's betrothed was none other than Sinclair Milne.

"Mr. Pennington! Mr. Pennington, you must allow me to explain!"

Benedict paused mid-step. Rude, it was, to dash down the pavement so, leaving Polly Adler to shout after him like a fishwife hawking her wares on the wharf. But he didn't think he could countenance speaking with anyone right now, especially not the lady responsible for all the conflicting emotions churning through his veins. He needed to be alone, to try and understand how he could have been so utterly wrong about Clair.

He shook his head and kept walking. Bad enough that Adler had abandoned their museum plans. But his idyll with Clair, would it soon be coming to an end as well? He yanked at his cravat, scrabbling against the sudden tightness constricting his throat.

Clair couldn't have been deliberately lying to him all this time about not wanting Adler's paintings. But perhaps his lover had been lying to himself? Any gentleman with even the smallest pretension to aesthetic taste would be ecstatic to find himself the owner of such a collection. And if he might please his father in the process of winning them, well, was it any surprise that his previous denials might fall by the wayside?

Yes, it was Benedict who was the one at fault, for putting so much faith in a man as unreliable as Clair. Foolish to believe him immune from the lure of Adler's paintings. Even more foolish to believe him so enthralled by the lure of Benedict Pennington that he'd turn away from a more conventional, socially acceptable life.

Somehow, though, he could not entirely banish the improbable hope that the gentleman currently chortling over his good luck in winning Polly Adler and her dowry was someone other than Sinclair Milne.

"Mr. Pennington!"

Light footsteps sounded behind him. What, was Polly chasing him down Pall Mall? And without a chaperone? Damnation!

"Mr. Pennington! Benedict, please!"

He had come almost to Cleveland Row by the time conscience forced him to a halt. Polly was not to blame here, truly. She could have no idea how the news of her pending betrothal would cut at his very heart. And only a blackguard would allow an unmarried lady to dash about the city unaccompanied.

"Oh, Benedict! I am so sorry," she said as she finally caught him up, her usually pale face ruddy from the exertion. "I *begged* grandfather to allow me to tell you. But he is so high-handed, he must have all his own way."

"It is true, then? You are engaged?"

She nodded.

"And the best paintings in his collection, those that were to be donated to the museum—excuse me for speaking so bluntly —they will now be given to your betrothed?"

"Yes, to Lord Dulcie. Is it not a happy scheme?"

His mind numbed, but his hands tingled with an unfamiliar need to strike out, to dash that easy joy from her face with a stinging slap. What a wretch he was! He fought the cruel urge, his fists tightening for a long moment.

"I see," he finally bit out, then turned and strode down the passage towards Green Park. Surely he could find somewhere to lose himself in its extensive wilderness, some place to hide away and mourn alone.

"No, I do not believe you do," she said to his back. Once again footsteps followed him.

When she caught him up this time, she slid a gloved hand inside his elbow, as if her small strength would keep him from fleeing. "How kind of you to join me for a stroll in the park on such a fine summer's morning, Mr. Pennington."

"Polly, please. You will not find me good company today." He tried to shrug free of her hand, but she only tightened her grip.

"Do not worry yourself on my account. I have enough conversation for us both, if you will just *stop running away and listen to me!*"

Benedict jerked to a halt, taken aback by the vehemence of her words. Her set jaw and furrowed forehead told him she would not take no for an answer. Girding himself against more painful revelations, he gave a curt nod.

She remained silent, though, as they turned onto the gravel of the Queen's Walk and strolled towards the Basin and

Piccadilly. The morning's fine weather had brought out myriad strollers, couples and groups of all ranks and degrees. A crowd similar to the one he'd imagined visiting a public art museum, gentlemen and shopkeepers, parliamentarians and clerks, all side by side, all drinking in the splendors of the finest works of art. He sighed. It would take months to cultivate another donor with as rich a collection as Adler's.

The park was still not as crowded as it would be later in the evening, when the well-dressed and the genteel thronged its paths. Thank heaven the daily parade of the guards, accompanied by a full music band, had already taken place. He didn't think he could tolerate such cacophony, not with the images, real and imagined, clamoring inside his own head. Clair kissing him until they both gasped for breath. Clair in Adler's gallery, expounding on the merits of Adler's Titian and Carracci. Clair laughing with Lattimer Leverett over how each could so easily manipulate a still painfully naïve Benedict Pennington.

Polly waited until they had passed a group of nursery maids and their young charges before speaking. "I know how upset you must be, Benedict, about this delay to your museum plans. But you must not blame Lord Dulcie. It was my idea, mine entirely."

"Your idea?" Benedict scoffed. "No doubt he made you think so. He has a gift, to make others believe him sincere. But far too often, all is mere artifice and show."

"Benedict, no! It *was* my idea. Indeed, he refused me at first, and for quite some time. Only after I explained how marrying me would allow him to help *you* could I bring him to even consider the proposal."

"Help me? In what way can his marrying you, and stealing away your grandfather's paintings for himself, be of the least help to me?"

Polly grabbed his arm and stamped her foot, sending small brown stones kicking up around them. "Benedict Pennington!

Stop jumping to conclusions! You may be quick-witted, but you're not always right, you know."

He opened then closed his mouth, chastened by her anger.

With an approving nod at his silence, she began walking again. "You know that Grandfather once thought to make a match between the two of us, did you not?"

Benedict nodded.

"But since our return to England, he has become more and more set on my wedding a gentleman of both property and of rank. Not just one with good connections, such as yourself, but a gentleman with a title, or at the very least in line to inherit one."

"And you could not dissuade him from such a course."

Polly's lips twisted. "No. He loves his adopted country so, and wishes for his descendants to be English to the bone. What better way to accomplish this than to wed his granddaughter to a scion of the peerage?"

"But must he also give away the paintings?" Damn, he hated the petulance that crept into his voice.

Polly huffed. "You know no aristocrat would ever offer for a girl of little social standing and even less beauty without proper recompense. But if the dowry that came along with her offered an unprecedented measure of prestige . . ."

"You underestimate yourself, Polly. Any gentleman would—"

"Any gentleman wouldn't," she interrupted. "And an aristocrat certainly wouldn't, not without the incentive of grandfather's best paintings."

The intensity of her scowl made him drop that line of protest. "But must it be Dulcie?" he could not help but ask, damning the pain and longing those words revealed.

"Yes, it must! What other man would agree to donate them to your museum project, rather than keep them to himself and his own kind? Do you not see, it is the perfect solution to all of our difficulties!"

Benedict closed his eyes, the sudden rush of hope nearly blinding him. "Dulcie told you he'd donate them? And you believe him?"

"Yes, I do. And I must say your doubt does him great disservice, Benedict. Because I can see where his true feelings lie. He may have agreed to marry me, but it is you whom he loves."

"Loves?" Clair, love him? Why would she think such a—?

Benedict stilled. "It was you! Last week, outside my studio."

"Well, I did not say your intuition was always wrong," she said with a chuckle. "I told your footman that I knew my way, and wished to surprise you. But instead it was I who received the surprise. And the answer to all of our problems."

He shook his head. How could she be taking this all so lightly?

"And still, you would marry him? Even after witnessing us —?" He couldn't bring himself to finish the sentence.

"He has agreed to let me pursue my art as I wish," she said in a remarkably even tone. "Why should I not grant him the same courtesy to pursue his own interests?"

Benedict stared at her. "His own interests?"

Instead of answering, she began to walk again, tapping her closed parasol against the light iron railing running beside the gravel path. "Have you heard the story of why there are no flower beds here in Green Park?"

He frowned at the sudden change of topic. "Because it was once a burial ground for lepers? Surely you don't believe such a foolish tale."

"No, not that one. The story I know is that during one of his daily constitutionals, Charles II picked some flowers here for a lady—a lady decidedly *not* his wife. Of course, the Queen saw him, and in a fit of pique ordered all the blooms removed from her husband's favorite park. A foolish act, I think, to deprive everyone of the beauties of nature just to spite a philandering husband. And he, no doubt, easily found both another supply of blossoms and another lady upon whom to bestow them."

She paused, and raised both her eyebrows. "I myself have always regarded jealousy a particularly unbecoming feature in a wife. And in a husband. Just one of the many beliefs Lord Dulcie and I share. Yes, I believe we will rub along together quite well."

His mouth must have been hanging open in shock, for her gloved hand reached out and gently pushed it closed.

"Benedict. After you take me back to my grandfather, go and have a word with your Lord Dulcie. He cares for you, and you for him. That is a rare thing, such caring. It would be a sin to allow doubt and fear to come between you."

CHAPTER 17

DULCIE PULLED OUT HIS POCKET watch and flicked open its case, then frowned. Had the blue steel minute hand truly only advanced a few scant minutes since the last time he'd checked? Perhaps his valet forgotten to wind it this morning. He gave it a shake, then held it to his ear. No, the damned thing still *tick tick*-ed away at an annoyingly steady clip.

Perhaps it was losing time. He'd send it in to be repaired, just as soon as he'd finished explaining to Benedict just why he had agreed to marry Polly Adler.

If Benedict ever returned to Pennington House to hear his explanation . . .

With a scowl, Dulcie jerked open the door of the bed chamber and called out into the empty passageway. "Hill? Hill, can you tell me the time?"

Quick footsteps tapped against the marble staircase before Hill, the tall, light-haired footman, reached the landing. "My lord? The clock in the hallway says ten minutes past two."

Just as did his own watch. He clicked its case shut and shoved it back into his waistcoat pocket. "And Mr. Pennington has still not returned?"

"No, my lord. As you instructed, I will tell him you wish speak with him as soon as he arrives."

"Yes. Very good."

The footman frowned. "Is there anything else I might do for

you, my lord?"

"No, I thank you." He nodded in dismissal, then turned on his heel and stalked back down the passageway. Polly Adler had solemnly promised to send Benedict back home as soon as she had explained their plan to rescue her grandfather's paintings. But hours must have passed since then. Damnation! He'd known Benedict wouldn't take it well.

Instead of returning his own room, he opened the door to his lover's. Dulcie had been given his own chamber at Pennington House, but over the past fortnight, they'd spent more and more nights—at least the ones when Benedict did not stay up until the wee hours painting—here, together, in Benedict's room. He often teased his lover over his refusal to employ a valet, and the subsequent disorder of his personal belongings, but today, he was glad of it. He could burn off some of this restless energy by picking up the coats and waistcoats Benedict had stuffed into his wardrobe, folding them neatly, gently placing the smaller items inside their proper drawers, the larger on their appropriate hooks.

As he tutted over a paint stain on a dark brown waistcoat—where did the fellow purchase his clothing? Dulcie truly needed to introduce him to his own tailor—the door to the chamber behind him slammed shut. With a start, he dropped the garment and whirled round.

"Oomph!" A large, warm body pinned him against the wardrobe door. Before he could even catch his breath, hands yanked at his neckcloth, then slid down and quickly slipped open the buttons of his waistcoat. And then his shirt was yanked from his breeches, and warm, nimble fingers stroked up his flanks with seductive intent.

"Benedict! What in the world—"

Hot, searching lips swallowed his words. A fevered tongue pushed into his mouth, then shifted to lick a lascivious strip up the cord of his neck.

Dulcie shuddered, almost unbearably aroused at the intensity of Benedict's ardor. In all their previous trysting, Dulcie had been the one who'd most often acted as seducer, most often directed their subsequent love play. And even though that astonishing bit of mouth-play last week had been at Benedict's urging, Dulcie had been the active one, the one to push his prick into his lover's body, the one to spend in his lover's mouth.

But to be almost attacked by a lover! No, by *this* lover. Pinned, undressed, worshipped by Benedict Pennington, the boy who had once looked up to him as hero. Now with arms strong enough to capture his hands and force them above his head, hips powerful enough to pin his own tight to the wardrobe— Dulcie nearly moaned at the heady rush of pleasure his own helplessness engendered.

With whom else besides Benedict would he have felt safe enough to allow himself to play *eromenos*, the beloved, the passive partner, rather than *erastes*, the active one? His body grew heavy, languid, his head tipping back to allow Benedict better access.

But when sharp teeth nipped at the lobe of his ear, his head banged on the wardrobe with a painful *thunk* that shook him free of the thick haze of pleasure.

Grabbing his lover's head, he pushed it up and away until he could see Benedict's face.

The sight that greeted him made him shudder. He'd expected disappointment, bitterness, even recrimination. But instead he saw only desire, fierce enough to singe.

"You spoke with Miss Adler this morning?"

"Yes."

"And you're not angry with me?"

"I was, yes." Benedict bit the side of Dulcie's neck, then grabbed the tail of his shirt and yanked it over his head. "I assumed the worst of you, until Polly explained your plan."

"That I'd betrayed you?"

"Not betrayed, exactly. Disappointed me, perhaps. By not living up to the promise of your best self. I thought temptation had proven too great." His hands moved to the placket of Dulcie's trousers.

"And now?" Dulcie asked, grabbing Benedict's hands in his own. He needed to see his lover's eyes, to make sure that he truly understood what Dulcie was asking of him, and what he was willing to give him in return.

"Do you pledge to give the artwork from Polly's dowry to the country to endow a national art gallery?"

"I do."

"And you will treat Polly with kindness, and never give her cause to regret her choice?"

"I will."

"And you will give yourself to me as well? And take no other lovers, for as long as we both shall live?"

Dulcie blinked against the tear that foolishly threatened to fall from his lashes at Benedict's echoing of the marriage ceremony. "I will."

Benedict's laughter echoed as he ducked and swooped Dulcie up into his arms. "Then prepare to be worshiped as you've never been worshipped before, my dearly beloved viscount. For I feel a great urge to expiate my guilt on the altar of your body."

And so Benedict did.

"And so I invite you all to join me as I offer a toast to the happy couple. Lord Dulcie, Polyhymnia, we wish you every joy!"

Even the denizens of the paintings on the walls of Julius Adler's picture gallery seemed to hold their breath in astonishment as the banker raised his glass to salute his granddaughter and the least marriage-minded bachelor in all the ton. But after Dulcie raised his own glass in confirmation, the hundred or so guests Adler had invited to celebrate their betrothal began to chatter and cheer, and then to throng about the couple, eager to offer their surprised congratulations before hieing off to gossip about the shocking development.

Dulcie's entire body fairly hummed, satisfaction effervescent in his veins. Tonight, all the players in his elaborate plans were falling neatly into place. His mother, her eyes sparking with tears as she pulled a surprised Polly into her arms to welcome her to the family. His father, smiling at Dulcie as he accepted the congratulations of the older gentlemen in the room, especially those with sons and daughters of their own still to marry off. And Julius Adler himself, puffed up with as much pride as any Punchinello at having snared the son of an earl for his wayward granddaughter, clapping an arm about Dulcie's back and even condescending to refill his glass himself.

Dulcie took particular pleasure in the sight of Lattimer Leverett, sulking over by Adler's Rubens like a spoilt child. Ridiculous, to take on so over losing a silly wager. But then Leverett never had liked to lose.

The only player not dancing to Dulcie's tune tonight was Benedict. He might at least have come over and offered his congratulations along with the other gentlemen in the artistic set. But instead he stood aloof, a delectably surly scowl warding off all attempts to engage him in conversation. Why could not he get into the spirit of the thing? A gentleman who cared for another man would never be able to openly declare it in public, as he himself very well knew. So why not take pleasure in the thrill of the secrecy itself, rather than chafe like a horse against an over-tight girth?

Lord Milne clapped his own hand to Dulcie's back, his color high with well-wishing and wine. "Well done, my boy, well done indeed. Knew you couldn't hold out forever. Done the family proud today."

"*Tam arte quad marte*," Dulcie said with ironic tilt of his glass. But his father's brow only furrowed in confusion.

"Come, father, don't tell me you've forgotten your schoolboy Latin? For I won't believe a man so proud of his lineage as you has forgotten his family's motto. *As much by art as strength?*"

"Don't know what strength or art has to do with a betrothal," his father said with a frown.

His mother's aunt, the Dowager Lady Davenport, who was a bit hard of hearing, squeezed between Dulcie and his father before Dulcie could answer. She took his hand and pressed it between her small, gnarled fingers. "Always said you'd come up to snuff someday. No fool, this son of yours, Milne. He'll not allow the earldom to revert to the crown, no matter his own peculiar tastes. Can always have a bit of something on the side, what?"

"Indeed, Aunt." Dulcie squeezed her hands, cutting her off before his father turned an even more alarming shade of red. No need to remind him that a bit of something on the side was far more to his son's tastes than any bride-to-be.

But his father's attention had been caught by a loud burst of laughter from the horde stationed in front of Adler's most highly regarded painting, Piombo's *Christ Raising Lazarus from the Dead*. They called themselves connoisseurs, Leverett, Carrington, Selsey, and the rest of the usual coterie of young British Institution members gathered about them? Philistines, each and every one, to stand about gossiping when they could be examining the glittering color and luminosity of that glorious altarpiece, or any one of the other masterpieces hanging on the walls of Adler's gallery. He'd be sure to tease Benedict later, telling him such disregard by the public was almost enough to make him change his mind about donating all the paintings from Polly's dowry to the new museum.

Where was Benedict? Dulcie gazed about the room, but his lover seemed to have disappeared.

"Have you been introduced to my betrothed, Miss Adler?" Dulcie asked, abruptly pulling his bride-to-be into their circle. "Polly, Lady Davenport has just returned from Bath, and would be happy to tell you all about the restorative powers of the waters there. And father, you've been as well, haven't you? If you will excuse me, I see Lord Carrington is eager to offer his congratulations."

Dulcie ducked away before his great aunt's old-fashioned manners could land him in any hotter water. At least Polly's promise that he'd not need to dance attendance on her all evening was proving true. Having the girl hanging on him like Venus on Adonis in that Titian on the wall opposite would prove most annoying. But if she'd be willing to distract his pesky relatives when he had bigger fish to fry, he'd be well content.

Now, where had Benedict hidden himself?

"Dulcie, at last brought up to scratch!" he heard as he approached the gossips milling by the Piombo. "I can hardly believe my ears."

"Yes, but only because parson's mousetrap was baited with a van Dyck, two Claudes, and a Titian," another offered.

"Only *two* Claudes? Doesn't Adler own four?"

"Our wily viscount must be losing his touch!"

Dulcie's nostrils flared as chuckles more appropriate to a pub than to a picture gallery split the air. Heavens knew he enjoyed a good gossip as well as the next man, but it was hardly good ton to speak so about a fellow at his own betrothal celebration. At least Benedict had not joined the tittle-tattling group. He'd no desire to break up a round of fisticuffs amidst Adler's priceless paintings.

"Adler has no other heirs besides that plain-faced granddaughter, you know," he heard another wag assert as he nudged Carrington to make space in the circle. "Dulcie won't have to wait too much longer for the rest."

"Just until the first great-grandchild comes along."

Leverett gave a particularly nasty chuckle. "*If* the first great-grandchild comes along. I've heard—"

"Gentlemen," Dulcie interrupted, his smile completely at odds with the unexpected churning in his stomach. Why had he ever confided his sexual antipathy towards women to a creature as heartless as Leverett? "So pleased you could join us on this auspicious occasion. It is not every day that one can gaze at length upon the genius of Piombo."

"Indeed," George Norton said, eyes fixed on the painting. "I did not expect to see such varied reactions amongst the observers of Lazarus's resurrection."

"I admire and honor the artist's choice," Dulcie said. "By showing us so many different people responding in so many different ways to such a strange and shocking event, Piombo doesn't tell the viewer how he should feel. He invites him to choose for himself."

"Even poor Lazarus doesn't know quite what to make of it all," Lattimer Leverett agreed, gesturing towards the reclining figure with a lazy hand. "His head turns towards the Christ, but his body twists back towards the cold stone tomb. Does he regret it, do you think, being so shockingly yanked from his heavenly reward? What is Mr. Pennington's opinion of the matter, Dulcie?"

Leverett's tight smile told him they were no longer speaking only of a painting. "I'm sure I don't know. Perhaps you should ask him yourself?"

"I would if he were in attendance tonight. But perhaps now that you are betrothed, the two of you will no longer be living in each other's pockets?"

"I saw him earlier," Norton piped up, then colored as both Dulcie and Leverett focused on him. "Examining the *Paradise Lost* paintings? The ones hanging in the far room?"

"Shockingly bad taste on Adler's part, to hang Fuseli's

modern travesties anywhere near these Old Masters," Leverett opined, wiping a handkerchief against his quizzing glass. "I've rarely laid eyes on anything so lurid."

"Lurid? Perhaps to the uninformed critic," Dulcie taunted. "But it takes a certain refinement of temper to recognize true sublimity."

Leverett's eyes narrowed. "Is that Pennington's influence I hear? Perhaps he was the one to advise Adler to purchase such monstrosities."

"Quite perspicacious of him if he had, considering Adler added them to his collection in 1799." Dulcie couldn't help but smile as he caught sight of Benedict out of the corner of his eye, taking up a position near, but not part of, the gossiping group. "Pennington would have been all of four years old at the time."

Leverett's hand flew to his chest. "Lord Dulcie, tender-hearted enough to recall the date of birth of someone besides himself? How womanly of him!"

Benedict's face colored. Damn Leverett for his persistent public insinuations.

"Yes, my memory is not my strongest point." Dulcie shook his head in mock regret. "Carrington, here, I believe you entered the world in '79? And Baron Selsey—in '87? And Mr. Norton, completely a child of this modern century, born in the year five. But for the life of me, my dear Leverett, I simply cannot recall when you first graced the world with your presence."

Leverett's face turned a remarkably satisfying shade of purple.

"Do you intend to marry in London, my lord?" Norton asked as Leverett sputtered. "Or will you and your lady travel into the country?"

"At St. George's," Julius Adler's self-satisfied voice answered from over Dulcie's shoulder. "Sinclair, my boy, you must introduce me to your friends. But first, I believe we have a portrait to unveil?"

Dulcie stilled. Had Polly found out about his portrait, and persuaded Benedict to display it?

"A portrait?" Leverett's eyes narrowed. "Of Lord Dulcie?"

Adler nodded. "Mr. Benedict Pennington was kind enough to paint a betrothal portrait of my future son-in-law. But they've kept it all quite a secret between them, these two. Lord Milne, I know, is almost as eager to see the finished work as I am."

"Yes, your mother is eager to cede it the pride of place at Milne House," his father said as he joined the group. "Only fitting, what? Settling down at last, siring an heir in due course. High time to take your rightful place amongst your progenitors. High time."

Of course his father would think of a portrait not as a work of art, but as a sign of status and lineage. Nothing more than a practical, dignified sign of a nobleman worthy of public responsibility, the typical aristocratic portrait. How surprised his father would be when Dulcie revealed the decidedly unconventional painting.

Dulcie's eyes darted to Benedict's, anticipation coursing through his frame. But his lover's face held none of the eagerness he'd expected. In fact, he looked rather ill at ease. Poor boy, was he truly worried about the reception the portrait would receive?

"Come, everyone," Adler boomed over the chatter of the crowd. "We've another surprise for you tonight! Out here, in the entryway. Lord Milne, stand here beside me, and your lady, too."

What he wouldn't give to take his lover's hand and squeeze it. He'd no idea Benedict felt so insecure about his own talents.

"Courage, sir," he had to content himself with whispering. "A raging success, I guarantee it."

But Benedict did not seem at all reassured. "How can you be certain? You haven't even seen it yet."

"Haven't seen it? But of course I have. And rewarded you for it quite handsomely, too," he said, raising his eyebrows suggestively.

Benedict grabbed his sleeve. "But I've painted more than one," he whispered.

"More than one? And you never showed me?" Dulcie tried hard not to preen. "Well, it will serve you right if Adler's got hold of something not quite polished enough to display."

"Dulcie, no, you don't understand—"

But Julius Adler's booming voice drowned out Benedict's words. "My dear guests. During our travels on the Continent last year, my granddaughter Polyhymnia and I were blessed to meet one of England's most promising young painters, a man who extended the hand of friendship to two lonely strangers, and generously shared his knowledge and wisdom as we toured the wonders of Europe's finest collections of art. And today, we are blessed again, to have this talented artist deign to set his brush to canvas to capture a likeness of my granddaughter's betrothed. Lord Dulcie, would you do the honors?"

Dulcie bowed, then strode to the easel. Playing to the crowd, he slowly reached for the cloth covering it, then drew it aside with a dramatic flourish.

Another silence, this one longer than the one that had followed Adler's original announcement, drummed in Dulcie's ears. Then, a gasp, and another. Twitters quickly covered by a restraining hand. And then, a loud guffaw. What in heaven's name?

Dulcie swung around, his eyes pulled wide. No bland, superficial rendering of his appearance and aristocratic appendages stood on the easel, as if he'd been painted by a more traditional portraitist. But nor did the muscular, dynamic portrait of masculinity that Benedict had revealed to him with such pride earlier in the week. No, the canvas unveiled in the midst of his fiancée's townhouse depicted an entirely naked male body lying on its side in a leafy bower, one arm flung wide in wanton slumber. Or no, not slumber, not with such exaggerated elongated lines, not with those sensuous curves of the back and the buttocks and the thighs. Rather, in the moment just before slumber, in the susurrating calm after the exultation of sexual climax.

Dulcie could barely believe the lasciviousness on the canvas in front of him. Lord, Pen had painted him as if he were an object of desire, not just inviting but demanding the viewer's touch. Open. Languid. *Vulnerable*.

As if he were a woman.

Damnation!

It must be some mistake. Pen would never have agreed to show such a revealing painting in public. Especially not without asking him first.

But when his eyes flicked to Benedict, his lover only scowled, defiant.

He had shown it on purpose? But why?

The question became irrelevant as his father stepped between them.

His father. Oh God, his face. The confusion. The hurt. The cringing distaste. Just as it had been after Copeland's uncle accused Dulcie of debauching his innocent nephew.

His eyes turned back to the painting, blood pounding in his ears. He had to deny it. Had to deny it was him, had to deny he'd had anything to do with such a shameful creation. Only the back of the figure's head appeared on the canvas, but with those guinea-gold curls, everyone would assume—

"How very singular," Lattimer Leverett proclaimed, stepping up to the easel, quizzing glass in hand. "The artist seems to have entirely disregarded anatomical possibility. No one who had actually drawn from life would have put so many vertebrae in a man's back."

Dulcie reached for Leverett's lifeline with both hands.

"I do believe you are right," he said, taking up a stance beside his fellow critic. "Nor would a competent artist have depicted the pelvis rotated to such an impossible angle. Not if he

271

had been drawing from a model. Exercising the imagination a bit too freely, I fear."

"And in exercising his imagination too freely, the painter also exceeds the bounds of good taste," Leverett added as he dropped his quizzing glass to his side. "An impatient style, not at all diligent or persuasive."

"This is not the portrait," Benedict said, shouldering aside Leverett to gather the sheet that had once covered the painting from where Dulcie had tossed it on the floor. "Only an experiment, something not ready to be shown in public."

"An experiment indeed. Too much poetry, and not enough painting," Dulcie said, pushing the cruel words out over the sudden lump in his throat. He would not look at Benedict. He would not.

Whispers rippled through the enthralled crowd as the other members of the British Institution set crowded round to offer their opinions of Benedict's painting.

"Excessive virtuosity," Carrington said.

"Artistic excess is never in good order," Dulcie agreed.

Leverett sniffed. "Almost vulgar, is it not?"

"Well, I think it sublime," George Norton said, his voice belligerent in disagreement.

Carrington turned to him, forehead wrinkling. "Sublime? Without a single feature of heroism or grandeur?"

"A style that proclaims sublime genius, rather than proves it," Leverett declared.

"Indeed. There is nothing here of the sublime, or of the genius about it in the least," Selsey agreed.

Dulcie shot a glance at his father. His lip still curled in disgust.

"Certainly nothing conducive to virtue or happiness," Dulcie added, his voice heavy with false regret. A small, disappointed shake of the head topped off the performance. There, that should appease his father.

"No, indeed. Nothing virtuous in that weak, effeminate thing," Leverett proclaimed, a sly, triumphant expression flashing across his face before it was replaced by a frown of moral repugnance.

"Far more likely to inspire vice than virtue," Carrington agreed.

"Best have a care, Norton," Leverett cautioned, his eyes fixing not on the younger man, but on Benedict. "It's never wise to publicly praise a work more suited to the libertine than to the gentleman."

Dulcie could barely maintain his studied composure in the face of Benedict's pained disbelief. His eyes pleaded with Dulcie, silently begging him to come to the defense of his painting.

After he'd just unmasked him in front of the entire company? He must be mad.

After a long, painful moment, Benedict's eyes dropped from Dulcie's. He flung the cloth over his painting and yanked it from the easel, then clutched it to his chest, as if it were a shield that might protect him from the scorn of his lover and his fellow connoisseurs.

With one last searing stare at Dulcie, Benedict turned his back on the jeering crowd and stalked from the room.

"Come, come, ladies and gentlemen. Far better offerings in the picture gallery." Julius Adler, having finally found his voice, began ushering his guests away from the site of the scandal. "Come away, Polly, immediately. Dulcie, you as well."

Adler rushed to follow his guests, assuming his orders would be obeyed. But Dulcie could not move. Should he follow Benedict and upbraid him? Or remain at the party and ignore him?

Before he could shake free of his paralyzing indecision, Leverett caught at his sleeve. "How amusing! You have won our little wager, but yet you give me the prize in spite of it."

"Prize? I won't pay you sixpence for this night's work," Dulcie snapped.

"A kinder man would offer far more than a few pennies to the fellow who singlehandedly saved his reputation from the heedlessness of a careless swain," Leverett said, patting Dulcie's shoulder in mock friendship. "But I've always had a soft spot in my heart for you, dear Sinclair. Your public set-down of Pennington's ridiculous artistic pretensions will be payment enough for me."

With a laugh, Leverett left Dulcie to stare at the door through which Benedict had fled.

Good God. What have I done?

CHAPTER 18

"A LOVELY DAY FOR A wedding, is it not, my lord? But then, I suspect any day which joins two people in the bond of holy matrimony must be a happy day to a clergyman."

The Bishop of London, who stood, long-faced and bewigged, beside Dulcie at the altar rails of St. George's, Hanover Square, gave a curt nod. "Indeed, my lord."

Dulcie sighed. For a bishop, the fellow was singularly lacking in conversation.

He fingered the gold ring in his waistcoat pocket, the ring that would soon bind him to Polyhymnia Adler. But the only hand he longed to bestow it on was far larger than Polly's. Rough with callouses from clutching paint brushes, a touch dry from the walnut oil he used to clean off the daubs of paint.

A hand that hadn't touched him in over a fortnight.

As the organist paused between songs, Dulcie heard the folds of the bishop's cassock rustle. Slim fingers pressed a latch on the enameled pocket watch, springing open its cover.

"Is not your eldest daughter to make her come-out next season?" Dulcie asked, pulling the bishop's attention back to him. Away from the time, and from the fashionably dressed, but increasingly restless crowd whose heads bobbed above the high-backed pews. Many had returned to town from their country estates specifically for this wedding, and were clearly growing tired of waiting. Polly Adler and her father were woefully late.

He tried once again to engage the bishop. "Your daughter is called Mary Anne, if my memory serves. You will surely enjoy presiding over that wedding when the time arrives."

"Yes, I will."

Ugh. Cold as a dead man's nose, the Right Reverend and Right Honourable the Lord Bishop of London. So different from Pen's reserved passion—

"Are you certain Mr. Adler knows the service was to begin at ten of the clock?" the bishop asked, his frown so deep the wrinkles on his forehead nearly set his white wig askew. "I've another appointment at Fulham Palace at eleven."

"Oh, you know how the ladies are, always primping until the last minute. I'm certain they'll be here shortly."

Truly, Dulcie had no idea. Since the debacle of the engagement party, he'd spent very little time with his future wife, allowing his parents and her grandfather to organize the entirety of today's spectacle. Instead, he'd spent the last fortnight carousing with his friends, fencing and boxing and riding by day, laughing and gaming and drinking long into the night. "Hell-bent on imbibing the last of a bachelor's pleasures to the lees," Leverett had joked, "before bending a docile head to the stifling yoke of matrimony."

Only Dulcie knew what his hectic revelry had truly been about. At first, to keep his roiling anger at Benedict from exploding like a shell from a mortar and decimating all in its range. And then, as his wrath cooled to a simmer, to keep himself from rushing to Benedict's side and demanding an apology for his rash, impulsive gesture, a gesture clearly meant to stake a claim on Dulcie even though he'd told Dulcie over and over that he had no objection to the marriage with Polly. And finally, as self-righteousness gave way to regret, to keep him from throwing himself at his lover's feet in abject apology. Because in the end, what truly haunted Dulcie was not his father's disappointment, or his own embarrassment or shame, but the shock and pain on Benedict's face as he and Leverett and the others heaped aspersion after insult on that horrifically revealing painting. If Benedict had betrayed him by displaying his longing and love in public, had not Dulcie betrayed him in his turn?

Yes, he had to stay away. To keep the world from guessing what he felt for Pen, when he could not even understand it himself.

He certainly didn't *need* Benedict Pennington. He didn't need anybody but himself.

Why, then, should he feel so restless, at such loose ends, after spending only a fortnight without him?

He scanned the pews, searching in vain for his tall head of dark, tousled curls. Foolish, to think Pen would come. After the wedding, perhaps, then it might be safe for them to meet—

The bishop cleared his throat. "I can only wait so long, my lord. You must realize that a man of my station has many responsibilities—"

The older man broke off as the door at the end of the spacious nave opened. Dulcie's stomach quivered. Silks and satins rustled as guests turned in their seats to catch the first sight of the bride on the arm of her proud grandfather.

But only one Adler strode down the wide carpeted aisle.

Julius Adler, sallow and drawn despite the finest tailoring London could offer, looked as if he'd aged a decade since Dulcie had last seen him. With a shaking hand, he pulled a thin letter from his pocket.

"There will be no wedding today," he whispered, handing the folded paper to Dulcie. Then he turned and said, this time in a carrying voice, to the guests assembled in the pews. "There will be no wedding today. My deepest apologies. If you will excuse me?"

Whispers and titters rose from the nave as Dulcie stared at the note in his hand. Polly wasn't coming?

His eyes fixed on the painting hanging behind the altar in an ornate wooden reredos. A depiction of the Last Supper, in the style of Poussin. Who had painted it? He could just make out Judas, in the dark left-hand corner of the canvas, scurrying from the room.

"Dulcie. Dulcie! Come away, before you make another spectacle of yourself." Lord Milne, his face as pasty as blancmange, pulled on Dulcie's sleeve.

"Don't, Father, you'll wrinkle it," Dulcie said, the words coming by rote. Had he truly been left at the altar? And by a young woman as unprepossessing as Polly Adler?

"I'll see to him, my lord. You attend to your wife and daughter."

A hand on his back guided him from the chancel to the vestry. Not the hand of the bishop, who seemed to have left, thank heavens, for his other pressing appointment. No, it was the hand of Lattimer Leverett.

"She left me at the altar?" Dulcie shook his head.

"What a fool. Doesn't she realize her reputation will be in ruins after such a slight?" Leverett moved to pull the note from Dulcie's fingers. "Would you like me to read it to you?"

Dulcie pulled his hand away. "No. No thank you. I would prefer some privacy, if you please."

Leverett nodded. "I'll wait for you in the vestibule."

Slipping his thumb under the seal, Dulcie broke the wax then unfolded the single sheet of paper.

22 September, 1822

My Lord Dulcie,

When we first discussed the possibility of a marriage between us, we agreed we would each allow the other the freedom to pursue his, or her, own particular interests without interference after we wed. But I find now that the time has come, I am not at all certain that I can rely upon your assurances on this point. Your treatment of our mutual friend, Mr. Benedict Pennington, suggests a certain willingness to put your own well-being above that of others, even others for whom you have a care. I cannot think it wise to risk my financial, nor my emotional, well-being on one who would act in such a manner.

If you had deigned to visit me since our betrothal party, I would have informed you of my decision in person. But perhaps it is better this way; you now have no opportunity to use your persuasive manners and abundant charm to sway me from my decision. And I do so hate to argue.

I remind you that the marriage settlement specifies that you receive three paintings of your own choosing from my grandfather's collection if I am the cause of our failure to wed. I wish you joy of them.

Yrs. Sincerely,
Polyhymnia Adler

P.S. Mr. Pennington favors the Carracci

Dulcie looked up from the note, his eyes fixing on the white vestments hanging like dull ghosts in an open wardrobe by the wall. Pen favored the Carracci? Why should Polly tell him such a thing?

Because she thought Pen just might give him a second chance, if only he offered the proper incentive?

He crumpled the note in a shaking hand. Lord, he felt almost giddy, as if Polly had tossed over each and every sandbag weighing down the hot air balloon of his soul. Who would have thought a man could be bubbling with hope, so soon after being jilted?

What a gift Polly had given him!

His chuckle must have sounded a bit mad, because Leverett leaned around the doorframe, eyes narrowed in concern. "Dulcie? Care to share the joke?"

"No time, Leverett," he said, shoving the note into his pocket and catching up his cane and his hat. "No time. I've a man—no, two men—to see about a painting."

Benedict closed the portmanteau and buckled its straps, pulling each one tight against the leather case. Satisfying, how many garments one could fit inside. Everything he needed to stand up beside Theo at his wedding, all in one small bag.

If only one might pack away pain as easily as one did clothing.

A discreet cough interrupted his melancholy. "Shall I bring your bag down to the carriage, Mr. Benedict?"

Benedict nodded to the footman. "Tell the driver I'll be down directly. I need to collect a few last things from my studio."

"Yes, sir." Hill hoisted the bag and slid its strap over his shoulder, then paused in the doorway. "Will you offer the best wishes of all the staff to Lord Saybrook and his new bride? It will be a true pleasure to have a lady gracing this house once more."

He nodded again, though he shared little of Hill's enthusiasm for his brother's impending nuptials. Oh, he was pleased for Theo's sake, of course. His brother seemed quite enamored of Harriot Atherton, and she, a kindly, practical young woman, would certainly make a fitting wife for avoidance-prone Theo. But the idea of any woman taking over his mother's rightful title inclined him to pensiveness, if not outright dejection.

And to stand and watch as yet another of his siblings took a spouse, knowing all the while that he never would—

"And don't forget to sleep with a slice of the groom's cake under your pillow, sir," Hill added over his shoulder as Benedict followed him down the passageway. "Dream of your future wife, you will."

"That old superstition? I thought it only applied to unmarried girls."

Hill paused at the top of the staircase and gave a cheeky grin. "Sure and it can't hurt. Besides, if you get to hungering in the middle of the night, then you've a bit of something right to hand, haven't you?"

Benedict mustered a smile, but doubted it looked very convincing. In the darkest hours of the night, it wasn't cake for which his body hungered. No, it longed for a certain angel-faced viscount, a man so charming on the surface, but so very afraid underneath.

Benedict had stayed in London up until the last possible moment before Theo's wedding, imagining hundreds of ways Clair might apologize. Arriving with a bouquet of autumn flowers in hand. Beating his breast while he declared *mea culpa, mea culpa, mea maxima culpa* on Benedict's doorstep. Scribbling "I'm sorry" in charcoals over every blank canvas in Benedict's studio. Anything to let him know that he'd only said those disparaging things about Benedict's painting to protect him, Benedict, and not just himself. That he hadn't meant to laugh at him, or to repudiate him in front of his family and friends.

But Clair had never come.

And now he was married to Polly.

With a snarl of frustration, Benedict yanked opened the door to his studio. But only two steps in, he jerked to a halt. An oversized canvas, one far larger than any he'd ever worked on, perched on an easel in the middle of the room.

Blank? Or already painted? He couldn't tell; he could see the stretcher bars, but a white sheet concealed its opposite side.

He stepped closer and drew aside the cloth.

Good God. The sheet fell from his suddenly nerveless hand.

Adler's Carracci! The rich blue of that sky, the deep red of the cloth, those smooth, barely perceptible brushstrokes. Saint John's golden curls, the reclining torso that had put him so in mind of Clair. What the hell was this invaluable painting doing in his studio?

"A little bird tells me you have some fondness for this particular canvas."

Benedict whirled to find the man for whom he'd been yearning, leaning with practiced ease against the frame of the studio door. Impeccably turned out, as always, from the top of his pomaded head to the tips of his champagne-shined boots. He held his arms loosely crossed over his chest; his mouth tipped up at one corner in his lazy social smile. Once, Benedict wouldn't have hesitated to reach out and wind his hands through those perfectly arranged curls, or run a thumb over those mocking lips until they forgot to maintain the pretense of indifference. Devour that mouth until it no longer kept him at a distance, but welcomed him into its warmth.

Not today, the hard knot in his stomach insisted. Perhaps not ever again.

Dulcie pushed off from the doorframe and strolled into the room, hands held loosely behind his back. Was offering a private viewing of his newly-acquired painting meant to be recompense for the cruel words he'd tossed out with such ease at Adler's party? Benedict's entire body clenched in protest.

"Your new father-in-law has given you the run of the collection already?" he asked as he turned back to the Carracci. "I'm surprised he would allow you to cart about such a priceless canvas as if it were a mere bale of hay."

Clair's footsteps echoed across the wooden floor behind him. "You've not heard the latest *on dit*, I take it?"

Benedict shook his head, but kept his gaze fixed on the

painting.

"Adler is not my father-in-law. Nor ever like to be."

Hope, sharp and swift, battered Benedict's ribs. "You jilted Polly?" he asked, whirling to face Clair.

Clair sniffed. "Would Lord Dulcie ever commit such an incivility? No, it was Miss Adler, the dear child, who failed to come up to the mark. Left me standing in the midst of St. George's, failing in every attempt to entertain that bore of a bishop Adler persuaded to conduct the ceremony. How such a fellow ever ingratiated himself with enough prelates to win the bishopric of London I'll never understand."

Polly had left *Clair*? "Why?"

"Ah, who can fathom the ways of women?" Clair shrugged with his usual elegance. "Especially ladies of an artistic temperament. Perhaps she did not like the cut of my coat, or the way I styled my hair."

Benedict grimaced. "Devil it! She must have been embarrassed by the scene we made at your betrothal party. It could not have been pleasant for a rival for your attentions to make such a public display, and in her very own home." Damn him for a blockhead. He'd been so wrapped up in his own hurts, he'd not given a moment's consideration to Polly's.

"It may have had something to do with your painting," Clair said with an airy wave of the hand. "But do not trouble yourself overmuch. Such a temperamental young lady and I would never have suited."

"Still, perhaps if I go to her and explain, apologize for making her look a fool—"

"No need, Pen." Clair grabbed his arm. "She's left London, fled in a flurry of petticoats and paintbrushes. Gone to stay with an aunt in Surrey, Adler tells me, far from the imprecations of both her disappointed bridegroom and her irate grandfather. May she paint in peace."

He shrugged free of Clair's grasp and turned his back on

him. His lover showed as little care for Polly's feelings as he did for Benedict's.

"And so, I am to play consolation prize, am I? And treated to a private viewing of a famous painting so I'll forget your careless dismissals of Polly and myself? Just how did you convince Adler to part with it, even for a few hours?"

Clair mirrored his pose in front of the easel, looking not at him but at the painting. "Do you like it? Polly insists the saint and I share a certain resemblance. I can't say that I see it myself, but I'd be flattered if that were the reason you've developed a fondness for it."

Benedict cursed his propensity to blush. "Damn it to hell, Dulcie. For once in your life would you please answer a question directly, instead of perambulating about it as if you were strolling in a garden of pretty words?"

"Very well." But he remained silent for a few moments, reaching out a finger to sweep away a few invisible specks of dust from the painting's frame. "Unbeknownst to me, the marriage contract specified that in the case of either party refusing to execute its terms, certain penalties were to be paid. On my part, a rather hefty sum of money. But on Polly's, as you see—a painting from Adler's collection. Three, in fact. Who knew my father could be so wily?"

Benedict recoiled. "Why would you bring your ill-gotten gains here?"

"Because it's yours, Pen. It, and any other two paintings from Adler's collection, both of your choosing. Not as many as I initially had hoped, I realize, but—"

"Keep it."

"Now, Pen. I know that three paintings aren't enough to start a museum, but in time—"

"I said keep it," he interrupted again, his voice tight and strained. "I don't want it. If it's meant as some kind of feeble apology, then I don't accept it."

Clair immediately stiffened. "Apology? For what?"

"For what? Do you not remember what happened at your betrothal party? How you mocked me in front of your friends? In front of Adler? In front of Polly? No, not all the paintings in the world would make up for what you said to me that night."

Clair jerked on the cuff of his sleeve. "What *I* said? And what of what you *did*? After saying you accepted my need to marry Polly, you put that damned painting on display in her house! A work that all but proclaimed you'd swived me like a bitch in heat!"

"I didn't realize!" Benedict nearly shouted. How did Clair always manage to turn the conversation away from his own faults and on to those of others? "I didn't think of it as lewd, or lecherous. It's just how I see you."

"As a wanton, effeminate slut?"

"No, damn you! As a beautiful, vulnerable man! A man with a soul so much finer than the one he shows to the world. One who not only inspires admiration, but who is worthy of the deepest devotion another human being may offer."

Clair recoiled, as if he'd been hit with a scattering of shot rather than with the deepest truths of Benedict's heart.

But perhaps for Clair, one was tantamount to the other.

What a fool he'd been, imagining that his wary lover might defend such a painting in front of the *ton*. And his dream had not just been about wanting Clair to champion his skills as an artist, had it, no matter what he'd told himself when he'd handed over his outrageous, rather than his merely experimental, portrait to Adler's footman to put on display. No, he'd wanted to make some public claim to Clair, even one as indirect as through a painting. And he'd wanted Clair to claim him publicly too, even if only in the guise of praising his artistic talents.

Idiot. Imbecile.

"I was jealous," Benedict whispered. He turned to stare out the window, sickened by the sudden revelation of feelings he thought he'd already understood. "Jealous, knowing that you'd soon be legally bound to another."

His rational brain had accepted the necessity of Clair's marriage, had even applauded it. But something far deeper inside had still rebelled.

How could he have not considered how Clair would feel to be confronted so directly? To be shown himself as Benedict saw him, in the aftermath of their intimacies—open, exposed, shorn of his usual wit and charm? Lord, it must have been his worst nightmare. No wonder fear had driven him like a hound from hell to deny any involvement in the painting's creation.

"I'm sorry, Clair," he whispered. "I didn't mean to embarrass you, or to put your reputation in danger."

Clair gave a short, stiff nod. "I accept your apology. And we shall say no more of it. Now, come and tell me which of Adler's other paintings you think I should choose."

Benedict sank onto the settee, his hands clenching between his knees. Understanding Clair, though, was not the same as forgiving him.

"Before you offer an apology of your own for lying about my work?" he asked.

Clair eyes widened. "You accuse me of lying? You should be thanking me, and Leverett, for redirecting the conversation towards the painting's artistic merits. Those lies all but saved you from a public pillorying."

"Saved *you*, rather. Leverett rode to your rescue, but trampled me into the dust. And you joined him up there on his noble steed, stabbing down at me with your cutting criticisms and stinging insults as if I hadn't just laid my heart out on canvas for you, as if it had been just any other painting hanging on Adler's wall."

Clair shook his head. "Resenting Polly, resenting Leverett— Why, you're as jealous as a barren wife! What a child, to be in need of such constant reassurance of my regard."

The sting of Clair's disdain hit him like a slap, and his first instinct was to hit back. But he paused as understanding washed over him. Clair *wanted* Benedict to argue, *wanted* to push him away.

He took a deep breath. "I know you're afraid, Clair, but do you have to make me so ashamed of my own feelings for you?"

"Afraid? Pah. You may imagine yourself the heroine of some stage melodrama, but pray, don't cast me in the role of your overwrought swain."

Benedict jerked to his feet. "Of course not. Charming Lord Dulcie is beyond mere feeling."

"Just because I don't wallow in the pits of darkest despair or soar to the heights of unbridled joy doesn't mean I feel nothing, Pen."

"No, you are not unfeeling. Pleasure, amusement, a touch of anger, a bit of disdain—all the lighter emotions are more than welcome. But even you must admit you never stand still long enough to allow any deep feeling, any meaningful emotion, to even tap you on the shoulder, never mind stop to ask yourself why it might be haunting you."

"And you fault me for that? Surely only a foolish man welcomes bad feeling with open arms."

"Bad feeling? Not all strong emotions are bad!"

"Yes, they are! For whenever a feeling is strong enough to overwhelm one's better judgment, it makes one forget one's obligations to others. To one's family, to one's good name."

Benedict took a step back. Surely Clair did not believe such a ridiculous thing. But his lover's face had taken on a closed, mulish look.

"Are those your words?" he asked. "Or are they your father's?"

"What does it matter, so long as they are true? You certainly forgot your obligation to me when you showed the world that painting."

"Obligation? What obligation do I have to you?"

"To keep our relations a secret."

"By suppressing all I feel for you?"

"When it is called for, yes!"

Benedict crowded Clair towards the wall. "And is it called for now? When we are alone together, as well as when we are in public? Are we to laugh, and tryst, and then go about our separate lives as if nothing we do together, as if nothing we *are* to each other, matters in the least?"

Clair's blue eyes frosted. "If that is the only way to keep both the Milne and the Saybrook family names from being smeared with the label sodomite—then yes."

"So you will pretend to feel nothing for me whenever we are in company together outside this house, disparage me and my finest feelings to my face, and not even give me the honesty of your own feelings when we are alone?" he cried. "You expect me to come begging to you like a dog for the meager scraps of affection you deign to drop from your table?"

"What a to do!" Clair sniffed. "Please, I beg, let's have no more of such irrational drivel."

Benedict's palms slapped the wall beside his lover's head. "Hell and the devil, Clair! I think you'd prefer it if I didn't love you. You certainly wish you didn't love me."

"Love?" Clair whispered, his face draining of color.

Benedict's breath caught. Had his declaration finally shocked Clair from his self-protective shell?

But before he could press his advantage, Clair shuddered, then donned his most dismissive Lord Dulcie sneer. "Love? What sentimental drivel you do spout, my dear boy. As if I could bring myself to care for anyone besides myself."

Even though he knew them for a lie, Clair's careless words stabbed him in the gut. He stared at his lover, eyes burning, waiting for him to hear how ridiculous his words sounded when weighed against all they had shared these past few weeks. Waiting for him to admit how wrong he was to be so afraid of his own feelings, and of sharing them with Benedict.

Waiting for him to admit that yes, he, too, knew what it was to love.

Long minutes passed, with neither of them saying a word.

"Mr. Benedict?" The voice of the footman outside the door finally broke them apart.

"Yes, Hill?"

"John Coachman says you must leave within the hour if he is to make Cambridge by nightfall."

"Very good. Tell him I'll be down directly."

With unseeing eyes, Benedict gathered up brushes and charcoals, shoving them indiscriminately into his paint box.

"You are leaving town?" Clair asked, his tone studiedly even.

"Yes. Theo is to be married to Miss Atherton next week. He wishes me to stand up with him." He shoved in one last tube of dry pigment, then latched the paint box shut.

"But when you return, you will come with me to Adler's to select two other paintings?" A question, but uttered in a tone that said he had no doubt Benedict would agree.

"I will visit Mr. Adler, yes. But not in your company." Benedict picked up the paint box and walked to the door. "Someone needs to convince him that his legacy will be better assured by endowing a museum than by tying his granddaughter to some other undeserving scion of the ton."

"And what am I to do with your Carracci, then?"

"My Carracci? You know it doesn't belong to me, or to you. It should be returned to Adler. But perhaps you think such an opinion just another example of my sentimental drivel."

"Self-righteous rather than sentimental, I'd say."

"Then perhaps you'd do better to hang it amongst your Milne ancestors and crow over your cunning in tricking it away from its rightful owner."

"Are you leaving me, Pen?"

Benedict paused in the doorway, steeling himself against that hint of vulnerability in Clair's voice. He couldn't settle for just a hint. Not any longer.

"If you're worried about being alone with your regrets, Lord Dulcie, I'm certain Mr. Leverett would be happy to join you."

He pulled the door of his studio softly closed behind him.

CHAPTER 19

"DULCIE, IS THAT YOU? A word, if you would."

Dulcie grimaced as his gloved hand grabbed the intricately carved newel at the top of the Milne House's grand staircase. He was in no mood to listen to his father's lectures about the importance of the entire family attending Sunday services together, as if he were still a child rather than a man of three and thirty. Not after spending all night staring at the portrait he'd stolen away from Benedict's studio, Benedict's self-righteous reproofs echoing in his ears. He'd been wrong to accept Adler's Carracci as payment for his public embarrassment. Wrong to hide his true response to Benedict's inflammatory portrait, even to keep their affair safe from prying eyes. Wrong to demand the least bit of discretion from his ridiculously idealistic lover.

Wrong to keep his own feelings for Benedict—liking, or admiration, or whatever the hell they might be—decently to himself.

How could the same man be so angry with him, yet paint him as if he were the most beloved being in his universe?

"Dulcie! Come and explain yourself, immediately!" His father, face ruddy, cravat rumpled, glared at him from the top of the landing.

Devil take it. No slipping out the back door today, no matter how badly he might need a bracingly restorative gallop through Hyde Park.

Dulcie walked slowly back up the stairs.

His father met him at the top of the landing, pointing an unsteady finger in the direction of Dulcie's chamber. "Sinclair Milne, what in the heaven's name is that, that—monstrosity doing here?"

Dulcie suppressed a sharp retort. He had no wish to discuss Benedict's portrait with his father, but he needn't antagonize the man, either.

"You deigned to visit my rooms, father? But did you not vow never to speak to me again after Miss Adler failed to keep her appointment with me at St. George's?"

"After you drove her away, more like!" Lord Milne huffed.

"Does the cause matter? The result was the same. I am still unwed. And I distinctly recall you promising never to utter another word to me until I managed to walk out of a church securely tied to some appropriate chit."

His father cleared his throat. "Yes, well. Your mother begged me to reconsider. Yet already I begin to regret my capitulation. If I'd only sent a footman to tell you to attend me at Mr. Adler's this afternoon, I wouldn't have had to look at that indecent excuse for a painting again."

"What, Carracci's St. John? Blasphemous, it is, to call one of the great masterpieces of Western art indecent." Dulcie gave a mournful shake of his head. "I fear we'll never make a connoisseur of you, Father."

"You mistake the matter, sir. It is not the painting of St. John to which I refer." His father flapped his hand again towards the bedchamber. "It is the other!"

"No, no, do not apologize," Dulcie said, waving a careless hand of his own. "If it is not to your taste, we may certainly return it to Mr. Adler. Especially as we seem to have an appointment with him this very day."

"Return it? When you said it was one of the most valuable in the collection? What, do you mean to exchange it for another?"

"No, father. I mean to return it to its rightful owner."

Lord Milne blinked. "But you are its rightful owner. Not only of that painting, but of two others. And you will come with me today, and select the ones you wish to add to your collection, as per the terms of the marriage contract."

"I will come with you today, but not to steal away any paintings. I will come to return poor St. John to his rightful place in Adler's gallery." The corner of Dulcie's mouth quirked. "I fear he has been missing his view of Claude's lovely seaport."

"What?" His father's eyes nearly popped out of his head. "Dulcie, have you run mad?"

Dulcie grinned. His declaration had been impetuous, yes. Yet, the longer it hung in the air, the more convinced he became that it was the only honorable choice. Benedict was right. The painting did not belong to him, nor to Dulcie. It belonged to Adler, and perhaps someday to the nation, if Benedict could convince Adler not to use his collection again as a bargaining chip in the marriage mart.

"Unexpectedly high-minded, perhaps, but certainly not mad," Dulcie said. "Why should poor Adler turn over three of his most prized possessions, just because his granddaughter had the good sense to toss me over?"

"Because those are the terms to which we agreed!"

"I did not agree to that. You never informed me when I signed the contract that such a clause had been included."

"Oh, do not quibble over trifles. You've never had any interest in the finer details of any legal matter. And even if I'd told you of the clause beforehand, I sincerely doubt you would have refused to sign."

Dulcie frowned. No, he probably wouldn't have refused, would he? He'd just have laughed at his father's unexpected cunning, and signed away with an extra flourish. Why now, then, did the thought of absconding with three of Adler's paintings weigh so uncomfortably on his conscience?

"Besides, the good Lord knows we need some incentive to entice another suitable lady to take you on," his father added.

"What sensible lady would agree to marry a gentleman jilted by another?"

"Now, now, son, do not worry about that." Lord Milne gave him a comforting pat on the back. How ready he always was to forgive and forget. "We'll try again next season, find a young chit just out of the schoolroom, one who didn't witness the unveiling of that improper portrait. Speaking of which, what is that thing doing in this house?"

What was Benedict's portrait doing here? How could he explain to his father, when he could not even explain to himself? How every shred of feeling inside him had cried out against allowing it to remain in Benedict's studio, just another bit of artistic detritus among the partially painted canvases and empty bladders of paint that his lover had left behind.

Just as he'd abandoned Dulcie himself.

Lord Milne shook his head. "Bad enough that painter tricked you into posing for such a thing—"

"He didn't trick me, Fa—"

"Now, don't bother to deny you posed for him," Lord Milne interrupted. "I recognized that scar on your calf from when you fell from the apple tree, and that oddly-shaped birthmark on the back of your shoulder. Misguided, is it not, for a painter to include such blemishes? A proper portrait depicts its sitter in the most flattering light."

"Not according to Mr. Pennington," Dulcie said with a wry twist of the mouth.

"Pennington? Oh, merciful heavens!" Lord Milne's eyes widened in sudden recognition. "Was not Pennington the name of the boy who sent that painfully revealing letter to you, just before you were off to Oxford?"

The devil and his minions! Why did his father have to recall that long ago incident today? Dulcie shook his head. If only one could pray to Saint Anthony to lose a memory, rather than to find something lost.

Lord Milne's frown deepened. "And here I thought it was you who was in danger of corrupting him! But now I see who was the true serpent in the garden. Did he think to shame you by sending that atrocious portrait here? Or to mock you, after you so roundly denounced it?"

"No! Benedict would never be so cruel."

"Then how did the appalling thing find its way into this house?"

Dulcie drew a deep breath and met his father's eyes. "I brought it here."

"You?"

"Yes. I stole it away from Benedict's studio after he left town."

"But why—" Sudden understanding lit Lord Milne's eyes. "Oh! You mean to have it destroyed. Painted over? Or better yet, burned! Yes, very wise, very wise. Just don't do it in the house, please. Poisonous, some of the things they use to make those paints, I understand."

Dulcie's pulse drummed in his ears. Destroy the most evocative painting Benedict had ever created?

He chased his father down the passageway to his own bedchamber. But when they reached the door, Lord Milne waved him back. "Now, now, Dulcie, don't trouble yourself. I'll send a footman up to take the noxious thing away, and you'll never have to look at it again. Thank heavens Pennington's parents are both dead and in their graves. How appalling, to think they might have witnessed their son so publicly shamed."

Their son? Or his own? Dulcie rushed after his father, grabbing his arm before he could reach for the bell pull.

"Are you ashamed of it, Father?"

Lord Milne frowned. "What?"

Dulcie gestured towards Benedict's portrait, which leaned against the wall next to the wardrobe. "Are you ashamed to see me like that? Ashamed for others to see me like that?"

"Naturally I'm ashamed! Who wouldn't be, to see their son posed like a, a—like the lewdest of courtesans? How dare Pennington insult you like that!"

"You keep placing the blame on Benedict, Father. But he didn't trick me. I posed for him of my own accord."

"But surely you never posed like that! Only a foul, disordered imagination would depict a future peer of the realm in such a manner. Why, you look as debauched as an odalisque in a sultan's harem!"

Dulcie stared at the painting. Lewd? Debauched? He'd thought the same, hadn't he, when Julius Adler had first unveiled it. But now, after staring at it all night, he saw something far different.

Satiety. Peace.

Love.

"He did only imagine it, Dulcie?" His father's words faltered, less a question than a plea. "Didn't he?"

Dulcie reached out a finger, slowly tracing the lines and curves of his own body on the canvas. "No, Father. He only painted what he saw."

Lord Milne backed away, shaking his head. "Still! No decent man would paint the heir to an earldom as an effeminate weakling."

"Is that what you see when you look at me?" Dulcie asked, his eyes turning to his father's. "An effeminate weakling?"

"No! You at least have the decency to hide what you are! Unlike that painter, who seems to wish to tell all the world of his unnatural proclivities, the damned fool!"

Dulcie stepped back, his lips pressed tightly together. All these years, all this effort to protect his deepest longings, and still, this was what his father thought of him. Weak. Effeminate. Less than a man.

And yet he would still rather blame someone else, rather

than his own son, for the weaknesses he deplored.

A bark of shocked laughter spilled from Dulcie's mouth. Why should he be surprised by his father's self-deceptions? Hadn't he himself always done just the same? All those years ago, he'd blamed both Benedict and his father for his being sent away to Oxford. But in truth, his own thoughtless demand that the boy write to him had been the real cause of the trouble. And he'd also blamed Copeland for betraying him, when it had been Dulcie's heedless behavior that had led to his uncle's discovery of their clandestine relations, and his subsequent confrontation with the Earl. Perhaps it was a family trait, to blame others for troubles that one caused oneself.

He thought he'd learned his lesson after those two painful incidents: keep his true self entirely hidden. Not only from the world at large, which of course one must do when one lived in a society which denied the validity of one man's love for another. But also from anyone for whom he'd come to care.

Just yesterday, he'd blamed Benedict, Benedict and the feelings he'd laid at Dulcie's feet in that portrait, for pushing them apart. But wasn't it his own unwillingness to stop hiding, his unwillingness to allow himself to be vulnerable, to love, that had led to their break?

"I think your anger misplaced, Father," he said as he covered Benedict's portrait in a protective cloth. "Mr. Pennington is not responsible for my, as you call them, unnatural proclivities. I am."

"I've no need to hear about your private doings, Dulcie." His father waved a hand, as if shooing away a pesky fly. "Just do your duty to the Milne name, and we'll say no more of it."

"But the two are inextricably linked. I cannot do my duty—cannot wed and sire an heir—because of my, as you call them, unnatural proclivities. It grows tedious, continually pretending that I can and will."

"But you are the only male heir. Surely you'll not allow the earldom to fall extinct at your death?"

Dulcie's heart gave a sharp jerk. But he could not allow his guilt and shame to drive him any longer.

"Father. The only way I'll ever sire an heir is if my mythical future wife cuckolds me. I'd rather not have that pleasure, thank you very much."

He bowed, then turned on his heel, Benedict's painting in his arms.

"A bland choice, white."

Dulcie drew the new Lady Saybrook and her party into the Assembly Rooms and sniffed at the parade of pallid gowns worn by the female attendees of Lincolnshire's Annual Stuff Ball. Long before his break with Benedict, he'd rashly promised Theo Pennington to attend him and his new bride during their first foray into society as a married couple. Saybrook thought his presence would send a message to his peers that while his new wife might only be the daughter of a steward, she did not lack for friends of influence.

Gossip about the scandalous portrait evidently had not reached the bucolic environs of Lincolnshire, for Saybrook had not written to rescind his invitation. And so now here Dulcie was, in company not only with Lord and Lady Saybrook, but also with the man who had turned his back and walked out on him not quite a month earlier.

As always, his eyes kept straying to Benedict, the most striking man in the room. His former lover stood a bit to the side of his sister-in-law's party, tight-lipped, unsmiling, but too damned handsome all the same. Why had Dulcie not realized how painful it would be to see him again? He'd owe Saint

Genesius, patron saint of actors, a boon if he could successfully maintain his mask of disinterested bystander for the rest of this blasted evening. At least the pulse that pounded in his throat each time he caught sight of Benedict was hidden by his neatly tied cravat.

How he longed to erase that stern, closed look from his lover's face, to make him smile and laugh. A few jokes at the expense of the ridiculous person who had first come up with the idea for this Stuff Ball—to encourage the consumption of local wool by allowing free entrance to any lady who came dressed in a frock made from it—would surely do the trick. Not to mention the one with the brilliant notion to name a different patroness for the ball each year, a local notable who would chose the color each and every lady was required to wear.

Dulcie's breath hitched when Benedict's brown eyes caught him staring. But his lover only frowned, then turned away.

Dulcie forced his attention back to the new Lady Saybrook. She, not Benedict, after all, was the reason why he was here tonight. Gazing with calf's-eyes at Benedict would do little to launch her successfully into Lincolnshire society.

At least Harriot had enough color in her face not to fade into insignificance under the dictate for white. Unlike Benedict, whom he could not but notice had grown decidedly pale in the weeks since they had parted. His sister-in-law had been wise enough to ask her dressmaker to trim her gown's neckline and sleeves with a dark green ribbon, but Benedict had chosen to clothe himself only in the starkest of white and black. And he stood as stiffly as his sister-in-law, as if they were both puppets with sticks up their backs, rather than flesh and blood human beings. If only they would carry themselves with a bit more ease! Harriot would convince these country gentry to welcome her as the lady of an earl rather than dismiss her as merely the daughter of a steward. And Benedict would avoid the crowd gossiping that his coldness signaled his displeasure with his brother's choice.

Well, he might not be able to please surly Benedict, but damn him if he couldn't tug a smile from the man's anxious sister-in-law.

He gave Harriot's arm an encouraging squeeze with one hand, then raised his quizzing glass with the other. "White? I do wonder what Lady Sheffield was thinking. Next year, my dear Lady Saybrook, when you are the Patroness, you should select a more flattering color. Cerulean, perhaps? Or hazel, to match your eyes?"

"And what should it matter to you, my lord?" Benedict's sister-in-law tapped her fan to his arm, making a good show of courage in the face of the crowd. Almost every eye in the room was on her. "The rules restricting gentlemen's attire have long been abandoned."

Dulcie stroked a hand down his favorite waistcoat. The gentlemen, praise Paul the Hermit, could wear whatever colors they chose. All they had to do was pay the price of admission to keep from being turned away.

"But when I marry, I must pay for my lady's new gown, in the appropriate color," Dulcie said, his eyes flicking again in Benedict's direction. "Or to purchase yards and yards of this hideous material in lieu of it."

Benedict stiffened even further at Dulcie's words. But he stepped closer, almost as if compelled against his will. "By the time you wed, Dulcie, the requirements are likely to have been dropped entirely," he said, his brown eyes snapping with annoyance. "And if you don't cease your complaining, I'll dress you in a lovely white shroud in this portrait you've forced me to paint."

A shroud? Dulcie's eyes narrowed.

"Lord Dulcie, have you a partner for the opening set?" Lady Saybrook asked, glancing back and forth between him and her brother-in-law. The air between them fairly crackled. "Come, allow me to introduce you to some of our local ladies."

Dulcie smiled at her attempt to diffuse the tension, all in the guise of a bravura show of confidence. He likely knew more of the local ladies than she did, poor girl.

"But am I not to dance the first with your charming self? We all know how little Lord Saybrook enjoys treading a measure."

"Oh, no, Dulcie." Theo Pennington, Lord Saybrook, cut between Dulcie and his new bride. "I may not be a dab hand at dancing, but no one but myself will lead out my lady at her first ball as my wife."

Dulcie stepped back in surprise. Knowing Saybrook's antipathy for dancing, he'd assumed he'd be the one to lead Lady Saybrook onto the floor tonight.

"Rejected again, Dulcie?" Benedict asked as they watched the couple move out into the crowd.

He wouldn't take offense, despite Benedict's waspish tone. For as Saybrook took his lady's hand, the wrinkles marring his wife's forehead disappeared. And as they waited for the dance to begin, she and Saybrook smiled at one another as if no one else in the room mattered at all.

Good girl. A public display of tender feelings would likely win over the sentimental half of the crowd.

And if he and Benedict could just keep from making a scene . . .

"My dear Sibilla," he said, turning to Benedict's sister rather than respond to his former lover's taunt. "Take pity on a spurned man, and dance the first with me."

But her husband, too, swooped in to claim his lady, making her eyes shine brighter than the gaslights on Westminster Bridge. Gauche, really, how openly these Penningtons expressed their affection for their spouses.

With such models of tender attachment before him, no wonder Benedict had found Dulcie's romantic professions wanting.

But before Dulcie could tease Benedict over the outré behavior of his siblings, his former lover turned on his heel and strode away towards the card room.

Dulcie graciously engaged another partner, even while he fumed in silence. Did not Benedict realize how refusing to dance would make things more difficult for his new sister-in-law?

After dancing the second with Lady Saybrook, and the third with Sibilla Sayre, all with no sign of Benedict, Dulcie decided enough was enough. With a gracious nod, he brought Sibilla to her next partner, then left the floor in search of her brother.

He found him not in the card room, but outside, leaning against the back wall. Foolish man, didn't he realize how dirty the stones of the building were? No, he was too lost in his own thoughts, pensively staring at the gibbous moon.

But Dulcie no longer had the right to ask of what Benedict dreamed. The realization brought a tight, melancholy ache to his chest.

"Pennington," he whispered, reluctant to pull Benedict from his reverie even in spite of his frustration with him. He placed a hand on his sleeve. "I hate to see you standing about by yourself in this stupid manner. You had much better dance."

Benedict jerked under his touch. "Dance? With you?"

Dulcie's imagination leapt at the image. "No, alas. We're at no military ball, where the lack of ladies might necessitate the forming of all-male couples. In fact, several ladies this evening have remained without partners while you've been out here sulking by yourself. Not the thing, Pennington, not if you wish Lady Saybrook to win over her detractors."

"I fail to see how my dancing with some lady I barely know can help Harry."

Dulcie shook his head. How could someone so intelligent be so oblivious of even the most basic of social graces?

"Does not your refusal to stand up with Lady Saybrook suggest your own contempt for her? And will not other ladies follow your example? Especially when they can take out their ire at being slighted by you by slighting your new sister in return."

Benedict glanced back towards the ballroom, then turned back to Dulcie with a wan smile. "Surely no one will dare slight her, not after the great Lord Dulcie has given her the stamp of approval."

"Come, such sarcasm doesn't suit you." Benedict's words may have been caustic, but their tone was more weary than bitter. Dulcie took a step closer. "If I can put aside our disagreements to support Lady Saybrook, why cannot you?"

Before Benedict could reply, an unpleasant laugh sounded from the doorway behind them. "Lord Dulcie and Mr. Pennington at odds again? Who knew tedious Lincolnshire would prove so entertaining?"

Dulcie whipped around. Lattimer Leverett stood by the back entrance to the Assembly Rooms, a thin smile sharpening his features. Over his shoulder Dulcie spied George Norton, his mouth agape.

Damnation! The last thing he wanted was to set off yet another scandal.

"Leverett. A pleasure, as always. I did not expect to meet you here."

"But you must know my lady wife claims relation to the Sheffields," Leverett answered as he stepped outside into the courtyard. "Failing to attend the Stuff Ball would be a decided slight to her family, as well as to one of the county's leading landowners. And of course, I'm always happy to visit my friend Norton here. But I don't believe you have any such connections requiring your presence, Dulcie."

"I am here to give countenance to the new Lady Saybrook. This is her first introduction to society."

"Ah, yes, a Miss Atherton, I understand. Shall I engage her for the next, Norton, do you think?" he asked, turning to his companion with a smile that set Dulcie's teeth on edge. Leverett, unlike Benedict, had sarcasm down to an art. "Or would I be risking the safety of my toes by stepping out with the daughter of a steward?"

"Stay away from my new sister," Benedict hissed before Norton could offer any opinion on the matter. "As if her standing in society would benefit from being patronized by the likes of you!"

Dulcie grabbed Benedict's hand, a fist tight under his fingers.

"And your presence lends her countenance? You, a painter who laid himself open to the basest of accusations by wearing his heart upon his canvas?" Leverett gave an exaggerated shudder. "How can you bear to be in his presence, Dulcie, knowing how likely the fool is to embarrass you with his sentimental attachment to your person?"

"How kind of you to fear for my reputation. Happy for you to never be in danger of such a fate yourself," Dulcie answered. "Your lady wife is notable for her lack of sentiment."

Leverett's eyes narrowed. "My wife knows her place. As do any others I choose to engage with, don't they, George?"

"On their knees before you, heads bowed and mouths shut?" Benedict taunted. *Damnation, why must he always be provoking Leverett so?*

Leverett took a step closer, lips twisted into a mocking sneer. "Mouth open, in your case, wasn't it, Pennington? Back when you knew what it was to respect your elders, as George here does. Go inside, George."

Beside him, Dulcie felt Benedict tense as Norton took a few cautious steps back into the passageway.

"Respect his elders?" he asked, glancing between Benedict and Norton. What the hell was going on here?

"I was once his fag-master, after all. Just as you yourself were." Leverett turned back to the doorway, his eyes narrowing as he caught sight of the hovering Norton. "*All* the way inside, George. Back into the ballroom. Now."

Dulcie laid a questioning hand on Benedict's shoulder as Norton ducked his head then disappeared from sight. Good God, the man was shuddering.

"Pen?" He gave his lover's shoulder a reassuring squeeze.

"He told me I had to serve him," Benedict whispered. "After you left Harrow."

Dulcie frowned. "But that was simply the way things worked there. You ran errands for me, cleaned my study, and had the chance in return to peep into my books and pictures, and to interact with a fellow in the sixth form. And when I left, you did the same for Leverett."

"But it wasn't the same! The kind of serving he had in mind had nothing to do with cleaning out his study, or carrying messages for him. He never wanted to talk, or debate, or just sit together in friendly silence, as we used to do. He only wanted—" Benedict bit his lip.

"What did he want, Pen?"

"He wanted what you had of me, he said. He wanted me to pleasure him. To make him spend."

"But you and I— we never—" Dulcie could barely shape the words.

"But did you brag to him?" Benedict's voice cracked. "Tell him how I hero-worshiped you? How I would have done anything for you?"

Leverett chuckled. "Dulcie never had to say a word. Such an expressive countenance you had, even then! Almost as pretty as a girl's. Such a pity you proved so squeamish about fucking. Why, Dulcie, did you never introduce him to the pleasure? I showed you how to go on, back when you were my boy."

Benedict grabbed Dulcie's arms and jerked his body to face his. "He fucked you?"

"Of course I did," Leverett answered before Dulcie could bring himself to speak. "It's what older boys do, if the younger prove amenable."

But Benedict seemed unwilling to take Leverett's word for it. "Clair?" he asked, giving Dulcie a gentle shake.

God, how excruciating. His initial enthusiasm curdling into distaste at the awkwardness and the mess of it all. The way he'd broken out in a sweat as Leverett's cock prodded his arse, the disgust he'd felt as Leverett's spend leaked out over the hours that followed—no, it was not a memory of which he was particularly fond.

But Benedict seemed willing to stand here all night until he answered.

At last he gave a short, sharp nod. He had agreed to it, at least that one time.

Benedict's lips thinned, and Dulcie could practically hear his teeth grinding together. Could he be jealous of Leverett? Angry that Dulcie had allowed the other man such a liberty when he'd refused to grant Pen the same?

But then Benedict's fingers dug into him, as tight as a vise, and he knew it was something more.

"Did you want him to?"

"I thought I would. But I didn't like it, didn't want to—"

"And did he make you? Even after you told him to stop?" The wildness in Benedict's eyes frightened him.

"No!" Dulcie shook his head with vehemence. "And I stopped visiting his room altogether soon after. He didn't hurt me, if that's what you're afraid of."

The hands on his arms suddenly loosened, and Benedict's head bowed. "I'd kill him if he had," he whispered.

Dulcie fought the sudden sick certainty rising in his mind. "But he hurt you. Didn't he?"

"Oh, please, Dulcie. Enough of such maudlin prattle," Leverett interjected. "You should come away, before he makes yet another scene."

Dulcie winced. He'd sounded just like Leverett when he'd repudiated Benedict back in London, hadn't he?

Ignoring Leverett, he turned to Benedict. "You didn't want him to. But he made you think you had to."

"He only wanted me to keep my mouth open while he shoved his filthy prick into it. Or to keep it shut while he spent in my hand. 'Dulcie may like to sport with a prattler,' he told me, 'but I prefer my boys to keep their tiresome thoughts to themselves.'"

Dulcie feared he might vomit. *He told me you'd given me to him.* How light he'd made of Benedict's admission all those months ago. Bloody hell, had the twelve-year-old thought he'd given Leverett the rights to his *body*?

"Why didn't you tell him we never did any such thing?"

"What should it matter?" Leverett interrupted. "Even if you hadn't, it was clear he wanted to. Disgusting, it was, the way he followed you all about the school, like a calf bleating for its dam! Why, he should have thanked me, for giving him what he was too afraid to ask for himself."

"I didn't want it!" Benedict cried. "Not from you."

"Then why did you let him?" Dulcie asked, touching his hand to the other's face.

But Benedict jerked away. "I didn't think I was allowed to say no."

A low moan sounded in Dulcie's ears. Where had it come from? Not from Benedict, surely? Lord, from himself?

With a shout, he whirled and grabbed Leverett by the lapels. "You bloody cur," he snarled, shoving him against the wall.

"I don't see what all the fuss is about," Leverett spat out, eyes fixed not at Dulcie but on Benedict. "You certainly *learned* how to say no."

"Only after you fucked me, then slapped me afterwards, saying it wasn't the same," Benedict said, then laughed wildly. "Oh my God! You meant Dulcie, didn't you? Fucking me wasn't the same as fucking Dulcie."

"Indeed," Leverett acknowledged with a cruel twist of his lip.

"A sniveling, puling coward hardly makes an attractive *eromenos*."

But Benedict only laughed again. "You wanted me because you were jealous, didn't you? Jealous of my friendship with Dulcie. If you couldn't have him yourself any longer, you'd settle for what he'd had. And turn me against him in the bargain."

"Leverett?" Dulcie asked, his voice unsure even as his grip on the other's cravat tightened. "Jealous?"

Leverett rolled his eyes. "Now Dulcie, don't listen to the ravings of an intemperate madman."

"Mad, am I?" Benedict's laugh scraped harsh in his ears. "Haven't you done everything in your power to keep us apart since my return to London? That ridiculous bet? Encouraging Dulcie to wed Miss Adler? Denigrating my art, and encouraging Dulcie to do the same?" Benedict pointed a finger at Leverett. "Who else but a jealous man would go to such extremes?"

"Dulcie, really. Will you allow him to make another scene?"

"What, were you afraid it would make you too vulnerable if you told him?" Benedict said.

"Told him what?" Dulcie asked.

"That he loves you, of course."

The words hung in the air for a long moment, stunning them all into silence.

But at last, Leverett spoke. "Me? Love Dulcie? You truly are mad."

His voice sounded as it always did, all scathing amusement, but still, his denial fell flat. And when Dulcie tried to catch his eyes, to read his true feelings, Leverett only looked away.

Good God. Leverett, nursing a *tendre* for him all these years?

Even if it were true, Leverett would never admit to such a thing. Hell, he'd never protested when Dulcie stopped coming to his rooms back at school, never asked him even once to return. He'd only striven all the harder to best him in the classroom, and on the playing fields, to prove himself the superior. Didn't Leverett use people, for status or financial gain, and insist on being the acknowledged superior in all his relationships? Tender feelings would make him seem weak, vulnerable, and he'd never stand for that. Admitting he loved someone would force him to be the supplicant, the subordinate. Why, he might even be rejected, if the one he loved did not love him in return.

"How ironical," Benedict said, his voice edged with scorn. "You both feel love, yet are both utterly incapable of admitting it."

Dulcie shuddered. Both? Could Benedict truly equate his feelings, his behavior, with Leverett's?

"Come, Dulcie," Leverett said with a scornful glance in Benedict's direction. "Such vulgar emotional displays are unbecoming a gentlemen."

Dulcie shook his head. By continually hiding his fears, pretending he had no weaknesses, it was *Leverett* who had made himself vulnerable.

Is that what Benedict had been trying to tell him, that night back in London when he'd left Dulcie behind? That hiding from the ones you love made *you* the vulnerable one?

"As you don't love me," Dulcie said as he dropped his grip on Leverett's cravat and took a step closer to Benedict, "it won't matter in the least when I give you the cut direct whenever we are in company in future."

Leverett's nostrils flared. "You wouldn't dare."

Dulcie smiled brittlely. "Care to wager on it?"

"Gentlemen!" a stern voice interrupted.

Dulcie turned and saw Theo Pennington, Lord Saybrook, standing in the doorway, hands on his hips. Even more surprisingly, young George Norton stood behind him.

"Norton told me I might find my brother here," Saybrook said. "Benedict promised my wife the next dance, and I'm certain he does not wish to disappoint her."

Leverett scowled at Norton, but the younger man only frowned. Had Norton finally realized some elders were not worthy of his respect?

"My apologies, Theo," Benedict said, brushing past Leverett and Dulcie without a backward glance. "My business is finished here."

"Then let us return to the ballroom." Saybrook laid a hand on his brother's shoulder. "Mr. Norton will partner Sibilla and complete your set."

Benedict nodded, then followed the two other men back into the Assembly Rooms.

Dulcie moved to follow, but Leverett grabbed him by the arm. "You'd best reconsider cutting me, Dulcie. No one at the British Institution will listen to your opinion at all, not if you think to champion Pennington's art. And certainly not if you set yourself up in opposition to me."

Dulcie stared pointedly at the gloved hand wrinkling his sleeve. After a long pause, Leverett finally removed it.

Taking a handkerchief from his pocket, Dulcie swept it against the spot where Leverett's hand had lain. "Perhaps it is time, then, for me to throw my lot in with those who champion an alternative to the British Institution."

Dulcie turned on his heel, leaving Leverett to sputter impotently behind him.

CHAPTER 20

"AND SO WE ARE IN agreement, gentlemen?" asked Sir Charles Long. "Sixteen paintings to be donated by Sir George Beaumont, and twenty-five to be purchased at the agreed-upon price from Mr. Julius Adler?"

The nods given by the cabal of gentlemen seated around a table at the British Institution should have filled Benedict with pride. It was he, after all, who had brokered the agreement between the government, represented here today by Sir Charles and Mr. Agar-Ellis, and Julius Adler, for the purchase of the most prized paintings in Adler's collection.

Benedict had assumed Adler would want nothing to do with him after the debacle at his granddaughter's engagement party. He'd not written to the merchant while he'd been in Lincolnshire for Theo's wedding, nor had he called in Pall Mall after his return to town in the middle of October. He'd kept deliberately away from all of Adler's usual known London haunts, not wishing to give his former patron the pain of having to cut him in public. But Adler, much to Benedict's surprise, had called at Pennington House, and asked him once again to serve as intermediary between himself and the government. Polly's doing? Or the fact that Sir George Beaumont, a member of the Board of the British Institution, had returned from his recent Italian travels determined to establish a national art museum in England, and Adler did not wish all the glory of being its sole benefactor to go to his fellow collector?

No matter. Adler seemed to think it best, in the interests of advancing his museum cause, to pretend Benedict had never painted the shocking work that had so rudely interrupted his granddaughter's party. So now, the combined gifts of Beaumont and Adler would serve as the foundation for one of the most illustrious public collections of artwork in all of Europe, a collection that could be viewed not only by those with wealth and privilege, but by Englishmen of all ranks and stations.

And Englishwomen.

But Benedict could not seem to summon any pride, or even excitement, at the prospect. No, not even when he imagined his mother, or Polly, or any other young artist of the future walking the galleries, their minds alight with wonder. Ever since his break with Clair, he'd felt as flat as the varnish on the paintings over which they bargained.

Nor could he bring himself to put a single brush to canvas, or even a pencil to paper.

"Very good, gentlemen." Sir Charles clapped his palms together and smiled. "Then I will ask the Chancellor of the Exchequer to request in his budget speech to the Commons the funds for said purchase, as well as for the purchase of Mr. Adler's Pall Mall residence, to house these works of art."

Adler only gave a wan smile. But Beaumont made up for all of Adler's lack of spirits, crying a lusty "Hear, hear," and patting the other man on the back.

Benedict stifled a laugh at the sudden memory of Clair, gossiping about Beaumont's practice of carrying his favorite painting about with him whenever he set forth on a journey by carriage, in a case he'd had designed for the purpose. Clair, a wicked mimic, had caught the self-important mannerisms of his fellow collector perfectly.

"Let us have a drink to celebrate this grand new venture," Adler said with a wry glance at his fellow benefactor. Dulcie had no doubt told Adler the story, too.

"Yes, indeed. Summon a footman, will you, Pennington?" Beaumont waved a hand in Benedict's direction, almost as if he had sensed Benedict's lack of deference and wished to repress his pretensions.

If Clair had been here, he would have given Beaumont a sly set-down, one so clever the fellow would in all likelihood have believed he was being praised instead of mocked. Damn, how he missed the way Clair had of easing their way in society.

He summoned the footman without comment.

"To Sir George Beaumont and Mr. Julius Adler," Agar-Ellis toasted after the footman had filled his glass. "There are few gentlemen of my acquaintance who marry so true a spirit of beneficence with such a care for the good of the country. Now, at long last, we will finally boast a collection worthy of our fine nation."

"And one which shall allow us to educate the public taste. By acting now, we may curb this strange taste for innovation that prevails in the present age."

"Strange taste for innovation?" Benedict asked, prickling. Dulcie had decried Beaumont's slavish veneration for the Old Masters. Would his conservative views keep more modern, experimental works from being displayed at the new museum?

"You may not be aware, Mr. Pennington, having spent so much time out of the country," Beaumont proclaimed with a self-important air. "But too many British artists of present day believe that all that has hitherto been done in the arts is fit only for the flames. Why, I've heard some call Titian, and even Claude, the black masters, and warn each other with earnestness not to paint like them! But now that they will have before their eyes the finished works of the greatest artists, they will surely learn the proper respect for their superiors."

Benedict's foot tapped against the carpet. "Can one not appreciate the accomplishments of those who have come before, yet still wish to explore new directions in one's own work?"

"New directions? Bah. Such pretenders to artistic taste simply dash away without any knowledge or reason, and thus produce the most disgusting nondescripts possible."

Beaumont turned to Sir Charles with a frown. "Now, you must be sure the Prime Minister appoints only disinterested connoisseurs to superintend the Gallery, gentlemen of taste who understand the hierarchy of artistic genres. None of us wishes to see such eccentricities as Hogarth's modern moral subjects, or Turner's dreadful landscapes, marring our Gallery's walls."

Benedict stifled a laugh. Beaumont must have been spending a good deal of time with Lattimer Leverett, to parrot his words with such accuracy.

"Indeed," Sir Charles said with an apologetic glance in Benedict's direction. Before Beaumont's arrival, they had just been speaking of their admiration for Turner's landscapes. "Your recommendations for suitable candidates will be most welcome."

"Thank heavens I returned from the continent in time to prevent one such unsuitable gentleman from cajoling his way onto the Board here at the British Institution. To think he believed his own bizarre collection would suit our national gallery! His Carracci would, of course, have been more than acceptable, but the Fuseli paintings?"

The skin on the back of Benedict's neck tingled. Another man had thought to join Adler and Beaumont in endowing the new museum? A man who owned a Carracci?

"A Carracci?" Agar-Ellis asked, longing edging his voice.

"Yes, but he wouldn't give it unless we accepted all the others." Beaumont gave a visible shudder as he threw a familiar portfolio onto the table. "Just take a look at these dreadful sketches. Some mad Frenchman, I understand. And there, outside in the passageway, an indecent thing he has the temerity to own is a portrait of himself. How dare he bring such rubbish here?"

"He's here?" The tingling shot down Benedict's spine.

Beaumont sniffed. "Yes, just out in the passageway. Wanted to worm his way into our meeting today, but I refused. You all agree, I'm certain, that we are not interested in accepting such dubious gifts. Pennington? Where are you going? We are not finished here!"

But Benedict had pushed back his chair and rushed through the door.

Dulcie's booted footsteps echoed hollowly as he paced the marble floor of the lower vestibule of the British Institution. The three galleries at the top of the stairway above were empty, the paintings on display during the spring and summer all taken down, carefully packed in boxes and crates to be returned to their aristocratic owners. And the works by so-called modern artists to open in January were still to be hung.

Dulcie doubted he'd be there to see them.

How strange, to feel almost like a ghost, the spirit of Viscount Dulcies past, haunting this familiar building. He'd not be welcomed here much longer, not after tipping his hand to Sir George with his rash offer to donate his truly modern collection of paintings to Benedict's museum. How shocked that hidebound traditionalist had been to discover that Dulcie's taste so differed from his own! He'd never support Dulcie being named to a seat on the Institution's Board now, not after seeing how Dulcie's tastes disregarded the tenets of connoisseurship Beaumont had spent his life espousing.

No, Dulcie would never see the word "Director" printed next to his name in the Institution's annual catalog. Yet somehow he could not find it within himself to mourn the dashing of his longtime dream.

No, what truly made his heart pound was whether Benedict would understand all he meant to say with his offer.

He stared again at the portrait he'd carried here himself, rubbing a restless finger across the new frame he'd had especially commissioned for it. No swags or festoons or cartouches, just a plain gilt moulding, one that would not distract the eye from the painting within. He hoped Benedict would think it the right choice.

How much longer would he have to wait?

The sound of footsteps on the floor above brought his restless pacing to a halt. He grasped the finial atop the staircase's post, squeezing tight.

"Dulcie." Benedict halted above him on the landing, staring down at him with those dark, intense eyes. Did he see a man he still cared for? Or was that beloved Clair only a ghost to him now?

With careful, deliberate steps, Benedict came down the staircase, then strode over to the wall where Dulcie had propped his portrait. Benedict stared at the painting for several moments, brow furrowed.

"How did this come to be here? I thought I had left it behind, in my studio."

"As you did me?"

Benedict frowned.

"Yes, you are right. It was only what I deserved," Dulcie quickly added with a wave of his hand. "But when it came time for me to go, I found I could not abandon it."

"Because you couldn't stand the thought of anyone else seeing you so?" Benedict asked, his eyes fixed on the painting. "Even the stray housemaid, come to straighten and dust?"

Dulcie gave a wry smile. "That is what I told myself at the time. I'd lock it away, hide its secrets from all the world. Maybe even destroy it altogether."

Benedict clasped his hands tight behind his back. "And yet here it is. You've held on to it all this time?"

"Yes." Dulcie moved to stand beside him. "Instead of closeting it away, as any sane man would have done, I hung it in my bedchamber. And stared at it, night and day. Marveling not over your talent, which of course is prodigious. But at how you were able to see something about me I was not even aware of myself, and then have the bravery to commit it to canvas."

Beside him, Benedict took a deep breath "And what is it that I saw, Dulcie? What do you see when you look at your portrait?"

"I see a man—" With the blood pounding in his ears, Dulcie could barely hear his own words. "I see a man who loves."

He slid his hand down Benedict's arm, then teased open his tightly-clutched fist. His fingers threaded through Benedict's, smooth against rough, frost against heat. Yes, this, this is where he belonged, by this man's side, hand in hand, together.

If Benedict would only take him back.

For a painfully long moment, Benedict's hand lay stiff, unresponsive, within Dulcie's. But at last, a shudder ran through his frame, and then his palm pressed Dulcie's and held fast, as if he would never let go.

How extraordinary, the lightness suddenly bubbling up inside him. He'd been so afraid of how vulnerable loving another person, loving Benedict, made him. And yet now that he'd said the words, he didn't feel vulnerable at all. No, he felt safe, and strong, and so full of joy he could barely contain himself, even in the hallowed halls of the British Institution. If Beaumont thought his taste in paintings shocking, just imagine how he'd react to finding Dulcie kissing Benedict Pennington in front of the noble bust of Sir Joshua Reynolds!

He took a step closer to Benedict and pulled their clasped hands around his own back.

With a sigh, Benedict pulled Dulcie closer to his side.

"Shall I tell you what I see?" Benedict asked, his eyes still

317

fixed on the portrait. "I see a man willing to throw away any chance he had of ever becoming a Director of the British Institution, making a foolish gesture when a simple apology would have done."

"Ah, but you underrate the grandeur of my gesture!" Dulcie laughed. "I also cast away any chance I have of serving on the committee appointed to oversee your new museum, too. In fact, I just may have to resign my membership in the British Institution altogether now that Sir George and Sir Charles know the extent of my rebellion against the tenets of correct artistic judgment."

"But it's your most cherished dream, Clair! How can you stand to give it up?"

Dulcie laid his head on Benedict's shoulder. "My dearest Pen. Don't you realize? The concern in your voice is more than recompense for any mere trifle I've lost by this morning's work."

"But will you not regret it? You could tell Beaumont, tell Sir Charles, it was all just a joke, and they'd welcome you back, I'm sure of it. I'd not gainsay you."

"But then I'd have to deny my true opinion of your work."

"Then you don't agree with Leverett? You don't find it vulgar?"

Dulcie pulled Benedict's arms more tightly about him. "Not in the least."

"And you don't blame me?"

"Blame you? Blame you for what?"

"For letting him fuck me. Or for refusing to allow him to keep fucking me."

A large lump rose in Dulcie's throat. Benedict thought he'd blame *him*, when it was all Dulcie's fault?

With a quick glance up the staircase to ensure they were still alone, Dulcie pulled Benedict behind the colossal plaster statue of Achilles that stood in an alcove by the front door of the British Institute. He'd heard it was meant to portray the hero mourning

318

his lost concubine, but Dulcie preferred to imagine Achilles grieving instead for Patroclus, his male lover. The way he'd felt all these weeks after Benedict had left him.

"Do you remember the passage from Xenophon I set you to translate, all those years ago?" Dulcie asked, reaching out a hand to raise Benedict's lowered head.

"*The sweetest of all and the most erotic is when he fights with you and argues,*" Benedict recited, color rising in his cheeks.

"Yes, but before that, Hiero says this: *But what I long for, I wish to receive from a willing lover, and with friendship.* How could I blame you? Leverett is the one at fault, or rather, Leverett and myself, for leaving you all unsuspecting to his care."

Benedict shook his head. "I thought you knew. All along I thought you knew, and wished me to do what he told me. I was so angry, but so ashamed, too, when I brought my brother's sword from home and threatened to gut him with it if he ever touched me again. I thought you'd think me a disappointment."

"A disappointment, for defending yourself? Never. I have no respect for Leverett, or for any boy or man, who forces unwanted attentions on another."

Benedict bent his head. "But can you respect me?"

"Respect you? Foolish man, don't you know I feel far more than simply respect for you?" Taking Benedict into his arms, Dulcie whispered in his ear. "*Man with a lover's glance, I seek you out, but you hear not, unknowing that you are the charioteer of my soul.*"

"That's not Xenophon," Benedict said.

"No, it's Anacreon. And as he writes elsewhere, *I am mad for Benedict, I gaze at Benedict, I love Benedict.*"

"You love me, Clair?" Benedict asked, not questioning his somewhat free translation.

"Yes, my wild, sensitive artist. Yes, for now and for always."

Throwing discretion to the winds, he cradled Benedict's face in his hands and kissed him before his lover could catch sight of the tears threatening to escape his eyes.

The touch of Benedict's lips, the feel of his thick hair threading between his fingers, the sound of his eager pants as Dulcie traced kisses down the rough column of his throat—he'd never felt such an intoxicating mixture of lust and liking and love. Saint Valentine, Saint Dwynwen, perhaps even Eros himself must be smiling down on him today.

A clatter on the staircase behind him had him pressing Benedict even closer to the wall. "Shhh!" he urged, more caution to himself than to Benedict, who silently took his earlobe between his lips and gave it a seductive tug.

"I do regret the loss of the Carracci," Sir George Beaumont's voice drifted through the entryway. "It would have made a fine addition to the treasures of the nation."

"But perhaps you may persuade Lord Dulcie to donate it without the others," Sir Charles answered.

"Perhaps. But not at the cost of a place on the superintending committee!"

"No, indeed! We need gentlemen of superior taste, gentlemen who understand what artistic subjects are most likely to be conducive to the virtue and happiness of the public."

"Such as the gentlemen currently serving on the board of directors of the British Institution?"

"Indeed."

Dulcie pressed his body closer to Benedict's as the door closed behind the gossiping men. Lord, how had he survived all those weeks apart?

"I'm sorry the new museum won't be interested in acquiring any works outside the currently accepted canon," Dulcie said with a consoling kiss to Benedict's own ear.

"Or any superintendents who espouse anything but Beaumont's views on what constitutes proper art," Benedict added. "I'm sorry if I've cost you your chance to be a founding member of the museum."

How correct the words of Tibullus: *Slide your shining arms around a young man's torso, and all the wealth of kings seems meaningless.* "No matter. I doubt I'd have enjoyed working with that conservative bunch."

"I wonder . . ."

Dulcie's breath caught at the sight of Benedict's face, dreaming of some amazing future no one but he could ever imagine. "You wonder what?"

"What if we opened a museum of our own? One which gives the new, the innovative, the experimental a place to shine? I'm sure I can find an artist or two willing to display his work."

"Benedict, this hardly seems the time for such a venture. Not when all the efforts of the artistic set will be focused on this new National Gallery."

Benedict's shoulders slumped. Dulcie had only just declared his love, and already he was not taking heed of his lover's feelings. Damn him for a blockhead.

"Perhaps not just now," he said, taking Benedict's hands in his. "But shall we dream about it for the future?"

A shy, pleased smile stole across his lover's face. "You'd dream about the future, with me?"

An image of two sets of bachelor rooms in the Albany, a connecting door between them, rushed through Dulcie's brain. Paintings hanging on every available wall space, except for in Benedict's studio. A constant stream of collectors and artists, all committed to celebrating not just what art had once been, but to the possibilities of what it could someday become.

And at the end of each day, a warm, loving Benedict, alive in his arms.

"The only dream I have is of a future with you. Be careful, Pen, you'll knock poor Achilles right off his pedestal!"

But Dulcie soon forgot his concerns for the plaster Greek hero, caught up in the wonder of being kissed, being held, being loved by Benedict Pennington. Ghost no longer, but flesh and blood hero, the love of his heart.

THANK YOU

Thanks for reading *A Sinner without a Saint*. I hope it gave you as much pleasure in the reading as it gave me in the writing.

Would you consider writing a review? Reader reviews on Amazon, Goodreads, LibraryThing, and other social networking sites are especially valuable for e-books. I'm grateful for all reviews, critical or admiring, and if you take the time to write one of *Sinner*, you have my thanks.

If you'd like to know when my next book becomes available, or to find out about discounts, giveaways, and other Bliss Bennet-related info, sign up for my newsletter at blissbennet.com, follow me on BlueSky, like my Facebook page at www.facebook.com/blissbennetauthor, or my Instagram page (http://www.instagram.com/blissbennetwrites).

AUTHOR'S NOTE

From the moment I first began to write the story of the Pennington siblings, I knew that Benedict, the second Pennington brother, had some unfinished business with Sinclair Milne, Lord Dulcie, the friend of Sir Peregrine Sayre. But it wasn't until I watched a BBC show about the Regency period and heard about Noël Joseph Desenfans and Sir Francis Bourgeois that the idea of a plot focused on the founding of England's National Gallery came into my mind.

Born in France in 1744, Desenfans emigrated to London and married the wealthy Margaret Morris in 1776. His new financial position allowed him to engage in the art trade, although he presented himself more as an art lover than as a professional dealer. How Desenfans became friends with Sir Francis Bourgeois (b. 1756 in London) is a mystery. Sir Francis's father intended him for the army, but Desenfans encouraged the younger man to pursue a career as a painter. We do know that Sir Francis helped Desenfans when he was commissioned in 1789 by King Stanislaus to purchase paintings for a proposed national art gallery in Poland. But before Desenfans could be repaid for the paintings, Poland was dismembered and Stanislaus divested of his crown. In 1802, Desenfans prepared a catalogue of the paintings he had collected on behalf of the Polish monarch, as well as an exhibition in London, both with a view to their sale. Many of the paintings were sold, but at his death in 1807, he willed all that remained to Sir Francis. Bourgeois first thought to bequeath the pictures to the British Museum, but then chose to bestow them on Dulwich College instead, his will stipulating that the paintings should be made available for the "inspection of the public." Upon Bourgeois' death in 1811, the Dulwich Picture Gallery—England's first art gallery built specifically for the public—was founded.

Sir Francis lived with both Desenfans and his wife from the late 1770s, and the BBC show I watched hinted that the two men may have been lovers. It was this hint, as well as the idea of exploring the controversies surrounding the proper role of art in public life, that inspired me to set Clair and Benedict's love story against the backdrop of the founding of the National Gallery.

Several of the secondary characters in *A Sinner without a Saint* are real people involved in the debates about public access to fine art: Sir Charles Long, art advisor to King George IV; George Agar-Ellis, a leading proponent of the arts in Parliament; and Sir George Beaumont, who donated his own collection of art to the National Gallery. Julius Adler is based on the other founder of the National Gallery, banker and art collector John Julius Angerstein.

If you are curious about debates about art in Regency period, or the people involved in the founding of the National Gallery, you can find information about the sources I consulted on my web site. And if you wish to see copies of the many real works of art referred to in the book, check out my Pinterest board for *A Sinner*. I've also put together a Pinterest board with as many of the paintings I could find of the British Institution's 1822 spring show, as well as a board for John Julius Angerstein's collection.

Writing this fourth book in the series, which takes place simultaneously with many of the events of the previous three books, proved a bit of a challenge. I know of at least one time discrepancy between *Sinner* and *A Lady without a Lord* that I made on purpose, for reasons of plot; if you find more than one, please do let me know!

ACKNOWLEDGEMENTS

No novel is ever completed without the help, encouragement, and good will of many people besides its author. My deepest gratitude to:

My romance writing friends and colleagues, in particular my fellow authors in the New England Chapter of Romance Writers of America. Thank you for allowing me to serve as your president for the past two years! Thanks too, to the members of the online RWA Chapter for historical romance writers, Hearts Through History, and the online RWA Chapter for Regency romance writers, the Beau Monde. I appreciate all the knowledge and expertise members of each group share with generosity and good humor.

Readers and critique partners who continue to praise, suggest, and criticize in just the right balance: Laurie Alice Eakes, Judith Laik, Jessica Gibbons, and Anne Marie Rothstein. I continue to grow and learn as a writer from each of you.

My publishing support team, including Sue Laybourn, my editor/copyeditor, and Jenny Q of Historical Editorial, for creating yet another gorgeous cover. You are the best!

The many, many readers who have commented on, and/or disagreed with, the blog posts my alter ego, Jackie Horne, has written at *Romance Novels for Feminists*. I love the way you challenge my ideas, and push me to think harder about the hows and whys of feminist romance.

My toddler dinner neighbors, especially now that our toddlers have all flown the nest. Thanks to Jessica, Trey, Anita, Norbert, Anne Marie, and Roger for *still* listening to all my talk about Romancelandia, self-publishing, and sex. And special thanks to Jessica for the lovely author and cover photos. And to Sam for being such an enthusiastic cover model.

Mr. Bennet (my own, not Elizabeth's), who continues to support me with funny comics and razor-sharp analytical skills. And my own young Miss Bennet, especially now that she is becoming an intelligent, independent woman. You are very right: there are not three f's in "sniffed." I love you both so much.

And last, but certainly not least, you, my readers and reviewers. Thank you for taking a chance on my books. There are so many romances of all types being written and published today; it is an honor to know that you've chosen to spend your time with mine.

SOMETHING ABOUT BLISS

Bliss Bennet writes smart, edgy novels for readers who love history as much as they love romance. Despite being born and bred in New England, Bliss has always been fascinated by the history of that country across the pond, particularly the politically-volatile period known as the English Regency. Though she's visited Britain several times, Bliss continues to make her home in New England along with her spouse and an ever-multiplying collection of historical reference books.

Bliss's Regency-set historical romances have been praised as "savvy, sensual, and engrossing" by *USA Today*, "catnip for the Historical Romance reader" by *Bookworlder*, "romantic, funny, touching, and extremely well-researched" by *All About Romance*, and "everything you want in a great historical romance" by *The Reading Wench*.

Turn the page for more books by Bliss Bennet

EAGER FOR MORE FROM BLISS BENNET?

THE AUDACIOUS LADIES OF AUDLEY

Sheba and Noel's Story: *Not Quite a Scandal*

An inheritance lost. A betrothal threatened. A scandal brewing...

Outspoken Bathsheba Honeychurch knows how difficult it is for an unmarried woman, even a Quaker, to successfully champion political change. Her solution? Wed best friend Ash Griffin and begin remaking the world. But the arrival of Ash's worldly cousin with unthinkable news puts Sheba's dreams for the future suddenly at risk...

The death of Noel Griffin's grandfather exposes an appalling betrayal: Noel is *not* the heir to the Silliman earldom, despite what the late earl raised him to believe. Still, the only honorable course is to accept his widowed grandmother's bitter charge: find the true heir, disentangle him from his religious community, and tutor him in the responsibilities and privileges of a title Noel assumed would be his. He certainly won't allow a presumptuous, irritating Quakeress to keep him from his duty—no matter how fascinating he finds her...

When scandal threatens both their reputations, can Sheba and Noel look beyond past dreams and imagine a new world —together?

Delphie and Spencer's story: *Not Quite a Marriage*

Spencer Burnett, Viscount Stiles, once swore he'd left England for good. Yet after five years of self-imposed exile in West Africa, he's no longer the same spoiled, selfish boy who ran away from a domineering father, a disappointed grandmother, and a decidedly unwanted wife. Proving himself to the family he abandoned will be no easy task. But he hardly expects his formerly docile wife will be the hardest to convince. When Philadelphia refuses to accept his apologies—or to allow him back into her bed—Spencer finds himself tempting her into a bargain he cannot afford to lose.

Philadelphia Burnett's desires were once as vast as the sky. But now, after suffering one devastating loss after another, the only thing she allows herself to want is a home. When Delphie's estranged rake of a husband returns from a five-years' absence to claim the estate promised to *her*, Delphie resolves to fight him every step of the way. Beechcombe Park will be a sanctuary for her, and for the wayward Audley cousins she promised her sister she'd always protect. She cannot, will not, suffer even one more loss. Especially not the loss of her heart...

THE PENNINGTONS

Kit's story: *A Rebel without a Rogue*

A woman striving for justice
Fianna Cameron has devoted her life to avenging the death of her father, hanged as a traitor during the Irish Rebellion of 1798. Now, on the eve of her thirtieth birthday, only one last miscreant remains: Major Christopher Pennington, who both oversaw her father's execution and maligned his honor. Fianna risks everything to travel to London and confront the man who has haunted her every nightmare. Only after her pistol misfires does she realize her sickening mistake: the Pennington she wounded is far too young to be her intended target.

A man who will protect his family at all costs
Rumors of being shot by a spurned mistress might burnish the reputation of a rake, but for Kit Pennington, determined to win a seat in Parliament, such salacious gossip is a nightmare. To regain his good name, Kit vows to track down his mysterious attacker and force her to reveal why she fired on him. Accepting an acquaintance's mistress as an ally in his search is risky enough, but when Kit begins to develop feelings for the icy, ethereal Miss Cameron, more than his

political career is in danger.

As their search begins to unearth long-held secrets, Kit and Fianna find themselves caught between duty to family and their beliefs in what's right. How can you balance the competing demands of loyalty and justice—especially when you add love to the mix.

Sibilla's story: _A Man without a Mistress_

A man determined to atone for the past
For seven long years, Sir Peregrine Sayre has tried to assuage his guilt over the horrifying events of his twenty-first birthday by immersing himself in political work—and by avoiding all entanglements with the ladies of the *ton*. But when his mentor sends him on a quest to track down purportedly penitent prostitutes, the events of his less-than-innocent past threaten not only his own political career, but the life of a vexatious viscount's daughter as well.

A woman who will risk anything for the future
Raised to be a political wife, but denied the opportunity by her father's untimely death, Sibilla Pennington has little desire to wed as soon as her period of mourning is over. Why should she have to marry just so her elder brothers might be free of her hoydenish ways and her blazingly angry grief? To delay their plans, Sibilla vows only to accept a betrothal with

a man as politically astute as was her father—and, in retaliation for her brothers' amorous peccadillos, only one who has never kept a mistress. Surely there is no such man in all of London.

When Sibilla's attempt to free a reformed maidservant from the clutches of a former procurer throw her into the midst of Per's penitent search, she finds herself inextricably drawn to the cool, reserved baronet. But as the search grows ever more dangerous, Sibilla's penchant for risk taking cannot help but remind Per of the shames he's spent years trying to outrun. Can Per continue to hide the guilt and ghosts of his past without endangering his chance at a passionate future with Sibilla?

Theo's story: *A Lady without a Lord*

A viscount convinced he's a failure

For years, Theodosius Pennington has tried to forget his myriad shortcomings by indulging in wine, women, and witty bonhomie. But now that he's inherited the title of Viscount Saybrook, it's time to stop ignoring his responsibilities. Finding the perfect husband for his headstrong younger sister seems a good first step. Until, that is, his sister's dowry goes missing . . .

A lady determined to succeed

Harriot Atherton has a secret: it is she, not her steward father, who maintains the Saybrook account books. But Harry's precarious balancing act begins to totter when the irresponsible new viscount unexpectedly returns to Lincolnshire, the painfully awkward boy of her childhood now a charming yet vulnerable man. Unfortunately, Theo is also claiming financial malfeasance. Can her father's wandering wits be responsible for the lost funds? Or is she?

As unlikely attraction flairs between dutiful Harry and playful Theo, each learns there is far more to the other than devoted daughter and happy-go-lucky lord. But if Harry succeeds at protecting her father, discovering the missing money, and keeping all her secrets, will she be in danger of failing at something equally important—finding love?

Turn the page for a preview of the first book in *The Penningtons* series,
A Rebel without a Rogue...

London, February 1822

Fianna Cameron—at least that was what she called herself today—slipped a hand inside her pocket and curled her fingers tight around the butt of her father's pistol. Her long, hurried strides sent it bouncing hard against her thigh, but even that pain wasn't enough to reassure her that the weapon hadn't disappeared, that she hadn't only imagined hiding it there before she'd finally tracked her prey to his lair. Still, she couldn't shake the fear that when the time came for her to act, she would find herself confronting the man empty-handed, shaking in impotent fury as Major Christopher Pennington offered her a condescending smile and walked on, just as he had so many times in her dreams.

The memory of Grandfather McCracken's soft, broken voice reading the Bible verse that had first inspired her—*For he is the minister of God, a revenger to execute wrath upon him who doeth evil*—brought her back to her sense of purpose. She could not fail, *would* not fail, not now, not when she'd given nearly everything for this chance to bring her father's killer to justice and redeem the honor of his name. And to prove herself, bastard though she might be, worthy of her rightful place in the McCracken family.

The only family she had left—

Eyes darting between strangers and shop windows, carriages and carts, she searched the unfamiliar street for her destination. She'd feared being followed and had altered her path to throw any pursuer off her trail. But the evasion must have pulled her off course as well. She'd come too far, missing Pennington's reputed favorite haunt.

Retracing her steps, she discovered the Crown and Anchor Tavern lay not on the Strand itself, but behind that bustling street's houses and shops. Stepping into the long, narrow passageway between two shopfronts, she forced herself to slow to a pace painfully at odds with the rapid beating of her heart.

The sight of the Crown and Anchor's spacious stone-paved foyer brought her up short. In Dublin, no place this grand would ever be termed a mere tavern. Ornate columns, a sweeping staircase with iron rails and what looked to be handrails of some dark, expensive wood—why, it seemed as elegantly appointed as the Lord Lieutenant's mansion. And so many people! How would she ever find her quarry amidst such a throng?

A man in dark livery broke through her dismay. "May I direct you to the Philharmonic Society concert, ma'am? Or Mr. Burdett's meeting to discuss the wisdom of abstaining from intoxicating spirits? Both may be found on the floor above."

Not just a tavern, then, this Crown and Anchor, but a public meeting hall of no small repute. What a lackwit, to call attention to herself by staring at its grandeur like the greenest bumpkin. Lucky, she'd be, not to be judged an impostor and thrown out on her ear.

Run! her body urged. *Hide!*

Instead, forcing her hand from the comfort of the pistol, she pushed back the hood that hid her face.

The footman took a step back, his eyes widening. How predictable, the catch of breath, the poleaxed, besotted expression. She'd long ago stopped wondering why God had gifted her with a face that no man could seem to pass without falling guilty to the rudeness of staring. Lucky for her, men only seemed to care about the deceptively lovely husk of her face, never giving a single thought to what ugliness might lie Benedicteath.

Lowering her voice to a murmur, she forced the footman to step closer. "It is so crowded here." She widened her eyes. "My footman seems to have gone astray."

"Might I send a man in search of him for you, ma'am?" he asked, a blush spreading over already ruddy cheeks.

"My uncle," she said, taking care to add a shy, embarrassed frown. "The footman was to take me to my uncle, Major Pennington. Would you know where I might find him, sir?"

The man took another step closer, as if drawn to her by an invisible wire. "Major Pennington? Ah, let me see. There is to be a meeting of military gentlemen in the Small Dining Room this evening, but I believe they are men of the navy. I do know of a *Mr.* Pennington, though, a Mr. Kit Pennington. Brother to Lord Saybrook, he is. Might he be the gentleman you seek?"

"Ah yes, *Mr.* Pennington. I nearly forgot, he sold out some years past. My mother always called him the Major, you see."

"Of course, ma'am. I believe he is up in the news room, reading the papers. I'll send someone to fetch him immediately." Reluctance and relief warred over his face as he turned towards the stair.

"Oh, please don't," she cried, placing a palm on the man's arm. No need to give the Major any warning.

She felt the footman start, watched him stare at the hand from which she'd deliberately removed a glove. "It was meant to be a surprise, you see, for his birthday," she added. "I'm sure I can find my way to this news room, if you give me the direction."

"But women don't typically frequent the news room, ma'am, and—"

Lifting her chin, she turned the full force of her green eyes upon the hapless servant. "You wouldn't spoil my uncle's surprise, would you?" she pleaded, adding the softest exhale of a sigh to draw his attention to her wide, full lips.

The quiver of his arm under her fingers told her all she needed to know.

Her mouth grew dry as they ascended the prodigious stone staircase and made their way across the second-floor lobby, passing a large assembly room. The strains of a tuning violin, its strings wound tight as her nerves, assaulted her ears. "Haydn's Requiem," the placard outside the room read. How fitting, that the Philharmonic Society should be playing a mass for the dead.

His death, not mine, she offered in silent prayer, even as a shiver slid down her frame.

"The news room, ma'am," the footman said, stopping beside one of the many doors lining the passageway and reaching towards its handle.

She raised a silencing finger to her lips before he could step inside.

"A surprise, do you not recall?" she whispered. He mimicked her action with his own finger, pleased to be privy to the secrets of such a creature as she. At her nod, he reached for the door and opened it just a crack. Then, with a flustered bow, he retreated down the passageway.

She stood for a moment, then another, until she was certain he had gone. Pulling the concealing folds of her hood back over her head, she forced her icy hand to push the door wide.

The floor's thick carpets and the door's well-oiled hinges allowed her to slip in unremarked. In her eagerness to finish the business, she'd stupidly assumed he'd be alone in the room. But she'd been mistaken; several groups of gentlemen were scattered about the large room. Damn, how her wits had gone astray since she'd arrived in London.

It would have been far wiser to leave before she attracted notice. But somehow, she could not pull her eyes away. Which of the room's occupants was the man responsible for her father's death? One of the knot of men debating earnestly around a table? The single man in a rumpled suit by the window, scribbling notes with a stubby pencil? Surely not one of the pair of gentlemen barely old enough to sprout whiskers, frantically pulling books off the shelves, nor their companion, dazed, even cup-shot, in a chair beside them.

She frowned. None had the stiff, upright bearing of the British military man, as had the soldiers she'd seen in Dublin and Belfast. Were they more relaxed, these English fighters, when in the safety of their own country? Her hand slipped back into her cloak pocket, feeling again for the reassurance of the pistol.

"Mr. Pennington?" she asked, taking a few steps into the room. Her eyes cut between the lone man by the window and the group on the left. "Is Mr. Pennington present?"

She could barely hear her own words over the pounding of blood in her ears. But her voice must have been louder than it seemed, for each man raised his eyes. Most seemed shocked to see an unescorted woman in their midst, although several looked as if they wished they could answer in the affirmative.

But none did.

Had the footman been mistaken, then? Her eyes narrowed, her teeth biting down hard against her lower lip.

Before she could draw blood, a supercilious English drawl caught her ear.

"Kit, how amusing. For once, a lady appears to want you, not me."

The voice had come not from the group on her left, but from the one on the right, the one now slightly behind her. She froze, waiting for the response.

"Pennington, pay attention. There's a *lady*, here, in this very room, asking for you," a second voice added. One voice to her left; the other to her right.

"A lady? Looking for *me*?" A third speaker. She heard one of the three take a step in her direction.

She cursed her shaking hand, clutching the butt of the pistol, her feet frozen to the floor. What, could she be losing her will now? Simply because this last act of retribution, unlike the others, demanded that she not simply humiliate or shame, but threaten real violence?

No. She steeled herself to charm Pennington into leaving the room. Once they were alone, she could beguile, or, if necessary, threaten, until the cursed man signed the recantation that would restore her father's honor.

Taking a deep breath, she turned to face him. In her pocket, the hand holding the hidden pistol gripped tight, angling the weapon away from her body. Upward, to ward off any potential threat.

But her finger, slippery with sweat, slid against the trigger

—

The unexpected force of the shot sent her reeling back towards the door.

Time hung suspended as, through the dissipating smoke, she struggled to make out her target.

Golden curls. Blue eyes, wide with shock. Blood, drip, drip, dripping from an arm to the carpet below.

A face even younger than her own.

A Mháthair Dé!

Mother of God. Not only had she fired too soon.

She'd fired upon the wrong man.

Eager to read more? Get your own copy from:
Apple Books • Amazon.com • Barnes & Noble •
Bookshop.org
Google Play • Ingram • Kobo • Powell's •
Smashwords.